The Dark Tomes

Eld of The Druid's Son

Written by Yoel M. Ellen

Skorpion Tribe Publishing

COPYRIGHTS

Dedication

I dedicate this first book to myself. A dream conjured in the darkness of my Savta's basement nearly two decades past. I did not give up.

To my grandmothers and grandfathers, especially to you Savta, because you raised me for most of my life. To my mother, never give up striving to better yourself and know that I always want to see you succeed. To my father, you gave me the discipline and drive to do more than I expect from myself. To my sister and brothers, and to my nephews, never settle for less than what I know you deserve. I dedicate this also to Isaiah Nelson, the son I never had and hope that you know I still think of you and love you as if you were my own. Let this be inspiration to achieve your goals.

Most importantly, I dedicate this to Evelyn Robbins, who now watches from on high, wherever that may be. For if not for you, I would have been lost to the abyssal depths of Cthulhu's watery realm.

The Dark Tomes
Eld of The Druid's Son

Table of contents

Chapter 1
Waking Beauty

Encircling a stone slab, upon which lays a veiled corpse, robed figures recite an unbroken chain of cabalistic phrases. Their voices reached out into the emptiness, echoing chillingly into the darkened and dilapidated chambers below Duldar's Keep. Only two simple tall braziers illuminated the gathering, but its light cast a blue and cold glow from the strange flames. Shadows that would normally recede away from light, almost appeared to have been summoned from further down the depths. Moldy aromas lingered amidst cool air, tickling the flesh coolly.

Where the light could not go there was only darkness. From within its endless veil, there watched unblinking reflective eyes of icy blue, and some observing from unseen elevations. Aside their cold burning intensity, there was not a sound uttered from these silent watchers.

The chanting lowered while the cultist's hovered their hands over the corpse, fingers moving meticulously like needles prodding flesh. With lax postures and bent necks, their lips worked in perfect unison, while their faces were hidden under the drape of their black cowls. And when they saw the ephemeral mist swirling from the husk, they slowly began tightening their circle. Beneath these chilling vapors, a glittering shell of ice formed over the body. Finally, with a single eldritch word, an exhale of power burst outward with a gale's force, causing the blue flames to stutter wildly within their braziers, and shattering the icy encasement.

An uncomfortable silence followed not soon afterward. While glowing eyes watched silently from the darkness, the cultist's widened their circle, slipping pale thin hands into their black robes. At their center, lying upon the cold stone slab, lay a sleeping woman seeping lustrously with the tight frame of youth. A long moment passed before the corpse gave a subtle twitch of a foot, then the jerk of a shoulder, soon followed by a waking moan as the pale lady stretched with crackling bones and snapping joints.

"Desdemona returns! The Masked Lady favors us again!" The tallest of the cultist's shuffled forward with the proclamation as soon as Desdemona rolled up like a rearing serpent. To some, it would look demonic and unnatural, but to the cultist's it was a sign.

Where a normal man would cringe in fear, the cultists instead recited a hymn of praise. "Blessed be She, blessed be Her champion."

Beautifully pale with skin the hue of cold death, Desdemona cast almond shaped eyes to those surrounding her. She both allured and hypnotized with but a single glance, while dark raven hair framed her heart-shaped face and cascade well past to tickle her breasts. With but a gesture from the High Priest who had announced her, another quickly brought forward a heavy fur-collared robe to drape over her slender shoulders.

She shrugged the garment away with a sneering twist of her kissable lips. Any sane man would not kiss them willingly, for they knew that those lips also held death. The cultist who had brought her such displeasure dropped immediately to his knees in supplication, where ordinarily such things would be punished with swift severity, Desdemona ignored him. She could taste his fear, however, she could smell his blood pumping through his very veins. Carrying through them such sweet nectar offering a bountiful feast.

Stretching arms until they could stretch no further, Desdemona clawed at the air and twisted her body with sexual inferences. Her eyes, aglow with cold yearning and accompanied by waking moans, looked askance to the supplicating cultist. Desdemona had been gone for too long without the pleasures of flesh, and there was a yearning to be satisfied, an itch to be scratched. Slowly, the pale lady eased herself down from the altar, reaching with frail looking toes until she alighted upon the cold stone floor. She stood short of stature, but she towered now over the one who groveled at her feet without ever taking her eyes from him.

Finding his obeisance stomach turning, Desdemona glanced back up to those gathered around her. Then to the setting to which she awoke, for none of it was the lavish return she had expected. A mere handful of her followers had assembled, with neither of her generals in their company. This led her to wonder how much time had passed. Desdemona glanced back down to the man betwixt her feet, breathing deeply of his scent. He dared not move, remaining as still as the massive pillars that filled the massive darkened hall.

"Get up," she commanded of him. He rose in an instant, keeping his hooded head low. Purposely, Desdemona positioned herself so that she peered up into his eyes. "Now kneel."

Standing much taller than she, the large youthful man brought himself to his knees. Such mindless loyalty was nearly disgusting. It was telling of weakness and it was something Desdemona found unacceptable, for there was no room for weakness in her court. Thus, was her reasoning to justify her next action. A single swipe of her hand swung past his face, disturbing the edges of his cowl. It almost seemed as though she did nothing more than swipe at the air in front his nose, but only blinks of time passed before a jet of blood arced out in a perfect stream.

Desdemona took a sideways step into its path, catching it in her mouth, relishing its warmth and taste. And as the Wulndarian bled out, she placed the ball of her foot to his chest, steadying him at just the right angle so his life's essence ran down the voluptuous contours of her body.

"Mi Lady," the High Priest risked her attention, fighting hard not to watch her rub sanguine over her face, breasts, and whispering eye. "The Chilling Hand welcomes yer return!" he bowed resplendently, maintaining it for a short while before lifting his head slightly. His accent was thick with the common brogue tongue native to Wulndar, just more faults in the people of this land the pale lady loathed.

"How long?" a question she would ask only once.

"A bit over a century, Abominating One," the High Priest quickly answered and soon professed, "the moment the air went cold and the rains became constant, we sent word throughout Wulndar—many were not easy to gather and those who dwell in the mountain passes have not responded."

"I see clearly your efforts," Desdemona noted, hiding nothing of her displeasure.

"Forgive me, mi Illustrious Queen," the High Priest bowed his ahead again until he could only stare at her toes.

"Are my personal chambers prepared, at least?" she held her eyes on him, hoping he would disappoint her further.

"O' course, yer Eminence. All is as it should be, with yer tasteful eye in mind," the High Priest straightened himself, then shrank back before sneaking a glimpse of her seductive beauty.

"What of my generals?" She asked with a sweep of her arm. Picking a servant at random, beckoning him forward with a curl of her finger. "Remove your robes and lay atop the altar."

There was no hesitancy in the muscularly youthful acolyte. He did so without question, settling his naked form atop the cold stone, starting into the swallowing darkness above. Desdemona moved to stand by his side, gorging her eyes with his athletically toned physique. Wandering further to his manhood with salivating fervor.

"Our fastest messengers have been sent to the Ghar'tul and Wolf-Kin clans who had honored the pact…" the High Priest's words trailed off, fearing to say more, and hoping he was not asked to do so.

"… But?" Desdemona had her back to him, sure that his eyes fell to her firm buttocks. She felt aroused by this and climbed up to straddle the naked Wuldnarian. He lay perfectly still, eyes up, but unable to control his own arousal. Desdemona smiled, licked her bottom lip.

"But the Duldarian's have grown stronger than before, and we weren't able to sever the bloodline that had delivered your unjust slumber," he watched as his queen played with her toy, feeling wrong and perverted doing so and yet he found pleasure in it himself.

"And where now does it hide?" Desdemona turned to meet the High Priests gaze, locking him within her own while riding the cultist below her.

Bowing deeply, the High Priest answered, "South from here, near the eastern coast. They have erected a great and lucrative port city, surrounded by impenetrable walls. I Fear, Great Lady, once they find out ye've returned, we will not have it easy."

Unconcerned laughter reached up to the watchful eyes above, stringing with it a haunting melody into the darkness. But it evaporated in an instant with a viper-like glare, "I care not for difficulties!" The High Priest lowered his eyes swiftly, not wanting to rouse her anger further. As for the poor man under her, he only groaned discomfort while his face was forced sideways. "What of the relic?" Desdemona began digging her sharpened nails into his flesh, using unnatural strength to keep him in place when he struggled.

"Locked in our highest tower, Abominating One."

Desdemona arched a brow, letting her eyes linger doubtfully over the High Priest, before tearing free the cultist's jaw with one swift yank. His blood splattered those too close, while the assembly watched as their queen drank heavily from their brother. Her tongue explored the wound and played with dangling flesh, then resuming her pleasures before the body went cold.

"What of the Duldarian's?" the High Priest dared ask as blood fell from the altar, on a straight path to be absorbed by the hem of his robes.

Desdemona threw her head back, blue eyes ablaze with the omission of her climax. Then, as though it had been nothing, she climbed down from the altar, leaving the corpse where it lay, and moved to stand before the High Priest. "The Duldarians of Wulndar will know of my return, one way or the other, leave that for me to deal with. Now, be gone, all of you. Except for *you*." She picked out another strongly built cultist, calling him to her.

The High Priest was already dreading the possibility of failure calling for the Warlords. Thwark Redeyes of the Wolf-kin and Bhar'daal of the Ghar'tul were longtime enemies, both scornful and stubborn. It was Desdemona's power that brought them to service. That, and a promise made that she never had gotten chance to honor. Now, with her return, the Feral Folk would rise again and continue her conquest that had begun those many years ago.

Chapter 2
Returning

What should have been a warm mid-summer day, was but a cloudy and miserable rainy afternoon. The turn in the weather had started a little more than a week ago and had not lifted since the ships left to lend aid to Es'lyhnn. The Druidic Circle claimed it to be foul witchcraft, and such dark magic had a way of traveling great distances. Whatever plagued the Northern Kingdoms across the Blood Sea must have blown something back, bringing on an early fall wind.

Truth be told, Flinn felt a tangible difference in the air as he walked through the narrow winding streets, nearer the docks of the city. He stepped around puddles, beneath the awnings of towering boat houses, small stores, and smaller personal domiciles stuffed between. Passing fishermen and woodworkers along his way offered subtle salute and greetings, reciprocated with an awkward smile and respectful nod. Every so often, he would stop and exchange a few friendly words with some of the merchants and dirt-ridden children at play. The rain continued to fall with a gentle misting, without pause or break. Yet, this was not bothersome, for it was the gnawing early cold that posed the true problem.

He pulled on the edges of his cowl, bringing it further over his head to stave off the cool air. On rounding a corner between two buildings creating a small alley, the corners of Flinn's mouth tugged into a restless frown on seeing a pair of dirt-ridden men at a game of bones. With a tug on his long, braided goatee, Flinn gave the unaware pair one last glance before turning to back into the street.

"Well, looks like we're graced with one of Hrothnir's

sons!" Ortheim called out at Flinn's back, the tallest of the two brothers. The Druid's son stiffened, if he kept going, they would call him a coward and then never hear the end of it. With a deep breath and a pulling back of his shoulders, the Druid's son turned to face down the unwanted exchange with a proud lift of his chin. The Port Master's sons were the same as they had always been, even in their youth they were a pair of bullying haughty louts.

The brothers made for Flinn, exuding an eagerness at the hazing that would ensue, exchanging low remarks to one another while chuckling. When they finally came face to face the brothers stood towering over the smaller Wulndarian. Ortheim was thicker than his twin, more muscled but with a larger belly from too much drink, while his brother Horthgir, nearly as tall, brought a meaty scarred hand to stroke a face flowing with dark thick facial hair. "Aye, that we are," he paused to slide his dark eyes to his brother, "Still the size of a wee bairn he is, however—I s'pose he stopped growin' from the lack of milk from 'is mothers tit."

Raucous laughter exploded from the two of them, holding their sides and nearly coming to tears. Horthgir even gave Flinn a friendly, but harder than expected, slap to his shoulder as though they were close friends. The Druid's son sorely did not consider either of them as such. Never had, and never would.

After Ortheim controlled himself, wiping away at the corner of his eye, he fixed Flinn with a studying glare. Tugging on his own bushy beard of strawberry-blonde, his lips formed a sly smile. "Ye're right! But he'd have to know what that's like to begin with."

The mood suddenly grew dark, its weight could be felt pushing down on Flinn as he set his jaw, staring up into Ortheim's taunting grey eyes. He was a massive tower of flesh that dwarfed Flinn by a few hands, and thought Wulndarians were naturally tall folk, some even reaching seven feet in height, it was an extreme rarity for any Wulndarian to be any shorter than six foot eight. In Flinn's case that gene somehow missed its mark, leaving him to be the smallest, no matter where he went. Some said it was due to the sickness his mother had developed during her pregnancy, of which some speculated played part in her death during childbirth.

Ortheim and his brother each took a step closer, bearing down on the much smaller man with intimidating glares. Flinn's father had raised him not to be fearful of any man, or any beast for that matter, for Wulndar's blood ran through his veins as well. Unfortunately, the brothers did not share that sentiment, seeing in Flinn no common traits that made these war bred people so renown. What Flinn lacked in size and strength, he more than made up for in agility and a sharp sense of awareness. He moved with such swiftness that Ortheim was unable able to grab for his shoulder as intended, instead snatching at the cowl covering Flinn's closely shaven pate, exposing it to the cold rain's chilling touch.

Finishing his low evasive spin, he came up to Ortheim's immediate right. Eliciting surprised and impressed expressions over the brothers faces.

"Ye're a quick one, I'll give ye that," Horthgir said, turning slightly with a tense posture.

Flinn watched him without looking at him, his eyes locked on Ortheim and ready to make a fool of them both. They would not be able to catch his evasive maneuvers, of that much he was confident in. They would tire quickly like the overweight oxen they were. The Druid's son shuffled a step to move past them, to leave through the other end of the alley, and found his path blocked by the repositioning brothers.

"What's the rush, boy-o? Can't take a compliment?" Ortheim reached out to make another grab at Flinn, rushing him with all the speed he could muster.

A larger man would have found themselves in a vicious bear hug. Flinn easily stepped well within Ortheim's reach and slipped beneath his arms, tumbling between his legs. He came up around from behind them and made for the end of the alley all in one fluid movement. The brothers turned in place, smiles broad as their teeth shown through their thick beards, each with amused chuckles.

"Ah, off wit' ye then!" Horthgir waved Flinn off, "Ye can't always hide in ye da's shadow, boy-o!"

Ortheim sniffed derisively, making his way back to where they had left their game on hold, "Come on, ye fool, let's finish before da comes lookin' for us." Meanwhile, Flinn rushed around the corner and continued his way.

He was glad he had avoided a tussle with the Port Master's sons, doubly so that they did not give chase. There had been times before where Flinn was not so lucky, finding himself lumped and bruised before the roughhousing and jibing words had ended. Continuing down the uneven cobblestones making up the street, and just up ahead, the docks came into view. Usually, the sight of them brought a certain joy to Flinn, memories of he and his brother Nelvedias staring yonder into the endless sea, imagining of going on grand adventures together. Lately, it was a sullen affair now, ever since the cold came and the skies turned grey; ever since his brother and father left with the ships for Es'lyhnn.

He hoped that today would be the day the ships returned, though. Months had gone by without any word, for no carrier bird came, only the gulls and the osprey who fished the Blood Sea's water. When they did return, Flinn was eager to hear the tales that came back with them, wondering what they had seen, and what they had done. Having never left Wulndar himself, the Druid's son could only read and fantasize about other lands to the east or hearing from those who visited Duldar's Port. And if who he met, what he heard, along with what he read about was just as exciting, then such lands were sure to hold grand adventures and all sorts of interesting folk.

Reaching the docks and pulling up his cowl against the elements, Flinn continued east and made a brief stop at the dock market. There was a small stall that he favored most, out of all the rest. Coincidentally, the only merchant to sell dates imported all the way from Isra'al. A land with vast seas of black sand and dread heat, where water was treasured. The merchant, an Isra'ali himself, spun tales of massive dunes like waves caught in time, of magical oases where ancient beasts and spirits often dwelled and offered boons and death. Such included stories of crazed sorcerers kidnapping princesses, and of the flying carpets they ferried them off with.

Often, the merchant spoke of great ruined cities and desert tribes that scoured the wilds, waylaying those whose pockets had grown too fat with greed. Whenever Flinn offered the due amount for his purchases, the merchant simply refused and instead requested a small telling of Wulndar and its people. Flinn was walking up to him now, the only stall erected at the corner of the street before deteriorating into the earth, with but a few strides to the docks left to traipse. Arl'at sat on a large, plush chair that looked more like a giant tomato, hemmed with gold and stitched with silver. His well-fed form sunk into the cushion's depths as his short legs draped and rested over its soft contours. In his one hand a long-stemmed pipe was held, whence a gentle slither of violet smoke rose, connecting its end with a long ribbed-hose into the base of an elaborately vase-shaped apparatus.

The little rotund man took a deep rushing pull from the pipe, blowing out a streamer of smoke as he bounced and wiggled himself out of the chair, waving excitedly towards Flinn.

"Ah, I am most pleased to see you again, my friend!" Arl'at ushered the Druid's son over with rolling and drawled enunciations. Moving quickly to grab another oversized chair of blue velvet and positioning it on the other side of what Flinn now recognized as a hookah. Arl'at had told him of such a thing in Isra'al, and of the potent weed they packed into its dish.

"I was hoping you would come visit me today, my friend, I have brought you the very thing I once described!" Arl'at bowed graciously with a wave of his hand towards the chair. "I welcome you to share under my canopy."

"How could I say no?" Flinn chuckled at the formalities, knowing that if he refused it would have been a great disrespect to the Isra'ali man. He returned the bow expressing gratitude and soon found himself sinking into the offered chair. This was the Isra'ali way, making for the best hosts, until made not to be so hospitable. "I think the ships will come today," Flinn said, shifting his weight deeper into the plush cushion, "what's in this?"

"Ah, I traded for these in one of the great palaces of Isra'al, filled with the softest feathers," dark bushy eyebrows rose on a sun-kissed face. His smile showed three golden teeth, complimenting the jewelry he bedecked himself with. Bracelets of silver and gold with such detailed engravings never seen before in Wulndar, and around his neck a thin rope of gold chain from which a star pendant hung. The exact number of points were hidden behind a dark beard, well kept, and moisturized with fragrant oils.

"No, this is no time to speak of feathers! Let us enjoy the Dervish Flower together, and I will tell you a tale of a desert prince who left his home," Arl'at shuffled across the thick carpeted floor as he spoke. "To leave behind a grand palace, filled with wonderous riches, and where women fawned over him." Maneuvering between a small eating table and matching chair, the merchant retrieved a loaf-sized lockbox from atop a larger chest. He brought it over before plopping down on the opposite side of the hookah, tittering excitedly.

Flinn was already intrigued by the tale, hoping it was not too long. The Blood Sea was within eyesight, though, so it was not as though he would miss the coming of the ships should they arrive. He got comfy, crossed his legs at the ankles and leaned back as he watched Arl'at open the box filled with overwhelming aromatics.

This was their relationship, for as long as Flinn could remember. Friendly banter, exchanging stories for history, and leaving with a small bag of dates. Of course, this was all after Flinn partook of the Dervish Flower, not unknown to it at all, for Wulndar had similar strains. Before leaving, Arl'at more than graciously gave the Druid's son a healthy amount of the herbs. After stepping out from under the merchant's canopy, now feeling light of foot and heightened of sense, the Druid's son went along his way, tossing another date into his mouth while walking the length of Duldar's Port.

The sun was high but fought to show through the grey sky, and yonder stretched the Blood Sea eastward, while rising and falling like a great breathing beast. Flinn reflected on the story told to him by the Isra'ali man. About how the desert prince realized no matter how far he ran, he could not outrun his destiny, despite the telling of how he wound up a thief and led a band of misfits to terrorize the desert sands. Yet, he had to return in the end, back to his palace, back to his father, and face his responsibilities both as a nobleman and a son. There was more to the tale, but Arl'at would save it for another visit.

Flinn headed to the furthest end of the docks where it was less frequented by dockhand, foreigner, and commoner alike. He looked askance, longing to sail the ocean, out to wherever the Fates took you. What adventures awaited him, Flinn wondered. And what battles were to be won? He wondered about his father and brother, praying to Wulndar for their safe return.

And even if Flinn had gone with them across the sea, what good would he do other than get in the way? He was too lean a man and not very skilled in terms of combat. The only weapon he owned was none other than his mother's dagger. Even that was more sentimental and ornate than anything, he would get better use out of it as a letter opener. No, Flinn was not a very imposing presence at all.

With eyes to the sea, searching the horizon for any shape that may resemble a ship, Flinn reached into his belt pouch and procured his pipe, stuffing it with the Dervish Flower. Igniting a tinder twig off the heel of his boot, the Druid's son held the flame to the pipe's chamber and pulled until a potent and hazy cloud formulated around him.

Euphoria washed over him nearly instantaneously, along with a calmness of mind and an understanding of self. Simplicity. Flinn filled his lungs up once more and let out a steady jet. Then, randomly, he thought about venturing into the Feral Lands, beyond the tall fortified walls of Duldar's Port. Traipsing through the mist of the moors beyond and across the lowlands to explore undisturbed forests. He fantasized over scaling coastal mountains to the West…

"Foolish," Flinn muttered, taking another drag of his pipe with a shake of his head.

The moors were filled with a shroud of heavy fog, and there were things that often hid there. The lowlands and surrounding forests were home to any number of Feral Folk who wandered its expanse, ripping anything apart either for fun or as food. To the west, where the mountains known as the Spines of Zhul'Tarrgan were found, were comprised of treacherous precipices and deadly falls, not to mention home to aggressive Ghar'tul clans who continually warred with one another—unlike their lowland cousins.

No. Flinn was not built for adventuring, he was not built for battle and he certainly as not built to survive the wilder places of Wulndar. Here, behind these walls he was safe. What did he care if he had to scrap here and again? He could handle himself in these streets, but out there was different and the laws within the city did not apply to those who called the Feral Lands home. Flinn did away with his fantastical imagination, eyes keeping to the waters beyond the docks.

As he stared longingly out into the ocean, something else caught his eye. At first, he thought perhaps it was nothing but shadows until the first image appeared on the Blood Sea's horizon.

And then there were two shapes! He squinted to try and make out the third ship, but it was nowhere to be seen. Perhaps it was further behind the others. Yet the ships had come! He knew today felt different, he just knew it! Flinn took off from his secluded part of the far docks and sprinted down where the ships would most likely put into port.

"They're here!" He shouted as he passed workers and fishermen, "the boats have returned!"

Those Wulndarians on the docks dropped what they were doing, some running towards the inner city with the news, while others crowded excitedly. As many crowded the dock's edge, hands to brows, Flinn looked well beyond the incoming vessels to try and see how far along the last ship was. Flinn's elation was starting to dissipate, while dockhands split off from the crowd, preparing row boats. They shoved off to find a spot to greet the incoming vessels or maybe offer any aid as they drew ever closer. Yet still, there was no sign of a third vessel.

With the nearing long boats, growing larger with the passing moments, there came a cold wind from the sea. The Wulndarians shivered against it, pulling tighter their cloaks and hide coats; assailed both by the chilling gust and the steady rain.

In time, the first ship neared the docks, some of the longboats that had gone out came back in while others drew up next to the vessel and climbed up rope ladders that were rolled down to them. Flinn caught glimpse of Dockmaster Jordt pushing through the crowd, his sons Ortheim and Horthgir flanking him.

"Make way, make way!" shouted the Dockmaster, as his sons pushed and shoved people from aside. "Get that darned gangplank up, ye dogs!" he shouted to his two burley sons.

Flinn watched as the two brothers handled the gangplank with ease just between the two of them, settling it in place so that those aboard the docked ship could disembark. His attentions went immediately to those who came down. Sullen, defeated people with haggard faces caked with dirt, grime, and dried blood came down the ramp. While others with wounds poorly dressed were ushered before them. Some clung to bags, others with nothing but the clothes on their backs, as these poor souls shambled along.

"Gods…" gasped a woman near Flinn as she looked over the sad lot.

Those from Es'lyhnn were far smaller in stature, leaner

of frame, and with eyes filled with hopeless despair as they filed out by the dozens and led by dockhands and arriving druids from the city.

These people, these refugees, were escorted by the Wulndarians who returned. They too looked battered and restless. Flinn searched frantically for his father and brother, even pushing through the crowd to get closer to the gangplank. As the refugees kept filtering from the ship, the second vessel soon docked. Longshoremen quickly helped tie the ship in, prepared the gangplank and went to assist where they were needed.

A messenger was sent by Dockmaster Jordt, sending word to High Lord Ranarek that the ships had finally returned. From the second vessel, Flinn watched as Warlord Joden made his way down, weary from the voyage and soon followed behind by several Druids all clad in their thick dark robes and pulled up hoods. There, Flinn's father was among them as they formed a circle around the Warlord. But of Nelvedias, his brother, there was no sign.

Forcing his way through the ever-thickening crowd as inner-city folk came rushing to the docks, Flinn at last managed to get closer to the small circle of Druids. He stopped short a few steps, allowing the Druids to complete their chant after a safe voyage and blessed the Warlord.

"Father!" Flinn called soon after the circle assembly broke and went to seeing that the refugees were led away in orderly fashion.

Joden gave the Druid's son a passing glance before he headed for the High Lord's Keep.

"Ah, there ye be, boy-o!" Hrothnir spread his arms wide and rushed to wrap his son up in strong arms. He held him a long moment, seemingly fearful to let him go.

"What's Nelvedias doing? I didn't see him get off yet," Flinn leaned to peek around his father, expecting to see his brother coming down the gangplank any moment.

Hrothnir took his son by the shoulders and eyed him solemnly. "There is much that needs to be told, lad." He gave

Flinn a loving squeeze before looking back over the scene.

The refugees were frightened, tired, and crying. Taken into boathouses soon after, where they would be cared for. Truly, they were the only buildings large enough to compensate for the swell of newcomers.

"What happened?" Flinn asked as his father led him away from the docks and towards the city, "How far back is the other ship?"

"First, I need ye to go straight home. I have to confer with the Druidic Circle in Duldar's Bastion," Hrothnir diverted, "High Lord Ranarek must be informed of what we saw."

They stopped as they reached the market, nearly empty since word of the ship's arrival. Arl'at had even gone, leaving his simple stall unattended. Hrothnir turned Flinn to face him. An old man in his son's eyes. Hunched over and aged, his father was still yet strong.

"What is it?" Flinn asked, seeing the hesitation in Hrothnir's eyes. He could tell something was bothering his father, something bad.

"Go home, Flinn—after I meet with the Circle, I'll explain everything to ye," Hrothnir placed a hand to his son's face and offered a nearly toothless smile. He turned and sauntered back to the docks, calling over two druids standing to one side, leaving Flinn to watch them go back to the ships.

Left with little else, the Druid's son turned and headed deeper into the city, making his way through its tightly woven streets with no intentions of going home. He wanted to see if he could muster up any information regarding what was going on, and there was only one place in Duldar's Port that provide such answers.

Just as Flinn had expected, the Bears Roar Pub was busy and rapt with rumor. He watched and listened as old men went back and forth with some of the returning warriors who came back on the ships, their eyes widening at the talk of black-skinned demons and lizard folk ravaging all of the Northern Kingdoms of Es'lyhnn. Spinning nearly incredulous tales of a flying being who had been sent down from the clouds at the final battle of Port Elzbar, the last stand before the ships made their escape. But theirs were the only ships that had made it out from the port. Sparing the refugees who returned with them from the fiends who ransacked the last standing city.

      Sitting at a table near the window looking out into the street, Flinn had been enthralled by the multitude of cross conversations buzzing throughout the pub. He had been there long after he had left his father at the docks, well now into noonday. Catching snippets of the butchery and horrors the warriors had seen. The serving girls rushed to and fro, bringing meals and refilling drinking horns, receiving solemn nods of thanks. The usually jovial atmosphere of this well frequented pub had been replaced with anger, shock, pity, and disbelief as one warrior after another stood to be heard and spin their own experiences.

      "I tell ye they be somethin' I've never yet seen," one such warrior supported the claims, a tall Wulndarian with his arm in a sling and a drinking horn held tight to his chest. He occupied the center of the pub, drawing everyone's attention to him. "Their skin dark as pitch, eyes aglow like raging blood and dark spittle threading from their toothy mouths! It took three of our warriors, at least, to take them down, many more if they be Es'lyhnnites!" lifting his horn, the warrior gave it a large guzzle before staring off to the floor, reliving the nightmare. "So many dead…"

      The pub had gone silent, each man or woman present envisioning the nightmarish demons described and the horrors they wrought. Even the serving girls had paused to look on the man with sympathy.

      "They made any Feral Man's ferocity look like a wee bairn's tantrum," spoke another suddenly, shoving from the bar's railing and coming to stand by his comrade. The two must have fought side by side, by the way he laid a comforting hand to his fellow's shoulder. "They did no' fight with honor, nor took pity on any—be they woman or child—they simply killed, feasted on the flesh of the dying, but that wasn't the worst of it..."

"They turned them, those they bit! I remember! Hauled them away until they came back just as dark as the fiends. It was too late," a veteran spoke up from the far side of the room, drawing eyes to him. His beard was nearly white, but he was far from frail with a strong build. A bandage had been wrapped around his head several times, yet his blood seeped through its fabric to make a dark stain. "We had to evacuate as many as we could, after falling back into the city, hoping they'd no' follow us into the Blood Sea."

Several nods from those who recalled the escape followed and then another lull of silence fell. The serving girls delivered their orders without a sound, setting down the meals or refilling drinking horns respectfully, not daring to disturb the quiet.

"What of the Druids?" Flinn blurted the question, unable to hold it at bay, and immediately regretted having done so. Every eye in the pub had turned to him.

"They fought with the Great Bear's fury, lad," came the warrior with his arm in a sling and rose his horn, "to the fallen!"

"To the fallen!" the pub shouted out in unison.

"What of Nelvedias?" Flinn asked, a question that made some nearly spit out their drink.

The Wulndarian who had led the toast slowly lowered his drink and set a piercing gaze over the Druid's son. "That I canno' say. I saw him once, fiercely hacking down the enemy, ye would've been proud, lad."

The Druid's son looked around the room, hoping for some other response from the others, but every one of them lowered their eyes, or hid their faces in their cups. Either they knew something had happened to his brother and were not forthcoming, or they truly did not know.

"The darkness that plagues Es'lyhnn is coming, for the same cold chill felt there now haunts Wulndar like a banshee," the white-beard warned, "mark me words, lads, something foul is happening and we'll no' be ready for its cold touch."

A heavy dread fell over the room once more. Each man feeling the weight of the white-beard's words while the pub seemed to have grown darker. The shadows seemed to press in to suffocate the warm glowing light of the fire pit, seeking further to snuff out the afternoon's light coming in from the few windows.

"Then we canno' let that be," spoke one warrior, slamming his fist that jerked each man from their sullen stupor. He was a younger warrior, hair of golden light as though spun from the looms of the Gods and stood from his place at the furthest and darkest corner to walk into the light of the pub. "The old tales speak of Duldar's sacrifice to make it so we can live in this city, how he drove the Lowland Witch into hiding at Duldar's Keep and spoiled her plans to corrupt all life—have we forgotten his mettle?"

The youth's piercing blue eyes scanned the faces of each man, waiting for any of them to discredit his words. None had, not even Flinn, who listened intently. He had heard the tales told by the elders and knew well the old stories of Duldar. A chosen champion who brought a civilized way to the peoples of Wulndar, a haven to those who did not wish to live as the Feral Folk.

Yet, Desdemona, the Lowland Witch had other plans and only sought to abominate life, convincing some of the Feral Clans to join her cause, making them believe that Duldar only sought to do away with the Natural Order. And blinded by this threat, they joined her readily—even those Duldar had once thought of as allies had turned against him. It was a tale long told, dating nearly over a century old. A story filled with adventure, betrayal, and subterfuge. Any Wulndarian youth grew up knowing that story, and as the years passed, it became legendary.

Flinn nodded, recalling the tale fondly, and lifted his drinking horn for a hearty swig. His eyes darted over the rim, gauging the reaction of the men as the young warrior went on. Noticing the mood changing from sullenness to a swell of pride. The serving girls had stopped to listen as well, enamored not only by the warrior's words, but by his comely and strong appearance.

"Duldar defeated darkness, and if this darkness from Es'lyhnn threatens Wulndar, then we too will defeat whatever may come!" he struck a strong fist to his chest to emphasize that point, and caused the patrons to sit straight, even stand up proudly holding their cups aloft.

"I say let them come! Let them come and see the might of Wulndar—death to our enemies!" the white-beard shouted, raising his drinking horn, emboldened by the youth's words.

"Death to our enemies!" the pub shouted and everyone man present were on their feet now.

A better mood took over the pub thereafter, somewhere a drum had been procured and a heavy resonant beat began. The men stomped their feet on the floor while some banged their fists to tables and started singing the ode of Duldar's Fury. Serving girls and the pub's proprietor fell into the overwhelming pride of it all, getting more drinks, bringing out more food, and refilling more cups.

Flinn found himself swept up by the song as well, stamping his foot and rapping his hand over the table in time with the beat, sipping his mead and bobbing his head with a smile. Warriors gathered around the firepit, beating their chests, and waving their drinking horns up high, spilling their mead with aggressive gestures, and slapping backs or gripping shoulders with shared camaraderie. Some of the serving girls were scooped up as they passed, grabbed by their waists, twirled about as they were lifted high in strong arms.

All the while, the Druid's son sang the song to himself quietly…

… His arms did swing twin mighty bits,

Hewing flesh and bone!
With badger's size and bear's strength,
More savage than the wolf!
The Feral Folk, no match they be,
For Duldar's newfound hopes!
No force by Lowland Witch could stand
And her allies he surely smote!
No fang, or horn nor claw could reach,
Duldar laid low betraying Folk,
For honor. For strength! His only creed!
Duldar freed us from the feral yolk!
Hail, Duldar!
For whom this song we sing!
Hail, Duldar!
For whom we keep his peace!

Flinn took a deep breath, letting it out slow before he finished his mead. A serving girl came quickly to refill it, giving him a wink before moving about the room. For him, and his love of mead, Flinn never had to worry of ever having an empty cup in this place. Yet, as the song repeated anew and the men became more confident and fearless with every imbibed drink, the Druid's son could not help but feel uncertain of the last few verses of the ode.

Stories were known to be embellished. Stories were meant to make a monster and a hero out of any man, but something deep within him made him feel contrary to the "freeing of feral yolks". That verse made Flinn feel as though he was told to hate the Feral Lands, but that hatred was unjustified for him. Other stories bespoke of beauty beyond imagination, of beasts great and small, tales of the Firbolgs and their hidden groves, of magics and adventures yielding great rewards. This reminded him of Arl'at's tales of Isra'al, leaving one's imagination to wander.

And if the stories told it right, there were only a few Feral Clans who joined the Lowland Witch, anyway, for not *all* of them rose to her cause. Which meant that there was good and bad to be found anywhere one traveled. Still, the Wulndarian's of Duldar's Port painted a different vision, one that struck fear into their children. Leaving them frightful to even go near the surrounding walls that separated them from the lands further inland.

Knowing his father to be busy at the docks, Flinn ordered two more horns of mead and a large parcel of deer haunch. When the steaming meat was placed before him, it shown with glazed honey accompanied by a smoked aromatic euphoria. A bowl of boiled potatoes, carrots and onions in an oily delicious broth had been set down also, filling his nostrils with delight. There was no harm in having a good meal before heading back home, and more besides, he had to soak up all the drink.

By the time he had left the Bear's Roar, Flinn staggered out into the settling dusk. Behind him was the uproarious merriments of the pub, soon muffled after the door closed behind him. Almost missing a step or two, Flinn found his equilibrium after a steadying moment and began his wavering walk home. The streets were nearly empty, and the chill of the day had heightened considerably now that the sun had nearly gone. Those few whom the Druid's son passed gave him soft greetings, hurrying along their way, eager to be out of the cold.

Flinn kept onward, following the worn uneven cobblestones of the street, imagining the warmth from the fire pit in his father's hall. Many stories were told around that pit, as vivid as they had been when he was young. And there had been many serious talks with his father as he watched his son grow into a man. Flinn looked forward to getting home, already eager for the serving girls to prepare him a hot bath, maybe one last horn of mead, before ending the night. Tomorrow would be a new day, one that would garner him the answer he was looking for concerning his missing brother.

Quickening his pace, Flinn followed the winding street, and just-so happened to glance between two shops forming a dark alley. His body stiffened with a flash-banging fear from deep within his being, expanding and needling the underside of his flesh, causing the hairs on his arms to stand on end. The pair of glowing orbs kept hold of him with hypnotic allure, flashing in the darkness, as all sound deafened while the edges of Flinn's vision clouded. It felt as though he was kept in a deathly cold grasp, unable to move no matter how badly he fought against it.

"Interesting." A woman's voice whispered harshly before the decaying image of her face leered from the darkness.

Flinn screamed, finally relinquished from the grasping hold, and took off at a hard sprint. The woman's hideous laughter chased after him, and when he dared to glance over his shoulder, there was no physical sign of anyone after him. By the time the Druid's son reached home, he had long since sobered up, and could not close the doors fast enough as the last remnants of twilight faded.

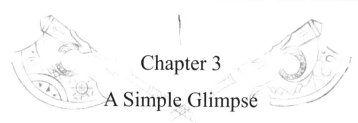

Chapter 3
A Simple Glimpse

The common architecture making up most of the city was built around wooden frames on simple stone footings with multi-layered roofs and entrances of ornamented decor. Walls were constructed of planks, logs or wattle and daub. Their interiors were much the same as far as decorative pillars and grand wooden carvings went. These were the more extravagant of the longhouses and were occupied only by those of the Druidic Circle and their staff.

The Druidic longhouses encircled Duldar's Bastion, a towering fortress overlooking the city to rival any in its complexity and breathless beauty. Each Druidic longhouse housed its own personal guard and servants, some would speculate that the longhouses also served as a barracks of sorts. It was a position of honor to head such a structure, and so here Flinn found himself in the great hall ignoring the boasts of his fellows who found comfort around the firepit. Large Wulndarian warriors all, spilling mead and swapping stories as the serving girls went about their business, while other warriors stood vigilant at specific posts throughout the building.

Flinn, shaken at what had transpired only moments ago, sat nearby at the center of the long hall, staring into the flames absently in silence reliving the horror he had been subjected to. It could well have been the mead crossed with the Dervish Flower. There just was no sense to be made of the occurrence. The image of the woman's face, as ghoulish as it had appeared, seemed both there and not, though her frigidly radiant eyes were solid enough. And what of the laughter that had chased after him echoingly, could it be that Flinn was the only one to hear it? He could not recall passing anyone else on the street, running as though the hounds of Hell were on his heels, not bothering to even look.

When Flinn had burst into the longhouse, surprising the guards momentarily until they realized who he was, he went straight up the long staircase to change his clothes without a word to come down shortly after to join the men by the firepit. An inquiry was made of his father's whereabouts but was told that he had not yet returned. The hour had grown late, with fatigue pulling down on Flinn's eyelids heavily. Dragging his hands down over his shaven head and his angular face, the Druid's son retired to his personal chambers. Tired, shaken and confused, Flinn was eager to leave the evening behind.

What he experienced continued to haunt him as he settled deeper into his mattress, pressing the back of his head further into the goose-down pillow.

"Duldar," Flinn whispered a prayer to Wulndar's long gone hero, "spare me these thoughts…"

Then, watching the shadows cast by the light from the small hearth in his room against the high ceiling, playing across thick supporting beams above his bed, the Druid's son soon fell unwittingly to sleep. There was naught but the sound of crackling flames to soothe him, sending his mind adrift, slipping into a realm beyond the physical. Even within the safety of his own mind, the image of the woman plagued him still, with much, much more.

His dreams were erratic. Jumping from one scene to the next with a constant theme of darkness ever present. He was looking down from a bird's eye view at Duldar's Port in flames, its streets filled with echoing screams and glistening with puddles of blood as shapes scampered throughout on all fours. Then the view rushed down into the thick of it, speeding through the grid-like thoroughfares, passing butchered people whose screams filled the night with their fear and agony. Great hulking creatures tore them apart with steel, fang, and claw.

Their features were difficult to make out in true details, for too heavily were they shadowed.

Flinn's subconscious sight panned out again, taken higher to scour over the ruination below, diving back down into the courtyard outside Duldar's Bastion. Stopping short to focus on a dark-skinned man—no—more than just a man, he was bestial with wolfish features, a standing mass of knotted muscle and obvious strength. His red eyes shown through the darkness concealing most of his features as he stood on the steps leading to the great doors of the fortress, while the glow of the surrounding longhouses burned violently. His hulking form stood over the slain High Lord Ranarek, with Warlord Joden not far off and Flinn's own father!

Behind this bestial Wulndarian, the silhouettes of more monstrous creatures gathered, slipping in and out of sight, leaping and bounding to fall over helpless victims attempting to make their escape from the fortress, all while brave warriors fought to buy them time. They fell to grisly deaths themselves, eventually overwhelmed and slain, posing no match for the sheer ferocity of the massive beasts who went from standing on two legs to all fours with ease.

But the red eyes of the bestial man suddenly flickered to lay over Flinn, considering him for a moment, unimpressed, as sanguine light softly illuminated the night while echoing howls called distantly in eerie song. Caught between the baleful stare of the beast-man and the screams of butchered Duldarians, Flinn could do nothing.

Then, without warning, the Druid's son was taken far above the mayhem, shooting up like an arrow at the red moon glaring its bloodied eye over the carnage. He shot across the high walls of the city, upon which the slaughter continued, and dropped down to speed through misty moors towards the north where Howler's Wood waited. Once more, as like a bird taking flight, Flinn rose high to skim the canopies of tall pedunculate oaks where in the distance there rose a ruined fortress. Up its towering mass to the top of its tallest tower Flinn scaled its height, stopping to hover before a black light emanating from its peak. Here was where a thick black tome was found floating of its own accord, and behind it the most beautiful pale skinned woman Flinn had ever laid eyes on.

Dark raven hair spilled down her shoulders, framing, and accentuating the breathtaking image of her youthful face. She stood before the tome nude, caring not for modesty, and freely revealing a lustrous body of deathly-hued flesh. Keeping intense glacial eyes on Flinn, paired with a deceiving smile playing over inviting lips, she lifted a finger as a mother would shush a child. She winked playfully, followed by hair-raising laughter as the dark book sent zapping tendrils and limned her body in its black-lit glow.

The sound of burning caught his ears, sending the sky into ruinous sanguine flames before thrusting him away so that the tower became smaller and more distant, all the way back into the burning city to plummet headfirst towards the uneven cobblestones. Flinn tried to scream against his descending fate, his stomach tying in knots to unravel as the street rushed up to meet him.

Flinn sat up with a great shout, crossing his arms and covering his face against the impact, but after several moments of exasperated heaving, he soon realized that he was awake and safe in his room. The sound of a low fire drew his attention to the hearth, finding his father adding more wood to the hungry flames.

"Ye've been tossing and turning for a bit now, boy-o, I tried to wake ye, but too deeply were ye gone." Hrothnir spoke into the flames as he fed them one last bit of wood.

Rubbing the sleep from his eyes, Flinn snatched back the sheets and swung his legs over the edge of the bed. He drew his hands down his face with some measure of relief, thankful that the nightmare ended, comforted that his father had come home, and yet remained haunted by the familiar laugh he had heard before waking.

"Tell me what ye've dreamt, boy-o." Hrothnir lifted a small chair and brought it over to sit across from his son. He sat, the chair creaking beneath his weight. With the light of the fire at his back now, Hrothnir's weathered and aged features were mildly masked, but the glow from its luminance only framed his strong build.

Flinn's father may be old in his years, perhaps nigh eighty, but he still retained a powerful youthful vigor. Looking into his eyes, their blue, almost hazel color still retained their vibrancy despite the shadow that draped over them. "Tell me, son," the Druid's eyebrows furrowed concernedly, edging forward in his chair to rest a bear's paw of a hand to Flinn's knee.

He followed the tracing creases marring his father's brow, the crows-feet foretelling of a man who enjoyed a good laugh, far more telling by furrowing lines around his mouth. They caused the Druid to appear as if he wore a constant smirk, plotting harmless mischief. Hrothnir stroked patiently at his long beard, a waterfall of peppered brown and grey, filled with woven braids and ornate clasps of silver and gold.

For a long moment, Flinn was not sure where to start. With the face he had seen in the alley, or the dream he just had, and he was damn sure that they both were related. Flinn sighed, the sound of the woman's laughter sounding so coincidentally the same from what he heard earlier that night. Worst yet, he had been awake for that, which did not make him feel any better.

And so Flinn told every detail, sparing not a one and even made mention of the experience he had in the street. During it all, Hrothnir leaned back so far in his chair that he was sure to fall backwards. As he sat reclining in silence, somehow maintaining balance, he quietly processed his son's ill portents. His eyes steeling into his youngest boy and became misted over as he continued to stare.

Flinn was quiet, waiting for some sort of comforting words from his father. "It was just a dream," he wanted him to say. "Too much excitement for one day," would also be a preferred response. But neither of those soothing phrases came to him.

"These visions," Hrothnir spoke his words with

confident factuality, "have they happened before tonight?"

"No, da, not until after the alley," Flinn shivered, hardly believing it himself, "now this." He shook his head, unsure of reality as he was with the sanity of his own mind.

To Hrothnir, Flinn was still a boy in his eyes, but he was not your typical ignorant youth lost in the primordial of teen years. Flinn was wise, more so than others would conceivably believe, his understanding of physical mechanics was uncanny, his understanding of the world around him unheard of, and despite the few things the lad did not excel at, they were but a blemish on the overwhelming greatness of this young Wulndarian man.

Flinn remained silent. He could not rightly think after waking from such horror. Should it be a vision, as his father intoned, then why was *he* receiving them? Flinn was a runt, scrawny to some, unassumingly quick and strong to others, and able to think under pressure. That was it.

Other than that, he had his nose buried in books, making friends with those who somehow seemed drawn enough to him to strike random conversation. Yet, he was bullied by some who were envious of his uneventful life, made fun of by others he grew up with, while wanting to come off as friends. Flinn had but few he called friends these days and could count them all on one hand.

"It was just a dream, Da," he waved the entire experience away, no longer wanting to be bothered by it. Maybe if he wished hard enough, it would all just go away and be forgotten.

Flinn removed himself from the bed, making his way across to the fireplace. His posture was disciplined, with pulled prominent shoulders and a raised head as he looked down the gentle slope of his nose into the flames. Their illumination revealed a physique of tightly packed muscle, sinewy and exuding an unassuming strength for one so small of stature. He blew out his nostrils, convincing himself further that he was no one special.

"Do not be a fool, boy-o." Hrothnir stood up, a cairn of

strength. "Do not think ye so little, son, someone or something allows you glimpses into what could be. Who that one is, I could only guess, but do not wave this lightly aside!"

Flinn's eyes held the flames still, not wanting to meet his father's irritated gaze. Why was this happening to him, of all times. With his silent denial, his next question came low and implicating, "Where is my brother?"

"Ye brother has been chosen by the Fates to travel another path, boy-o, but he is not alone," Hrothnir revealed what he had fretted revealing, but knowing it would come to pass eventually. Flinn's attachment to his brother was profound, their connection radiated intense complimentary energies, and when together were inseparable.

Flinn made to ask more, but he thought it best not to prod any further. By way of his father's apprehensive stance, it was a clear sign to lay the matter aside. The pain was clear in Hrothnir's posture, it was not easy letting Nelvedias go.

"The Dark Tome is the heart of this, with it comes horrible power to the one who wields it—and that woman only brings further concern, for it was in her hands last and is so again…" he looked away into the flames, recalling older times, "You know her, lad."

Flinn whispered, "The Lowland Witch…"

"Aye. Desdemona apparently was not killed utterly. Whatever it was that gave you these visions, or whoever it was, has reached out to you with a warning."

"So, what now?"

Hrothnir's thick eyebrows rose, accompanied by a tight-mouthed line of thoughtfulness. "We must bring this to the Druidic Circle's attention, but first to High Lord Ranarek."

A look of incredulity draped over Flinn's face. It was just a dream. Hardly anything to bother the Druids with, let alone the High Lord! He shook his head, becoming more and more confused by the moment. While yet maintaining his gaze over the dancing flames in the hearth, images of his nightmare replayed themselves, emphasizing the book and the sanguine moon.

If it meant anything to Flinn, he did not show it, he would not have any idea how to react even if it *did*. A fetid feeling, though, sat churning in his gut. He knew full well now that something bad was going to happen to Duldar's Port, especially if Hrothnir thought it important enough to involve the Druidic Circle. Maybe that was the reason for the early approach of fall; if so, did that also mean the darkness that plagued Es'lyhnn had already settled into the city?

"What's happening, Da?" Flinn finally asked, turning for guidance.

"That's what we're going to have to find out, boy-o—for if I've interpreted correct, then all Wulndar will soon see darker days ahead." Hrothnir nodded solemnly and tried his best to offer his son a comforting smile, but Flinn knew it only for that.

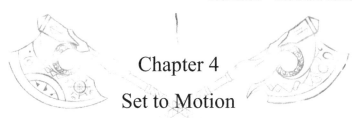

Chapter 4
Set to Motion

The dimly lit hall was quiet. At each of the decorative pillars flanking either side, there stood a hooded guard gripping in one hand a spear and a round shield strapped to the opposite arm. No sound escaped them; it was a wonder if they even breathed at all. Desdemona sat on a comfortably plump cushioned throne, draping herself over the arms of the obsidian craftsmanship. Spikes of dark ice lanced upwards to fan out like the wing of some foul creature, clawing inward in a pitiful attempt to cage her.

Her thoughts were not entirely on what was happening presently, for she had sent her astral form to traipse and haunt the forest beyond her ruined keep just yesternight. Traveling as a specter towards Duldar's Port, to probe this new *city* honoring a long dead fool. That accursed man that he was, the thought of him angered her. Knowing he was dead offered a small pleasure, but something had caught her attention to raise alarm. The young drunken man, who had staggered through the streets that night, exuding on him an unmistakable scent; however, faint as it was, but enough for Desdemona to make note of. And that bothered her immensely.

Meanwhile, seated as her guests at her banquet table, centralized in the long hall, there watched Baar'Dahl and his rowdy kin. Most watched a slave girl dance, laughing whenever she stumbled, taking bets as to when her fatigue would eventually kill her. Sometimes the end of their words trailed off into a wretched bleating, as if having no control over it, *especially* when they laughed. It brought a disgusted sneer to their hostess's lips, distracting her and breaking her contemplations.

Desdemona found the Ghar'tul crude and even more aesthetically displeasing with their goat-like legs, pointed ears and small horns protruding from their foreheads. Even in this form they were filthy creatures, yet she could not deny that they were unmerciful warriors. Especially, in larger groups. Unfortunately, only a few of the lowland clans answered her beckoning call and while still waiting for another clan to respond. She hoped that Thwark Redeyes would soon arrive, and if he should not, then Desdemona knew what to do with him.

Directing her thoughts onto the slave girl, who danced to a dark string of notes from an enchanted violin, the Pale Lady quickened the tune with a twitch of a finger. The melody picked up maddeningly, sending the girl into fits of sharp turns and spinning twirls led by the violin itself. It circled about her, forcing her in step with relentless grace.

After a simple arch of Desdemona's eyebrow, the possessed instrument strung faster. The slave girl could barely keep rhythm and fast becoming clumsy and less sure of foot. Then faster still did the violin play, throwing the slave girl off completely and narrowly rolling her ankle.

She had thought herself clever, though, while attempting to mask her mistake by stepping into another routine. Desdemona smiled deviously, amused by how hard this pathetic creature aimed to please. Of course, when death was imminent and dependent on performance, one often strived for perfection.

The music stopped suddenly much to the dancer's relief, collapsing to the cold stone floor heedless of banging her knees. She was happy to alleviate her aching feet, but her utmost concern was muffling her weeping into brilliant fiery hair. She was a frail thing at the center of an unjust audience, reinforced by sitting naked in fear, hugging bruising knees to her bare chest. And though faint, her whimpering shudders caught the Pale Lady's eye.

Desdemona picked herself up from lounging over the

throne, rising to stand elegantly and imperially. The long hall fell uncomfortably quiet, the Ghar'tul and the Pale Lady's court watched in silent eagerness. Baar'Dahl himself had seen the extents of the woman's cruelty, and more yet knew her not to a native of Wulndar. How she had come to their island, the Warlord could not recall. Only that after she had arrived on the far coast, she had wrought unspeakable horrors after finding her adrift those many years ago.

Descending the small dais, scantily clad in a black robe that left nothing to the imagination, Desdemona approached the girl with calculative steps. She wore no shoes; revealing black frostbitten toes. The Pale Lady nearly seemed to glide across the floor, her robe trailing behind like spilled ink until she was standing over the pathetic wretch.

Reaching to prick the tip of her sharp claw-like nail beneath the slave girl's chin, Desdemona lifted fear-filled eyes of emerald to be caught in her own stony gaze. A nervous sound escaped her when realizing that her body went into a state of paralysis.

Desdemona smiled as she lowered herself down to her haunches, delighting in the girl's frantic stare as nervous perspiration beaded across her brow. The stink of it filled the Dreaded Queen's nostrils, tasting the essence of life held within them. She reached down teasingly between her thighs, tickling them with the tips of her fingers, before reaching into the darkness of her robes. Soon retracting a small hidden blade. Its steel glinting wickedly in the brazier's light as the Pale Lady held it up at eye-level, causing tears to well up in the slave's eyes and sweat to trickle.

Desdemona, while smiling, drew the blade beneath the girl's chin with a surgeon's precision and opened the underside of the girl's jaw. Blood washed down her neck, painting smoothly the Pale Lady's hand while her fingers worked into the wet and sticky wound. Fiddling fingers searched for the girl's tongue as though picking for a worm, and when once found, pulled from the gaping incision to hang limp and bloody.

While licking blood stained fingers, an obnoxious banging came from the other end of the hall. Desdemona sprang to her feet in an instant, wiping blood from her lips and leaving a large smear across her face, before moving quickly back up the dais to spin and plop into her thrown. The slave girl had since been released from the paralytic spell, sprawled out in an expanding pool of her own blood.

Allowing the impatient banging to go on a bit longer, pleased that she had the power to get under someone's skin, especially if that someone was Thwark Redeyes, Desdemona gestured to two guards. They set into motion immediately, leaving their posts to admit whomever it was entry into the Pale Lady's long hall. They were swallowed instantaneously by the shadows after leaving the light of the firepit, where not long after old hinges groaned as the doors opened.

Desdemona watched as dark shapes sauntered into the shadows from long distance. Their bare feet slapping heavily against the stone floor, following a larger shape whose glowing red eyes led the way towards the light of the flames. The Pale Lady was not fond of fire, making sure that her throne sat far enough from its uncomfortable heat.

As the large Feral Wulndarian and his ilk came up short of the table at which the goat men sat, some of the Pack Master's kin hung back just outside the fire's light. Desdemona made note of the obvious look of disdain the Pack Master held for the Ghar'tul, especially for Baar'Dahl. Too long had the two been rivals and wondered what went on between them during her long slumber.

She tilted her head amusingly, able to feel the tension between them thick enough to stop a fine edged blade. "Thwark Redeyes comes at last," she did not hide her contempt for the bestial man's late arrival, "I'm afraid you've arrived too late—our entertainment has retired early." She gestured to the corpse of the slave girl.

Thwark was indifferent to the scene. Had had slain many Duldarians fool enough to wander from their stone walls. Seeing the slain girl did not bother him in the least, nor intimidate him anymore than he would allow, which was not at all.

He was a large Wulndarian man, seven feet of pure hulking muscle, clad in a great kilt of black, grey, and white. Strong wolfish features made him seem more beast than man, however, with a squared jaw and thick lips barely able to conceal his upper and lower canines. His pointed ears rotated forward and flared out from a thick head, were a mohawk of dreadlocks ran down the center and hung between gnarled back muscles. A prominent brow hung over the crooked bridge of his nose, broken many times over from battles. Thwark Redeyes, Pack Master to the Wolf-kin of Howler's Wood, was not one to be taken lightly.

He grunted at Desdemona's words, heedless of provoking her displeasure while his personal guard, seven of his strongest and fiercest warriors, skulked in the shadows. Once and a while, their eyes reflected the firepit's light, flashing amber to let the occupants of the long hall know they were still there.

Desdemona cared not for their arrogant predatory mannerisms, knowing full well she could end any one of them should she choose. If they were not such ruthlessly efficient warriors, the Pale Lady would have done away with them long ago. Just as she had done to another such defiant group. She had eradicated their clan outright with a swift hand. Until recently, she believed their destruction absolute, and now realized they had not *all* been wiped clean from this filthy island.

Baar'Dahl remained seated, glaring over at Redeyes but Thwark paid him no mind, a greater insult had he said anything at all. Instead, the Pack Master held his sanguine eyes to the cold stare of Desdemona's own. Amused, her smile returned, daring Thwark to move against her. Much to her disappointment, he only waited in silence.

"We have a problem that needs to be resolved before we renew our campaign and I may finally honor my promise," her words held no hint that she was troubled, but she had been ruffled tremendously with recent events.

Redeyes and Baar'Dahl both listened, waiting for more elaboration.

"Despite our failings in the past, I will ensure our victory," the Dreaded Queen tilted her head as she shifted her eyes between the two Clansmen, waiting for idiotic inquiries to blubber from their mouths. Still, they spoke not. "We must first mobilize a raiding party and retrieve a particular youth just entering manhood, once he is here with me, we launch a full-scale attack, thus finally erasing all memory of Duldar and his ilk."

Thwark lifted his chin, intrigued.

"And who be this young man of interest, Dreaded One?" Baar'Dahl inquired.

A derisive snort escaped her, waving the question aside and silencing him all at once. Her next words were for Thwark, "You'll know the scent, and once you do, you'll realize my concerns. I want this man alive, Redeyes, be warned. If he is anything but, I will be highly displeased."

She proceeded to describe a short statured Wulndarian no more than twenty summers, emphasizing his fiery goatee, "And green eyes—the bastard whelp may prove useful if under the right influence… perhaps entertaining. Yet there is—"

"I can see it done," Baar'Dahl interrupted in declaration, of which dropped a mask of doubt over Thwark's bestial visage.

Desdemona simply smiled and held up a hand before Baar'Dahl had chance to speak any more. "Yes," she approved, "I did have you in mind, but there is a level of discretion that only the Wolf-kin can execute, I have no use for brutish tactics and stubborn strategies..." she let her words trail off thoughtfully.

Baar'Dahl exuded visible frustration that brought a chuckle from his rival. It took all that he could muster to keep himself not to turn and spit into Thwark's face. Retaining eyes over Desdemona, Baar'Dahl bit his lower lip and dipped his horned head in obeisance, saying nothing further.

"The blessings of Zhul'Tarrgan are still with me—the task will be done," he had no need to say it, but Thwark did anyway. He wanted to add salt to the wound of Baar'Dahl's pride, along with casting him a sly sidelong glance.

Desdemona arched an eyebrow with a judicious lift of her chin, "It's been a long time since then, *old friend*." She smiled after that.

Redeyes eyed her dangerously, a low growl rumbling warningly at the back of his throat. He made no attempts at hiding his dislike for her, but their alliance was mutually beneficial; at least, it once was. He had no time for her games, though, and dared to say, "My actions have upheld me end of the bargain, what say ye o' yerself?"

The smugness Desdemona had just exuded dissipated within a blink. The Pale Lady may be powerful with her ways of dark magic and forbidden necromancies, but she could be offended easily, made to check herself. For if she allowed herself to strike Thwark down, before his guards and all else, not only would she have lost an effective ally, but would be hard pressed to accomplish what she had started long ago. She needed an army, and these fools provided it.

For Thwark, her fuming silence was answer enough. and grunted for his bodyguards to follow as he turned his back on her. The Ghar'tul watched the Wolf-kin with incredulous stares, shocked by the brazen air Redeyes carried. He was no slave of hers and he knew he played a pivotal role in the Witch's plans.

Let her continue to believe she had him at heel, for when the opportunity reveals itself, the Pack Master will leap to deliver a killing blow. Then, not only would he have slain her, but have possession of the Dark Tome. With it, Zhul'Tarrgan would find him worthy still, and bless him once more with abundant boons.

Shadowed silhouettes of trees swayed in the cool night's breeze, encircling a small glade within Howler's Wood not far from the ruined keep. Redeyes and his bodyguards met here with the rest of the pack. Whether Desdemona needed to know that Thwark had brought with him every able-bodied warrior or not was of no concern of his.

They stepped out from the darkness of the forest surrounding the clearing, astride ruddy brown dire wolves. One wolf trotted over to meet the Pack Master, darker than the darkest pitch, with a pair of brilliant yellow eyes, sniffing and nuzzling Redeyes as he stroked her muzzle and patted her flank. Taking hold of the saddle's pommel, he swung himself up and gestured for his helm and long handled bearded ax.

A smaller likewise weapon he kept tucked in his belt, and ready to use it at a moment's notice, it was a test of loyalty for his weapon bearer, a pup in the pack's eyes but nearly fifteen summers and still green along the edges. After adjusting his great kilt, Redeyes turned his mount to address The Pack.

"We ride for Duldar's Port!" he bellowed before fitting his horned helm over his head, flaring large nostrils.

There were no adrenaline rushing cheers or salutes, there were no questions asked nor demands made. The Wolf-kin simply waited until Redeyes gently tapped his mount's flank with the heels of his bare feet. She went where he led her, feeling the intention of his subtle movements, and the connection ran deeper than that.

Beneath the full moon's light, always watchful, ever bright; the pack traveled through the rest of the night until daybreak, finding rest and food in a maze of briars, using it as cover and protection. They were but a night away before reaching Duldar and returning Wulndar to its former glory. Back to when the clans embraced Zhul'Tarrgan's gifts, not casting them aside to build cities and invite foreigners into their lands and making it weak.

As his pack rested, taking picket shifts throughout the day. Thwark lounged against the base of a strong oak, its branches thick with changing colored leaves, clear sign that the shift had occurred once more. Things were different now, though, he could sense it. That was why he needed to bide his time, figure out how best to turn this opportunity to his favor. The Pale Lady's interest in this Duldarian youth rose more than his eyebrows but piqued his curiosity.

The dark wolf lay beside him, deep in slumber, not a care in the world, as Thwark stared in the distance of a sun-shafted forest towards Duldar's Port. Very soon, he thought, things were going to change drastically for the Island of Wulndar.

Chapter 5

A Somber Breakfast

That same morning Flinn woke in a cold sweat. The nightmare had persisted in all its chaotically twisted darkness. The same images, the same faces, the same laughter, and the same Dark Tome. His father's words echoed at the back of his mind and wondered still what it all meant for him specifically. Hrothnir had not even elucidated that fact and had simply left his son alone in his room after they had talked, giving him the same cliché comforts any parent would their child who *had a bad dream*.

Sitting up in his sweat soaked sheets, the Druid's son stiffly removed himself from his bed and made for an antique armoire. He adorned his great kilt and went to his writing desk and opened the drawer where he stashed his mother's dagger.

He slid the ornamental piece into the inside of his boot and left his room to take the stairs to the long hall on the base floor. He found his father at their banquet table, plates of food both cold and hot spread before him. At first sight of his son he waved him over hastily, "Come, eat, eat, we have a long day yet."

House guards stood attentively motionless, ready at a moment's notice, stationed, and evenly spaced at either side of the hall itself, whilst two others stood guard at the double doors leading out into the city. Flinn descended the last few steps and crossed the space as early morning light struggled to filter in through apertures above. He took the chair adjacent his father, taking a moment to settle and look over the selection of food.

"Today we meet with High Lord Ranarek and Warlord

Joden," Hrothnir informed.

Flinn nodded solemnly, as a serving approached to prepare whatever he wanted for breakfast. Yet, he settled for the simplest of things that he did for himself. A bowl of oats, raw honey, nuts, berries, cinnamon, and a hemp pressed milk concocted of his father's own recipe.

He stared down at his meal while his father droned on, becoming more distant by the second. His thoughts retracted back to the tales told at the Bear's Roar last night, of what the men in the pub described having seen while trying to assist the Es'lyhnnites. Of dark demons who slaughtered with extreme prejudice, killing, and spreading their evil like a sickness. With dark magics nearly forgotten and rampant, leaving an inviting trail for those who normally hid from the light, they emerged from the darker places of the land.

It had to be the reason why all of this was happening to Flinn, and physically changing the very fabrics of energy that bound life, somehow perverting it. There was something Flinn had read about in one of his father's books, about how the lands became sour during a previous dark age. Was it happening again, during Flinn's time; and if so, what would happen to the people of Duldar's Port, or of the foreigners who came for trade supporting such lucrative business?

"Eat, boy, ye'll need yer strength for what today brings." Hrothnir gestured to the food sitting under his son's far off stare.

Blinking from deep thought, Flinn stirred his food with sparing glances to his father who busied himself with another helping of eggs and beef. He washed it all down with a horn of mead that dribbled down his thick beard, never bothering to wipe it away.

The stiffness from a restless sleep left Flinn with irritating aches in his back, shoulders, and neck, and tried to work them out as he poked about with his spoon at his food. He ate as much as he was able, though he did not have much of an appetite. He hoped what he consumed would help loosen him up and fuel him for the day ahead, not that he was much looking forward to it.

After his father had finished filling his belly, he announced that it was time to leave. He gathered what he needed, leaving specific instructions to the captain of his guard, and led Flinn out to meet with the High Lord.

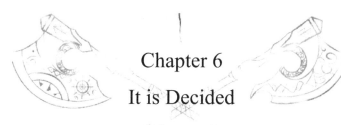

Chapter 6
It is Decided

It was a gloomy and wet morning. The rain had ceased for a time, but it threatened to start again at any moment. Flinn glanced up to the grey sky, making note of the suffocating sun attempting to warm the day, but the muffled light could do nothing to break free and relinquish the chill air. The aggression of this early fall weather was daunting, heavy with a depressive weight, and it showed in the faces of every Duldarian and foreigner who walked the city streets.

This did not stop usual business, however. Folk went about their daily duties much the same, either working down by the docks, opening their shops, or setting up their merchant stalls in the Tradesman Quarter, a few blocks south from the docks. Guard patrols made their rounds, relieving others, and kept an eye out for trouble. There rarely ever was any to be had, maybe a drunken brawl here and again, but for the most part Duldar's Port was a peaceful place with little to no crime at all.

Sometimes, the foreigners got themselves into trouble, earning themselves an uncomfortable night in the detainment garrison. Depending on the severity of their crime dictated their stay, or something added they would not soon forget about Wulndar's ways and customs when handling matters of theft, unnecessary violence, or murder. Thankfully, Duldar's Port had yet to deal with such a crime.

For all its sights, however, it was the Druid's Quarter that was off limits to visitors, unless on important business or with an urgent message that needed High Lord Ranarek's attention. Keeping the quarter divided from the rest of the city was a circle of high iron fence, topped with barbed tips. There were only three gated entrances, which were guarded by a quartet of armored guards.

Each of the Druid's longhouses had their own paved path to Duldar's Bastion, all met at a small outer road of smooth shale stone, of which circled just outside the Keep. This circling path wrapped around outside the stone walls of the fortress, coming to a singular iron gate flanked by large pillars topped with roaring bear's heads. The guards noted the approach of Hrothnir, snapping to attention and saluted him as he and Flinn neared.

The gates opened silently, well-oiled, and consistent maintenance. Flinn kept in step with Hrothnir, sparing a glance to one of the guards who watched him from the corner of their eye.

Once well enough inside, the gates were barred shut by the interior guards. An open courtyard of brightly green grass laid a carpet before them, filling gaps between smaller paths leading away and around Duldar's Bastion. Flinn, eying the majesty of the fortress, had only been inside as many times he could count on one hand, marveling with each visit over the complex architecture. Certainly, it was the jewel of all Duldar and many attempted to mimic its illustrious image. They all paled before the strength and steadfastness its presence exuded.

Hrothnir led his son past fountains and small gardens being tended by caretakers, passed between stone statues of proud warriors atop enlarged pedestals, and fantastical hedge sculpted beasts scattered all over. Beekeepers tended hives off to one side further away, as their bees buzzed about them harmlessly. Birds sung their songs in the boughs of trimmed trees springing up throughout the expanse, and flowers grew in controlled clusters, filling the air with floral aromatics.

Soon large stone steps led up to a pair of colossal wooden doors, while two guards heavy with muscle and hard leather armor, were the only thing between Hrothnir and Flinn. There was no need to announce themselves or ask for an audience. The Druid and his son were expected, for the guards hurried to admit them long before their ascension up the large steps.

Once within the well-lit greeting hall, servants rushed to offer horns of room temperature mead and clean damp towels to wash their hands with. Thereafter, Flinn and his father were led to a larger corridor that stretched into an even bigger chamber, where a pair of twin curving stairs rose to an upper level. A large door waited ahead between them where guards stood stolid and patient,

Hrothnir approached, handing his used towel to one of the servants who fought to keep up with the larger man's stride. Flinn followed a step behind, taking his time and prolonging it. The moment they stopped before the doors, one of the guards saluted and opened it.

"Hrothnir!" A commanding voice boomed excitedly at the other end of the greater hal and snapping Flinn from his thoughts with a jolt.

"I see ye've brought the young lad! Good, good!" High Lord Ranarek was an even larger man than his father. A mane of red hair, wild and unkempt, grew out and fell from the silver circlet crowning the High Lord's block of a head. He was rotund, save for a few telling features that hinted at once being a fit man.

Garbed heavily in robes over his great kilt, and animal furs that made him seem bigger than he was, Ranarek nearly leapt from his throne of thick oak and banded gold, hurrying down the small dais to greet his friend. His arms went wide, like the wings of a golden eagle as a fat-cheeked smile fought through a bearded forest.

Behind him, from the shadows beneath the colonnade, stepped out Warlord Joden. With a clean-shaven head, druidic ruins tattooed over most of his body, head and face included. The hilt of a great sword poked over a well sculpted shoulder as the large man stepped up beside Ranarek. Joden offered an acknowledging nod to Hrothnir, before sweeping stone-grey eyes over Flinn.

The Druid's son felt meek under that hard gaze, studying him with as much intent as one gauging the distance before shooting an arrow.

The High Lord's paw-like hands fell heavily over Hrothnir's shoulders and the two of them embraced. "Couldn't get enough of my mead yesternight, eh, came back for more did ye!?" his laughter was an encompassing storm that filled the hall and gave Joden a playful backhand to his chest.

Both the Warlord and Druid shared in the mirth, but Hrothnir's had gone out quickly and not without notice.

"So, what's it ye need to tell?" the High Lord looked up and glanced to Joden and gave him a commanding nod.

"Everyone out!" Joden boomed.

The guards and servants quickly rushed from the hall, disappearing through side doors. The guards made sure, for themselves, not to stray too far from earshot. And once the last door had shut, Ranarek gestured to the gargantuan banquet table that nearly filled the entire hall itself. They seated themselves comfortably with offers of food and drink, but the Druid refused with a quick glance to his son.

"What is it, old friend?" Ranarek sat back into his lavish chair at the head of the table, leaning into one arm and settling his chin atop a meaty fist. Flinn's eyes were attracted to the cerulean pinky ring he wore, wondering where he acquired such a rare piece of jewelry. Joden stood by closely with massive arms folded over his strong chest.

"My youngest," Hrothnir gestured with a hand to Flinn, "has had some disturbing visions ye need to know about."

Ranarek's neatly trimmed eyebrows rose.

"Tell him, boy-o," Hrothnir ushered.

Flinn nearly fought to even look the High Lord in the eyes and made all efforts possible to not meet the stone-cold stare he felt from Joden.

"Go on, there's nothing to fear from me—speak to ye High Lord and know me to be a sound man," Ranarek said soothingly. Joden shifted behind him, turning his head slightly as he observed Flinn's manner.

Feeling on edge, Flinn finally did admit to his nightmares, explaining it just as he had explained it his father last night. And just as Hrothnir react, so too did Ranarek and Joden. The Warlord's eyes flashed as the description of the red-eyed man specifically, as if he knew him. Ranarek looked extremely troubled, looking to Hrothnir several times during Flinn's telling, looking for confirmation in his words. The Druid nodded every time, affirming what was said was true.

"The Darkness that plagues the Eastern lands is making its way here," Hrothnir informed, "as I've spoken with you last night about our campaign—and these visions," he waved a hand to incorporate Flinn, "he speaks of no other than Desdemona."

"The Lowland Witch and her dog Redeyes return, then." Joden affirmed, his eyes studying Flinn.

Hrothnir nodded. "Apparently, the horrors across the Blood Sea were already stirring here on Wulndar—something terrible has set things in motion."

"What then do we do about it—can't very well send our men wandering the Feral Lands aimlessly, even though we know where the bitch is hiding, it would leave Duldar's Port weak and ripe for the plucking—ye know damn well that that witch will come of us."

The three large men deliberated at length, by which time Flinn had drowned them out completely. He wanted to lock himself up in his room and away from all this talk off Feral Folk, witches, horror, and evil books. He was perfectly fine just days ago, and now his life was spinning out of control. And instead of his father trying to soothe him by saying it was nothing, and that Wulndar was safe, he instead the complete opposite! It was too much.

"Ye know where the damned thing can be found and you know *what* it truly is," Hrothnir said in a foreboding tone, "need I remind us all of what nearly happened those years ago?"

Ranarek scoffed, waving the potential history lesson

away, for he knew damned well. The question was what needed to be done about it and for whom would be tasked to do it.

"It must be retrieved," Joden opined the obvious point, "but it must be done quietly—ye canno' send a war party out into the wilds, they'll be seen and ambushed in an instant."

High Lord Ranarek threw up a hand and looked incredulously to the Druid at that. "Retrieved, just like that," he snapped his fingers, chuckling nervously, "we'll skip across the Moors, tip-toe through Howler's Wood and knock on the front door and ask for the book, then, just us three!" he scoffed then, casting his eyes to Joden with a shake of his head.

"My days of adventure and battle have long gone, lads," Hrothnir hated to admit it, "and Joden speaks true, it *must* be retrieved and locked away under our watchful eyes."

"I'll go," Joden offered.

"Like the Fiery Hells ye will!" Ranarek waved the absurd notion aside, "besides, I need ye here to help, I've got refugees up to my neck, and I've got Duldarians demanding what's to be done with the dockside houses being filled with them—there's bound to be a brawl or three. No," he paused a moment, "we'll need someone who can move quickly and without notice, a two-man party." He sat back with a hand to his chin in thought, "maybe one of the foreigners, I oft times see sturdy looking folk among their ships, hard-edged and steely eyed. We could pay—"

"No." Hrothnir flat out shot the idea down and look pointedly to his son

Flinn pretended not to notice that he was now pointedly being stared at him, until it was too obvious now to ignore. He looked between them, with eyes ending to linger over his father.

"Ye've been given sight, boy-o," Hrothnir laid a heavy hand to Flinn's shoulder. "Ye'd be the least expected for the job—trust me."

Flinn's faced screwed up alarmingly, looking just as confused, "What're ye talkin' about, da?"

But Hrothnir kept talking, "I've see ye run, lad, I've seen how quick ye, mindful of step, always looking to avoid the avoidable when ye see that ye can avoid it—that's what we need right now!"

"I'm no adventurer, Da!" Flinn leapt from his chair, startling his father, while Ranarek's reaction was an observant one, and with Joden appearing annoyed with the adolescent behavior. "I'm no warrior either! What if I run into Feral Folk, or worse!? God's sakes, da, I don't even know how to wield a blade!"

Weaving himself from around the chair, Flinn moved away from the table as if making for the doors. Joden started to intercept, but Ranarek held up a hand before standing from his chair. He patted Hrothnir's shoulder in passing, both to keep his friend steady and assure confidently that he would handle the boy.

"Aye, an unfair charge, indeed! If I could, I'd make the journey with ye, lad!" Ranarek slapped his large belly, "But I fear me legs wouldn't support the added girth over such large tracks of land."

A hard chuckle between the three men ensued but succeeded in lightening the mood, halting Flinn's steps. He turned, not wanting to be disrespectful towards the High Lord, and bowed his head shamefully. "High Lord Ranarek, it's just…" he shook his head, unsure as to what he was even trying to say. "Ye don't understand, I'd sooner die out before I could be of any use. Then what, after putting ye're hopes in someone so weak and small, to be left to whatever doom ye foresee…?"

The High Lord looked down on Flinn kindly, sticking his thumbs into his girdle loops, rocking back on his heels with a smile, and with a twinkle in his eyes. He glanced over his shoulder, before taking a step closer to speak just soft enough for Flinn to hear.

"Listen, lad, ye're the only one who's been given these visions. And ye know how ye're father and the rest of those old fools are. But, if being afraid stopped us from doing anything, nothing would be done at all. Realize this, boy-o, whether by Almighty Wulndar, or perhaps by something we don't yet understand, ye've been given a glimpse of something that may well be diverted." He leaned back a bit, speaking slightly louder, "besides, he with the sight bears its weight! Isn't that right, Druid?"

"Aye," Hrothnir said with a tinge of sympathy, "that's correct."

"What if I don't want to?" Flinn asked softly.

Ranarek only offered a wink, looking back towards his friends at the table, "I have confidence in the lad, Hrothnir, see that he is given all that he needs for the tasks ahead, and I will see to his escort." The High Lord gave Flinn one last smile before turning for his throne.

An ornate furnishing constructed of sun-bleached bones, said to have once belonged to the largest of the drakes that scoured Wulndar. Its massive skull hung high above as a trophy, secured against a supporting beam rising from behind the high back of the elaborate chair. It was a testament to Ranarek's strength and courage.

"Gather ye in this hall," Ranarek's usual playful tone had turned authoritative.

This was a characteristic of Ranarek Flinn always found fascinating. In the streets the High Lord made a point to mingle with the commoners, joked with his guards, visited the docks, and played harmless jokes on his closest advisors. His behavior generated social exchanges that begot the best results as far as morale and efficiency were concerned, leaving him to be loved and respected by all. But with matters of great import, he was a heavy-handed ruler whose decree was finalized with but a breath.

Joden, Hrothnir, and Flinn now stood before him, the great firepit roiling behind them to outline their frames, with the Warlord and Druid flanking the much smaller Flinn between them. He was a gnome among giants, waiting for the king's order.

"All Wulndarians are tested before they may call

themselves a true man," Ranarek said while adjusting his posture, "Flinn Druid's Son, ye are no different. As ye're High Lord, Ruler, and King, I charge ye with the task and fate of my people, of *ye're* people. He who has sight bears its weight. Now know this, to fail in your task to retrieve the Dark Tome and bring it to the Druidic Circle, means our doom."

Flinn felt like he just received a death sentence, for all the misery and fear that came along with it. There was no arguing the decree, he knew the High Lord's command was final.

"He shall not fail us," the Druid promised and bowed reverently before Ranarek. An elbow to his son's side reminded him to do the same, before leading Flinn from the Great Hall.

Once Hrothnir and the young man were gone, Joden let out a distressful sigh and shook his head. "I don't know about this, Ranarek," he said, stroking his short-kept beard, "I canno' say that I share yer confidence in the lad."

"Good thing ye're not me, then," the High Lord chuckled but his humor quickly subsided. "Hrothnir raised the boy well, but there's no denying his destined role in all of this. That, coupled with all these dark tidings, he may well be our only hope."

"Or our greatest threat. Should the Pale Lady get her hands on him—" Joded started to counter, but Ranarek was quick to interject.

"Which is why she musn't."

Not once had he ever left the safety of Duldar's Port's walls, only ever looked beyond them from the parapets. Flinn's father went over possible routes for him to take, as he led his son from Duldar's Bastion back to their longhouse. The safest would be traveling through the Moors, circling wide of Howler's Wood and brave the Spines of Zhul'Tarrgan, to approach the ruined fortress of Duldar's Keep from the west. Getting inside of it, though…?

That thought unnerved Flinn to his core. There must be something he could do to protest further, somehow get himself out of this whole mess. The more he thought it over, the less likely that seemed. If he refused the High Lord's command, he would shame his father, become an embarrassment to the people, and not only disappoint the High Lord, but also be criminalized for treason. Instead, he only half-listened to his father's rambling, praying to whatever gods that listened to help him.

These were not the only thoughts plaguing Flinn's mind as he followed his father, trailing behind him. Flinn had hear tales of the Dark Tome, in fact, it was believed there were many scattered throughout distant lands as well. For it was said the books possessed a will of their own, calling to any who would be tempted to use its power, but in so doing slowly be bound to it. Slurping the spirit away like the last few drops from a drinking horn, until there was no soul left to drink. All in exchange for power beyond imagining, Flinn doubted very much he was one of those to resist such a thing.

But there returned his curiosity to grasp the unknown and live out adventurous daydreams. Was this the excitement he yearned for, the need to go out into the Feral Lands as he always wished? Perhaps. For the mere thought of it suddenly excited him.

That excitement soon washed away after he and his father finally made it back to their longhouse. There was much preparation to be had before nightfall, and they had yet to meet with the Druidic Circle. Something about specific rituals needing to be performed for safe journeys, blessings, and charms to be gifted. It only made everything that much more real for Flinn, shaking him like a trembling leaf on a brittle branch about to snap.

"I'm to do this alone?" Flinn asked while following his father into the entry hall, and on into a large chamber at the back of the hall used to study druidic magics.

"Ye won't be alone, boy-o, ye heard the High Lord say it himself," Hrothnir said after finding the most travel worn pack his son had ever seen. Then proceeded to visit various shelves, collecting small glass vials filled with dark liquids, maps, a compass, and other such necessities for the road.

"The heavy cloak in yer room, go get it," the Druid pushed his sputtering son out of the room and into the main hall.

Flinn came back down moments later, cloak in hand. The door was ajar, making it easy to slip through without being heard. Hrothnir stood at his massive desk, littered with parchments, quill pens and ink jars, stacks of books and half melted candles. Indeed, the entire room looked like his father's desk, with the shelved walls jammed with oddities only a druid would find interesting.

Atop the disarray of the desk, there lay a long sack-cloth bundle wrapped and secured by hemp rope. Flinn walked over to stand via his father, following his eyes to the bundle. Curiosity wrinkled his brow, which initiated Hrothnir to take a small dagger and cut away the hemp bindings.

"Ye've been chosen, my son, chosen to save Duldar's Port from unspeakable evil," the Druid spoke as he unwrapped the cloth, "but, there is more to ye than ye're knowing and much I have kept hidden."

Once again left confused, the deepening furrows of confusion crossed Flinn's gentle brow.

Hrothnir turned the bundle over several times before he set it down gently. He pulled back one-fold and then the other, revealing a twin pair of gorgeously forged hand-axes. Their strong polished handles were of bleached bone, ornately carved with druidic knots around the carved likenesses of a wolf on one and a bear on the other. While the axes remained to lay side by side, they showed the beasts locked in combat while together. Fit into the poll of each were two garnet gems, and the ax heads grew out narrow at first, then widened masterfully.

The cheek and beard of each blade had been engraved

with a series of runes stopping short of both the toe and heel of the bit. Whoever crafted these weapons had forged them in a strange ancient silver that was cold to the touch. Hrothnir picked one of them of them up, leaving its twin behind and held the weapon out for inspection. His eyes flickered to his son, holding the ax for Flinn to take and examine for himself.

Hesitant at first, still in awe of the labor that went behind it, Flinn at last reached out and relieved his father of the art-like piece of weaponry. He found it light, remarkably balanced, and cool but there was something else he felt. A distant something, like a far-off call, an echoing in an empty space, the waking of something long slept. And there then came a gradually warmth that swelled through his hand to climb up his forearm. Flinn set the ax down quickly, afraid to hold it any longer.

"I'm no warrior, Da, I wouldn't even know how to swing those things if I had to," Flinn shook his head, swallowing hard.

"These weapons will guide ye, boy-o, don't fight them. Allow these weapons to lead yer hands true," Hrothnir winked, adding, "tomorrow ye leave for Duldar's Keep, and along the way ye may face challenges," his father smiled and gestured to the twin axes, "these were once wielded by one of the most skilled warriors ever known to Wulndar—they served him then and they shall serve ye in the times ahead. "

"Da, I—" Flinn's words were cut short in an instant.

"It is said his last breath was given into these axes. Heating the blades so fierce it split winter clean in twain. A Feral warrior though he was; was also one who sought a change from the life he led. With these, he hacked and chopped his way to such a path..." the large man's words trailed off, his eyes staring into the axes distantly.

Flinn noticed the reminiscent twinkle in his father's eye before the old man quickly rewrapped the weapons and gathered them up. Hrothnir collected one last item found in a dust-ridden chest in the corner closest to the portal and set a plated and studded girdle with the rest of the provisions and equipment.

"This here, lad, will help keep yer gut form being skewered, along from a few other things ye'll find out on yer own," Hrothnir stepped back from his desk, inspecting the wares he had set out. With an approving nod, he brought both hands together into a loud clap.

"Now, we eat and speak no more of tomorrow. It will be nightfall soon, and we've yet to see the Druidic Circle," Hrothnir led his son from the study and into the main hall, signaling to the servants for food and drink. Flinn let out a heavy sigh, taking a seat while still trying to register everything that was happening, food was certainly not what was on his mind.

A serving girl came with a large decanter in one hand and two drinking horns awkwardly held in the other. She handed one to Hrothnir, then to Flinn before filling their horns with delicious mead.

"I think we need to discuss this further, da, I'm not built for anything like this," Flinn took the horn and drank from it hastily. His father simply eyed him a moment before a broad smile spread over his weathered and wrinkled face. He laughed. Flinn wrinkled his nose, failing to see the humor.

As the servants came and went, setting down plates of roasted meats and bowls of fruits and pastries, the Druid leaned forward with a taunting smile so that only Flinn could hear him, "Are ye scared, boy-o?"

Flinn's silence and incredulous expression was answer enough. As if his father could not already tell.

"Use it. It'll save ye life, allow ye to make quick decisions and act fast without thinking—use it, boy-o, because all warriors are lovers to fear—it's what drives them to battle in the first place." He leaned back into his chair, a quieter chuckle escaping him.

Shaking his head, unsure why his father expressed such confidence in him where Flinn lacked it in himself, the Druid's son could say nothing. His protests went unheard, his concerns offhandedly ignored, and there was only offered a false sense of hope. Sometimes he wondered about his father, curious as to what he saw that some did not.

The rest of the evening was done in small talk, subjects that had little to do or nothing at all with current events or those to come. Food eaten, mead ever flowing, and moments passed between father and son were as if he were not leaving at all. Forgetting momentarily of what the morrow would bring, Flinn was not entirely swept up by the merriment.

This was to be their last meal together, and Flinn could feel, more than see, that his father was coddling it for as long as he was able. Studying the large man's face, noting his blue eyes and warm smile, Flinn felt a sadness deep at the center of him. One born of the mere thought that after the next rising of the sun, he may never see his father again…

Chapter 7

Lunar Gifts & Roaring Passages

After dusk settled under the comforts of night, a dark blanket of ominous clouds pulled over the land, stretching from the east across Duldar's Port, the surrounding moors, and the outskirts of Howler's Wood. Peeking glimpses of a straining moon attempted to bless the night with a cool glow, replaced instead with momentary flashes of lightning. Their illuminated the bloated, swollen clouds from within, making their presence more foreboding.

The rain started lightly at first, with a strange warmth that perverted the cold air, and fell harder as the mist scouring the moors rose and thickened. While within the camouflaging darkness just beyond the edge of the forest, pairs of blinking amber eyes watched silently. Thwark's Redeyes stared off across the expanse that lay between he and Duldar's Port's walls. With the fog, an extra provision of cover, the Wolf-kin would be able to move ease ease.

Redeyes blew out his nose once, signaling his closest chief s to pass it along, and moved out from the tree line with their dire wolves remaining behind. The Pack Master glanced upwards, for just a moment, feeling the radiant power and catching a glimpse of the moon before clouds shrouded her once more. She would be needed this night.

His Wolf-kin began to spread themselves out as Thwark picked up the pace, his strong legs digging into the soft earth, or splashing through pockets of water, as he removed his great kilt. A few of a select few of his warriors did the same, with their eyes skyward, searching for the moment. They could feel the moon's power, feel its intense stare, and were eager to honor her.

And there she was, for a stationary moment that was just long enough. The Wolf-kin reached for the moon as they ran, yearning to touch and feel her soothing caress as her light silhouetted their splayed hands, making them more horrifying with the sudden growth of their fingernails.

After a sickening symphony of crackling bones, popping joints and defiant growls against the transformative agony, there now ran a nightmarish array of hulking dark-skinned werewolves. Redeyes, a towering beast nearly twice the size of the average, snorted and thrusted his salivating muzzle in the direction of the city as it grew closer. From around him, the werewolves loped ahead at a steady run. These were not mindless beasts, Wolf-kin were highly intelligent, and no clan on Wulndar dared believe they were stupid creatures.

They moved with purpose, using brute strength and cunning along with a ferocious savageness unlike any experienced. But most of all, they were ruthless on the battlefield, and that was particularly known of Redeye's Pack. He prided himself in their barbarism, their merciless tactics. Anything that had nothing to do with the Feral Lands he despised and seen as a threat that deserved *no* mercy.

As the main host of the lupine pack crossed the fog-blanketed moors, they picked up speed and split off into three different groups. When they neared the base of the great stone wall, they started their climb up, using protrusions and displacements making for easy handholds, with Thwark leading the way. Nearer the top, the soft glow of torchlight traveled from the left, a patrolling guardsman no doubt, though the Pack Master halted his progress nearly by the parapets edge.

The rest of the pack, on seeing their leader, froze in place as well with amber eyes looking upwards. The torchbearer stopped directly over where Thwark clung just blew the wall's edge, peering into the moors from the parapet with a scrutinous stare. Searching for anything out of the norm in the dead of night beneath the storm. A flash of lightning with an accompanying robust roar of thunder created the opportunity the Pack Master wanted, justifying that it had been long enough for a nightly gaze, and quickly made the rest of the climb as silently as he was able.

The hulking werewolf clawed into the lip of the wall and leapt up and over, clipping the nearby guard to send him staggering back. He almost lost the grip on his spear, but held tight to the torch for dear life, seeking asylum in its protective light. He kept it thrust before him, turning about in vain attempts to cast light on the large shadow that had spooked him, for how fast it had all happened. Then, the most extreme force of pressure clasped around the top of his skull, lifting him from his feet and screaming surprise.

Several other of his packmates found purchase on the wall, leaping over the lip to land on all fours before taking off towards the guardhouses. The Duldarian firmly held in Thwark's grasp kicked his feet amusingly, waving his torch uselessly, and swung his spear franticly, all while screaming has the pressure around his head tightened and tightened. Thwark turned so that the fool could see as the pack began their onslaught, meeting the response of guards as they came rushing out, not expecting to be overwhelming by the Wolf-kin.

And O' how they killed with silent effectiveness. All save this poor fool who screamed his fears, to which Thwark found disgusting and weak. With a frustrated snarling growl, he crushed the guard's skull, helm, and all, with the closing force of his clawed hand. Releasing the body, landing heavily atop the stone wall, the Pack Master threw back his head releasing a piercing howl, proclaiming his pack's presence, and heralding the city's doom.

A crash of thunder drummed, streaks of lightning crawled across the clouds, and a brief glimpse of the full moon peeked through momentary spaces while slowly passing overhead. Made more ominous with the responding howls of the Wolf-kin, who were now nearly well within the city walls.

Thwark leapt away to join them, to help ensure that the streets were red with Duldarian blood. The distraction would be needed if Thwark was to find his charge. He howled again, clambering up a rooftop, boosting the morale of his pack, then dropped down to street level and began sniffing the air immediately.

A group of guards rounded the corner of a building, spears rattling, swords and shields clanking. They stopped short on seeing Thwark in the middle of the street, and then three other werewolves dropped down.

"Alright, lads! Let's give 'em a good Duldarian welcome!" the captain of the group, a broad sword already in hand, shouted courageously and led the charge.

One of his warriors initiated the first attack, thrust the shaft of his spear over the top edge of his shield, hoping to skewer the red-eyed beast. Thwark slapped away at the spear and destroyed the weapon in an explosion of splinters. The look on the guard's face was priceless, a mixture of surprise and momentary realization that he may die this night.

He was right, of course, as Wolf-kin rushed past him to engage the others with furious claws battering shields, tearing clean through armor links, thick hides, and beyond to until rend flesh. The Duldarians screamed as they were torn apart, and the Wolf-kin howled their triumphs! As for the guard before Thwark, a broad sword held shakily in his hand while he hid behind his shield, he swallowed and accepted his fate before rushing in to defend.

An easy enough kill for the Pack Master, swiping wide the man's shield to expose his torso, while battering aside his blade before disemboweling him utterly. Thwark pulled his intestines out from the grisly wound, the guard screaming all the while his disbelief, and shut him up quickly with a slash that took off half his face. His packmates fed on the corpses, consuming the strengths of the fallen, while Redeyes sniffed again in the now empty street.

Desdemona said he would know the scent if he caught it, however faint. As of now, however, all he smelled was blood, sweat, and fear. Putting his nose to the uneven cobbles, Thwark started off in no direction specifically, and keen eyes searching for whom the Pale Lady described. During his prowling, the city was alive with screams, battle, and howls. It would not be long before the element of surprise dissipated, and the Duldarians mobilized into an effective defensible force.

Redeyes snarled, his ears rotating at the harsh whistle of an incoming arrow. Lodged deep in his bicep, he snapped his jaws in agitation at the imbedded missile and brushed it away as easily as one would a flea. In a single leaping bound, Thwark rushed the rest of the distance towards the one daring enough to think himself brave. The guard fumbled nervously to nock another arrow to his bow, even taking a knee in an attempt to steady his nerves, but soon his agonizing scream was all he managed to let loose just before Thwark sunk his fangs into the Duldarian's shoulder. He left the man to bleed out, his legs kicking away in pathetic attempts to deal with the pain.

Scaling up the side of a building, Thwark disappeared into the rooftops as alarms began to ring all throughout, ordering shouts and screams of confusion echoed throughout the streets. The city guard started to become more organized once they caught their bearings, but it did not prepare them for the descending death the werewolves delivered. Keeping from sight as the city guard began to rally towards the Northern Wall, Redeyes stalked through the shadows as his pack ravaged freely.

The storm would provide enough cover, just the right amount of disorientation to confuse and surprise. The Wolf-kin of Howler's Wood were a ferocious bunch, taking pleasure in in the anticipatory build up to the final kill. Unlike their cousins further south, Thwark's pack often killed for the sport of it, and tonight provided a perfect outlet to let loose some pent-up angst.

The Warlord sniffed at the air again. Nothing stood out to him at first but as he continued to slink from shadow to shadow, the smells of the city became stronger. All manner of scents assailed him, from rotted refuse to mouthwatering meats.

Until, that is, one scent suddenly stood out from all the rest. A scent that Redeyes had nearly forgotten and then recalled Desdemona's words. It had been nearly over a century since last he smelled that stench. Despite how faint the smell was, it managed to jog Thwark's memory of what had once been a long rivalry between clans. Now, there were none left to even remember they ever had a place in the Feral Lands. Was it possible that there yet remained a descendent of that thought-to-be exterminated lineage?

No, he thought. It was not possible. Yet still…

A low throaty growl rumbled from Redeyes. He sent a series of sequential howls, calling those nearest him to his side before he leapt off and followed the familiar scent. Answering calls returned, closer than he had expected; but now they had a target. Now they knew whom it was Desdemona had taken such an interest in, and now Thwark knew that the old blood feud continued anew—but instead of exterminating it, he sought to mold it, for the scent was filled with youth and green yet to life.

Hrothnir burst into his son's room in a rush, his breathing erratic. Flinn launched himself upright, tumbling from his bed in confusion. It took only a few blinks to realize the alarm was sounding. "Quickly, don ye traveling vestments and get that girdle on!" his father was already out from the room before Flinn could even orient himself.

After dressing as quickly as he could, Flinn nearly sprinted down the hall and flew down the stairwell. He took three steps at a time with one hand to the railing, while the other continued fiddling with one of the buckles of the girdle. His father at set his gear up on a chair, placed for an easy time of putting everything on in an orderly fashion. Well, it certainly worked, because Flinn could not recall the last time he dressed so quickly.

Downstairs, he found his father stuffing a leather sack into the traveler's pack and stuck a scroll in before securing it shut. Guards positioned themselves at the main entrance, forming up and positioning themselves along the decorative pillars and made a shield wall before the longhouse doors.

Hrothnir turned just as Flinn came up to him, reaching for the twin axes, but he froze at the sounding of distant howls outside. There was a shared moment of fear and urgency between father and son, before the old man quickly took up the axes and slid them into the belt loops of Flinn's girdle.

"Ye keep these close, boy-o, ye hear me?"

All Flinn could do was nod.

Without any more time to be wasted, Hrothnir tugged his son to follow him. Something had happened, something big and those howls outside were the cause of it. Another howl instilled the sense of urgency to move quickly, but they sounded right outside the longhouse, which made Flinn's spin tingle. The guards tightened the shield wall. While others pulled back on bows who positioned behind it.

"What's happening, Da?" Flinn had to ask, but Hrothnir did not respond other than taking him by the arm and led him to the back of the long hall. Behind a less extravagant throne than what was seen in High Lord Ranarek's hall, there was a sanguine tapestry that hung from the rafters above and covered the wall behind it, emblazoned with a bear's head and two clawed paw prints slightly raised at either side of the symbol, and below that a knotted circle of runic symbols that represented the Druids and their sacred pact.

Hrothnir pulled the tapestry aside, revealing the stone wall behind it. Flinn's puzzlement did not last long when he looked up suddenly hearing loud landing thuds on the roof of their longhouse. Hastily, the Druid felt for the correct protruding stone and pushed it inward with some effort. A portion of the wall set into itself, sliding downward with the soft grind of stone and crank of gears. A long, dark tunnel moaned before them, waiting patiently to swallow them whole. Gauging Flinn's reaction, Hrothnir knew there was just no time to explain.

Instead, he directed, "Follow it down until ye can't go any further, High Lord Ranarek and Warlord Joden will already be expecting arrivals," Hrothnir's words fell short when there came a crashing and splintering of wood back the way they had come. Whatever was out there was trying hard to get in as quickly as they could.

"What do I do once I'm there, and what about yerself?!" Flinn gripped his father's slumping but broad shoulder anxiously.

"I'll be right behind ye," Hrothnir smiled behind the lie, and placed a hand to the side his son's face. The warmth from his touch soothed Flinn as he whispered a prayer to first Wulndar and asked protection from Duldar, then drew a sign of protection in the air before him. "Go, boy-o, go!" and shoved Flinn into the passage, sending him stumbling and fighting for balance.

Flinn started to go back for his father, but he froze fearfully with what he saw happen next.

Shouts of warning went out as werewolves plummeted and dropped from above into the long hall, scrabbling over furniture and guards alike as their claws reached out menacingly. The terrifying beast-men who now ripped into the longhouse's men, came in strong. The front doors were next, bursting inward as the monstrous creatures barreled through, engaging the shield wall while taking arrows.

They were savage and unmerciful. The screams of agony from the guards made Flinn's blood run cold but there was one towering beast that stood out from all the rest that made his heart quicken, and it looked directly at him! Its eyes shown brilliant red, like twin reflective garnets, and the beast lumbered forward, hopping down from the ruined banquet table it had landed on.

"Go!" Hrothnir stamped the floor with the heel of his

boot. The grinding of stone becoming audible and the entrance to the passage beginning to rise upwards.

"Wait, da!" He moved as quickly as he could, hoping to get through in time.

Hrothnir smiled his near-toothless smile as the passage sealed shut at last. Flinn was left in darkness and rushed the stone door to beat against it with a fist. With a quick thought, and blindly, he frantically felt around for any odd protrusions in the surrounding stone walls and floor. Hoping he would soon discover the mechanism that would allow the door to open from this side of the wall.

The Druid's son beat again against the cold rock, dismayed and angry at his failure to do so. The faint muffled sound of struggle could be heard through the stone, only resulting in tying Flinn's stomach up in knots further. Flinn searched again, more thoroughly and less frantically and soon surmised, as much as accepted, that his father never intended for him to get back out.

He stepped back a bit from the sealed door. Torn between traveling the corridor to Duldar's Bastion or waiting to see if his father would be standing on the other side if the portal finally opened again. But would that not defeat the purpose his father had fought to accomplish? Defeated, Flinn swallowed the lump in his throat and turned his back to the sealed entrance. It was time to get moving, and enough of it had been wasted already standing and hoping.

Fighting back the swell of tears threatening to fall, Flinn fought down his angst and conscious turmoil as he sped through the darkened corridor. It was a straight run, but he could not go as fast as he had liked, out of fear of tripping on uneven stone. The thought of busting his knee or even his face was not on his list to-do. Eventually, however, he could see the glow of torchlight ahead after some time, but so spaced were they that the darkness in the gaps between them was thick. So the rest of the corridor went, out of dark shadows into momentary pockets of light, as Flinn quickened his pace with images of the red-eyed werewolf perverting his father's longhouse.

  "Stay alive, da," Flinn whispered to himself, "just stay alive."

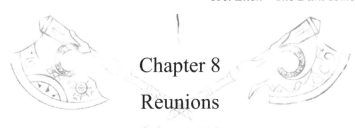

Chapter 8
Reunions

Redeyes clambered over the wreckage but was too late as he watched the stone slab rise and seal the Duldarian youth behind it. All that was between him and the door was the Old Druid, of whom Thwark knew well of olden times. Hrothnir Stand-Stone, and he looked much as he had back then, save for being weighed down by nearly more than a century of life.

Thwark made quickly for the old man, and any who crossed his path were batted away like foolish children, either by opening their soft bodies with knife-like claws, or driving them through their bellies, gutting them and pulling out their insides as one would a boar.

"I thought ye dead!" Hrothnir squared himself as Redeyes growled through his snarling fangs.

He gauged the Druid's searching eyes, spotting the disheartened sheen as he drank in the scene within his longhouse. Most of his house guards had been taken care off, moaning their pain or being outright cut short in gurgling blood.

Several who had been left rushed to Hrothnir and formed up a tightly packed wall before him, there was only one archer left and he fumbled to fit arrow to his bow. The shield wall rested the hafts of their spears on their shield's edges, pointing their leaf-shaped blades towards the Pack Master as he lumbered closer to them, his claws slick with blood.

"Not one for talk, eh?" Hrothnir removed his great kilt and heavy robes to fall at his feet. He kicked them back with his foot, planting himself into a firmer, wider stance. Despite his near ancient age, the old Druid's body was like that of a young mid-adult man! Scars littered his torso as his muscles bulged and accentuated by the shadows cast by the torchlight.

"Do ye remember when we last tussled, dog!?" the Old Druid challenged and made to push his guards aside, but that only urged them to push him back for his safety. "O', I think ye do." Hrothnir smiled, adding, "Returning to be put on yer back for a second time, are ye?"

Thwark roared defiance and charged into the shield wall, swatting the spears aside with ease. Some crashed to the stone, losing their footing, and others merely stumbled to regain their balance. Any of them who stumbled away too far were snatched up by the werewolves who hung back, allowing their leader to have his fun.

Redeyes turned in place with a snarl, raking out with a right, left, right swiping of his claws. Taking two of the five guards down quickly, while the rest pedaled back into the Druid, herding him out wide, attempting to get the pillars between them and the beast. Werewolves followed closely, stalking shadows, but they insured that the prey could go no further in any direction.

"Ye remember, Redeyes!" the Druid called again from behind his men as they fought to keep the hulking beast in front of them and the others at a bay.

They jabbed with their spears when Thwark came too close, who kept just out of reach of them, or when one of the others were overcome with impatience, lurched forward with his spear leading, only to snatched and tossed away for the Wolf-kin who lingered back hungrily.

Hrothnir pushed through his guards, ignoring their horror-stricken faces and pleas to do otherwise. But the Old Druid placed himself between them and Thwark, having it no other way. "Remember me as I once was!" he shouted, beating his fists against a strong chest.

The Pack Master snapped his jaws, threw back his head with a roaring howl and lurched forward. He would tear this old man apart before he could do anything, but as luck would have it, there shone the brilliance of the full moon, always full, ever bright.

It was all Hrothnir needed, offering him a window in time as his physical form began to change beneath her power. Within the instance, Thwark had closed the gap, but he quickly had to change his course, lest be wrapped in a vicious werebear's hug.

Running hard and fast, Flinn followed the illumined passage ever forward. How much distance he covered could not be speculated; besides, his mind was too focused on getting there to worry about something like that. Before long, the passage started to widen ahead. As he neared, a well-lit chamber could be seen and he could hear someone shouting, giving warning. Flinn slowed his approach, standing at the portal before leaving the passage, looking into the stone chamber with a singular door across the small space. The two guards posted at the door visibly relaxed, relieved to see who it was.

"My father," Flinn flung the point of his finger whence he came, "he's back there—we have to gather a force and take back the longhouse!"

The guards gave each other a concerned look, but otherwise did not seem too surprised by the news. One kept looking past Flinn, worry and hopeful expectance filling his eyes, while the other bit his cheek as if trying to make a hard decision.

"That's it then," the thinking guard decided and reached over to pull Flinn along with him as the other cursed and rushed to open the door where a spiraling staircase awaited.

Flinn pulled back from them and argued, "We have to go back and get him!" The guards were more forceful now, the other aiding his comrade in getting Flinn up the stairs. Their echoing boots scuffing the worn stone steps as they tugged their now squirming charge. "Unhand me!" Flinn insisted, "what're ye daft!? My Da's—"

They stopped, the guard who had decided their path thrusting Flinn up against the wall and baring his teeth in agitation. He was a large man, one incisor missing as he glared down on the young man.

"Right now, we're charged to get *ye* to the High Lord as quickly as possible—ye're father is far more stronger than ye give him credit for, believe ye me—and now ye're going to *shut up* and get up these damned stairs!" The guard eased back, loosening his hold on Flinn, and then nodded to his comrade before ascending at a quicker pace now.

Flinn blinked, dumbfounded, and glanced up to follow the larger man with his eyes, then back to the other who stood a step below him.

"Please, Druid's Son," the waiting guard spoke patiently and gestured with his chin upwards.

Setting his jaw with a subtle nod, Flinn went the rest of the way hastily and without protest. Yet, every few steps or so, he shook his head angrily at himself, wishing he had fought a little harder before allowing himself to be separated from his father.

Finally reaching the top of the stairs, a heavy iron door left open greeted them. Two guards stood at either side, as men and women moved hurriedly back and forth in a large circular chamber in the next room. White marbled floor and walls made the chamber feel important, along with several doors leading out form the centralized room. Some were open, while others had been barred closed, if the same tunnels led back to the other longhouses. People came and went through them, coming out more than going in and were directed up a flight of stairs leading up from the chamber beneath an ornate archway.

A large roaring bear's head had been emblazoned and set in gold on the floor, and at the center of it stood High Lord Ranarek. The rotund man was seen clad in a breastplate specially made for his large size and a vicious looking ax over one shoulder. Warlord Joden was nearby, directing his men hither and thither but when he noticed Flinn he shouted out one last order to double check the sealed doors before he made his way over to him, along with the High Lord.

"Where's ye father?" Ranarek peered over Flinn's shaven head. His brow knit together in disappointment when the door to the Druid's longhouse was closed and barred shut. The High Lord laid a sorrowful gaze over Hrothnir's son.

"My condolences," Joden laid a hand to Flinn's shoulder, "but I know yer da, and he's more ferocious than those dogs outside!"

Flinn acknowledged the kind words with a nod.

"Right!" Ranarek boomed, catching the attention of all in the room, "if the remaining Druids aren't through those last doors in fifty beats, close it all up and secure the main stairwell here—I want every man in this damned keep ready!" he looked to Flinn, sadness still in his eyes, and wrapped a bear-like arm around him while leading towards the wide staircase.

"Joden, you know what I need from ye." Ranarek said over his shoulder.

"Aye." Joden acknowledged.

It was not hard to keep pace with Ranarek, who was breathing heavily with every step the large man took. After they reached the top, a simple opening in the middle of a stone floor surrounded by a small railing of stone, the three left the small chamber and into a larger corridor where more guards were found standing their posts or rushing about. There was seen a group ahead of them escorting a Druid to a door at the end of the hall. Others were similarly escorted, either the Druid's wife and children, or a family member that had been taken into their care.

Instead of following them to that door, Ranarak turned down a smaller corridor to the side that led to an archway. Down a small flight of steps, another chamber greeted them. However, this one was far different than anything Flinn had ever seen. The walls were aglow with Wulndarian runes, each shimmering with their own power. A circular dais rose at the center, short steps leading up to it as natural stones created a miniature colonnade around it. They too were carved with runes, but they were aglow with a different power. Theirs pulsed with a black light, radiating ancient power.

Flinn froze in place, eyeing the eldritch runes on the cairns.

Sensing his hesitancy and anxiousness, Ranarek finally had a moment to look the lad over. "By Wulndar's beard. He looks the part now, doesn't he?"

Flinn's cheeks flushed, unsure how best to respond. He stood as though ready to go on a distant hike. But with traveling pack, girdle and axes looped at his hips, the Druid's son felt less ready than ever, he had no idea what was going to happen next and thoughts of his father's welfare kept pervading his concerns.

"On ye go, boy-o" Ranarek directed and pointed to the center of the cairns. Joden was already there, waiting as he slung over his shoulders his own traveler's pack. Was he to accompany Flinn on wherever they were to go?

"But, my father…" Flinn had to make one last try.

Ranarek offered a tight-lipped smile, truly understanding, but knowing that this was not the time for worry. "I'll make sure he's alright, lad, but ye have to go and quickly—Joden will be by yer side, ye'll be in good hands, I promise. Now, off with ye!"

Flinn was gentle shoved in the cairn stone's direction and was not so trusting as to go skipping up the center of them. Too many scary and supernatural stories came from mysterious cairns, for they held old magics filled with unpredictable power.

"Trust me, lad, not all dark things are evil—it's how ye use what ye know that makes the difference," High Lord Ranarek smiled after the boy, through his wild beard and waved him on.

"Where will we go?" Flinn asked when he stood with

Joden now.

"Close to the Moors's edge," Joden readjusted with the response.

They both watched as Ranaraek lifted his bejeweled hand with the cerulean ring and pressed it to the cold stone of the nearest cairn. The runes both in the room and on the standing stones flared to life as crackles of swirling energy emitted. The power reached out from one to the other, arcing and fizzing, snapping, and popping as dark light began to limn Flinn and Joden.

Flinn's jaw slackened with wide eyes as his heart thumped anxiously. He looked around him, ducking beneath leaping energetic streams of black light, afraid of the magic jumping through the cairns. Meanwhile, Warlord Joden stood as solid as one of the standing stones, without a bother. The High Lord watched, stepping back, and looking on as he shielded his eyes.

"Be brave, Druid's Son." His words were a dissipating echo as the chamber faded in and out.

The worst had yet to come, for suddenly everything around Flinn began to wink in and out, between the chamber and a field covered in fog and flooding from rain. The stone ceiling disappeared and reappeared, offering quick glimpses of a storm-filled night's sky. The stones remained untouched during their powerful conjunction, however, maintaining their solidity. And when Flinn believed he would be burned up from either the dark colored magic or the madness his eyes witnessed, it all simply stopped.

Mist-filled Moors surrounded him, beneath the heavy rain of the storm. With a slow scanning circle, Flinn could see Duldar's Port vaguely through the thick soup of mist, and even from this distance the howls of the Wolf-kin could be heard. Joden quickly stepped from the center of the cairns, out into the surrounding low-lying wetlands. Flinn could not believe it, it was as though the pair had not been at Duldar's Bastion at all. His eyes dared to linger on the city a moment longer, frightened for his father and the people subjected to the horrors within its walls.

"We have to move," Joden's deep voice startled the young man from his thoughts, "we go west."

Flinn was still trying to process everything that had just happened, but he got to moving with a shrug of his pack. There was nothing else now for him to do but follow and trust. He watched Joden readjust his claymore across his shoulder before starting off in the chosen direction, and with nothing left for the Druid's son to do but follow, he matched the Warlord's pace.

"We're near the narrowing handle of Augustinah's Mirror," Joden referred to the largest lake in Wulndar, northwest of the Moors, and the river that ran and trailed along the length of Duldar's western wall. "We'll cross the start of the river and continue from there."

"Aren't there Feral Folk clans that side of the river?" Flinn was confused. It would make for difficult travel should they run into any Ghar'tul. Especially with it being well into the night.

Joden shook his head but answered thusly, "we need to find shelter on the other side of the river. We need supplies other than what we provided ourselves. There're many things other than Feral Folk who roam these lands, boy-o."

Before Flinn could say anything more on the matter, Joden held up a silencing hand—a clear indication that the conversation had ended. The Druid's son resigned to walking the rest of the way to the river's edge in silence. A few sparing glances behind him showed only the thick fog whence they came, with no sign of the cairns in sight or the great walls of Duldar's Port.

Flinn trudged on with the sodden march of his boots towards some unforeseen fate. At least, he traveled with one of the most renowned warriors Duldar's Port had yet known. Surely the Warlord could fell a werewolf with ease, especially with that large claymore strapped to his muscled back.

Flinn rested his hands absently on the heads of his own weapons. It was odd, though, for the longer he laid his hands to rest atop them, the more he grew eager in the adventure at hand—confident in the company he kept, if not of himself. He felt emboldened, steadfast, and inviting of danger, wanting to experience the thrill of it. He quickly removed his hands, and the feelings swept away instantaneously. Flinn had fell behind, washed up with the strange emotions, and picked up his pace a bit more.

With the bone carved handles of the axes slapping at his legs, the strong and determined gait led by Joden and the sudden excitement of travel, Flinn gave into the moment to leave behind his fears and worries.

"Keep up, man! We've a little bit more to go," Joden's voice brought the Druid's son back to the Moors, away from his reliving of the attack only moments ago, reflecting on his nightmares, recalling the instance in the alley's shadows the night prior. It only continued, the spinning of Flinn's life, a maelstrom of sequences that had no apparent reasoning for happening other than to throw him into chaos.

Back to the chilling rain and the cold night, not at all the ideal environment Flinn had imagined for his first adventure, he walked on in silent misery. He kept his hooded head low, looking over his shoudler often, expecting to see a pair of red eyes loping up from behind him any moment. With that thought in mind, the Druid's son quickened his pace once more, nearly surpassing Joden who placed a hand to the young man's chest.

"I'll lead, lad, what good is an escort if ye don't let him do his job?" An apologetic dip of the head was all Flinn made in answer, falling back a step to allow the Warlrod to lead on.

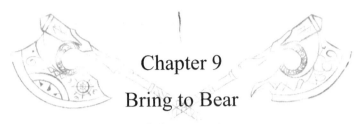

Chapter 9

Bring to Bear

Hrothnir clobbered another werewolf with two powerful strikes over its skull, after forcing Thwark back with his massive bulk, roaring defiance that shudder the pillars of the longhouse and loosened debris. Another clubbing attack followed, with a loud crunch. The Wolf-kin's skull smashed into the floor, caught beneath stone and fist. Turning in place, the towering beast that was part man and part bear, flung thick strands of pallid saliva with another thunderous roar.

His transformation only momentarily brought a pause to the Wolf-kin's advances, but Thwark was no fool in forgetting whom he was dealing with. The remainder of Hrothnir's guards, however, had scurried off as far from the werebeasts as possible, unsure what good they would do as they watched and protected themselves against the werewolves who sought easy prey.

Thwark Redeyes saw no more reason to remain in the exchange, and while snarling at the ill turn of events, worked his way to the back to the door. Hrothnir was not his prerogative. The Wolf-kin leapt, clambered, and climbed over the gargantuan werebear; clawing and biting into the thick hide of fur and flesh. Like children, Hrothnir reached and grabbed at the hounds from his hunched back with clawed hands, tossing them aside and flinging them great distances. One werewolf, unfortunate enough to land in the firepit, scrambled and yelped frantically to pull itself out.

Eyes of polished jasper gleamed over the backing werewolves, as they now were hesitant to engage after so many had fallen beneath the werebear's might.

Another roar, punctuated with monstrous flexing arms and claws, exuded an air of superiority over the Wolf-kin. Hrothnir knew it would take more than this parcel sum to take him down. He charged them, barreling through their ranks. Wrapping the slowest of them in great arms and cracking spines in gruesome hugs and placing on them fanged kisses, biting, and tearing asunder their hides.

The corpses were piling around Hrothnir now, as more of the Wolf-kin went down under the swipe of his claws and beneath heavy blows, opening deep fissures in their flesh and slamming some to the floor in crumpling heaps.

A singular howl went up into the longhouse, further back from the skirmish. The werewolves snapped their jaws, snarling at one another but not a one hesitated to be rid of the werebear's company. They retreated up into the rafters, out through the ruined roof and fought over one another through the busted door. They were too few to take this beast on their own, while the rest to their pack terrorized the city.

But as they dispersed, Hrothnir's jasper orbs settled over Thwark Redeyes who was found perched on a high rafter, growling back down towards the Druid. The opportunity had been lost, and now the search would begin for the Druid's son.

Distant howls echoed outside, drawing the Pack Leader's attention away from the werebear. Before he made to climb from the longhouse, Redeyes laid his sights back upon the werebear, making clawing gesture from left shoulder and down across his chest. A promise that their battle was far from over.

As Hrothnir made to climb up after him, Redeyes barked his amusement and left quicker than the werebear could even begin to reach. A resounding howl pierced the night yonder and the Druid was then left alone to let loose one last furious roar. The sound of triumph came from his remaining guards as they eased from the shadows. For now, the fight had been won and Flinn had been given the time to escape. At least, that was Hrothnir's hope. With a willful thought, the Druid returned to an old, strong man. Absently, he began sniffing at the air and moved to finish off any Wolf-kin left who struggled against their wounds, his guards did likewise and making quick work of it.

The Druid then directed his guards to follow him to the ruined door of the longhouse, wary of any Wolf-kin that may be lying in wait for them. Fortunately, there was no sign of the werewolves. Other than, of course, the citizens they had slaughtered and the poor guards who had given their lives to protect them. They would burn on high pyres this night, to honor their sacrifice. First, however, Duldar's Port needed to be secured and the Druid immediately burst into a run deeper into the city streets, never bothering to dress should he need to shapeshift once again.

The sound of the dying or the mortally injured echoed, carried on through shifting winds of slanting rain that came down mercilessly, creating pools in the streets and washing away spilt blood carried off down through the gutters. There was something else that was uplifting to Hrothnir, however, the sound of war-horns and drums. Above them, too, directing shouts as orders were issued from the city's guard. They were sweeping their way through, hunting the hunters.

Hrothnir met with one such group, a contingent of shield bearers and spearman aided by a handful of archers and two fellow druids. They came together at the middle of darkened street, where few bodies laid splayed out in their deaths poses. The small contingent welcomed Hrothnir and his few guards and openly cheered at the sight of them, ignoring the fact that the old man was naked. He took command, leading the way, and with his fellows keeping up with a confident stride bolstered by their conjoined ranks.

A few skirmishes had been fought at certain areas of the city, but for the most part things were beginning to settle. Less sightings of the Wolf-kin were seen, except for scant peripheral glimpses of shadowy shapes leaping from street corners or alleyways to the rooftops. After nearly an hour of patrolling searches, there was no sign of any of the Wolf-kin left.

Hrothnir was offered his robes by one of his guards, shrugging them on without fastening them securely. He limped somewhat, pinched his face at times, and let out a low grown from the wounds he endured form the werewolves. They would heal, faster than most. Much faster than most. But they would only add to his collection of many scars before morning. Eventually, after confident the city was safe, the Druid led his small force back to Duldar's Bastion to seek out High Lord Ranarek. They met him halfway there, with a handsome force behind him. There was no sign of Joden, who would ordinarily be by Ranarke's side. So, that only meant one thing.

"I see Wulndar bribed Delthos to spare ye once again, old man!" despite the High Lords jesting, there was no jovial expression save for concern creasing his brow. Stopping to stand close to his friend, Ranarek's guards spread to secure the area vigilantly.

Hrothnir had no words, too busy concentrating on his healing and feeling his age now once returned to his weaker state. He only looked to Ranarek questioningly, unabashed by his physical state.

"Joden's with him, big brother, and far enough now from the city—too blood-filled are the Wolf-kin's nostrils to pick out the lad's scent," the High Lord assured and called over for one of his guards.

A waterskin filled with mead was brought to the Druid and he took it graciously. The large retinue of city guards escorted the High Lord and the Druid back to Duldar's Bastion, while the rest patrolled the streets, ever watchful for the Wolf-kin.

Just before reaching the gates, Hrothnir felt the full effects of fatigue settling into his aching muscles and bones. He could walk well enough on his own with minimum effort, but that did not mean he was not hurting. Hrothnir hid such discomforts well, but not well enough from Ranarek's eyes who constantly glanced over at him worryingly.

Eyes to the street, the Druid offered a prayer to

Wulndar, for without him there would be no stone and then up to the sky to recite a blessing for Flinn's safe travels. It was all on him now, for there would certainly be a much larger force next time the city was attacked. One that he doubted Duldar's Port would be able to repel a second time.

Another dark age had fallen upon them with the tipping of the balance. One that would seek to cut down the people of Duldar to the very last and ensure that any hope for civility was stamped out. Flinn had to succeed, for if not, all was lost, and the ferocity of the encroaching wilds would see Duldar's Port's stone walls razed to the ground.

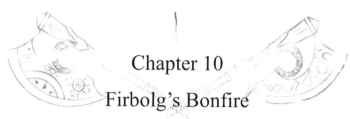

Chapter 10
Firbolg's Bonfire

Crossing the neck of Augustinah's Mirror was not so difficult a feat, yet there were minor dangers should one misplace a step. The lake itself was one of two, the second largest from the Northern Crook into which the Blood Sea fed. It ran into a river that ran into three impressive waterfalls; each of them feeding from the other before it spilt into the rushing river and sped south. The least and smallest, but no less spectacular of these river running lakes made Augustinah's Mirror, Neck and a few short hurrying miles through her Handle before lengthening into a straightaway.

Due to the rushing water, it was easy to find false purchase and slip from the sleek stones and fall to a skull-battering doom, but the Warlord and Flinn both picked their way carefully without incident. The Warlord glanced back occasionally, making sure the young man was not too far behind. The last thing he wanted was to haul Flinn's weight in addition to his own.

Getting across the river felt like it took an age, though by Joden's approximation, they were moving at a considerable rate. Flinn managed a few slips that could have saw him deep in cold water, and ye the most he suffered was an annoyed glance from the Warlord, a wet sleeve, and of course very soggy boots.

Finally, Joden made it to the other side first, and despite being soaked from his boots to his knees and showing no sign that the waters discomforted him. He grunted to himself, after watching Once Flinn made it across, they both removed their boot. Wriggling toes in the earth to work some feeling into them.

Joden led Flinn west, towards dark open fields of low rolling hills, where the dark shadows of forested land waited yonder. The Druid's son cast his eyes across the river towards the moors one last time. Watching as the storm raged on, its distant flashes and rumbling thunder clearly seen. Not so where Flinn stood, for the rain this side of the river fell as a gentle shower and the night had cleared mildly, save for the scattered rain clouds dark against the sky.

"Come on, then!" Joden's shout jolted Flinn. "Ye've the heart of a chicken, boy-o," he said, "come on, I know a place we can find shelter until daybreak. And food."

"Out there?" Flinn was incredulous as Joden made for forested hills ahead. "Aren't there Feral Folk in there?" he tried to keep up with the Warlord.

Joden grunted. Whether in affirmation or indifference, the Druid's son could not tell. "Spirit's Retreat isn't any ol' forest, lad, ye'll see."

Flinn remembered the name of the forest, but only through old stories. It was a place of peace and reprieve where heroes would find rest, to heal their wounds after fierce battles with Drakes and all other manner of beasts. Of course, those were just stories. But there was something about everything thus far that made Flinn feel like maybe they were not just tales told around a fire.

"Not all Feral Folk are conniving and battle hungry, or whatever else drives them," Joden spoke over his shoulder, "there are gentler things in these lands." He continued through, the forest getting closer with each stride.

Before Flinn could register, the two of them were standing at the forest's edge, peering into its shadows. Fireflies, blue and green, blinked in and out just outside the alder trees, blackthorn shrubs and brambles; even more-so the deeper into the forest, making the confines therein appear magical. A sense of power permeated from it that Flinn could immediately feel, a warm serenity with a subtle warning. Power could be several things, and all of them a matter of perspective hinged with perception, and here there lingered a power that was to be respected.

Joden's hand went to the hilt of his claymore, resting it there in a light hold—even after all that he said of gentler folk and the like, he continued through in search of an easy entrance. In these times, anything could be waiting to strike. Only a few blinks passed before the Warlord found a narrow deer trail leading. He looked back, signaling for Flinn to keep close. Sliding his hands from the straps of his pack, the Druid's son rested his hands over the heads of the twin axes and stepped in tandem.

Making their way deeper into the forest, guided by the grace of the high moon, the temperature difference was a marvel. The chill in the air had left, in fact, it was non-existent, but there was a soothing tranquility. Cool and soothing, as well as comforting. Crickets paused their orchestral melody as the Wulndarian's went by, quieting only long enough until they felt safe to start anew.

"This is remarkable," Flinn whispered with wandering eyes. He had never visited a forest in all his years, and now felt as though it was done purposely. And wondered if all the people of Duldar's Port were robbed of this serene experience?

Caught up in his own brain, Flinn bumbled into Joden who had stopped moving. It was more like walking into a cairn stone, for all Flinn could tell. But the Warlord was staring at something before them. Peeking around him, curious at the sudden halt, the Druid's son's eyes widened and lifted to see the tallest living man he had ever seen. At the very least ten feet in height! Flinn's jaw went slack and immediately tightened his hands around the Twins.

Built with the musculature of a Wulndarian, dressed in the skins of bear and wolf with deer-hide breeches and boots, an earth-toned giant looked down on the small pair with. One hand rested on his hip and the other held a great birch staff into which he leaned.

"Do these ancient eyes deceive me?" the giant's voice

was deep and calm as he spoke through a large moss-colored beard, reverberating like tumbled stones down a soft hill. Small red-capped speckled mushrooms grew from it, with pieces of bark weaved in some places, speckled with nightshade flowers. Yet, it looked alive.

As Flinn looked closer, narrowing his eyes as though it helped him, he could make-out the march of orange ants. Perfectly in line with one another, working in unison as they traveled an assortment of different paths all throughout the beard. A scent of sour lemon wafted into his nostrils, cast by a northerly wind behind the giant. He then reached into a small pouch, removing a large crumb of perhaps cake, or biscuit, and fed a chipmunk who popped out from his beard to accept the treat.

Joden spread out his arms heroically. "Aye, a shame ye're Elders did not carve me into their trunks of history!" he turned immediately, revealing Flinn and introducing him, "I present to ye Flinn son of Hrothnir."

"Truly?" asked the giant, a flash of intrigue crossed over large acorn-colored eyes. Suddenly, his large pointed ears flared out and rotated forward, as if catching a sound in the cool air. His face grew sullen and then there was a glossy sadness over his round eyes.

"Come," he beckoned and turned with careful steps around the scattered flora, "you will dine with Firbolg's this night, young Flinn and come to know our fire's hospitality."

Joden cast a glance to his smaller companion with a gloating smile and said, "We'll be safe here until morning, supply accordingly and be off. They'll want to know about what happened tonight and ye'll be the one to tell it first."

"Me? Why?" Flinn scrunched his face against the suggestion.

The Warlord held up a hand and shook his head, clear indication he would speak no more of it. Joden hustled after the Firbolg, having covered more than half the strides that either of the two Duldarians could gain. With but gentle shooing waves of his staff, the shrubs, brambles and barring branches parted before him in respectful retreat, providing a clear path for its guests. Crossing limbs making natural gated barriers lifted and away as though the forest itself was alive, adhering to the whispered words of the gentle giant.

Flinn watched Joden's back for a moment, allowing himself a spell of thought while the older man gained ahead. The Druid's son glanced back where they had come, his hands coming up absently to rest over the axes. *The Twins.* He liked calling them that. With them, he felt that he stood a good chance daring to venture back to the city, just to see if his father was alive. That was the very least he could do to settle his worries concerning the Old Bear, then he could hoof it straight through Howler's Wood. The Wolf-kin would never expect such a bold move. And if any did get in his way—if any of them were responsible for doing *any* harm to his father—Wulndar help them, for Flinn would cut them down into the hereafter!

"Boy!" Joden's voice brought Flinn out form his fantasizing thoughts with hands leaping away from the axes.

As he moved to catch up, his left-hand shot to his hip and grasped the head of the ax fiercely with a mind its own. He froze in step, lost to present time to be thrown someplace else. The image of a dire black wolf filled his vision, its eyes glinting like two ambers, standing in a field of swaying grass betwixt two weeping willows. Behind it, there glared a Sanguine Moon. Angry and hot, filled with a bestial rage—an unblinking eye permeating savage power.

"Wulndar's sake!" Joden exasperated, "don't go embarrassing me in front o' these Firbolgs—at least pretend this isn't ye first time out." He stopped short, however, seeing the angst clear in the young man's tense posture. "Flinn...ye alright, lad?"

Within that winking moment of time, the sounding of a name stood out most. Flinn blinked several times, a bright white silhouette of the image burning behind his lids, haunting his vision even after his eyes opened, attempting to orient themselves. But a name had been engraved into his mind, echoing like a distant howl. The name of *Wulfax*.

Flinn nearly collapsed, Joden there to catch and steady the lad in the same instance. His head swam dizzy, and his body felt dehydrated. "Well, lad?" Joden asked peering into Flinn's eyes.

After a moment, the Druid's son nodded with a glance to *Wulfax*. The weapon remained snug in the leather loop of the girdle, as plain an any ol' ax could. "I think so, but… I saw something." Joden listened as Flinn explained the vision and the name he heard. Instead of looking surprised, Joden only nodded, accepting of what he was told as though it was given to him by some oracle.

"Aye, I know the name." it was all that Joden said before gesturing for Flinn to follow him down the path. He stayed in step with the young man, though, making sure he was alright to walk on his own.

The Firbolg was so far ahead now that he was lost within the forest, but the trail was all the Duldarians needed. Flinn took in a deep breath, feeling and looking as though he had just lifted the heaviest rock he had yet to try, and walked as carefully as he could.

The Pack managed to make it back to the edge of Howler's Wood that same night, some licking their wounds, with few losses. Others waited for an opportunity to shift when the clouds cleared from the sky, eager to be back in less monstrous forms. Redeyes angrily shifted himself, storming in search of his mount. The dire wolf growled as he drew nearer, both sensing and sharing her rider's fuming mood as he donned the great kilt, having left his belongings with her, and fastened his girdle. Once he was properly fitted and dressed, the Pack Master mounted and cast his red glare over his pack as they started to gather around him.

Looking for the right words, Redeyes replayed the

night's events. Finding the younger man was easy, for now the scent was known, but getting to him was a different matter. He had not expected Hrothnir to be there and that certainly spun the blade on its point, and there was needed some time to regroup and reassess. Thwark wiped at his nose, smearing coagulated blood across his face with the back of his gnarled forearm. He sniffed the coppery scent of it, giving his arm a lick before he reached for his water skin and downed its contents. He rubbed his face clean, blowing out dried blood from his nostrils and palate.

"We do not return until the runt is found," he announced, "he's got the Blood in him and I don't want that bitch tainting it," Thwark growled out his ambitions, "I want him for The Pack, Desdemona be damned," he smiled balefully, "and when we do bring him to her, it won't be in the way she thought."

With a glance to the moon, pulling his hand over his face, as if painting it with her light, a sign of devotion before he spurred his mount forward. He and his Wolf-kin rode deeper into Howler's Wood, breaking to make camp to clean themselves, tend those who needed looking over. A watch was set before Thwark settled by a warm fire, food and drink were passed while using this time to heal and regain their strength. Their losses were not so great, but they felt it. Dire wolves without their riders howled moanfully away from the camp, their calls haunting the forest.

Next to Thwark was his own mount, the beautiful black beauty that she was, resting by the warmth of the fire unbridled and free of cinches. He fixed his eyes on her, boring them deep so she could feel his thoughts. She raised her head, holding held his concentrated gaze.

The penetrating and unblinking stare lasted several moments before the black wolf rose and licked Thwark's forehead before departing. She went south with the mental image of a frightened young Duldarian behind a rising stone door, and a remarkably familiar scent filling her nostrils. Into the darkness where the fire's light could not penetrate, the she-wolf disappeared into the night.

Thwark watched long after she had gone, begging Zhul'Tarrgan to lend her expedient strides. She would find him, the Pack Master was confident in that, and follow him until the pack was able to catch up. And should the lad respond ill to Thwark's singular offer, then a worse fate awaited him in the hands of the Pale Lady. Redeyes had seen what she did to others that were added to her ranks, an abominating process that left them less than who they were. He shuddered at that thought, as unnatural and aberrant as it was. He prayed the lad had sense enough to join the wilds when the offer was given him…

Spirit's Retreat lived up to its namesake, as Flinn marveled at the natural beauty of a massive encampment found in a grove deep at the heart of the forest itself. The hilly elevations seemed to all meet at this centralized point. To them, this was only a small camp, made to pack up and go at a moment's notice. To the Wulndarian's, however, it was like attending one of the spring festivals in Duldar's Bastion's inner bailey.

The only difference between them was that the nature here was untamed. There was beauty here and peace, nothing like the tales heard as a child. Stories made the Feral Lands seem a place filled with monsters, foul things that should not be and evil witches making themselves appear as helpless women calling for aide—only to ensnare those naïve enough to be blinded by the ruse.

But this? No, this was not some nightmarish horror. This grove, this natural living force, was harmonic. A place that stood amidst rings of broom, dogwood and elder shrubs, beneath towering silver birch, crabapple, and wild cherry trees; cupped between a carpet of soft green moss dotted with phosphorescent toadstool rings and a ceiling of dancing fireflies above. No, this rivaled the Festival of the Grand Gardens. In fact, this place made it seem like a pauper's child's birthday party.

The Firbolgs welcomed them gladly around a giant bonfire. A great blaze at the center of their grove. Yet it was not a fire that burned on wood. The flames were of black light, all at once warm and cool and comforting. A great ring was raked around the radius of the pit, itself surrounded by large round natural stones. The forest floor of the grove did not cross the pit's earthen circumference, instead encircling it respectfully.

Around it sat nearly two hands of Firbolg's, making ten as the one that greeted them led a clear way to the circle. Before he stepped onto the raked dirt, the ten-foot giant bowed.

"Fjorik enters this circle, and I bring two guests," he added his next words in a side-ways manner, "one ye already know!"

The nine Firbolg's responded simultaneously in a strange tongue Flinn had never heard before. It sounded old, with some of the familiar harsh rolling and brogue sounds of the common Wulndarian tongue. Joden was fast to announce himself and the greeting he received was one held for one of high esteem. Next, was Flinn, who was nervous and worried that his voice would not impress the giants. He was new to these customs, to which Joden seemed more than familiar.

Flinn removed his boots, as he had witnessed Joden do and then stepped close enough so that his toes barely crossed the threshold of the circle. He tried his best to mimic Fjorik's bow, all as the Firbolg's watched quietly and attentively. Joden eyed the Druid's son sharply, judging his manner.

Maintaining the bow, thinking maybe the length of it may show a greater respect to the giants watching him, Flinn announced himself. "Flinn Druid's Son enters this circle," there was no inflection on his name when announcing himself, and no air of superiority. He spoke plainly, in an unnaturally calm and deep tenor.

Their unified voices ushered him to cross the threshold and when he did, the instance his bare feet touched the soil, a revitalizing relief absorbed into his feet, spreading through his entire body. Everything made sense just then, the land and its inhabitants. The natural order of it all, the importance of life, no matter how big or small. All of it came flooding into his being, connecting him to it. It was all meant to be simple, without complication. To live and die and be reborn into and of the land. The feeling was an awakening one.

Was it this understanding of the natural realm that made these giants so lax? Flinn would have liked to believe so, as he moved to an offered chair gestured to him by Fjorik. It was a think that grew from the soil, entangling itself to form arms, a seat, and a back all cushioned with vibrantly green moss. A likewise table sprouted to his left as the Druid's son sat, with but another minute gesture made by Fjorik. Jolting in surprise, Flinn's his feet suddenly lifted, when a footstool grew beneath his heels.

He noted the amused expressions on the Firbolg's bearded faces as well as Joden's, smiling sheepishly himself.

A pipe was passed around between the Firbolgs while small ugly big-headed creatures appeared from the forest, offering drinking horns filled to the brim with sloshing mead. One such creature, wearing a mischievous grin over its child-like face, came to stand at Flinn's side, startling the young man at first but when he saw the others go about their duties, the Druid's son offered a nod of thanks and took up the horn.

The spriggan, as was later found out to be, skipped away with a melodic and hauntingly child-like giggle. Supposing it was amused by Flinn's reaction altogether, or perhaps even taking some small joy in it as well. Flinn watched the small figure dance away, disappearing into the surrounding forestry and meld into the trees and underbrush. Flinn blinked several times, glancing to his yet-to-be-sipped drinking horn, and then back whence the spriggan had gone. Strange magic was afoot here, he realized, and of the likes he had never seen done before.

Things were getting stranger by the second, Flinn thought, and decided it would be best to keep his thoughts to himself and his mouth shut. Besides, he did not want to say anything that may offend the Firbolgs, let alone Joden. Of whom appeared to be having the time of his life, jesting, and exchanging stories, or reminiscing of past times once shared. The Firbolgs certainly seemed to know well of the Warlord, engaging him in conversation with a renewed kind of spirit, asking him questions of Duldar's Port, querying of the sudden change in climate, and what Joden's thoughts were on affairs concerning the happenings of the Feral Lands.

Flinn listened politely to the rumbling tones of the Firbolg's as they conversed—comprising of haughty guffaws, noisome boasts, and rowdy jubilations. But all of it ended with shared laughter, raised drinking horns and billows of coughed-up smoke from whatever it was they were all partaking. Through it all, the Druid's son could not help but feel caught up in the jovial air that filled this sacred grove, seeing how easy it was to be caught up in the shared mirth of the gathering. These giants, so intimidatingly large, expressed a peaceful aspect of themselves that Flinn was fortunate enough to witness. Which left room for speculation as to what they were like when angered. A shuddering thought that.

"Ye're lookin' older, Joden," Fjorik pointed out, as he reached behind him for a set of drums and began slapping a beat to it to punctuate his words. A rumble of low laughter traveled around the fire as all eyes went to the Warlord. One of the Firbolg's began packing again the intricately carved pipe they had been passing around, and always seemed to skip over Flinn. It was a fascinating piece and looked to be made from bone, the bowl of which capped in polished bronze as the rune-engraved stem tapered to a fine point at the mouthpiece.

"Old age does nothing to stunt my strength, Fjorik," Joden lifted a hand and reached for the offered pipe. The acridity of its aroma soon twined with the birch scent of the flames. After a hefty pull, blowing a stream of expanding smoke, the Warlord finally offered Flinn the apparatus.

Flinn looked at it in disbelief for a moment, figuring this to be a great honor extended to him by the Firbolgs. His momentary shock and hesitancy made Joden lean in close, saying lowly as shadows played heavily across his visage.

"If ye wait any longer, they'll be mightily offended, lad—just so ye know," Joden gestured for Flinn to take the pipe, and the mischief in the Warlord's eyes did not go unnoticed by the Druid's son.

He realized too that the gathering had gone observantly silent. They watched with their anticipatory acorn-colored eyes at Flinn's hesitancy. For some reason, he believed they knew he would take it. Perhaps they were feeling him out before offering him the pipe earlier, and now wanted to test him further to see what sort of man he was. If he refused, would they think less of him, even more of Joden for bringing such poor company? The awkwardness was tangible. A glance about revealed some of the spriggans and other strange fey folk of the Grove peering out from the surrounding forestry. Their eyes twinkled with excitement, balancing on the precipice of expectancy.

The Druid's son took the pipe, placing the stem to his lips, while eager eyes watched. Glancing doubtfully over to the Warlord, all Flinn received in support was a raised eyebrow and nod.

There were only two other occasions Flinn had shared a peace smoke before, once with this father after his twelfth spring—of which did not end well whatsoever when he believed his lungs would collapse. The second, when he met with one of the local girls, hoping to use it as an excuse to see her immaculate breasts.

A drawn pull from the pipe's stem ensued, siphoning the smoke so that a cherry glow in the chamber grew brighter. The Firbolgs joined their voice in an encouraging droning hum, keeping to the the steady beat of the drums, all while Flinn continued his drag of the pipe. Finally, when his lungs could withstand no more, he coughed out excruciatingly. Clouds of smoke shot out in great puffs, billowing, and spreading wide into dancing shapes.

Joden and the Firbolgs laughed raucously, with Fjorik in the background changing the rhythm of the drums to a much fiercer beat. Somehow it almost sounded *fuzzy* to Flinn's ears, if such a thing was possible. Fading to stretch and waver like a ribbon caught in the wind; along with it, a hazy lightheadedness. In fact, the Druid's son felt he had entered a realm where substance was but an airy mist. Creative juices began to stimulate imagination, racing through Flinn's mind without break or pause.

Envisioning himself running wild through moonlit forests, surrounded by the natural beauty the land offered. He was free of worry, free from the bonds of civilization. Flinn could feel the moon's cool embrace, her gentle caress. He could hear the individualized crickets and peepers joining in their orchestral banter, harmonizing with Wulndar. Adding to their song, the rustling leaves high in the boughs of the trees, tickled by the soft nightly breeze, hushes a soothing lullaby. Through it all, Flinn saw himself running on all fours, naked and free, with nothing to hold him back.

Laughter ensued, snapping him away from the most imaginative and sensory experience he had ever had. How long had he been left in that daze? The question had immediately flittered away, the moment Flinn's attentions were drawn exhaled streams of smoke adding to a carousel of images ringing above the firepit. Like puppets, they moved with the swirling storm of purple-black haze, painting pictures of battles, huge mountains, open fields, ancient beasts, and celebrations.

Was it only Flinn that could see these things? He looked around himself, noting that Joden and the giants continued their revelry. Whatever they discussed came out inaudible, nothing they were saying could be understood. Flinn's ears felt extraordinarily warm and his eyes were heavy. He blinked several times, attempting to focus his vision as he continued surveying.

Making note of the spriggans along with small pointy-eared creatures of woodland brown skin, clad in leafy garments, dancing a ring outside the Firbolg's bonfire. They giggled, snickered, and whispered to one another when they noticed Flinn's gawking. Each joining hands as their pace quickened, spinning round and round and round, faster and faster, until it became too nauseating to watch anymore. Flinn looked away, to his bare toes and wiggled them, and nearly leapt from his reclining posture when a spriggan popped up behind his feet.

"Ye dream of wild things," the small creature separated Flinn's feet like pushing aside two leaves, its eyes wide and black. "Ye've got the blood in ye." The spriggan gestured with her chin to the smokey shapes made over the fire.

The young man's eyes glittered with fascination, watching the images play around him. Yet, there was no fear in the Druid's son's eyes, just pure fascination and wonder. He knew and felt he was in no danger here, and these creatures, as monstrous as they may appear, were kindly spirits.

"Sleep now, Druid's Son," The Spriggan said in an undertone that somehow inspired such fatigue to occur. "Let dreams guide yer spirit."

Stones must have been tied to his eyelashes, for he could not keep his eyes open any longer, and Flinn soon fell into a deep sleep. Far away sounds of the Firbolg voices faded away, along with the rhythmic drums. All that remained was the wind through the trees, and the cool whispering caress of its breeze.

Flinn opened his eyes, feeling refreshed, sitting up in a great relieving stretch. As he looked about him, the giants were gone, along with Joden and the other fey creatures. But the seats remained, hauntingly empty. As he moved to stand, he realized then he was without his clothes! Face reddening, the Druid's son cast about embarrassingly, and yet there were none present his nakedness. Little did that do to alleviate his exposure, however.

He was alone.

There was no way he was asleep for that long. It was still dark, in any event, but all sense of time eluded him. Only shadows offered any company, thrown about the grove by the black light of the bonfire. Besides its soft crackling, all other sound was absent. That only added to a gathering ill feeling.

The fear of being alone suddenly gripped him, for something deep inside of him suggested that he was the only one in existence here. Dare he call out for Joden, or perhaps the Firbolgs. Hells, he would have even called out for the spriggans or any of the fey folk if he thought it would help. Flinn, frightened, vulnerable, and nude, turned slowly in place. He was stricken over the thought of even venturing out into the forest as his eyes fought to peer into its dark depths. He gazed up at the canopy of the trees, swaying from a noiseless and unfelt breeze that terrified him further. Yet, all of it paled as a sanguine moon glared down at him. His heart beat quickly, increasing in its rapidity while the unease in the pit of his gut squirmed and grew.

Then the black light of the fire extinguished, leaving Flinn bathed in a bloody veil under that red burning moon. Panic now wracked his body. whatever had happened while he was asleep had drastically taken a turn for the worst. But there then sounded the snap of a twig, spinning Flinn around, lowering his weightbearing into his legs, and tensing with a loaded posture. He was ready to run for it, though something in him told him to wait and see what it was first.

Peering across the grove, through the sanguine night, a shadowy shape stood silent, and still within the dark of the wood. Hungry amber eyes stared back from the darkness of the forest, piercing into Flinn, marking him with an intense stare. Whatever it was it was big, much larger than Flinn, with an equally large growl that rumbled and rolled towards him. He backed up a step, then two, then frantically several more. His mind flashed with an image of gnawing fangs tearing into naked flesh.

The growling intensified, reverberating the environment around Flinn. He could feel the vibrations, tickling into his toes, running up his legs, to spread throughout his body. His mind began to reel, more images of running wild, but this time beneath the blood moon, and he was no longer alone. Shadowy shapes ran along with him, darting through trees, leaping over logs, dashing ahead of him to cut across his path.

The image vanished, leaving him to stand before a large black wolf. So close that Flinn could feel the moist heat of its breath on his face, hear its panting, almost hear its voice...

Flinn sprang awake to the sudden roar of triumph and cheers. Groggy and sleepy-eyed, the Druid's son blinked away his confusion, picking his head up to look over at the blurred shapes moving strangely in the bonfire's light. I thought he saw a Ghar'tul among them, playing a panpipe, skipping about on his goat-like legs while other fey creatures danced to his cheery melody.

It may just be his own eyes playing tricks on him, but it almost appeared as though Joden was locked in a grappling match with one of the Firbolgs. Confused, tired and having no energy at all for any other strange sights, Flinn settled back with a moan, and draped an arm over his eyes. He prayed he dreamt of other things other than red moons and giant black wolves.

Chapter 11
Rocky Hills & Trailing Shadows

Waking sunlight flittered down, filtering through the branches, sending dappling shadows across the mossy floor of the Grove. Early morning song twittered through the canopies, filling the forest with refreshed perspective. It was to this harmonic and undisturbed peaceful space that Flinn eased from sleep. The smell of fire-smoke lingered in the air, bringing a nostalgic memory of the Firbolgs, but they were nowhere to be seen. Nor was there any sign of any other fey creatures ever being by the bonfire that night.

All the sudden a thrusted speared haunch of meat appeared before Flinn's face, smoking and sizzling. After eliciting his surprise, the aroma quickly overtook the feeling of shame from his lack of awareness. He took the spit gladly, salivating in anticipation of tearing into warm cooked muscled flesh. The skin was browned nearly perfectly, save for a crispy area or two, but that only added to the overall flavor. Sitting up as he tore into his breakfast, he continued to look around him. Flinn's wonderment was easy to decipher.

"just as the wind blows, so too do the ways of the Firbolgs." Joden stated as he packed his things into his traveler's bag. It sounded to Flinn like some recitation he should have heard as a child, sounding old and new.

Flinn stood up from where he slept on the chair, realizing with surprise, that it was a log covered in thick spongey moss. He looked up to Joden who shrugged back at him, leaving it up for Flinn to believe or not. Yet, despite his elusive memory and confusion, Flinn found himself completely revitalized.

He Felt springier in his step, well balanced as he crossed a short distance to his traveling pack. He bit into the cooked boar carefully, trying not to burn his mouth with but a periphery glance to the rest of the spitted beast over a considerate bed of coals. Once again, there was no sign that a giant bonfire had even existed. He shook his head, bending to gather his things.

"Make sure ye have everything, lad, there'll be no more Firbolg Groves along the way," Joden cast about with a concerned look, adding, "This was the easiest part of our journey, and with what I've just learned from my friends, the Highlands be restless."

Flinn scanned the surrounding trees warily, expecting to see amber eyes in the shadows, his stomach turning in knots. "Maybe there's another way 'round?"

Hefting the straps of his pack over his large shoulders, Joden offered a glancing response, "If ye mean for an easier way, there's aren't any. And among any of them that may even be considered easy, would be through the Spines of Zhul'Tarrgan. And that, lad, is no easy trek."

Flinn had a feeling that was the case, with naught but accepting the long road ahead as fate deemed it.

"Now," Joden fidgeted some more with his pack while straightening his posture, "we go."

"What of the coals, and the meat?" Flinn started for the roasting boar, intent on rationing as much as he could and to see the coals properly doused.

Joden shook his head, halting Flinn's advance. "No. Let the coals be, lad, they'll go out on their own—besides—the meat be for the enjoyment of another. Our tribute for having stayed the night. Now, let's go, we've wasted enough time." There was nothing else said as the Warlord turned and melded into the thick of the wood, leaving Flinn behind in the small camp.

Shaking his head, baffled by yesternight, and left flabbergasted after waking, the Druid's son hurried after the Warlord with hasty steps, and already worrying what the day would bring.

Redeyes mounted one of his fallen warrior's wolves, meanwhile his own kept pace with the Duldarians. He had seen the images clearly through her eyes when she finally found their prey. Having found sanctuary in Spirit's Retreat. Redeyes wanted her to continue and follow them. While waiting for the rest of his pack to saddle their mounts and prepare for the day, Thwark bowed his head and closed his eyes—pushing his consciousness through.

The images he saw through the eyes of his wolf were of the Duldarian pair moving north from the forest. He was curious where they were heading, for their course would lead them through the rolling hills before rising into the mountain cliffs of the Ghar'tul clans. If the roving hill clans of the goat-folk did not capture them first, then the much fiercer of the mountain clans would. Either them or the banshees and dead sinners would have them if they did not make it through the night. A sad afterthought, more because it would have been a waste.

It was all an unfortunate possibility, either way, Thwark thought it prudent to head north also but up along the other side of Northern Crook Lake, cross the River Serpent's Bridge, and there wait in the likelihood that the two Duldarian's made it that far. For why else would they keep such a heading? They must be trying to make for the Dark Tome, thinking to take it for themselves before Desdemona sent the Feral Folk to war.

Thwark Redeyes focused back to his surroundings, casting a surveying glare over the Wolf-kin, measuring their preparedness. With a thrust of his fist and a rallying howl, the Pack Master spurred his wolf mount northward. Behind him, his pack stirred and followed with eager howls of their own.

Through Spirit's Retreat, using the forest as cover, the pair of Duldarians made their way until they reached the edge. A great expanse of lowland hills rolled northeast, dwarfed by the jagged coastal mountains distant as the terrain rose gradually into the highlands yonder under a grey sky that muffled the sun. For a few blinks, Joden studied the environment while Flinn leaned against a tree a few strides back.

A sea of open land stretched and spread up for leagues, green and sodden looking. To the west, a herd of great elk meandered across the vast plain, taking their time as they grazed, ever-alert against impending threats. Across the sky flew a flock of greenfinch, shimmering and shifting like a great emerald cloud, changing altitude and direction as spontaneously as the winds.

"It's going to be rough country here on out, lad," Joden reiterated over his shoulder, before pressing forward.

They walked for hours until the sun was at its highest, leaving Spirit's Retreat far behind them. There was a momentary rest, found at the crest of a large hill that shielded against the east-wind by way of a jutting slab of natural rock. It breached on a sharp forty-five-degree angle, leaving Flinn to wonder if the Firbolgs had erected it to serve as a marker. Which left him to wonder further, if they even had the collective strength to move such a massive formation.

In any case, Joden used it as a vantage point, sweeping his eyes from the sky to the roving lands below. While Flinn consumed dried meat rations, he contemplated whether the Warlord searched for Ghar'tul, Wolf-kin, or possibly mapped out their next stretch by eye alone. Whatever the case, he was glad for not being the one to do it.

After their short break, the pair set off again. Picking their way across rugged terrain, as it shifted and changed from leveled expanses, to steep slopes, and into high rises. The land surrounding them looked the same in every direction but was becoming rockier and increasingly more precarious to traverse, not to mention the pressure change in altitude. Flinn's ears, on more than one occasion, popped from an involuntary yawn or by simply swallowing.

At one point in their journey, he had chanced a glimpse behind them and could have sworn he saw a dark shape in the distance, something large and quadrupedal. But as quickly as he had seen it, the shape disappeared. His recollection went back to his dream yesternight, the pair of amber eyes in the shadows.

"Duldar's sake, boy-o, quit your daydreaming and keep up!" Joden warned harshly, "this is no place to let ye mind wander. We'll be making camp as soon as the land is giving." He grunted at his own words, seeming unconvinced that they would find worthy shelter. There was nothing out here but rocky hills, open field, and sparse vegetation. Aside the occasional spotting of a hare or perhaps a red fox hunting shrew, there was nothing around for leagues. If there was danger, Flinn or Joden were sure to see it long before reached them.

But the terrain only continued to become challenging, offering a long and painful fall that would send them tumbling and crashing into sharp rock. Finding themselves scaling short faces of stone and clambering over steeper ground as they made their way deeper into the highlands. Mountain goats were soon noticed, scattered in spacey clusters, perched precariously on insanely narrow ledges that no creature should be able to balance on. That was when Joden slowed their pace, forcing a more cautious approach now. Not simply due to the arduous footwork, but because they were well within Ghar'tul territories.

Of yet, there had been no sign of the half-man, half-goat folk, and for that Flinn was grateful.

Stories described the brazen, ill-tempered Wulndarians easy to provoke, impetuous to act and were said to eat just about anything if circumstances permitted. So foul were their habits that not even Wolf-kin could stomach their presence. The Ghar'tul were vicious and filthy, without a shred of compassion or honor. Of course, so said the tales, from what Flinn could recall, he remembered the panpipe playing creature of last night. He looked like a milder version than what the stories told, with nothing about him that seemed threatening in the least.

They at last rested at a small escarpment overlooking an embankment that sunk into a depression where a small lake could be seen. A coat of mist clung over the water, but all around there was nothing to show that anything made it a highly trafficked watering hole, if that was what it was at all—the water beneath the mist looked brackish and undrinkable. In fact, there was nothing other than the mist and the lake.

"I take it we'll make camp by the lake?" Flinn guessed.

Jodan shook his head slowly with a forborne look in his fierce eyes. "No, lad, not down there—" he glanced back over his shoulder, gesturing with his chin further back from where they stood, "we'll camp back a ways. Come morning, we'll trace the outside of the depression." He glanced to the dwindling light of the day, "we'd best get a fire on."

Flinn leaned forward, peeking over into the depression. "Looks… dead."

"Trust me, lad," Joden assured, "that is not a place ye wish to poke around in." He pointed to a sole island at the center of the lake where a singular tree grew, where the mist gathered thickest. The tree was a mangled and twisted thing bent like an old crone, surrounded by tall leaning cairns, untouched by time.

The sight of it would be something Flinn would not soon forget. His sense of curiosity was dashed away after slapped at his shoulder, but something drew his attentions back to the depression where the lone tree stood. So strange that it should be found here, and so lonely a place at that. The Druid's son followed Joden back down until the ground leveled some and helped prepare a small fire, readying themselves for a cold night as the day waned further.

When night arrived, casting a black blanket fixed with a singular opal eye, the highlands became a ghostly place. Strong winds moaned around them, playing over the cliffs that made the hairs on the back of Flinn's neck stand on end. He rubbed at his hackles, readjusted his seating, sore from being poked by sharp rocks, and unable to be at ease while feeling so vulnerable to the surrounding darkness. Anything could be watching them right now, perhaps some roaming beast waiting for them to sleep and satiate its hunger. Or a fist-sized contingent of Ghar'tul slinking in for an ambush, waiting to cut their throats.

Joden had set a small kettle over the fire after filling it with mead, just something to warm their bones aside from the cool waterskins they carried. "This'll lighten the mood," he said, pouring the steaming drink into a small cup made from a hollowed-out hoof. Rations were divided between them, just enough to settle the rumbling in their bellies. When that had been finished, they both sat crossed legged facing one another with the fire between them. Both sipping from their steaming cups, but with Joden studying Flinn.

Uncomfortable, Flinn shifted beneath the Warlord's scrutinizing stare. He tried not to meet the man's gaze, but it was difficult to do when he was glaring right at him without a word. Clearing his throat, Flinn sipped his drink and swallowed before breaking the silence. "Ye don't think I can do it?"

Joden downed a great portion of his mead before answering. "Ye do, or ye don't. We won't know until it happens."

Nodding in response, in truth not knowing what to say to that, Flinn blew out a breath and downed the rest of his mead. His yes went to the fire, lost in their dance.

"Has yer da told ye anything about yerself?" the Warlord suddenly asked casually as he reached forward, using a thick scrap of hide to lift the kettle from its purchase over the small flames.

The Druid's son knitted his eyebrows together, thinking on it, but he was unsure to what Joden was referring. "Should he have?"

Joden grunted incredulously while pouring himself a second cup, then set the kettle back over the flames.

"Do ye know something I should?" Flinn eyed the Warlord a moment, trying to gauge some sort of tell.

Another grunt and sip from his cup were all the response Joden gave. In a single gulp, the Warlord finished, shaking the remnants free, wiping it out clean, to then stuff it back into his bag. After that, he went about situating himself to get some sleep, laying with his back to the flames. "Rest now, and be warned, whatever ye hear this night, do not go seeking."

With a restless sigh, the Druid's son tossed the last of his mead with a flick before he situated himself for sleep as well. Other than the wind, he thought, what else was there to possibly hear, Joden's snorting, his own? He shook doubtfully, for if there were something to worry about seeking, it would be that damned Dark Tome they were out here to get.

Flinn's eyes finally became heavy and fell shut, sending him into an exhausted slumber with his axes snuggly in their belt loops. He laid a hand to their handles, comforted by their smoothness as they diminished all worries, all doubts, and especially his fears.

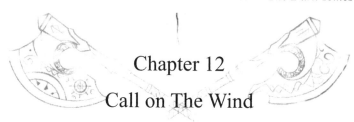

Chapter 12
Call on The Wind

Flinn woke suddenly to a strange moaning of wind, almost siren-like and with a faint calling melody. It had gone as quickly as it had roused him, and for several heartbeats there was only the wind itself. Until that distinct call echoed down from the escarpment again, carrying over him to wisp into the night. He turned over, finding Joden fast asleep, ruling him out at once. The night laid in silence for a few more moments before the calling rose again. Flinn remained still, peering out into the night as the sound faded once more, staring askance whence it came.

But the ghostly call came again, with a clear woefulness that was for Flinn specifically. He could not mistake the sounding of his name. Without misinterpreting the distressful intonations, Flinn leapt up, hands on the heads of his axes, and bunched his shoulders against the chill, sporadic winds. He moved past the sleeping Warlord, traveled the distance away from the camp and rushed for the escarpment, following the call for help.

Whatever you hear, do not *go seeking.* Joden's warning seemed far away, a whisper now, drowned out with another wailing wind and the haunting cry that rode along with it. The safety of the camp was far behind him now, the light of its fire small in the sloping distance, and at last stood looking down over the edge of the escarpment.

The wind's howling, its wailing and ghostly song had led the young man on as well as one was pulled by a length of rope. The call of distress seemingly increased its tempo with an edge of eagerness, as if sensing his nearing presence. As the song became clearer and louder, echoing below, Flinn lowered himself to his belly as he edge closer to the lip of the escarpment and used the light of the moon to try and make out the island at the lake. Could it be that the distressed party was stranded somehow, Flinn wondered?

Much to his surprise, the lake appeared to glow beneath the mist, creating an underlying light reflected by the moon. The cairn stones seemed to glow themselves or possibly reflecting the light that emitted its soft luminance altogether.

Stranger yet, the bent tree was no longer bent, but lively and thick of trunk. Its branches grew wide and splayed lushly with autumn colored leaves. But there, on that lonely island at the center of that small misty lake, there came the sad calling of a woman in white flowing robes. Her red hair moved as though she danced beneath water, a back glow of light making it glow like flame, and her robes clung scantily to her body in fluttering shreds like wisps of silks. All while she waved for Flinn, beckoning him to her, asking for his help to save her.

Her voice traveled back up to his ears, filling his head with the need for urgency. She was trapped, that much was obvious, but how? Maybe if he could figure out how to free her, the woman may lend aid to their cause. The Druid's son was already searching for a way down, spying a questionable area where he impetuously clambered down safely enough, save for a misplaced toe or hand hold. He was lucky Joden was not there to see it, it was bad enough he left the Warlord alone by the fire

For whatever reason, the woman's call for help trumped all other responsibility. Eventually, Flinn made his way down at a steady pace. The nearer he came to the bottom, the less concerned he was of hurting himself and half-slid and half-skipped the rest of the way down until he landed on a bed of spongey soil and loose river rock.

Flinn moved towards the lake's edge, his eyes locked on the woman's form. And for a moment, he thought she was floating, until she beckoned him once more, distracting him with her sweet voice.

His gaze kept to the island and the woman mesmerizingly as she now danced around the tree, obviously ecstatic about being rescued. Tendrils of mist went unnoticed coiling below Flinn's knees. Whenever the red-haired woman made a pass across his sight, she turned an alluring smile his way and pointed. He followed the line she created, noticing the sound of slapping water against the hull of a small boat tied off a few feet away. How had he not noticed that before?

Flinn made quick work of untying it from its anchor point. Shoving it off it into the water after a momentary struggle. He pulled himself into the small craft, rickety as it was, relieved to find two oars waiting. They looked as though they had not been touched in an age, rotted as the wood was, and Flinn was not so sure that they would hold.

Flinn fit them into the rowing stations and began paddling towards the island. He was determined more now than ever to reach the woman. Her dancing drew him to her, her calls for help now a song of jubilatin. Flinn's eyes were able to pick out more details as he neared, following her slender and curvaceous body as it swayed and gyrated alluringly. Like the shimmering autumn leaves rustling above her, so did the woman's arms and fingers.

It did not appear to Flinn there was any danger here, by way this woman danced so carelessly and sang so melodiously. But he had come too far now just to go back, or maybe he should? The song intensified, bringing his thoughts back from straying, back to the matter at hand. That woman needed help, stranded as she was. Flinn continued rowing until the stem of the boat's transom slid into the gravely sore of the island.

The wind howled again, and for a moment Flinn thought he heard the Warlord's voice calling for him. But that could not be, for Joden was too deep in sleep and Flinn had left the camp as quietly as a serpent. She wanted him to dance with her, share in her elation at finally being saved, turning her sorrow into joy.

His eagerness to get to the woman had intensified, adding to his quickening stride. Only a few more yard to get to her, a few more steps up the small incline and within those glowing cairns. But now the woman no longer danced, and neither did she advance to meet Flinn, but instead continued to sing with her eyes locked intensely with Flinn's own. Her arms were held out to him, her hands straining to touch him, and so too did Flinn yearn to bring her close to him.

There was one thing yet strong enough to direct Flinn's attentions elsewhere, and that was his natural curiosity of things both strange and odd. His attentions went to the glowing cairns he had yet to reach and pass through. Each had been inscribed with a single rune permeating with an icy blue radiance, but the aura that limned the stones was a ghostly white. A raw power thrummed between them like an unseen drape of energy, its radiating power could be felt with only being a few steps away. And though the woman's voice kept the urgency in Flinn to come and take her away, his interest in the cairns called him hither. Their power, he could feel more than he knew, was ancient and with something else…

That was when the woman's intonations turned desperate and angry, as she stood within the encircling stones frustratingly. Her green eyes were fierce with determination, focused on the young man but went unnoticed while he stared at the cairns. The tempo of her song climbed, her words coming off more harsh and rapid, much as Flinn heard his father chant sometimes in his study.

Chanting!

Flinn's sudden interest in the stones vanished, turning to the milk-skinned woman with emerald eyes. She could but reach out now and touch him if she wanted to but made no move as her words were likened to rubbing parchment. Now, with glacial orbs blazed within hollow sockets and her fiery hair gone to a stark blue/white, her ghoulish appearance was unveiled. A sudden forceful gale suddenly inhaled from within the cairns, pulling the Druid's son in closer. A few more steps and he would be well within their parameter.

The banshee's song had stopped, now a hungry wailing. With flesh stretched taut over gaunt features and dared an attempt to snatch out a near fleshless clawed hand as Flinn pitched forward and staggered close enough to step a foot between the stones.

She gripped his wrist, sending biting cold running up his arm to the elbow, but he pulled back against her. The banshee floated from the ground, propelling herself backwards, yanking on Flinn as if he were a child's doll. Fear gripped, frostbitten and fearing for his life, the Druid's son leaned back as hard as he could and dug his heels into the ground without purchase. They dug deep furrows into what looked like blood-soaked moss, spongey and swelling from the violent tearing. And in moments, he would be beyond the cairns, within their encircling agelessness, and in the clutches of the banshee.

Flinn crossed his right hand over to his left hip, feeling the head of Wulfax and fought as quickly as he could to slide it free its holster. The moment his fingers played over the cold silver, surety in arming himself with the weapon became even more ubiquitous. Flinn found a firm grip around its bone handle, the runes on the blade suddenly aglow with cool light and sending a sudden repulsive nova of unseen force from it.

The banshee screeched, releasing her hold after one last attempt to pull the Druid's son into the circle, and flung herself away from him towards the twisted and mangled tree. Its autumn colored leaves now gone, leaving only barren clawed branches. But Flinn was not so fortunate to keep from within the cairns. The last valiant attempt to pull him in had been successful and he stumbled headfirst to the blood-soaked mossy bed of the island.

Flinn scrambled to his feet in a kick of soil and rocks, Wulfax ready at hand and hungry to rend and tear! With his free hand, trying his best to keep the undead thing in his sights, he reached for the second ax but found it missing. Frantic searching eyes found it a few feet away from him; it must have slid free during his fall. But it was nothing against the scream that pierced his ears and froze him in place. Racking Flinn with a compelling fear that made his knees tremble, suddenly feeling too weak to support his own weight.

A quickening heartbeat caused for the Druid's son to break into a cold sweat, sending warning pangs in his gut as he watched the undead creature float ominously towards him. As much as Flinn wanted fight against the banshee's hold, he found that his body would not obey. The scream turned into a sobbing, a rasping weeping that did not elicit empathy from Flinn, but instead only heightened the frightening experience of his predicament.

But Wulfax was fierce. Fiercer when faced with fear and dispelled of it in a single washing wave. Meanwhile, the banshee floated left to right, burying her rotted face into her hands, and sobbing as she sneakily closed the distance between them. But the ease of confidence in Flinn's heart spread like flaming wings throughout his chest, soon catching the rest of his body with the fires of determination. Sensing this from her prey, the banshee crackled her neck and turned her head to lay eyes on him, shrieking angrily as inky tears poured out from hollow sockets.

She rushed the last few strides, reaching out with clawing hands. Ordinarily, Flinn would have pissed himself and turn to run, but Wulfax felt intent on bringing his arm up and around, biting into one of the banshee's reaching arms and hacking it cleanly away. The scream that escaped her was unmistakably one of anguish, as she held up a stump with hate-filled glacial eyes. She lashed out swiftly in response, slashing at Flinn's gut, but the silver plating of his girdle was large enough to shield his midsection. Her attack only resulted in bringing back fingered nubs still sizzling and burning as the stench of charred rot wafted in the night air.

Whether she was incorporeal or not made little difference as far as Flinn's girdle and weapon were concerned. For they did her as much harm as though she were made of flesh and blood. She flung herself backwards in response, hovering behind the mangled oak, peeking around it though she never to lay scornful hollows on Flinn. It was clear that the dead hag had not expected her victim to be so well prepared. Hells, Flinn had not expected it himself!

Then an ear-piercing screech doubled him over, gritting his teeth and flexing his jaw against its pain, while gripping Wulfax's handle for dear life. Flinn refused to part from it. His ears began to bleed, while fighting to keep his eyes from popping from their sockets. The Druid's son felt the building pressure in his head, his brain threatening to burst through his skull.

For the banshee, as she came from around the dead oak, bearing down on the young man with her crippling voice, victory for her was nigh at hand. She now floated above her prey, reaching for him with one almost-fingerless hand. Flinn braced himself beneath the weight of her voice, fighting to keep himself on one knee at least, noticing now for the first time the collection of bones that scattered the island like a carpet.

For Flinn, this was the end. He had failed. Duldar's Port was doomed, and its people would know only cruelty and torment. But most of all he had failed his father. As his mind trembled, shaking to soon shatter utterly, there faintly came a heavy trampling from behind. A hulking shape rushed past the enfeebled young man, and the banshee now directed her attentions on the unexpected intruder. The whoosh of a heavy blade swung down over her, splitting her form, and causing her to shriek painfully as she dissipated and solidified by the dead tree.

She lingered close by the base, hissing at the monster of a man that placed himself between her and her prey. With her scream gone and after a few blinks of reorientation, the Druid's son recognized Joden's sodden form. He must have swum the lake! The man stood with a two-handed grip on the claymore whose runes of black light ran down its broad length. The banshee shrieked again her outrage, swiping a clawed hand out towards the Warlord from where she haunted. He scoffed, gathered up throaty phlegm and spat in her direction.

She then began to sing, but her words were not for the ears of the Duldarians this time.

"Get on the boat, lad!" Joden directed in earnest, never turning his eyes or the edge of his blade away from the banshee. Wherever she floated, he was sure to keep her in front of him.

Gripping his axe, Flinn forced himself painfully to his feet, scooping up matching weapon on his way towards the boat.

"I say ye, back!" Joden rebuked the undead woman, taking backward steps.

Stopping short of the boat, Flinn's hesitancy was not due to his desire to stay and fight alongside the Warlord, it was the lumbering, shambling dark shapes rising from the misty murk of the lake. They began surrounding the island, dragging their feet against the stones, bones, and soggy muck, with more of them wading and swaying depressingly, dripping wet as their animated forms slowly advanced. Wherever Flinn glimpsed, there they were. Some clearly Wolf-kin, others Ghar'tul and there were even those few seemingly stuck in their hybrid forms, but all nothing more now than decaying husks.

Gripping tight the bone handle of both axes now, Flinn forced himself to utter a warning at the same time he felt an overwhelming surge of power through his opposite arm from his reclaimed weapon. He felt unstoppable, he felt larger than life, and he felt like he could swing through those old shambling bones with one swipe.

Joden dared a quick glance over his shoulder, cursing through his short beard and past the long-braided mustaches hanging at either side. He backed into Flinn, pressing his weight into him and suggested the lad do to the same.

"Fight back to back," he directed, "I'll keep the banshee occupied, but ye'll need to take care of those damned Sinners if they get too close to my back—where I go, ye go! Do ye understand me, boy-o!?"

Flinn gave a curt nod, muttering acquiescence, his axes held in fierce grips. Sending through him an excitement for battle he had never felt before. He was eager for the bloodletting, intent on hacking into long dead flesh and bone. With the Twins in his hands, there was no force that could match his might.

"They're slow, dull witted—aim for their heads, if no' they'll just keep getting up," Joden waved his claymore threateningly at the banshee who tried her hand in closing the distance, but he succeeded in keeping her at length with his runic claymore.

The Druid's son felt better with Joden at his back, adding to the inspiration his weapons gifted him. But that did nothing to slow the Sinner's advance. As the first neared, holding a rusted and jagged short sword, Wulfax tugged Flinn roughly to the left, forcing his step and then raising his arm up high to slash down at a vicious angle. The Undead Sinner could not have brought its weapon up quick enough, so fast had Wulfax tugged at its wielder and executed the attack. Flinn felt Joden's weight shift to the right, and he pressed back into him lightly to make it easier to keep with the Warlord's movement.

Another test of distance from the banshee, her voice still calling to the shambling Sinners closing in around the Duldarians. Yet the tip of Joden's claymore nearly pierced through her had she gotten any closer. A hateful hiss escaped her, pressing the stump of her severed arm to her boney chest.

Caught between a horde of soggy skeletons, and zombies, and a gods damned banshee, this would be a story to rival all! That was if Flinn and Joden even made it out of this alive. As the undead gained ground, the shriek of the banshee filled the night and somehow forced them to move faster with their unstable gaits. Flinn hunkered down his stance a bit, widening his footing, waiting for one to get close enough.

With his shoulders bouncing with his steps, relaxed and loose, the Druid's son allowed Wulfax free range to guide his hand. Likewise, with its twin, which had yet to reveal its name to him. Perhaps after wetting its bit in a reacquainting dance of battle, mayhap.

The second to feel the axe's bites was a Ghar'tul hybrid. A monstrous creature, taller than Flinn, with a head and lower half of a grotesque half-decayed goat, came charging in swinging down with a spiked club. The twins pulled Flinn to step in low and pivot around the reckless Sinner, swinging one with an upper-cutting angle, and sending the other to chop into the undead flank. The top half of the Ghar'tul's head suffered a clean cut, almost immediately deactivating whatever dark magic animated it, as its ribs collapsed and splintered into itself. Small minnows, black leeches and lake water fountained from the wounds in the place of blood, making a putrid smelling mess.

Wulfax pulled Flinn further to the side as the Ghar'tul corpse fell lifelessly forward, but he resisted the suggestion. There was the Warlord's back to consider and the promise to watch it. Surprisingly, the axes did not feel as though they disagreed.

Another Sinner stepped in, lunging lazily behind the tip of a reaching blade. Flinn felt his left hand pull straight back behind him, forcing his shoulder to dip back and evade the Sinner's sword thrust just-barely. The right-handed ax whipped him around, guiding him into a spinning step complimentary to Wulfax's guiding pull. And though the sword did make a glancing blow, it did nothing to mortally wound the Druid's son. He was certain that if not for the axes, he would have suffered a fatal blow.

Flinn dropped low mid-spin, guided by his weapons, and was yanked up in a springing motion to deliver with generated momentum an exploding blow with his secondary ax. The Sinner's shoulder took the impact, blasting clean through, and sending bits of bone and leathery, soggy flesh before the husk collapsed. Flinn marveled at the weapon for but a moment, the ax working his hand as a puppeteer to twirl it dexterously.

"Oh, I think I like these, Warlord!" Flinn called over

his shoulder, his face pulled into a maniacal grin.

Joden swung out to the side with his blade, hewing the shaft of a spear that suddenly reached out for him. With a quick turn of the sword, the Warlord brought the claymore back up on a harsh angle severing the forearms of the Sinner wielding the weapon. Both spear and limbs plopped into the ground, leaving the Undead Sinner's head exposed as the sword shifted back again. This time, taking the head of the abomination, falling with a thud at its own feet before Joden turned his attentions onto the onrushing banshee. She stopped in an instant, floating back casually nearest the tree while her undead horde tightened around her victims.

"We have to push to the boat, lad!" Joden called, waving his sword to ward off the Undead Sinners. He pushed back against Flinn, forcing him to move in the direction of where the boat waited.

Flinn tried to keep his footing, but the Warlord's strength was like trying to hold back a horse from getting to its trough. His boots dug and slid across ground, now muddy and turning it up to cause blood to seep and swell. Meanwhile, allowing his weapons to guide his hands, swinging at unthinkable angles that boggled Flinn's mind. Clawed hands and arms were hacked away, weapons deflected and redirected only to expose openings for counter strikes. Heads flew free, gone rolling about at the undead horde's feet to be kicked about.

The banshee followed at a leisurely pace amidst the Undead Sinners she had called to her, with a voice droning on with a dreadfully unending ballad, pushing her animated fodder to press the Duldarians harder. With great left to right sweeps of his claymore Joden cut those too close like too much wheat in a field. Along with Flinn's directed attacks possessed by the Twins, the pair painstakingly cut their way through the cairns. And by the sudden heightening of the banshee's song, resulting in the hungry impatience from the Sinners, it was apparent that she did not want for the two barbarians to make it to the boat.

As Flinn hacked and swung with the axes, cutting down reaching claws or batting away pathetic attempts with rusty weapons, there rushed one such Sinner unexpectedly from his right. The poor bastard had half a jaw remaining, clipping, and clapping against the underside of his skull with every awkward step. It closed the distance easily enough, despite its shambled gait, and lunged with grasping decayed fingers. Latching hold of the Druid's son's great kilt and digging its claws into the flesh of his opposite shoulder, the undead thing pulled itself close so that Flinn bore all its rickety weight. A noxious green cloud spewed within blinks, right into his face.

Fighting the undead Wulndarian—both out of fear of being so close and in attempts to relinquish its hold—Wulfax shot upwards, angling to bury itself into the Sinner's skull and pulled it to the ground before yanking his arm back to free its bit. In the same instance, its twin followed through with a wind-milling chop that brough it down into the Undead Sinners face. Staggering back from the fumes that assailed his lungs, Flinn fought against an intense coughing spell. His green eyes bulged while the veins in his neck and forehead looked about to burst, reeling clumsily as the axes swung of their own accord, heedless of its wielders plight. Teetering on the edges of suffocation and unconsciousness, Flinn would soon become an unworthy vessel for the axes.

The Warlord halted his steps, risking a quick glance over his shoulder, noticing Flinn's sorry state of being. The banshee's shriek alone was enough to bring Joden's attentions back again, cackling through her weeping at Flinn's ill turn of luck. With a roar, and powerful rushing steps forward, Joden made it seem that he was loading up to charge but stead swung his sword in heavy circles. He left Flinn vulnerably alone for but a few moments, but neither did Joden had to worry about him being in the radius of his powerful swings.

Fearful of the weapon's harmful touch, the banshee flung back, bringing her arms up to shield herself. Joden stepped back one step at a time, never ceasing the circling swings of his claymore. Cutting down the ever-swarming Undead Sinners, catching them up in the devastation of his whooshing blade. Their heads flew clean off, cutting cleanly through shoulders, through rib cages, and if angling the weapon just-right, swiped away their legs with ease. More yet, with every one of them that met the edge of that vicious weapon, the runes on the sword flared with black light, leaving behind in its wake a silver trail of light.

Finally, near enough to Flinn to stop swinging and close the rest of the distance, Joden rushed and narrowly missed being beheaded himself by the lad. He ducked low, coming up hard to scoop the young man up in one strong arm and holding the length of weight of his claymore in the other hand. A front kick to the sternum of a less than threatening Sinner sent a cloud of mortified dust in the air, doing nothing did nothing to stop the Warlord's momentum towards the boat. He flung the Druid's son none-too-gently into the vessel, pushing it so that it took to the water.

"Stay ye down, boy-o!" Joden boomed as the boat drifted from shore, gripping tight the hilt of his double-handled blade as he faced down the encroaching horde of undead.

He swung again in great circles, producing the silver trailing line, and then went into a powerful dance of swordplay. A moment for Flinn gave him reprieve from the coughing fit, but he felt extremely nauseated. This did not stop him to prop himself enough to see Joden demolishing the encroaching Undead Sinners that swarmed him. Unable to support himself any long, the Druid's son fell back down into the bottom of the boat, loud splashes soon fading further away.

Joden had retreated into the dark murk of the surrounding, placid water as he made towards the boat before it had gotten too far. Behind him the undead clambered over their fallen, disentangling themselves from one another with arms still reaching for the living, and with voices harsh whispering rasps. As for the Banshee, she continued her woeful song, pushing her minions beyond their limits, watching them give chase

At last Joden reached the boat, only bothering enough to settle his claymore next to Flinn and began kicking his powerfully to propel the boat with his own legs. Behind them, the Undead Sinners were even more clumsy in the water than they were on land, slow in their pursuit. The banshee's screams echoed back to them, wailing of her defeat and the missed opportunity of adding the Duldarians to her collection. Joden set his jaw, focused on getting back to the other side and as far from this unholy place as possible.

Flinn lay unconscious at the bottom, unaware of Joden's toiling. Other than his raspy breathing, there was nothing else to say he was coherent, and as pale as he looked, he was alive. After shoring up, Joden reclaimed and sheathed his claymore before reaching for the Druid's son, throwing him over his shoulder. Getting up the escarpment would prove difficult, and there was no telling if the Undead Sinners would come ashore or not, so time was of the essence.

For Joden, Flinn was not heavy, feeling like a child ready for bedtime, with another hundred thirty pounds of weight over him, Jodan made for the escarpment and began to pick his way up carefully. He did not waste time in looking back or down, all that mattered was getting Flinn by the warmth of the fire back at camp.

Any slight redistribution of weight could very well mean a horrific fall. But as it was, Joden was no novice adventurer. A skilled and experienced Wulndarian who had seen time pass and did not look a day over forty. Once over the lip of the escarpment, the mighty Warlord tossed Flinn ahead of him to clamber the rest of the way unhindered. Taking up the Druid's son once more, Joden trotted the rest of the way back down the slope towards the distant fire. When at last they reached it, and once there the Warlord laid Flinn near its warmth.

He would be fine by himself a moment, Joden believed, before drawing his claymore and rushing back up the escarpment to peer over its ledge. Joden expected to see the undead climbing their way up by the light of the moon, but there were not to be seen. A glance towards the island, now hidden by heavy fog, appeared undisturbed. Only the howling winds moaned, traveling across the open highlands, dipping down into the depression, to be lost within. Just like so many who had perished, lost within the Banshee's assortment of undeath. Leaving the depression, forgetting it as it should be forgotten, Joden made his way back down the camp, balancing his sword over his one shoulder.

He later added wood to the coals, stoking the flames hotter, before checking on Flinn. The lad was deathly pale, and his breathing came out ragged and wheezing. Not at all a good sign, especially so early on their road. There was only one thing that may possibly help the Druid's son stave off the sickness, but it was a long way from here and unlikely that they would be able to reach the place without harassment. Joden sighed, covering the young man up with his own bedroll and blankets, perhaps hoping that he could sweat out most of it out. Of course, the Warlord knew that to be fool's hope.

"Banchee's callin', leadin' me to an end—a cry for help turned deadly song—her touch breaks the heart while decay takes my breath," Joden quoted the old song, worrying about what the morrow might bring. If Flinn did not get the help he needed to fight this, then the Warlord feared he would die before the next moon.

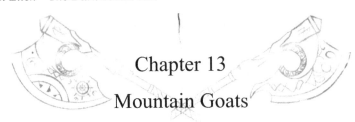

Chapter 13
Mountain Goats

Joden woke to a pile of ashes that next morning, but he hardly slept as his worry for Flinn kept him up to check on him periodically. He blinked several times, staring for a moment at the slithering streams of smoke rising from the coals. Rousing himself, the Warlord quickly went to work at gathering their belongings and covering up the firepit as much as he was able.

Not far laid Flinn, wrapped as tightly as possible to insulate his body heat. He appeared worse in the daylight, his skin pale and having taken a greenish tint. The orbits of his eyes were dark, bruised, and slightly sunken. He had not stirred since yesternight, and his breathing came out even shallower than before.

Joden scanned the area, looking across the pre-dawn illumination, wary of the soft blanket of mist that covered the rolling highlands before finishing collecting his belongings, and those of Flinn's. The rising sun was able to peek over the high and jagged landscape, casting its light before the grey sky drew over it.

The trek ahead would be cumbersome, frustratingly so, and hard pressed for time as it worked against the pair of Duldarians; especially, with Flinn in no shape to travel, but they had to keep going. Back tracking now would only waste more precious time. But the lad needed help, and if not soon then there would be a dangerous possibility of him never gazing on the next full moon. Had the young man suffered mortal wounds, perhaps Joden would be of more help but the fatal blow of a more sinister sort There was only one thing that would help, but to reach it meant to enter the Spines of Zhul'Tarrgan by a different path.

Emptying Flinn's pack into his own, Joden fit as much as was necessary to keep before using the empty pack and the rope to form a makeshift litter. Using the rope to create a securing line that tied the litter at one end and the other to his girdle, Joden pulled his burden along and moved north towards the high mountainous range and jagged spires of green splayed, dark capped stone.

It would set the Wulndarian's back a few days, perhaps two if Joden kept a reasonable pace, but he had to reach those mountains first before they headed to the eastern side of Wulndar. Half a day's travel was ahead of them, and that was just to reach the mountain pass. Hopefully, keeping to the west, the pair would be able to avoid the Ghar'tul who roamed the harsh environ. The Warlord had to move quickly and without being noticed, which may prove more difficult than originally thought. An encounter with the goat-folk would most likely be inevitable.

As Joden pulled Flinn across uneven terrain, sometimes sloping upwards, other times mindful of sudden declines, the leagues traveled only became far rockier and more precarious. Exaggerated jutting stones, boulders and vibrant greenery carpeted the rising and falling expanse as the Spines of Zhul'Tarrgan rose high in the distance. Mid-day would soon approach, placing the sun high and glaring if not for the grey sky and chill in the air, making for miserable travel.

The Warlord trekked on, however, mindless to the aching in his thighs, the burning in his calves and the fatigue in his glutes. He listened carefully, cocking his ear, to make sure that the Druid's son was still breathing and often glancing back every once and a while to see it for himself. When at last the sun was at its highest, the Wulndarian truly felt the pain of his travels.

When the land started to climb higher, that was when the Warlord took his break. He set Flinn carefully to one side, well within sight, and then rummaged through his traveler's pack. He procured a waterskin, pouring it carefully into Flinn's mouth while lifting his head gently forward, but it trickled out and down the corners wastefully.

Heaving a sigh, the large man made sure the lad got *something* before he deciding he had done all he could, the next option would be to force Flinn's mouth open and pour the water down his throat. Joden replenished his own strength with rations, water, and cold mead, allowing himself a few extra moments of rest. He took the time to observe the steep inclines and the passes that wound up and sometimes disappeared into the mountains. This landscape was harsh living, and it came to no surprise how most Wulndarians, be they Feral Folk or Fey, survived such climes. Maintaining his sweeping gaze, Joden soon froze on a dark shape to the south, high on a ridge silhouetted against the rain-grey sky, close enough to see the cold wind play against her fur and far enough to know she would be gone before he could even reach her.

She was a dark shadow starring back, resolute, and proud, unafraid, and imposing. She was Lunesesse, the Dire Mother. And had seen more than three centuries, far more than the Warlord. With that fact, there came respect. An undeniable feeling came from the piercing glint of her amber eyes, an old oath unspoken but never unknown to the Feral Lands. Joden brought himself to his feet slowly, careful not to appear overly anxious, and neither wanting to present himself as a foe but nor did he look away.

It was then that there came a descending whistle from above. The arrow that landed between Flinn's motionless body and Joden's feet brought his claymore to hand. The Warlord spun on the ball of his foot, turning in place. A trip of Ghar'tul approached from the north, horned forms trotting warily while others prancing excitedly. Joden winced at their sporadic bleating, calling to one another in their guttural and ugly language as they slowed upon nearing.

Another arrow suddenly whistled past Joden's ear,

meaning to frighten him. But he simply shifted slightly from its line of fire without a flinch. The Ghar'tul were easily excitable, bullying in nature and brash—especially when the odds were in their favor. They had the numbers, the power to overwhelm easily and all rights to this land, but as they neared some of their excitement began to waver, replaced with taut wariness. Joden knew some of them wanted to cut him down, but the fact that he was not a pin cushion and Flinn was not yet put out of his misery, meant the Ghar'tul had other intentions.

Another arrow whistled past, piercing the ground just a mere few inches from Flinn's head as if in response to that realization. The Warlord caught the message all too plainly and thrust the tip of his sword into the dirt, the weapon wobbling angrily at the audacity of being thrust into dirt.

Their approaching hooves thudded into earth and clopped against stone while fanning out to form a crescent shape around the Duldarians. Some were in their hybrid forms, standing taller than their faun-like kin. Whatever form they chose to wear, Ghar'tul nature remained to be the same.

A scrappy looking warrior stepped forward, keeping distance from Joden, but showing also that he was not afraid to engage him should it come to that. A short tangle of facial hair grew from the sides of the goat-man's face, meeting to form a lengthy plaited beard. Dark tattoos, bleeding patterns of tribal knots inked the Ghar'tul's brown and weathered flesh, signaled decades of tribulations. His hand gripped the hilt of a club, smacking the gnarled length of bone into his meaty palm.

Joden maintained a calm resolve, keeping his palms out and raised, knowing that he could close the distance and snap the clansman's neck before the others could react. He kept a sharp peripheral eye on those around him, ready to act if any of the rest decided to ambush, and confident enough to reach his sword in time to swipe a few heads.

The Ghar'tul stopped a run's distance from Joden, speaking in thick highland brogue and nearly too fast to comprehend. "Ye're oot an' 'boot, eh?

Fighting not to cringe, Joden stomached the compulsion to lurch forward. Instead, minding his intonation, he answered, "My companion is sick, I'm on my way to collect an ingredient." Joden told the truth. If he had to, he would make the first move. But if these Ghar'tul wanted them both dead, then they would have killed them already. The fact that they were polite enough to send three warning shots was surprise enough.

The apparent leader of the troupe leaned to the side, peering past the Warlord a bit to look Flinn over. He snorted through his nostrils, as though expelling an undesired scent, before focusing his attentions back on Joden. "Si'ner's?"

Joden nodded only once. Muscles tight and ready to spring. None of which went unnoticed by the Ghar'tul. They kept their bows half drawn, hoping for the city dweller to make the wrong move. Others held loosely to their axes, swords, or maces; equally prepared to kill.

The Ghar'tul placed a hand to his chest, over the dark green and brown plaid great kilt her wore, introducing himself, "Larrluc o' th'Pass," he waved an arm all round them and finally settled back to the mountain pass clearly seen in the distance.

"We're not here to invade—" Quieting Joden from saying anything further, Larrluc patted at the air with his hands. "Ye've trey b'yoot, then?"

There was plenty the Ghar'tul would find of value. The Warlord knew if they demanded the weapons in exchange to continue, that it would be an open challenge to fight for them. He had to think quickly and when the idea came to him in that same instance, Joden's smile caused for Larrluc's brow to crease and eyes to squint suspiciously.

"I am Joden Bear-Blade," Joden placed a gentle fist to his chest with a gentle dip of his head.

Larrluc needed no more introduction, Joden's name traveled these lands as well as any. He swallowed away the dryness that had settled in his throat, and then sniffed derisively as though the name did not impress him.

"I'll challenge ye to a match in exchange to pass," Joden went on, delighting in the widening of Larrluc's eyes, "I win, ye give me right of passage and if I lose—well, ye get braggin' rights."

The Ghar'rul were already murmuring among themselves, causing irritated twitches of Larrluc's pointed ears. If he did not accept the challenge, then he would look weak and thus provoke opposition from his kin, thus risk losing status among them. Not only that, it was the chance at besting Joden Bear-Blade and that would elevate Larrluc even further!

Slapping his war-club in contemplation, Larrluc swung it out for one of his scouts take. I fhis action was to elicit a reaction from the Warlord, it did not appear to work as he stood statuesque, watching as the Ghar'tul leader slid out from his mantel to flex filth-ridden muscles and backed away from where Joden and his burden took respite. The other scouts pranced away to form a wide circle around them, creating a ring from which to spectate.

Larrluc beat upon his broad chest, stomping at the earth and stone with cloven hooves, turning in place for his kin as they cheered for him. And Joden simply slipped from his mantel, coming to the circle as well, stretching like a great bear. He gave Flinn a final glance, making sure he was still breathing but the snapping of bone and popping of joints drew his attention back to Larrluc. Any feral transformation was difficult to watch, for it was an unnatural sight, but it was nothing Joden had not seen before. Yet what made this transformation unique was that the Ghar'tul had no need for the moon to do so, in fact, they were the only Feral Folk Joden knew about that could change during the day.

"Ye've not a taste o' Larrluc, Dool'darian!" Larrluc boasted, now with the head of a goat and five times the size he was before. He stepped forward, standing slightly taller than Joden, with one hoof after the others while a great hairy chest heaved with snorting breaths. Another bleating escaped the

Ghar'tul before he stamped the earth and charged, his horns leading the way.

Joden stepped aside, grabbing Larrluc by the horns as he passed, and steering him into a wild spin, and tossed him embarrassingly into a spinning tumble. Larrluc rolled with the momentum, springing back to his hooves in an instant. Roaring frustration, the Ghar'tul came rushing in again, faster this time.

Around them the others of the circle bleated displeasure while others laughed openly in the same manner. Only a madman would find their excitable sounds pleasing to the ear, for they surely grated on Joden's. Instead of waiting for Larrluc, the Warlord rushed the space and speared the goat-man with his broad shoulder, scooping and gathering his legs in a powerful takedown. Larrluc was driven to the ground violently, fighting to scramble out from beneath Joden's weight. But Joden scrambled into a side-control position. One arm coming up under the far-side armpit and making ninety-degree angles with his legs, pressing himself into the Ghar'tul further and forcing him to bear his bulk in weight.

Kicking and scrambling, turning in and hipping out, Larrluc tucked his legs into the tight space generated and shot both hooves into Joden's hip and lower back. Succeeding in managing to launch Joden away before getting back to his hooves. The Warlord rolled backwards, coming up effortlessly into a low three-pointed stance and wearing an exhilarated smile.

Joden circled around and brought his arms in tight to the inside of his body. Palms out and fingers down, tucking his elbows in and ready to grab or defend. Larrluc stamped at the dirt, kicking up earth and rock before circling opposite the Duldarian. An irritated snort escaped the slits of his flaring nostrils, long drooping ears twitching in annoyance, all the while watching Joden smile at him eagerly. Bleating a war-cry, the scout leader yet again charged headfirst, his rectangular-shaped irises held Joden keenly in his sights.

Shooting in to gain hold of Larrluc's leading leg, the

Ghar'tul instead redirected his momentum with the slightest of shifts and pivoted around to come up and down with a heavy headbutt. The thick base of his horns crashed into the Duldarian's temple, sending him slanting down and having to catch himself with one hand. Larrluc was on him in an instant. Bearing down on his opponent with tenacity and driving force as he locked up with the large city dwelling warrior.

Stars flashed and shimmered over Joden's eyes as he stumbled to keep Larrluc from taking him to the ground, his head thrumming from the impact. What would have put a lesser man down, the Warlord was one who quickly oriented himself enough to take Larrluc by the horns and neck with a single arm, keeping his forearm tight against the Feral Folks head, and dropping his weight down suddenly to jerk the beast-man to the ground. Larrluc was forced to post with a free hand, the other grabbing stringing of Joden's singular arm about his head and neck.

But that was the ruse, for Joden quickly switched tactic, using the disruption of balance to shoot underneath Larrluc's outside arm and pass the same side leg. He popped up to his feet, pulling the Ghar'tul in by the waist and wrapping a tight hold about his gut.

Those spectating cheered on, with a few exchanging silver coins between themselves. Their cheers amplified as Joden lifted Larrluc up and over, bending backwards impossibly to slam the Ghar'tul scout leader onto his head. Joden got back up to his hands and toes, scrambling forward to lock to stave Larrluc from reorienting himself. But the poor bastard lay motionless, and those around them who watched had gone dreadfully silent.

"He's dead, then?" asked one curiously while another skipped forward to inspect their leader's vitals.

Joden backed away slowly, rising to his height but kept ever alert. There was no telling what the Ghar'tul might do should their scout leader be dead.

"Nah, he's out cold, he is!" the one doing the inspections laughed, and emphasized that fact by rolling

Larrluc over, producing a not-so-flattering gargling snorting sound.

Never taking his eyes off those in the circle, Joden spoke, "Looks like I win, friends, will ye honor yer word and let the lad and I pass?"

The entangled Ghar'tul growled in response with a curt nods and baring teeth. "Off wit' ye, then, Joden Bear-Blade. We'll haul this one back, I doubt he'll be comin' out with us again after the chieftain has 'is way!"

A final nod from Joden, and the circle parted to let him pass as several of them moved forward to drag their scout leader away, all while making jokes at his expense.

One of the smaller scouts broke away from the group herding themselves back whence they came and clopped lightly to stop a short distance from the Warlord as he saw to Flinn. Seeing clearly that this Ghar'tul was a youth, most likely his first time out in the field with the others. Certainly, an experience he would not soon forget. Joden watched him warily, however.

"It's true ye fought during the days of the Chilling Hand and slew scores o' the Pale Lady's abominations by yerself?" the young Ghar'tul asked excitedly.

"Those days are long gone, I'm afraid, and stories can be embellished some," Joden smiled, offering a teasing wink.

This brought a smile to the Ghar'tul's face, though faded with but a glance towards Flinn. "Lavender avas grows closest to the base of the mountains, but these darker times suddenly make them wilt and die in the cold quickly—ye may not find any worth using." He shrugged apologetically, sad he could not offer more help, then turned to go.

But Joden stopped him, asking, "What's ye name, lad?"

The scout turned about quickly, the smile returning to his face, beaming with admiration. "Mi name's Ghlaaric, Son o' Yami."

"I'll remember yer name, Ghlaaric, Son o' Yami," Joden nodded once and then went back to securing the lines to begin dragging his companion towards the passes.

"Here, Duldarian," Ghlaaric, skipping back to the Warlord, reached into his girdle, and pulled out a red piece of twine.

Recognizing it, Joden gratefully took it and awkwardly tied it around his wrist. It served as a sign of protection, signaling that he was not to be harassed on his journey by the nearby Ghar'tul. There would be no fear from this clan, should they be scouring about, but there were other clans roaming the mountains who did not honor such ways. Here in the wilds of Wulndar nothing was ever guaranteed.

He bowed his head slightly, making note of Ghlaaric's respectful glare and watched him turn to hurry off and catch up with the rest of his trip.

Joden watched them go until they grew small in the distance, disappearing moments later behind some rising elevations to the south and peppering rock formations. He wasted no more time, and quickly hauled Flinn away where they had to retrieve the only thing that may save him before nightfall. Precious time had been wasted dallying with the Ghar'tul, leaving a hurrying Warlord hoping there was still enough of it to save Flinn's life.

Chapter 14
Promise

A natural vibrancy, unlike anything ever seen before, made up most of the forest with tall pines and birch trees sprinkling alongside lone oaks. Elder shrubs, with their wide heads of creamy flowers hanging in clusters of dark red and black berries, grew up from the cushioned bed of pine needles carpeting the forest floor. A tranquil breeze could be heard, sometimes felt, while shafts of sunlight shifted and filtered down from above, dappling the carpet below with camouflaging shadows. Serenity and ease were an unseen, but very much felt drape that fell over the atmosphere to give Flinn the calm he always seemed to seek.

How long he had been traipsing through this seemingly endless forest, however, and with no true knowledge as to how he arrived in the first place. That was not the first time that question had crossed his mind, as he walked barefoot over the thick cushiony bed of pine needles. They felt cool and soft beneath every step, refreshing him, and connecting him to something that made this forest more than what it was. He continued his vivid exploration, following in whatever direction his heart pointed him.

There *was* something waiting for him to discover it, he could not explain why, only that he could feel it. As to who or what that may be Flinn would just have to wait and find out. Feeling more receptive, sensitive even, to his surroundings, the distant flap of wings of a bird settling on a branch caused him to pause in step, taking the moment to search for the creature. Then, the soft bounding hooves of a deer passing far off from sight urged his eyes to try and follow. Smells of sweet flowers carried on through the gentle breeze, could be seen swirling and sparkling through the shimmering shafts of light, casting a magical sense to this peaceful realm.

Whatever this place was, it was exactly the experiences he sought to revel in. Flinn had always yearned to surround himself by nature, reveling in its purity, free of outside complication, and immersing in the simplicities it offered life. How could the Feral Folk be looked upon with such negative nuances, if they were all truly evil then why would they be free to roam such environs? It left Flinn to deeply question all the old stories he read of the ravaging people.

Everything around him tugged at his senses as he continued traipsing through the magical wood, following no path other than what he felt and spotted a line of ants to his right. No common eye should be able to pick that out amid twigs and underbrush, but he did. He kept going, passing through the wilderness at a steady gait, drinking visually of the artistry the forest painted before him.

Soon, the forest suddenly opened into a small clearing. Filled with thin tall grass, and scattered bushes. Flinn stopped short of the forest's edge, sweeping his gaze warily left to right. Specifically searching the shadows of the surrounding tree line, hoping not to spot a pair of watchful amber eyes. Much to his relief, the black wolf they belonged to was not found.

Cautiously, Flinn pressed forward to wade through the grass, slowly turning in place and taking the opportunity to admire the serenity of this place. A pair of birds fluttered a few strides away, spooked by his coming, but even their flight aroused a sense of appreciation from Flinn. Tilting his head back, looking up with eyes shut, the Druid's son bathed in the warmth of the sun. Absorbing its rays and basking in its soothing luxury.

Breathing deeply with a renewing inhale, Flinn opened his eyes and nearly jumped out of his skin. Not but twenty yards from him now grew a large fairy-thorn tree that assuredly had not been there before. The tree was remarkable, by way of natural design. Firmly rooted into the ground, rising strong, forming a thick trunk whose growth could be traced into its lower branches. The subtle twisting and turning at their base could prominently be seen before their limbs shot out, taken along their true paths.

Round red berries held a glow of their own, glistening with early morning dew and sparkling like garnets. The large branches wavered after a caressing breeze and with that a soft tinkling of windchimes. Flinn only then realized he had been holding his breath this entire time, so enraptured with awe, and finally let it go.

And with that exhaling breath there stepped out from behind the tree one of the biggest badgers he had ever seen. The noble beast lumbered out, offering but a glance to Flinn, before rising onto its hindquarters and placed a massive clawed paw to the trunk to steady itself. The giant badger sniffed at the dangling berries within reach. Its tongue reached out, snagging a cluster to snap them free of their anchoring branch, and as the animal consumed their succulence, a growing glow of shimmering golden light appeared around the beast. The aurora intermingled with the tree, highlighting it and causing the garnet color of the berries to have a glow of their own. But their color bled into the golden aura, causing their garnet tone to be absorbed into a decadent light.

The aura only grew bright, so much so that Flinn had to turn and shield his face from the blinding golden-garnet light that now outshone the day. Lasting for only a few blinks of time, and soon the faded died away, leaving Flinn to dare and open his eyes. The fairy-thorn tree remained and badger nowhere to be seen, instead a woman stood in its place. She stood tall, brown-skinned with a main of wild red hair worn long and intricately braided in patterned knots, and a face kind to the eyes. She wore no clothes whatsoever, unashamed of her beautifully curvaceous body accentuated by thickly toned muscles.

The forest floor was alive beneath her feet, bringing a moment of incredulity from Flinn, but as he looked on as vines coiled and reached from beneath her feet, sprouting between her toes, and climbing halfway up her sculpted calves. Brightly colored flowers budded and bloomed and died away only to be replaced and birth anew, creating an accumulating bed of flower petals at her soft feet.

"Come closer, Wulndarian," the woman beckoned, her voice sweeter than mead and more comforting than the warmth of the sun.

Without hesitance, Flinn found himself moving to stand before her, unafraid. Emerald eyes captivatingly over the young man, paired with a smile that would disarm the most fearsome warrior. Tresses of her fiery hair blew with a relaxing breeze, only adding to the overall beauty this woman kept about her.

"Do ye know me, Druid's Son?" she asked softly.

Flinn nodded. The stories of Augustinah were well known, especially that of her favored form of a vibrant red-haired woman. Known as the Green Woman, she who made the forests grow, and changed the seasons, associated with the cycle of life and its harmonic balance. All Wulndarian children learned of her, even those of the Feral Folk. Flinn new her particularly well, learning of her through Hrothnir, as one of the gods that the Druidic Circle often gave praises.

Augustinah smiled warmly, laying a gentle hand against Flinn's face. "Ye've much to accomplish yet, young kit," she said, never taking her green eyes from him, "and though ye may be smaller than yer kith and kin, ye hold great strengths." She slid her hand from Flinn's face, trailing it down to his chest.

"Here, is yer mettle," the Lady of Harmony then tapped the center of Flinn's forehead, "here is yer resolve," then proceed to trace a small line over his navel, "and here is yer instinct.

"Remember that the smallest of us are destined for greatness, Flinn Druid's Son, and even the small can be mighty. Keep upon yer path, for ye shall yet accomplish great things before yer time is done." Augustinah's words lit a fire within Flinn's gut, igniting and burning away self-doubt.

"Great change is happening, my child, and ye're the one to bring it—how ye choose to do so, however, will either cause further disarray, dropping Wulndar to a lowly state, or ye will bring about harmony and peace for all."

"What if I can't, what if I fail?" Flinn spoke for the first time since standing before the divine being. He felt meek before her, wondering if he had spoken out of turn.

Augustinah's features smoothed and instead of a reprimand she offered a smile in response. Placing both hands at the sides of Flinn's face, leaning in, pressing her forehead against his. There came a warmth that washed over him, like a mild summer afternoon. He felt like a budding flower blooming betwixt her palms, waking anew into existence. Then, it was gone, as Augustinah leaned and straightened.

"Promise me to maintain natural order, no matter what excitements sway yer heart." Her never seemed to leave her face. "Can ye promise me that, my child?"

"I…" Flinn started to answer but felt overwhelmed with emotion. Looking on her gave him joy, reminding him of someone he had never met and then he felt shameful for looking on her naked form. This woman deserved the utmost respect, but when he tried to look away, Augustinah took his chin and gently turned his eyes back to meet her leveled gaze. There was nothing angry about her features. Only her offered warmth and love.

"I promise." Flinn breathed.

"Follow your instincts, Druid's Son," Augustinah said, her voice nearly echoed as the aura surrounding her began to brighten.

Flinn found himself shielding his eyes from the glare again, else risk his sight. But no matter how hard he squeezed shut his eyes, the brilliance of that light was too much to bear. Surely, anyone unworthy of Augustinah's presence would burn them away into nothingness. For Flinn it was not so, and even after the brilliance dissipated, she had gone. Her beauty left a scarring imprint that would live on in Flinn's mind. Such an an encounter, whether it be a dream or not, would not be forgotten. Dreams held truths, and dreams could be foretelling of one's fate.

In Augustinah's absence, the tree remained. The trunk split as if struck by lightning and offered a portal of shimmering green light that glowed from within its wound. Approaching the opening warily, Flinn drew near enough to reach out with a hand and touch it. His curiosity had gotten the better of him, which it sometimes did, but here and now it felt like good a place as any to be daring.

The moment Flinn's fingers touched the light an unseen force yanked him into the portal. Swallowing him up like a great river drake of old, he was thrown into a disorienting corridor through space and time. Assailed by a spiraling green kaleidoscope of confusing patterns, Flinn's capacity to make sense of what was happening was overloaded, shorting his reason and grasp of reality. Tumbling and fighting hard for equilibrium, the Druid's son only succeeded in making himself spin faster.

Motion sickness gripped him, his stomach heaving and ready to vomit. Everything was happening so fast, throwing Flinn further and further down the dizzying hall of colors. He could do nothing but accept the climbing irrationality of the experience. Making things worse, his stomach finally decided to empty itself, and instead of half-digested chunks of food, bile, and acid, there puff out a cloud of butterflies.

"God's sake." Flinn's words somehow echoed ahead of him, breaking away into harmless laughter not his own.

Chapter 15
Of Wolves & Goats

It was nearly nightfall; the full moon was already against the dimming sky when Redeyes and his pack approached North Bridge. A wide crossing of hewn stone blocks spanning the expanse over an oceanic river feeding in from the north, and on the westernmost side rose the Spines of Zhul'Tarrgan. Thwark decided to break for camp, giving their dire wolves time to rest and feed.

After the Pack Master unbridled his wolf mount, he went off on his own for some solitude. His pack knew not to follow him, and if he were needed, their call would be enough to stir his action. Thwark need a moment, however, to catch up with what Lunyrr had to show him of the Duldarian's progress. Beneath the bridge, with the river rushing by, Thwark finally brought himself to one knee and bowed his head. While closing his eyes to the sound of the passing water, he sent his mind across leagues of land, following the thread that connected him to Lunyrr.

Images of the Sinner's Tree, the young lad's misfortune, and the exchange between Joden the Ghar'tul scout captain flashed into Thwark's head. Painting vivid pictures with brevity in mind. If he wanted to, Redeyes could have Lunyrr grant him the wider scope of her observations. He required the bare minimum, for she knew the extent of his patience. And just like that, Thwark severed the link and opened his eyes. He stood slowly, creases of reflection forming across his contemplative brow.

Just as he moved to return to his pack, a sudden gust of cold wind blew in from the other side of the bridge.

Desdemona stood in all her deathly beauty, the stench of her rot reaching Thwark's nostrils even from where he stood and blew them out to rid himself of her decayed stink.

Thwark's demeanor immediately turned to one of annoyance. "Breathin' down me neck won't get the job done any faster."

Pouting mockingly, Desdemona tilted her head with a hand to her hip. "Is that why you think I'm here?" she said, and the mocking features of her face changed menacingly. "Where is he?" Desdemona drawled the question, each word dripping with venom.

Thwark was no pup to be cowed. He stepped towards her with eyes tracing the voluptuous form of her body. "A hare naturally runs from danger, in fear of being eaten—but so does it become fatigued, making it easy prey."

Desdemona rolled her eyes, glancing up to the bridge. "Then I assume the *rabbit* has outrun the wolf?"

Thwark blew out his nostrils contemptuously. "No."

"You've failed me, Redeyes," Desdemona began, "and not just failing to fetch my prize, but failing to report of its loss. What am I to do with you, Thwark Redeyes?"

Thwark nearly leapt on her right then, thinking to strike her down before she could utter a spell. Desdemona was indeed powerful, equipped with magics of the darkest kind at her disposal. Especially so with the Dark Tome, but she had to be within its vicinity to absorb its power and Thwark did not see it in her possession. Yet here she was, leagues from her ruined keep, leagues away from her precious book. He could very well tear her apart, piece by piece, calling for his pack in the same moment.

Did Redeyes dare put his swiftness to the test, to dare strike her down and claim Duldar's Keep and lord over its surrounding lands? He could sense that she knew what he was thinking, simply by the smug and daring smile he wore. Surely, Desdemona wanted him to try.

"The one ye seek is poisoned, and if Joden is quick—"

Desdemona flared at the mention of the Warlord's

name. "Joden Bear-Blade is with him!?"

Thwark lifted his chin, looking down his large nose smugly. "Aye, and if he saves the lad in time, ye'll have ye prize well in hand."

"See that I do and see that you kill Joden Bear-Blade in the process," Desdemona snapped back, "I want the other alive and unharmed. Bring him to me, Thwark, this is your last chance."

Desdemona lifted her chin thoughtfully with a soft calculating hum. "Send a small force to collect them while the rest of your pack waits here," she ordered and quickly added, "I'll be giving the order for Baar'Dahl to mobilize and prepare—the moment I have the boy in my care, is the moment we unleash the attack."

The news caused Thwark to step forward angrily. "That is my honor!"

"Well, then the faster you retrieve my prize, the faster you can join your beastly kin in the mayhem," Desdemona responded liltingly. "Now go and see the task done and be sure that this time your *rabbit* doesn't get away from you!"

Redeyes growled low in his throat, deep and rumbling, watching as the Pale Lady stepped out from under the bridge into the dusk of coming night. She was gone in a blink, disappeared, and carried away unseen on the cold wind. His eyes never left where last he saw her, seething that Baar'Dahl would be at Duldar's Port's gates long before he and the pack.

The Pack Master peeled his lips back against his teeth, nipping at the air to give his frustration some substance, eying after Desdemona and wishing he had taken his chance to end her. But the time was too soon, he had to wait and see. If he could convince the youth Duldarian to join him, with the blood that ran through the lad's veins, then the Pale Lady stood not a chance.

"Pack Master?" came an inquiring voice that turned Thwark around.

A high-ranking male peeked halfway around the arching base of the bridge, head tilted at an exaggerated angle and kept his posture low, baring his fangs in supplication. For a moment Thwark was silent, anger still fresh in his eyes and waited for it settle to a low simmer. "Gather a small hunting party and meet me on the other side of the bridge."

Bobbing his head obediently, the male sauntered off to spread the word.

Thwark looked towards the mountains, both angry and eager to spill blood. Once the Duldarians were his, then Desdemona would be next to feel his wrath with Baar'Dahl not far behind. After that was taken care of, with the Duldarian youth at his heel, then all of the highlands would belong to the Pack Master.

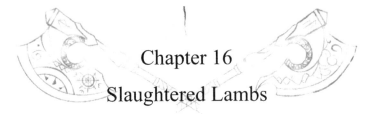

Chapter 16
Slaughtered Lambs

Joden had not seen any wandering Ghar'tul along the mountain pass so far, but he was not about to rule that out solely on that basis. Joden made a show of fidgeting with the red twine whenever possible, hoping that doing so was the reason that kept them from sight. Lumbering up the pass was a challenge, posing to be more of an obstacle course. At some points Flinn had to be dragged, pulled, or carried to traverse the ever-changing landscape. Each change offered its own treacherous outcomes, because with one misplaced step both would go tumbling back down.

And that is not to say the outcome would be any less pleasant. The rocks were sharper, like dark spines of some greenish beast as they sliced up through the earth. The mountain was uneven, making some elevations nearly impossible to scale. As Loose shale proved to be a far more dangerous obstacle than anything else, slipping on them would result in deadly consequences. Joden took his time, even though time was against them, and still there was no sign of the five petaled lavender avas.

The Warlord's eyes desperately swept the terrain for them, trying to remember what the Ghar'tul youth had said about them. Already it had fallen dark, the moon full and somehow pierced through the grey night's sky. Green grass grew nearly all around, breached by the jutting solidity of bare stone, making shelves sometimes that could hide the flora in shade, but nothing grew under them other than brightly capped mushrooms. Joden was becoming worried.

It was cold the higher they climbed, trying to keep to

the lower elevations of the mountain, yet the curling unseen fingers of the wind clawed around and slice against the Duldarians' bare flesh. Joden would need to build a fire soon, camp along the pass, if it could be considered a pass. Then again, the Ghar'tul were nimble of hoof and if this was considered an easy way, then he would hate to find out what proved a challenge to them.

Shivering against the cold air, Joden let the heat of his determination drive him forward. To find the avas and get it to Flinn pushed him, to save the lad's life before he became something *else*. If he could not get Flinn to the lavender avas within the next few moments, then the journey would then be the Warlord's alone to trek.

The pass continued to wind up wide and disappeared around a face of protruding stone. Sight came easy to Joden, never having a problem seeing at night, especially with the full moon's brilliance unchecked. As he now carried Flinn, the Warlord was careful coming around the protrusion, placing his steps carefully and mindful of his weight distribution.

The pass straightened abruptly to round another bend between twin towers of high rock, looking more as if the stone itself suffered a terrible blow from Wulndar's own ax. But the path, despite its treacherous stones jabbing upwards, soon opened to form a large circle where a thin layer of mist spread over a carpet of green moss, fern, and other uncommon flora. Most of all, the bunches of lavender avas grew in clusters all throughout, with some even from the patches of moss crawling up and across the stone walls. The air here had substance, sparkling softly wherever moon light chanced to grace, and kept the chill of the east winds away.

Joden collapsed to his knees with thanks to the powers that be and settled Flinn down gently. He then quickly went about harvesting the lavender avas, plucking them three at a time, yanking them up with urgency. With what he thought was enough, he scanned the area for loose shale to use as mortar and pestle. Finding what he needed in no time at all, the large man dexterously went to work grinding the petals and leaves into a paste.

"Just a wee bit longer, boy-o, I'll not let ye go so easy—yer da would sooner take me head if so!" Joden glanced nervously back to Flinn. He had not stirred since their arrival, and difficult was it to tell if he breathed at all. Hurrying over to him, the Warlord fed the unappetizing paste to Flinn. The young lad lightly groaned at being disturbed, while his face contorted from the wretched taste herbal muck.

It was no easy task force feeding the Druid's son, but Joden managed to get enough of the poultice into his mouth to hopefully bring him back away from death. He just hoped it was not too late. Retrieving his waterskin, Joden poured some of its contents over Flinn's lips and down his gullet. He coughed from that, sputtering up the water, but at least he was alive when he did.

Joden fell back, settling against a large smooth stone that seemed out of place not far from Flinn. He sat there a moment, with making a fire on his mind, but needing the moment's reprieve. All he could do now was wait through the night and hoped Flinn would be rid of the sickness come morning. A few moments more, Joden thought, and he would prepare the fire. He just needed to close his eyes for a few moments and let his body catch up with his mind.

Night came to the hunting party in a cool arctic blue of differentiating shades of shadow and light, allowing the Wolf-kin to see perfectly and with aid of the moon. Seeing just as clearly if it were not. Some had chosen to alter themselves into their hybrid forms, loping alongside their mounts as they followed Redeyes through the winding and nearly hidden eastern mountain passes to the west.

They moved with little sound issuing from their advance, taking their time as they skulked like stretching shadows. Whenever they were downwind, their noses turned up, inhaling deeply through flaring nostrils. It was faint, but the scent was there. Thwark could not mistake it. He quickened his stride, leaping silently over smaller rock formations or scrambling up sheer masses. He traveled by foot, preferring to do so when the pack went out hunting.

Those mounted had to take alternate routes whenever the terrain changed, either circumventing higher or bringing themselves to lower ground. They kept pace, no matter what path they chose. Trusting in their dire wolves not to be impetuous, else they and their rider would take a fall.

Redeyes was just climbing over another elevation when he stopped dead still. Slowly, he waved a hand behind him quietly, signaling for his Wolf-kin to hunker down and be silent. Peaking over the escarpment, Thwark could see the light of a fire. He watched dark silhouetted figures by the flames, some large, others smaller of frame. But Thwark knew them, could smell their stink from his vantage point and felt the rumble of his low growling.

He *hated* Ghar'tul. More so now that Baar'Dahl would reap all the glory when the final assault was launched—but these were Mountain Folk, their clans did not concern themselves with lowland affairs—so long as the lowlanders kept from the Spines of Zhul'Tarrgan. It did not matter, for they would all have to know their place eventually. They were prey and prey were to be hunted and eaten, or in this case, killed for sport. The perfect outlet to release his frustrations while they went off in search of Joden and his nearly dead charge.

Looking back to his hunting party, Redeyes made three decisive gestures. His Wolf-kin dismounted, those already in werewolf form divided themselves to join the others as the group split off into three. Two groups scaled the jagged rocks without making a sound at either side, placing themselves into flanking positions, keeping the large group of Ghar'tul in sight. This was most likely their main post, patrolling leagues of the surrounding mountains in this area and often made small camps. As to what clan they belonged was of little consequence to Thwark, for they were Ghar'tul, and they all died the same.

Wolf-kin hearts quickened as the thrill to commence their onslaught overwhelmed them. Hunkering down now while some flattened themselves against the rock, they eagerly waited for the word to initiate the attack. Thwark watched one of the Ghar'tul, drinking from a horn, suddenly lift his nose to the night. Sniffing at the air as a soft bleating of agitation escape him. Redeyes remained still, observing now as the Ghar'tul spoke quickly between themselves and made it seem they were none-the-wiser. Thwark Redeyes knew better, watching as they eased themselves nearer their weapons, or positioning themselves so that their backs were to the fire.

In that moment Thwark's howl pierced the night, splitting the chill air in twain as the sound of it bounced between the rocks. The Ghar'tul sounded alarm, quickly arming themselves with cruel axes, and broad swords, reaching for spears, while also fidgeting with fitting arrows to their bows. Futile attempts all, scrambling frantically to mobilize as the Wolf-kin descended from the high rocks. They crashed into the Ghar'tul like water with blade, tooth, and claw. Thwark and his warriors were merciless in their attack, exuding an extreme sense of prejudice towards the goat-folk.

Blood curdling bleating added to the snarls, grunts, and growls of battle. Agonizing screams reached high to the moon, some begging for mercy, while others voiced their fears. Such sounds would make a normal man shiver, but to Thwark's ears they brought satisfaction. Reaping the delight of the slaughter as he raised his bearded ax up and down, hewing flesh and bone. Sweeping the weapon like Death's own scythe coming to collect the souls of the vanquished. Filthy Ghar'tul blood splattered his face, staining his great kilt, and satisfied the thirst of his ax as he and the Wolf-kin were now acting as executioners.

He hoped that word of this reached the other clans, even Desdemona herself, for he cared not. All that mattered now was to slay as many of these fools as possible, as the strong copper scent of spilt blood filled the Pack Master's nostrils. It was a scene of cruel, raw, and deliberate violence. A clear message that maintaining honor was of no concern, along with the absence of respect. Thwark wanted that known first and foremost. It would be the first of many acts before he took over all of the Highlands.

Until there was one that stood alone, surrounded by fallen clansmen and hungry Wolf-kin whose amber eyes glittered in the night. The Ghar'tul survivor was but a frightened lamb as the wolves snapped and salivated. Redeyes pushed his way through, snapping at some of his packmates who did not move fast enough, and came to stand before the Ghar'tul with a look of disgust.

Redeyes made note of the pattern of the Ghar'tul's great kilt, and of the dried blood painted at the base of his horns, marking the warrior to be of the Blood Horn Clan. Thwark knew of them well, a fierce clan when in greater number, but even this patrol could have proved a challenge had they been prepared. All the more reason to make this moment memorable.

"I hate Blood Horns," Thwark broke the silence and sliced another strand from the growing tensions.

The Blood Horn snorted through his nostrils, tightening his hold on a pair of twin blades until he held in white-knuckled hands. His eyes swept feverishly to the surrounding Wolf-kin, seemingly tightening their half-circle, and forcing him to back up into a rockwall.

Thwark turned from the Ghar'tul with eyes to the moon, saying, "So much that I won't touch such filth!"

The pack needed no signal from their leader and rushed over one another for the Blood Horn. His bleating screams had but a fraction of that time to be heard before meeting a brutal death. The only sound left was the ripping of bloody flesh along with crunching, snapping bones.

While the pack fed on the corpses of the slain, Thwark had his eyes to the western pass. Somewhere in that direction were the Duldarians, but their road was that much shorter now.

Soon, their paths would meet, Joden would die, and the young Wulndarian in his care would be Thwark's to mold. With but a singular call, the Pack Master rallied his warriors and continue through the mountain pass, leaving behind them a massacre no different than had these Ghar'tul found their way to a butcher's block.

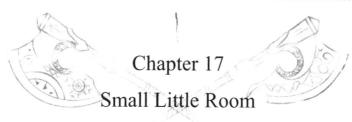

Chapter 17
Small Little Room

Flinn opened his eyes. A high ceiling greeting him
before he sat up to find himself in a small room. A low fire
burned in the hearth, popping periodically, and giving off a
soft light. Looking over to the foot of his bed, he saw a night
sky and a red moon glaring through the window. Sitting up,
swinging his feet over the edge of his soft mattress, Flinn
glanced down and picked at a bleached night shirt he did not
remember ever putting on. His green eyes peered beyond a
singular window, bringing himself to stand before it.

A vast city sprawled out before him. The roofs of
longhouses and lesser buildings stretched on, as the red moon
silhouetted Duldar's Port with its sanguine glow and casting a
more nightmarish ambience of a once otherwise welcoming
city. Had he returned to Duldar's Port, Flinn wondered? If so,
was his father near? After a glance about the room and a quick
search through a set of dresser drawers, a closet, and a trunk at
the foot of the bed, Flinn found nothing to change into. He had
all intents on searching for Hrothnir, or anyone for that matter.
But something felt off.

The Druid's son cast a suspicious glance once more
around the small room.

He made for the closed door leading out and came into
a dark hallway. He followed it until a flight of stairs greeted
him. A warm glow illuminated the bottom floor below, casting
vertical shadows from the supports of the railing, drawing on
Flinn's curiosity. The Druid's son waited a moment longer
before deciding to take the stairs, one by one, with some
trepidation making for a slow descent.

When Flinn stopped at the last step, gazing into a shadowy basement-like chamber illuminated by the fireplace on the other side of the room, there were two chairs sitting before its warmth. Each tall backed and ornately crafted in the traditional Wulndarian style. Flinn cautiously walked wide of them, at first notice of the clawed hand, sun weathered and hairy knuckled, resting on the arm of one of the chairs.

"Come, find warmth by me fire, Druid's Son," a deep voice bellowed in welcome, almost animal-like. It reminded Flinn of the boisterous Firbolgs, but that last tinge of animosity made the hackles of his neck rise.

The sound of it sent a wash of anxiety through Flinn's body, but he found the courage enough to make his way to the hearth and stand before the one who had beckoned. But when he saw to whom the voice belonged, he was at a loss for words and stood stricken stiff in disbelief.

A bearded man sat powerfully in the chair, broad of chest, wide of shoulders, naked from the waist up. But this was not just a man, for there were other features about him that made him otherworldly, supernatural even. Flinn recalled childhood stories describing such a being, of both man and beast, not like the Feral Folk of the wilderness, but with slight similarities.

"Sit," Zhul'Tarrgan offered the empty chair with a large hand, his fingernails like bear's claws.

Flinn did not wish to rouse the Lord of Beast's ire, fearful of what consequences may follow. Zhul'Tarrgan was known to be wild, short tempered and easily agitated but so too was he a protector of the wilds, both zealous and graciously rewarding to those who gave him praises—but there was always an ultimatum. Flinn looked upon the god in awe, crowned with a twin pair of ibex horns sweeping and curling back from his brow, over the top of the chair's back, which amplified his regal disposition.

The Druid's son's eyes were fogged by disbelief as he sat but ever removing ahis eyes from Zhul'Tarrgan's serpentine orbs staring back him hypnotically. The kilts he

wore were of gold, black and silver plaid, and wore no shoes
to hide his bear-clawed toes. The Lord of Beasts sat observant,
calm, and studious.

Flinn cleared his throat, adjusting himself better in the
chair. He did not know what to say, or how to say it even if he
did, but one thing was for sure; Zhul'Tarrgan did not look like
the demon he was painted out to be. A simple man, thick with
a mane of brown hair falling over his shoulders, almost hiding
the pointed tips of his ears that peeked out and rotated slightly
forward. His nose however did give Flinn a sense of unease,
for it was strange in appearance much like that of a wolf's
nose, and though it was small it still felt wrong.

A smile pulled at the corners of Zhul'Tarrgan's
mustache, finding obvious amusement by Flinn's reaction
towards him. "I feel me sister has wakened something in ye,"
the anthropomorphic Beast Lord began, "but that's not me
concern, in fact, had she not done so I surely would have—
ye'll need more than that to deal with Desdemona's
abominations."

Flinn swallowed, sitting back into his chair a bit, and
licked at his lips with unease, unsure how best to respond, but
Zhul'Tarrgan limply raised a hand to halt any such thing.

"There isn't any need, I know all things that happen on
Wulndar—indeed—all of the Sphere. Ye saw the city from yer
window, yes?"

Flinn answered with a delayed nod.

"All of Wulndar will look like that, perhaps long after
yer time and perhaps a bit differently from what architecture
ye're used to seeing," Zhul'Tarrgan tilted his head, his eyes
looking Flinn over a moment to gauge his manner, "there will
be nothing left of the Wilderness as we know it, and though I
don't like Duldar's Port's staining the wilds, it too will be
changed for worse. Desdemona's vision is one of death, or
undeath rather, and would rather see all life on Wulndar
trapped in an eternal winter." Zhul'Tarrgan sniffed dryly and
slumped in his chair, appearing perturbed by that thought.
Even turning his eyes to investigate the flames, resting his

bearded chin atop a mallet-sized fist.

Flinn sat quietly, more so because he had no idea what to say. Visited by one god only to be in the presence of another? It was ludicrous! He swallowed hard, letting his eyes linger over Zhul'Tarrgan a moment longer before tearing them away out of fear of being caught starring.

"'Tis not madness that takes ye, boy-o, ye've been given sight and with that sight comes the attention of many others who would use ye for their own schemes," Zhul'Tarrgan answered that thought without removing his eyes from the hearth. "But I digress," the Beast Lord straightened before growing a tad more serious in his words. "Augustinah has opened the door for ye, and it is for me to offer ye further passage."

The confusion over Flinn's face caused Zhul'Tarrgan to smile further. He turned now, relinquishing his gaze from the fire to settle them over the Druid's son. "Thwart Desdemona's plans any way that ye can, and I shall reward ye tenfold."

What exactly was the Lord of Beasts offering, what did he consider to be a reward for serving him? Flinn did not know, but he was afraid to even ask, content that whatever the god bequeathed him would be something fantastical. Or maybe, something twisted. If that were so, then why was Zhul'Tarrgan so concerned about Desdemona and her plans for Wulndar? So many questions ran through Flinn's mind, and he had not the courage to inquire for an answer from he who sat before him. There was one question, however, that Flinn did have the mettle to ask.

"What of this Dark Tome, what do I do about that?"

"Use it, don't use it, I care little," Zhul'Tarrgan sensed the Druid's son's contradicting mind, "but ye *must* put an end to Dedemona's plans before it's too late, and as for Duldar's Port itself… well, in time the Duldarians and their city living will encroach the rest of Wulndar—they will no longer be satisfied with their piece of it and only become more greedy, thus destroying its natural beauty in their ignorance. Already, they have forgotten the Feral Ways—I charge you with the preservation of the land and to protect it with as much ferocity as ye'll soon discover in yerself."

The Druid's son's gaze was held as Zhul'Tarrgan spoke, making him feel like a child shrinking back in the chair under fatherly advice, coming off too aggressive.

"Make this promise to me, Druid's Son, and I will see that ye remain strong and ferocious against any who offer challenge," Zhul'Tarrgan's eyes glittered as he spoke, leaning forward with eagerness at the edge of his seat, "I know ye desire to run wild beneath the moon, boy-o. To know the boundless laws of nature itself!"

Flinn's heart was beating so fast in his chest it felt like it was about to pop right out. How could any of this be happening? What happened to him that brought him here, where was Joden?

"When the time comes, I will call on ye. Whatever ye desire, in exchange for yer fealty and oath to protect Feral Wulndar—think on this and when I call, remember that you have been chosen for this task by the Gods." Before Flinn could ask any more questions, the Beast Lord and the room itself started to stretch further and further away from him, or was it he who fell back from everything else?

He tried to leap out from the chair, but found that he was stuck fast, and no matter how much he struggled his body would not obey. Instead, he watched Zhul'Tarrgan and the small chamber become smaller and smaller until he could see only a continuously stretching corridor of darkness.

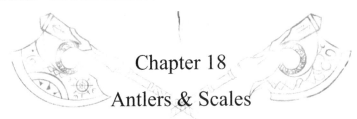

Chapter 18
Antlers & Scales

Coming back to consciousness, Flinn looked up into a night sky from his back. The moon, full and glowing, showered its soft light down into a mountainous clearing. Natural walls of stone towered above him, shadowy and silent. Soft crackling drew Flinn's attention to find Joden sitting on the other side of a low fire. His blue eyes were like a hawk's, watching the Druid's son rouse himself slowly. At his side, sheathed within reach, lay the Warlord's weapon restfully.

"I told ye not to go wandering." Not precisely the greeting Flinn was expecting, but then again, the warrior was right.

Confusion wrinkled Flinn's brow and then made the attempt to prop himself up on an elbow, he immediately eased himself back down. His muscles were too stiff and sore, feeling as though he had been dragged about by a Firbolg.

Joden reached for a small iron pot hanging above the fire, using a ladle to scoop and pour the its contents into a bowl, filling it up with a beefy broth. Afterwards, he moved around over to Flinn and helped lift the lad's head as he brought the bowl to his lips. "This will help get ye strength before morning, until then ye must drink and rest. Otherwise, ye'll be no good to either of us."

"How long was I out for?" Flinn asked.

"Too long. We're far into the wee hours of the night, but with enough time for ye to rest before sunup," Joden helped the Druid's son once more with the broth before setting the bowl nearby. "Drink it all, or ye'll regret it come the morrow."

Flinn watched silently as the Warlord went back to where he had been sitting. His body felt stomped and twisted, but the broth was a welcomed comfort. Fighting to keep his eyes open, Flinn's thoughts returned to the dreams he had experienced. Wondering why he was being bothered by them at all, the irony of it was baffling. He even questioned whether they were worth mentioning or thinking more on at all. Maybe they were just dreams warped by his overactive imagination afterall. It did not much matter, for Flinn's thoughts flitted away as he gave way to sleep. The sound of the fire lulling him into a deep stupor and once more drifted away.

That next sunrise, just before it had chance to peek over into the Spines of Zhul'Tarrgan, came with a dull ache that assailed Flinn's entire body. Doubtful that he would be much use to Joden should trouble find them, the Druid's son *did* feel better albeit weak compared to yesternight. For now, though, he simply lay there watching as the beams of filtering gold pour into the small ravine. Everywhere there were lavender five-petaled flowers, nestled in vibrant greenery. The early morning mist had risen higher, consuming the small open area in a stew, and reminding Flinn of the Moors surrounding Duldar's Port.

Flinn continued to get his bearings, looking around the small clearing Joden had chosen for their camp, he realized that he was alone. Joden nowhere to be seen. And then panic sunk its fangs into Flinn's heart, generating outlandish possibilities that could explain the Warlord's absence, as he simultaneously made attempts to rationalize his overreaction.

Anxiousness taking precedence, Flinn brought himself achingly to his elbows, propping himself up to garner a better look around him. The high mountainous walls were as fencing to protect the garden of lavender flowers that speckled the small clearing. Their traveling packs were both there, which could be a good or a bad sign. Worst yet, everything around him was quiet save for the chill wind that moan and whistled.

Fear pawed at the fringes of Flinn's being, and his hands went to his twin axes which caused his stomach to drop, for they too were absent. Panic flared. The Druid's son wrestled the blankets from his body but was reminded of how pained he still felt, washing over him as he attempted to bring himself to his feet. His head swam for just a few blinks with the movement, coming up too quickly and had to take a moment to steady himself. Slowly, he made to stand with all intents of looking for his weapons.

"Breakfast first, boy-o," Joden's voice came from the side, leaping down from the low escarpment of the ravine. He landed lightly, a pair of hares jostling in either of his hands by their hindlegs.

Flinn wondered if the Warlord had caught them barehandedly or not, for the only tool he carried with him was that giant claymore strapped across his back. And though the young lad tried to hide it, he was nearly ecstatic to see the large bald man. His fears and unease had been dashed away nearly immediately from the initial surprise.

"I have 'em, don't ye worry," Joden pointed to his traveling pack not far off from where Flinn stood. "Both of o' them. Besides, how're ye feeling?" Joden could see it took much of Flinn's willpower to keep himself steady.

Flinn simply lifted his eyebrows in response, blinking his eye wide trying to clear away some blurriness from his vision. Joden chuckled, shook his head, and made his way to the smoldering bed of ashes from their fire. With some set aside kindling, Joden set the hares down and knelt into the mist and sparked some flames with both with flint and steel.

"Either Wulndar has plans for ye yet, or the gods guide ye well, because ye're extremely fortunate to have opened ye eyes at all," Joden spoke casually as he carefully placed some gathered wood over the small conjured flames.

Flinn watched the Warlord at work fanning the fire, giving more life to it as it licked upwards. Once the fire caught, Joden saw to skinning and cleaning the hares. A messy business and one the Druid's son had no desire to do himself. Meanwhile, watching quietly, his mind went back to the two separate dreams he had had, or perhaps they were more like *visitations*. Whatever the case, he found himself periodically trying to make sense of them.

"Ye mind is troubled, I can tell by the crinkle of ye brow, what ails ye?" it took a moment for Flinn to realize Joden was talking to him.

Snapping himself out from his thoughts, the young man answered. "I'm not sure I'm cut out for this sort of life, is all." His own reflections of recent events caused doubt, and Flinn found himself wanting to grip firmly to the bone carved handles of the Twins.

Joden said nothing to that, instead focused on finishing his bloody work.

With the pot hanging above the fire by means of a tripod, Joden put the meat into the water and began adding various spices he had brought along with him. Every once and a while looking at Flinn, studying him thoughtfully. A few moments of silence pervaded as the sun continued to rise in the early morn, causing filters of light to shimmer over the Spines. Soon as the two ate their breakfast, they would have to be on the move again.

Before they left, Flinn had thrice the amount than Joden did, but the Warlord had seen to that purposely. Whenever the young man offered anything left in the kettle, Joden kindly declined, encouraging Flinn to get his fill. It took a short while to prepare their packs and see to it that Flinn was strong enough to walk, but with some effort and a full belly, the Druid's son was able to stand on his own. A bit shakily at first, but once Flinn got his legs moving and his blood flowing, he would be fine. At least, that was what Joden had hoped.

They followed an easterly pass, over nearly impassable terrain as the elevation increased and the air became not only colder but thinner, which made breathing difficult for Flinn.

Often, Joden was forced to slow his pace and sometimes help the lad over difficult impediments. Traveling at such a rate surely affirmed that they would not reach the middle of the Spines of Zhul'Tarrgan until early evening, and quite possibly forced to break for camp (of which the Warlord was not looking forward to). The deeper into the mountain passes they ventured, the more likely they would soon find danger. It was his hope that Flinn would have regained more strength by then, an extra pair of weapons were better odds against trouble making Ghar'tul, or other creatures known to hunt the Spines.

They stopped a moment, Joden seeing that Flinn needed a short moment to catch himself and chose that to be the time to hand the axes back. "Here, lad, I fear ye'll be needing these soon enough—there are worst things in these mountains than Ghar'tul." He procured the axes from his pack and crossed the short space and held them out for the young man to take.

Leaning against a large stony protrusion, Flinn gladly took the weapons and no sooner had he made contact with their bone handles, there came an empowering reuniting charge that traveled through the fingers and into the lengths of his arms to his shoulders. The feeling left behind a tingling sensation that climbed up his neck to warm the lobe of his ears, but his right-handed ax bestowed an image that flashed into his mind, and though it happened in the blink of an eye it felt as though an entire age had been lived.

He felt the powerful, large, and unstoppable presence the beast exuded. The intensity of its eyes as the monstrous animal looked directly at him. That same feeling washed over the right side of his body, transferring itself into his very being and with it the echoing power of a name roaring within the confines of Flinn's mind. Ursarctos, The Great Bear.

"Did ye hear me, lad!" Joden said harshly, bringing Flinn back from wherever his farsightedness led him, "are ye alright?"

Flinn, emboldened, snatched the axes free from the Warlord's offering hand and slid the weapons into their respectable loops at his right hips. "If I were ill, ye'd know." Once his hand left the head of the weapon, even *he* was shocked at the bluntness of his tone.

Joden frowned, unsure how to react to the sudden change in manner.

"I'm sorry, I—" Joden walked away before Flinn could finish.

"Just be ready to use whatever became o' ye when the time calls," Joden said irritably and gathered his traveler's pack.

Flinn pushed from the stone protrusion, feeling strength and confidence in his steps now as he rested either hand over the Twins.

Progress was made, if by a little, as the pair of city dwellers scaled through the inconsistency of rising and falling green mountains. They rose in massive formations, then were dwarfed by even larger highland rock. The sky above was grey as it had been since the ships had left for Es'lyhnn, the warmth of the sun straining to pierce through. It made Flinn think of Augustinah's forest she had taken him to, how the heat of the sun felt against his face. The cold air here had only increased. They happened upon lakes, both small and great, nestled in great depressions, looking like a spill of dark blue. And from them a conjoined river slithering eastward from the Blood Sea.

Yet Joden kept his wits about him. His eyes darting to the faintest tumble of rock, the sudden howl of wind, or the slightest scampering. As the day went on, so too did Flinn's strength, whether from the weapons he now carried or the stewed hare he consumed earlier that morning. Yet his moving was still at a steady gait, not wanting to risk too much should he truly need to call on himself to act.

The river soon fed into a valley below, as the pair of Duldarians stood on a high elevation that offered a clear overlooking view where another lake could be seen distant. Cresting foothills with towering mountains to the left and right stretched in every direction, a sight to behold and one that Flinn would always remember. The river bent around and disappeared behind a wall of crags with no visible way to follow, other than cross and hope that the path was clear on the other side.

The way down proved treacherous, deadly even. For a moment, Flinn feared making the attempt, but after feeling for the Twins at his hips, his confidence of overbearing sense of strong will overcame him, assuaging his uncertainty.

"There's a bridge down there closest to the bend, there's a way down by an unseen pass but river's too deep to cross without being swept by the current—and we need to get on the other side…" Joden had yet to move from their vantage point, however. He seemed hesitant and his stare was intent on something below in the valley.

Flinn moved for a better eye and observed the valley below. He saw the bridge but there was little else he could discern from the greenery and intrusive rocks that would make the Warlord look so concerned. No, wait. Flinn *did* see something.

On the other side of the bridge there was a small encampment of domed huts. How Flinn could have missed it was embarrassing, but that was not the least of it. It was the sudden roar that startled him, causing him to nearly stagger and made the hackles on his neck stand on end. His eyes were drawn to a gargantuan and exceptionally thin antlered beast sequestered and guarded away from the small encampment. Its skull and skeleton tearing through its life-less colored skin. Another roar from the frightening beast escaped it, past a muzzle of sharp fangs.

A test against the chains holding the monster to the rock wall was a reminder to the captive creature that it was not going anywhere. Its wrists and neck sported iron clasps that held the beast at bay. Only two of the goat-men guarded the beast, but even they appeared not wanting of the duty.

"What the Hells is *that*?" Flinn had lowered himself down instinctively, not wanting notice from below.

Joden lowered to a kneeling position, never taking his eyes from the scene. "Abominable."

"Surely."

"No, lad," Joden looked to him, "That thing there *is* Abominable.

Flinn's eyes widened and a new wash of dread washed over him. His eyes turned back to the valley, to the Abominable and the many Ghar'tul camped on the other side of the river. Once again, childhood stories came back to him in a flood of memory. The Abominable was a wretched, fetid undead creature that parents used to frighten their children to their beds. A consumer of living flesh, a destroyer of life. How could fantasy turn to reality, it was only a story used to frighten children!?

There would no avoiding that *thing* or its Ghar'tul captors, not from what the Druid's son could surmise. He flinched after another roar carried its way back up the overlooking foothills that burrowed beneath his skin to make him shiver.

Joden shook his head thoughtfully. Cursing the days under Desdemona's rule of the last era of darkness. It was a sad thing to look upon, a creature that had once been a magnificent beast, glorious to behold—now cursed and haunted by deathly spirit. The Abominable was a stark reminder of things to come should the Pale Lady regain a fraction of power over Wulndar. Nor did he look back fondly on those darkened times.

The Warlord had an idea, as dangerous as it was. Slow and steady was the name of the game here, moving silently and unseen. He looked to Flinn, meeting his calculative gaze in turn.

Before the lad could inquire, Joden instructed, "Follow me, stay low and stay close—*do not* make a sound and be mindful of where ye step. That beast can hear anything and can smell ye blood leagues away…" he took a moment, eyes up as if looking at the air itself, "well, we're not downwind, we can work with that—let's go before it shifts."

Joden turned, making his way back down the foothills overlooking the valley, and picking a path to the river below and through a very narrow pass only a Ghar'tul would dare trek. It was a precarious descent, but they both managed to make it to a lower altitude where the river rushed through the valley, leveling to cut a swath around the mountain's bend. They followed the river upstream, until the mountain rock itself blocked their path, forcing them to have to cross. The Warlord set down his pack, unfastening its buckles, and rummaged around inside until he pulled out a bundle of strong looking corded rope. He immediately looked on their side of the river for an anchor point.

With the rushing current, the wide expanse from one bank to the other, attempting to cross without any securing line would make for a dangerous gamble and result in being swept back violently the way they had come. Being dragged over river rock like wet clothes over a washboard was not an ideal outcome.

Dark jagged crags breached the greenery their side of the river and slid away from the sand and river stones of the bank, reaching up to form the climbing escarpments. There was not much for Joden to secure the rope to, but he walked up and down the length of the riverbank anyway. Meanwhile, Flinn looked about him, studying the environment and taking this moment to appreciate the landscape.

It was never a thought in his mind that he would one day find himself amid the Spines of Zhul'Tarrgan. An echoing call brought Flinn's eyes skyward, recognizing a gliding northern goshawk circling high above. There were several instances where the Druid's son fantasized about flying. It seemed so freeing. But it was Joden's grumbling curses that brought Flinn's attentions back to what was now a dilemma.

He would not bring mind to it, however. It seemed to him that Joden was not enjoying this stall in their journey. The occasional roaring from the Abominable was a constant reminder of the potential dangers that surrounded them. Instead, Flinn gazed out across the river. Watching from where he stood as the cool water went rushing by. Nervousness was beginning to set in, with thoughts of the undead antlered beast and the Ghar'tul up the river and what they would have to do to sneak by them.

Flinn had one nightmarish scare too many since leaving Duldar's Port. There was no need for any others. He hoped that Joden had a plan to sneak them past the encampment. If not, there was a high probability that their journey would take another dismal turn.

Frustrated, Joden came to stand next to the Druid's son, the rope held loosely in one hand in defeat. Flinn glanced over at him as the Warlord moved as close to the river's edge as he dared, kneeling to cup his hand into the rushing water to take a drink and wash his face. But then went completely still, his eyes transfixed on the appearance of fin-shaped rock rising from the water, creating a backboard of resistance against the current.

Flinn was quiet, watching the Warlord's strange behavior, until he followed the man's gaze.

But there was something else other than that strange rock formation that held Flinn's eye. A strange scaly shape rose subtly, long, large, and sleek. More fins created three rows length-wise that diminished in size the further back they ran from the arrow-shaped head of the creature now glaring at them from beneath a brow of plated scales, just peeking up from the rushing river's surface.

Flinn did not need to exclaim what he saw, for Joden very well had the creature in sight.

"Get back, boy-o, slowly," the Warlord said carefully as he himself started to inch his way from the river's edge carefully. His hand reached for the hilt of his blade, but doing must have triggered what happened next.

An explosion of water issued forth after a burst of forward momentum came from the river towards Joden. Amid the chaos of the splashing, Flinn was able to make out the frightening shape of the beast.

"Run, lad!" Joden shouted, pivoting as he turned and sprinted back, "run, damn ye, run!"

Flinn managed a moment to glimpse the thirty-foot

long River Drake as it roared after Joden, its long body moved easily through the water, with a finned tail propelling it, webbed clawed feet aiding its propulsion without any hindrance. The sheer bulk of the monster could not be impeded by the rush of water and once it reached the shallows, its movements became no less graceful in its slithering and fluid gait as it moved swiftly across to the river's edge ashore.

The Druid's son focused on pumping his legs into a sprint, screaming at such torture, but the sense of flight was too strong in him to take heed of the painful tearing he felt in his muscles and joints. His body had not yet fully recovered, and it showed when Joden rushed past him, giving his arm an encouraging tug as he ran by and began to pick and climb his way back up the narrow pass leading into the higher elevation of the mountains.

They had managed to gain some lead, but Flinn's vitality waned, realizing then that he was falling behind the Warlord. Fear of being caught by the dragon-like creature sped him onward, heedless of the pain racking his body, however. And when he reached the pass, Joden had to stop and pull him along. Behind them the dark scaled Drake snapped its jaws for the heels of Flinn's boots, barely snapping down on them. The creature was already scrabbling up the rocks, but the terrain proved difficult for the beast, forcing it to take some caution in the chase.

Flinn half climbed and was half pulled up by Joden as they scaled higher, putting more of the unforgiving terrain of the climb between they and the Drake. Flinn's legs kicked feebly, his boots slipping and scrambling, barely finding purchase, but despite whatever obstacles the mountain pass offered it did nothing to assuage the fear gripping him. For not far behind, the sounds of the scrabbling River Drake made his spine tingle and his back tighten anxiously.

Joden, meanwhile, hauled Flinn along as he used his power and sheer strength to bring them both higher and higher until they would come to a relatively leveled plane. At least then, he hoped, he could somehow make a stand against the beast and give the Druid's son some time to pick his way back down into the valley. Well, that was his idea in the moment, and that is not to say it was even a good one. But in the interim of their plight, it was all they had.

He glanced back to see how far they had climbed, and his gut dropped to find that the River Drake was keeping up, if not for a few strides behind. Joden growled frustratingly, tugging on Flinn, gripping his wrist tighter, and redoubling his efforts to get as much distance between them and the River Drake as possible. They just needed to get from the narrow pass to the top of the escarpment and then find a way back down into the valley, the Ghar'tul and their Abominable be damned.

Another idea suddenly came to him and the Warlord prayed it would be enough. The saying "*out of the pot and into the fire*" came to mind, but the hope was that the pot came crashing down into the flames and left two little morsels alone to roll away from the tumult…

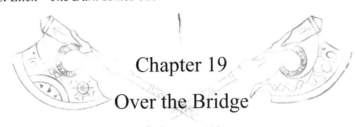

Chapter 19
Over the Bridge

The snap of jaws came too close to his heels as Flinn involuntarily screamed, now frighteningly aware of how close the damned River Drake was. He peered over his left shoulder while being hauled up the last few feet of the escarpment, he and Joden finally reaching higher ground. Flinn's left hand brushed against Wulfaxe and immediately brought the weapon to bear without realizing his right hand had already gone for Ursarctos. Now, armed with the Twins, Flinn managed to get his feet under him with no mind to Joden who frantically moved to where the escarpment fell off overlooking the valley.

The dark green scaled River Drake scrabbled and clawed furiously up the mountain, sending loose debris tumbling back down under its weight. A few times it had lost its footing, but found secure purchase just as quickly, regaining the ascent and yellow serpentine eyes locked on its prey.

"Here, lad!" Joden beckoned, waving the Druid's son over to him. But when seeing how Flinn waited at the edge of the cliff, looking down and seemingly *waiting* for the beast, the Warlord's eyes widened in panic. "Flinn!" He bellowed commandingly, jolting the lad out of whatever foolishness cropped up into the lad's head.

Eye fluttering as though waking from a dream, loosening his grips on the bone handles of the Twins, Flinn shook away whatever stubbornness overcame him. Turning quickly, he rushed to Joden and then followed him up to take the mountain ridge along the river. As they picked their way as quickly and as carefully as they could, a single glimpse over the edge foretold a deadly fall. Flinn wondered if hitting the water at this altitude would be the same as landing on solid ground before being swept by the water itself.

The climb proved more dangerous with each moment, climbing higher and higher, making the drop over the edge that much more unnerving. The terrain did nothing to dissuade the Drake, however, and after daring a glance behind them, Flinn saw that the beast stalked them at a steady pace. It too mindful of the dangers of following this path, but not longer needing to rush after its prey.

But then the mountain became too high to climb safely, offering no feasible way to ascend any further. Caught between jagged rocks and a hungry Drake. The beast slowed its approach now, its stance wide to displace its weight evenly among the rocks. It knew the chase had finally came to its end and a hearty meal was imminent.

"Are ye afraid of heights, boy-o?" Joden asked, never taking his eyes from the approaching monster.

Twins in hand, Flinn bit at his lower lip after risking another glance over the edge to the river below. Even the Ghar'tul encampment looked small from this height. But he knew what the Warlord had in mind. It was either fight on the precarious mountain and perhaps risk being mauled to death or taking a literal leap of faith with hopes that there were no hidden rocks beneath the churning waters.

"On my count, Druid's Son," Joden said lowly, waiting for the Drake to near enough.

Flinn slipped the Twins home in his girdle loops but found even doing that was somewhat a challenge, for they felt resistant to his wishes.

"One…" Joden started the count.

The River Drake snapped its jaws, slavering at the maw and tilted its head inquisitively. Each step it took brought it ever closer to its prey.

"… Two…"

Flinn swallowed the dryness away collecting at the back of his throat, also maintaining complete rigidity in his posture. He did not want to do anything that would provoke the beast too early. Most likely, savoring its triumph.

"THREE!" Joden shouted so loudly that it caused the Drake a moment of pause before scurrying to catch the Duldarians before they had both gone over.

Flinn pivoted to his right, scurried the last few strides it took that would send him over the edge and sprang forward in a kicking of legs and a windmill of arms. The Drake had thrown itself into a leap, its long toothy jaws open wide and webbed clawed feet outstretched. But it was a blink too late and had to force its momentum awkwardly to follow the Duldarians.

Flinn and joden both plummeted hundreds of feet over the mountain, the rushing river came up faster than they could think. The Druid's son prayed and hoped the water below would be deep enough. They plunged feet first into the chilling, churning, rapid depths. First Flinn, followed half a blink after by Joden.

The water stole Flinn's breath away, barely having time before to catch it before hitting the river's surface, but as he was being thrown, rolled, and tossed violently beneath the current, he managed to breach the churning rapids. It was a fight to keep himself from going under again, after a few struggling moments, he managed to keep his head above the water and allow the current to take him.

Joden sprang up moments later further behind, his powerful arms pumping to make it to shore while the hilt of his claymore hit him in the back of his head with every stroke. While doing so, he searched frantically for the Druid's son, finally spotting him upriver, quickly being carried away.

Flinn was not a large man, with no true weight to him which worked against him when trying to swim for the shoreline himself. And though he made some progress, he was being taken further and further down river and would eventually go too far for Joden to be of any help.

Using his weight and bulk, coupled with determination and strength, Joden redirected his efforts and swam along with the current, helping him speed his progress to reach Flinn. His legs and feet kicked furiously, his arms and hands working in unison to propel the Warlord speedily along.

"Swim to me!" Joden shouted, directing his words to Flinn, but doubtful of being heard over the rapids and redoubled his efforts.

He could see Flinn fighting against the current, no more than a bobbing head and flailing arms. The lad was being taken away faster than Joden could reach, making poor progress. He kept on, however, using all his strength and conditioning to reach the Druid's son. He would be damned if he let the lad slip away so easily. With his resolute determination, Flinn's form appeared to be getting closer, and closer still. The shortening distance only drove Joden to swim harder.

But there was something else, a large splash not far behind Flinn that did not go unnoticed by Joden as he saw the River Drake rise to break the current and speedily snake its way for the much smaller morsel. Its sharp spines running down the length of its back were as sails cutting through wind, making its propulsion that much easier.

The Druid's son was nearly within reach, and Joden aligned himself so that his own trajectory would ensure that he could catch him in one grab, but at that same moment the River Drake submerged into the rushing depths. Joden swam harder than ever now, trying to keep the water from his eyes and working as best as he could with the claymore strapped to his back.

Flinn fought to swim as best he could, catching glimpse of Joden but unaware of the danger that lurked behind him. Fatigue overcame him, however, no longer possessing the strength to fight against the river. And just as he was about to give up and allow the waters to take him, Joden smacked into him. The Warlord kept a firm hold around the lad, using his legs and arm to steer them towards shore on a sharp diagonal and ever watchful for the River Drake.

With Joden's strength and sheer willful determination,

sped along by the rushing waters, the Duldarians managed to get to shallower waters at last. A hard-fought battle to be sure, but one that brought them both out alive. Joden dragged Flinn until they were well ashore, sodden, and cold. With his claymore already in his hands as he turned towards the water. Flinn scrambled to his feet, checking to make sure the Twins had not somehow slipped free from his girdle loops; with much relief, they had not.

The danger was not over yet, as the River Drake suddenly appeared rising out from the river and turned his m towards the shoreline. Joden stepped in front of Flinn, facing down the encroaching River Drake. "Get ye gone, boy-o!"

The beast slowed its approach, yellow elliptical eyes darting between Joden and the Druid's son who now took off running up the riverbank. Joden stepped into its line of sight, his lips pulled back to bare his teeth.

Glancing over his shoulder as he ran, expecting to see Joden overcome, his attentions were brought back in front of him by a blood curdling bleating. A group of Ghar'tul came rushing from their encampment several yards away towards the riverbank. Without a thought, Flinn slipped the Twins free as they twirled themselves in his hands, his fingers and wrists moving complimentary to their desires. Confidence seized the Druid's son, eying the incoming Ghar'tul, coupled with a rapacious want to defy them.

Flinn dared once last glance over his shoulder, in time to witness the River Drake rushing Joden further down the shoreline. Circling him while the Warlord swung mightily with his sword, missing the creature as it darted to one side. It shot back in; head rotated to snap its jaws for Joden's legs. He managed to step aside, swinging up and over with his claymore, but once again the beast proved faster and avoided a chopping end.

Flinn hauled his small frame to close the distance quickly between he and the Ghar'tul. Ordinarily, he would have bene running the opposite direction, but with the Twins in his hands he felt confident in their ability to see him through. Or die trying, but even that grim thought had no influence in the Druid's son's course of action.

The Ghar'tul spread themselves out, creating space as they advanced with but a few more strides left to cover before they crossed blades with the shorter Wulndarian. Until a bone chilling roar echoed from their encampment, carried down to the river's bank, and eliciting a brief pause in their advance to exchange worried glances between them.

It had been chained to the rock for longer than it could remember. But any concept of time was trivial, irrelevant even, for it was the constant suffering of living that caused the creature to detest its servitude. A foul, twisted thing with no memory of what it had once been with only the knowledge of pain and agony and the heavy chains that kept it bound. The Abominable was not meant to be held for safekeeping, it was a tool for destruction and a deliverer of death. Once more, the abomination fought against its restraints, letting loose a low eerie rumble that clambered from the depths of its inner self to release a chilling roar.

But now, with a familiar scent in the air, the Abominable had gone berserk. Thrashing at its restraints wildly, pulling on them to cause the manacles clasped about its wrists, ankles, and neck to bite into rotted flesh, resulting in a dark oozing of blood that seeped from the wounds and stunk of decomposition. A sweet and sour stench of fear wafted from the two pathetic forms guarding the Abominable, sending it into even more of a frenzy. The plates bolted into the living rock had loosened over the aging of time, rusted, and stripped, clanking against both stone and iron.

Another powerful thrashing of the chains occurred as they Abominable threw itself forward to reach the Ghar'tul guards. They backed away nervously, exchanging concerned glances and continued to create space. They knew this time the chains would not hold, but that was only a matter of time before this day. Again, and again did the unnatural creature work at its holds, loosening the plates and pulling the bolts a little bit further out from the stone. Bit by bit. The scent, however faint, called to the creature, called it to freedom, and with that freedom there would be slaughter and an age long task would continue anew. The blood of a champion begged to be spilled, and in Desdemona's name would the Abominable see that task done.

The group of Ghar'tul, momentarily disturbed by the roar of the Abominable, resumed their approach of the Duldarian, three of which moved synchronously shoulder-to-shoulder, bearing round wooden shields held by iron bands. Their spears rested on the upper rounded edges, ready to be thrust with deadly efficiency. Skipping its grotesque bulk behind them, a hybrid followed wielding a wicked looking bearded ax. While bringing up the rear, a crossbowman fought to keep up with the pace of his fellows as they closed in on the scrawny Wulndarian youth.

One of which drew the attentions of its fellows to look further down the shoreline, bringing attention to the intense exchange between the River Drake and the larger man who fought it. A command was given, and one of the crossbowmen splintered off from the rest, rushing back towards their encampment. No doubt to inform the others and gather more forces, of which would not be ideal in Flinn's case.

He swallowed, a small part of him doubting a victorious outcome if more of the Ghar'tul returned. That meant he had little time to dispatch these warriors, outnumbered six to one, and with that came self-doubt. Flinn was no warrior. Never had been. His hands tightened around Wulfaxe and Ursarctos, the images of the wolf and bear flashing vividly into his mind's eye.

No, Flinn corrected himself, he *was* a warrior, the Twins assured him of that. As the Ghar'tul continued their slow advance, now forming a crescent around him, the Druid's son narrowed his gaze as a menacing smirk painted his lips. His axes lifted his arms slightly, spreading them out wide from his hips, telling him to keep a soft bend in his knees and stay light on his toes. None of which was new to the Druid's son, his small size and light weight was built for this sort of play.

It was all him now. Flinn would not be able to rely on Joden, who was engaged with the River Drake, and wondered how he fared. There would be no time to glance over his shoulder a third time, but Flinn sorely wished the Warlord had dispatched of the thing already and came to stand beside him. Caught between the Ghar'tul and the serpentine creature seemed unreal, but the adrenaline pumping through Flinn's veins could very much so.

He realized then that the edges of his vision clouded, obscuring his peripherals so that only the Ghar'tul were his concern. This was something Flinn had yet to experience while holding the Twins, but it did nothing to lessen the eagerness he felt. Or was it the eagerness bestowed on him by the obvious enchantments inherent in the weapons? Something to ponder for later perhaps, for now all the Druid's son seemed to care about was the ensuing battle to come. The Twins tugged at him when the first of the Ghar'tul warriors came rushing in, hungry to initiate the first swings and draw first blood.

Wulfax swung up and down, hooking the top edge of the shield-bearer who stepped first to dance with him, yanking it forward to throw the Ghar'tul off balance with staggering forward steps. Ursarctos came up on a short but sharp crossing angle, deflecting a spear thrust that would have skewered Flinn's throat as another Ghar'tul followed, seeking to bombard Flinn. Ursarctos swung back nastily, too fast for the spear wielding Ghar'tul to react, and clipped the warrior at the side of his face. He bleated out its pain, shocked by how quickly the attack occurred, and stumbled sideways into another warrior at his left.

A second spear thrust came in at the left side of Flinn's face, but Wulfax proved quick to deflect it. The Ghar'tul were all around him now, the axes direction his actions and turning the young man's body so that his movements were complimentary to their guidance. They weaved themselves in a fierce display, hacking, slashing, and chopping relentlessly.

One of the Ghar'tul, in its imposing hybrid form, waded through its fellows, bringing its wicked ax overhead to come down with a powerful descending chop. The Twins spun Flinn around, bringing him low to thrust his arms up in the same instance, driving into the haft of Ghar'tul's bearded ax. Flinn stepped aside to the warrior's left, throwing its weapon forcefully to its right. The Twins swung around and down to burry their bits into the nape of the Ghar'tul's neck.

A spray of dark essence showered in a fanlike spray, painting Flinn's face in a mask of blood. With the largest of the Ghar'tul put down, dead and dying as its hooves kicked and scraped against the riverbank, the others spread themselves out wide from the unnatural dance of Flinn's wild movements. Incredulity plain on their faces at the unexpected outcome, where there was once confidence in the small troupe, there now was caution. It had all happened in the blink of an eye for them, but for Flinn it was as if time itself had slowed.

The sound of a crossbow clicked, sending a whistling shot towards Flinn, but the Twins were ready. Ursarctos tugged slightly to the right, guiding Flinn to step subtly from the line of fire, just as Wulfaxe shot up and hit the missile to send it spinning off course. Flinn agreed with the feeling his weapons shared with him, that the crossbowman needed to be taken out as quickly as possible. But the Ghar'tul still outnumbered him and with the shot they came rushing in once more. Flinn was led backwards, circling out wide to the right closer towards the river's edge, keeping the goat-men in his sights.

Snorting their frustrations, one of the warriors taunted, "Ye'll not outmaneuver us, city dweller!"

Three more clicks from crossbows sounded off, but Flinn was pulled so fast by the Twins that he placed the warriors in line of their comrades' fire unwittingly. Two dropped to their deaths, receiving mortal blows from the bolts, meanwhile Flinn successfully deflected the last that snuck between their ranks. As the Ghar'tul worked quickly to reload their crossbows, another hybrid rushed in spear first. What should have been a panic-riddling moment for Flinn, was instead one of exhilaration.

An easy parry of the spear thrust by Wulfax swung the length of the weapon wide, turning the warrior with it, and exposing the Ghar'tul's mid-section. Ursarctos pulled Flinn left of the warrior, coming back in mightily to swing through flesh, bone, and disrespectfully destroy the soft insides of the Ghar'tul. Another warrior added and sent to the land of the dead.

The Ghar'tul ranks had thinned, playing out in Flinn's favor. But there were still three with crossbows and one shield bearer armed with a nasty looking flail, dragging a heavy flanged head at the end of a seven-linked chain. He wished Joden was beside him sharing in the excitement of the exchange. He dared a glance down the riverbank, noting Joden's heavy swings that kept the beast at a distance. The Drake bled freely from gash found in its hindquarter, which caused for the River Drake to be less eager in throwing itself at the Warlord.

Joden was not without injury himself. Bearing claw marks across his chest and back, coating his torso in bright blood. He seemed unperturbed by them, however, for he never relinquished his focus long enough to pay them any heed.

Until now, the Druid's son never thought he would enjoy such deadly back and forth, but the Twins instilled in him a newfound love for battle. That would all change, however, after returning his attentions back to the threat at hand and noticing another contingent of Ghar'tul underway from the encampment. They had some distance yet to cross before they came to join their fellows, and though the Twins

allowed Flinn the ability to slay his enemies as if he had
trained all his life using them, they did nothing to stave off the
fatigue he felt.

Lifting its flail with a powerful arm, sending its weight
up and swinging back down, the Ghar'tul followed the weight
of its pull down with all intents of bashing the Druid son's
skull in. Flinn stepped aside, yanked back by Ursarctos, to
watch the head of the flail thud heavily into the sand where he
had been blinks ago, sending sand and river stones in a nova
from the impact. In the same moment, Wulfax went with the
turn, using the momentum of Ursarctos to lash out and up on a
wicked angle. Its bit would have buried into the Ghar'tul's
shoulder, if not for its shield taking the brunt of the attack with
a resounding crack. Shouldering behind the shield, the
Ghar'tul rammed in behind it and forced Flinn backwards in a
frantic backpedaling stagger.

Flinn lost his footing with a last second bashing from
the shield, sitting him down and sending him skipping back on
his posterior like a stone over water. He fell backwards from
the momentum, landing hard on his back and nearly smacking
his head. The Ghar'tul, bleating triumphantly, quickly
followed up with a spin that brought the length of chain of his
flail swinging up and down, bringing the weight of its head for
the final blow that would end the Druid son's life.

Wulfax threw Flinn's arm over his right side into a fast
roll, missing weapon's impact by mere inches. He scrambled
to his feet, the clicking of crossbows urging him faster in
getting up. Two bolts landed where he had been, the third
skimming across his calf and opening a gash. It was not a
mortal wound, but it was enough to put the fear of the gods in
him.

Further down the riverbank, Joden delivered three
more powerful swings of his blade, forcing the River Drake
backwards. It snapped and hissed, its frills fanned out and
shivering, expressing its desire to down the warrior but not so
impetuous to risk being hewn by the powerful blade he
wielded. War drums sounded in the distance, their sounding

and the distant roar of the Abominable spurring Joden to turn and run upriver. The River Drake gave chase once more, hot on its quarry's heels, nearly nipping at Joden's heels.

Joden bore witness to a pit-falling feeling when he saw Flinn struggling to evade the heavy swings of the Ghar'tul, narrowly being missed several times from a fateful end. Yet, to much his own surprise, many of Ghar'tul lay day around the Druid's son already and by the way he moved, pulled by his own arms into awkward positions, turns, and evasive maneuverings, Joden was left impressed. There was only one other instance he saw someone move like that, but that had been nearly over a century ago.

The River Drake could be felt getting closer to Joden as he sprinted in a hurry to get to Flinn's side. He turned mid-run, however, never losing speed, or impeding his own progress, as his sword swung around with him with a single strike. His claymore whooshed horizontally, aiming for the River Drake's serpentine head. The beast lowered itself bodily, squinting its eyes, as it just-barely ducked underneath of the swing.

River Drakes, or Drakes of any kind, were not mindless creatures. Yet the sudden attack did slow the creature's advance, and Joden a little extra time to gain some ground. His heart sank once more on noticing a larger contingent of goat-folk closing in on Flinn's skirmish and that was when Joden recalled his maddening idea. He would lead the River Drake right into their midst.

Flinn kept the hybrid busy with his movements, turning him so that the crossbowmen did not have an easy shot and risked harming their fellow. One happened to glance in Joden's direction and then quickly shouted to the others. The four remaining skirmishers backed off, forgetting about Flinn altogether. It was not Joden they feared, but the damnable creature that came in after him.

The crossbowmen redirected their aim, backpedaling towards their reinforcements, calling for their flail-wielding comrade to pull back. But he was as stubborn as their kind came and refused to let against Flinn. Coming up fast, Joden shouted for Flinn's attention as he came near, telling him to make a run for it now or never. Not far behind, was the River Drake.

Relieved by Joden's presence, even for but a moment, Flinn's eyes went immediately wide and took off past the flail-wielder. The crossbowmen's focus was now on the River Drake, still shouting out in warning. But for their comrade, lost in the confusion of Flinn's sudden cowardice and again by Joden racing by, did not see the impending danger.

The River Drake came upon the Ghar'tul warrior in an instant, caught within its path and taking the poor soul up in its jaws and thrash him violently to and fro. The warriors's blood sprayed as his torso began to separate from his lower half, bleating agony at such an unfair end to his life. His comrades released their missiles, all three thudding into the River Drake's side, with all but one bouncing off its hardened scales. The Ghar'tul reinforcements slowed their advance, torn between giving chase after the Duldarians and aiding their comrades engaged now with the River Drake. But their predicament only became more perilous with another echoing roar from the Abominable in their custody.

With the River Drake distracted with the Ghar'tul, Joden finally caught up alongside Flinn at last, falling in step with the young man while bleating screams of anguish and panic sounded from behind them. The riverbank started to rise, taking them uphill and closer to where a waterfall crashed loudly into the river. But there was a clear beaten path that eventually disappeared into the mountains veering off to the left.

Joden bellowed encouragingly to keep going, with glances over his hulk-like shoulders. Flinn pushed himself to run faster, forcing himself through fatigue and aching muscles with his ally back at his side once more. The pair sped ahead, leaving behind them the tumult of what had been at first a hopeless situation.

That was when a chilling roar was heard, calling for

attention. Flinn dared a glance behind them, witnessing both the struggle between the River Drake and the Ghar'tul now enveloped in taking it down, but most of all at the lumbering, fast moving Abominable that made its way down from its place of confinement from deeper within the encampment.

"Joden!" Flinn shouted, drawing the Warlord's attention back whence they came.

The Warlord shouted back, "Gods' sake, boy-o, quit gawking and keep running!"

Chapter 20
Navigating the Spines

The roar of the Abominable split the air, dulling the battle cries of the Ghar'tul and the ferocious calls from the River Drake that tore into them with fang and claw. Flinn and Joden kept at a steady run, but the Druid's son's legs were screaming for him to stop. Yet, with the Abominable throwing itself through the Ghar'tul ranks, there was even more urgency to be gone and get the hells out of the valley.

Joden veered into Flinn, scooping him up with a massive arm and slung the Druid's son over his huge shoulder. "I'm getting tired of carrying ye arse, boy-o!"

They left behind the screams, the roars, and the animalistic sounds of battle echoing from the valley, but Flinn had a feeling that their escape would be short lived.

"I don't think I like being carried off like a child either!" Flinn shouted into the Warlord's ear.

All that was offered in response was a growling grunt as they continued to run as quickly as Joden could. Following the long bend of the pass into the mountains, and after Joden had been convinced they had put as much ground between themselves and the Ghart'ul, he finally slowed.

"Do ye think they'll come looking for us?" Flinn had to ask, finally being set down to stand on his own. Only a throaty grumble issued from Joden, leading them higher and deeper into the Spines.

The Druid's son was sure that these mountains had eyes, sending forth its horrors from whatever rivers or caves they came from, watching one failed attempt to stop the Duldarians after the next. So far, Flinn had survived but that was mainly due to Joden's company and the strange hand axes his father had gifted him. Both of which he was thankful for.

After a while, Joden brought slowed their trek, giving them a moment's reprieve. They had lost their gear long ago since jumping into the river, save for the great kilts they wore and their weapons. Flinn wondered now how they would survive without food or water, but he figured Joden would remedy that problem as he seemed to do with everything else.

Then, the pair continued to pick their way up and lost themselves deeper into the shadows of the mountains. The river, although unable to be seen here, could be heard off in the distance to the east and that seemed to be what Joden was using to help navigate their way through. If they followed the river, then perhaps they would soon find their way out, or at least that was what Flinn thought.

As he followed, Flinn's mind returned to his dreams. Wondering what waited for him at the end of all this. He thought about his father, the people back at Duldar's Port, and the mess they had just left behind them. After all he had experienced thus far, a miracle that he was even still alive, would he be successful in the end of it all? Flinn hoped to return home, Dark Tome in hand, and stave off any dark doom that was creeping over Wulndar. Yet, there was the possibility of failure. What then would happen to the people of Duldar's Port, what would happen to *him*?

linn shook his head, for there were no answers readily available. He could very well speak of this with Joden, but there was a chance that the Warlord would not have the answers either. So, here Flinn was, deep within the Spines of Zhul'Tarrgan, headed to a place only told of in stories. And it did not stop here, oh no, for there was Desdemona to deal with and the Wolf-kin and whatever else that waited.

Flinn's hands went to the heads of his axes, snug within their designated belt loops, and feeling that renewed sense of courage and confidence, of power, the fierceness and steadfastness whenever he touched them. A warmth swirled about his gut, flowering upward to bloom throughout his chest until his arms, legs, fingers, and toes all felt that familiar tingling sensation whenever his hands contacted the weapons. He *was* chosen, for to wield such instruments and survive this far, one had to be. But to be chosen meant to be a champion of one of the many gods of this island. The question, however, was to which did Flinn owe allegiance, for he had been given two choices.

"Liven up, lad!" Joden called back, "ye'll wind up misplacing a step and roll an ankle—I don't' look forward to hauling yer arse over my shoulder again, I'll need a damned back readjustment at this rate."

Flinn blinked out from his thoughts, more aware of his surroundings. Each step would be a vital one, for the terrain was ever turning unkind and dangerous.

The Duldarians continued to pick their way through, keeping the river's rushing sound to the east as they continued north. So far, they had not run into any other Ghar'tul or hungry beasts. Both of which Flinn was grateful for. He was hoping, however, they would stop soon for a quick respite. They had been going at it for hours and the day grew long, beginning to wane. Joden seemed adamant on covering as much ground as they could before dusk, and always was he looking back to check on Flinn's progress, making sure the Druid's son was keeping up, and to see if they were being pursued.

There was another reason, however, one that both Joden and Flinn knew without verbalizing. The Abominable. Whatever happened back at the Ghar'tul encampment was sure to have ended in horror. Flinn could not imagine anything that could stop such a creature. The stories he heard of the beast did nothing compared to having seen it for himself. Flinn knew he would have nightmares about the thing in nights to come. He prayed that they had gone undetected by it, for there was no telling how well Joden, or himself, would manage against such a creature.

The pass became more harrowing, jutting out from the western natural wall of the mountain and forcing the

Duldarians to trek singly. To the east, the mountains fell into the cutting river at a sheer drop. There would be no jumping over into the waters this time, for only a sure death awaited. The pair would have to watch their steps, looking for loose stones or unexpected drops along the path.

The trail led them straight on for a long time in a subtle ascending manner until the river to one side was replaced by rock once more and jagged crags and vibrant green patches of life reached up before them. Eventually, the path descended, leaving Joden and Flinn to pick their way down, following a sudden slope until the land region leveled slightly.

"We've been at it for hours," Flinn said in a huff of exasperation, "my legs won't carry me any further if I go another step."

Joden let out a sigh as well, knowing full well that they needed to find someplace safe to relax. Besides that, he needed to address his wounds, caked in his own dried blood. "A little bit further, boy-o," the Warlord assured, "a wee bit further and we'll have our rest."

"How do you know the Spines so well?" Flinn asked.

Joden grunted without looking back, answering, "Great battles had been fought all over Wulndar, stretching up down from the Lowlands up into the Spines. Back in the days of the Pale Lady. I led many excursions."

"You were alive then? That was nearly over a century ago." Flinn was slow to fit the pieces together until his mind reeled, "you'd have to be just as old to have fought then!"

"Aye, lad, I certainly don't look it, do I?" Joden chuckled gruffly.

"That doesn't make any sense…"

"Many things don't make sense on Wulndar," Joden returned, leading all the while, "even so, that doesn't mean it's not so."

As the Warlord led the way, clambering over large rock and letting Flinn lull over his words, picking over precarious foot and hand holds, he soon found a small cropping of natural rock that depressed into the wall to form a small depression that more or less formed a cave. They would be away from prying eyes, but to make a fire now could attract unwanted curiosity. After Joden had inspected the cave and the immediate surrounding area, he beckoned for Flinn to follow him and make camp. They needed rest and would have to do so before they traveled any further.

Without their traveling pack, there would be no water, mead, or food to sustain them and the terrain around them was unyielding to anything bountiful in terms of sustenance. Joden did manage to fashion himself bandages by tearing strips from his garments, but as Flinn watched, the Warlord's wounds strangely appeared to be fast healing since their skirmish.

"We have some wretched luck," Flinn muttered, settling himself down against the stone wall of the cave after releasing a heavy sigh.

"Eh?"

Flinn shook his head and stretched, "Just everything so far. Not precisely the adventure I envisioned."

"Life's no fairytale, boy-o, but think how unexciting life would be without a few perils thrown in," Joden offered a smile over his shoulder and scratched at his beard before looking out into the Spines.

Flinn supposed the Warlord was right. Many tales told of conflict, and always the heroes came out on top. Would it be so for them, however, would the Druid's son's tale end with a similar happy ending? He hoped so.

"Rest, lad," Joden bade as he sat near the mouth of the cave, "I'll keep watch."

Late afternoon settled, lengthening into the early evening while Redeyes and his pack traipsed at a leisurely pace through the crags and foothills of the green mountains. To some, the Spines of Zhul Tarrgan were an imposing sight, many Wolf-kin clans stayed away from it both for their dislike of the Ghar'tul and for the savage beasts that dwelled therein. Not to mention, it was not kind terrain nor an ideal environment for their ilk.

There were extensive cavernous systems if one was unfortunate enough to discover an entrance, and although some Wolf-kin clans used caverns in the lowlands, they never dared make their homes in the Spines of Zhul'Tarrgan.

Especially not after Desdemona sent her undead scourge across Wulndar those many years ago. Offering alliances to those feral clansmen who were smart enough to take the offer, killing the rest who did not. Thwark did not want to see that age pass again, not this time. It was an age of unnatural disorder, an age of abominations. He kept his designs to himself this time around, vowing that he would not be Desdemona's lacky again. No, this time a new age would dawn, and he would be at the center of it all. An age of ferocity, an age where the predator reigned and preyed on those too weak to withstand the might of the strong.

For now, Redeyes would play along with Desdemona's plans. With her power and leadership, she will do away with Duldar's Port completely and while she is too engrossed in her mobilizations, that is when he would strike. After taking the Dark Tome for himself, Redeyes would send that witch back to whatever Hell she crawled back from and then Duldar's Keep would be his. Thereafter the cult of the Chilling Hand would be put to death and only his pack would remain.

Redeyes smiled wolfishly, already visualizing the Ghar'tul bowing before him, either willingly or in chains. Perhaps he would just have their clans wiped out. His pack would have to have plentiful reserves of fresh meat, after all.

Many leagues yet had been traveled, up steep slopes, clambering over jagged rises and picking their way down dangerous declines. Since their slaughter of the Ghar'tul, they had not crossed paths with any other clans. Word must have traveled of the slaughter, for there were many ears in these mountains. The goat-folk of the Spines were always warring with one another, always spying and conspiring. They were a numerous people, but their clans were small and tightly knit and loose alliances here and there were not unknown, but it took a great amount of effort to unite them.

During Desdemona's short-lived reign however, she was able to bring them all together granting them power and promising great rewards. But this time, the Ghar'tul of the Spines did not heed the Witch's call, for they were not so foolish as they once were in the past. Redeyes grunted that last thought, for the Wolf-kin would not be so easily fooled either. He remembered how difficult it was for the Pale Lady to convince the many different clans to aide her, doubly so now after so many years gone by.

The pack was skittish as they went along following the winding river westerly. The ears of their mounts constantly twitching, as did their own, making rider and mount increasingly paranoid. They wanted to be ready for anything, not desiring to be caught off guard. It was an embarrassing after thought, and a sign of inadequacy among the pack. Each wanted to have purpose, offering their strengths and none of their weaknesses.

"Keep on," Thwark Redeyes ordered, turning to look behind him with thrusting sanguine orbs.

"This is no longer a holy place, Pack Master" one of his captains expressed aloud while keeping pace beside Thwark. "The taint remains on these mountains."

Redeyes sucked at his teeth, expressing his irritation at such words. When he twisted back around, without looking to his captain, he said, "To the Hells with the taint, the Champion of Zhul'Tarrgan fears nothing! Is it so with those who follow him?" This time Redeyes pointedly looked to his captain. Meanwhile, the pack howled and barked their bravery, showing that they had no fear of the Spines.

Thwark's eyes remained dead fast on his captain, waiting for a reaction. Of which was a dip of the head and an aversion of the eyes, before pulling his mount back to fall behind his leader.

Grunting satisfaction escaped the Pack Master, then a

given command to scouts to break off to higher ground. The Pack slowed as Thwark brought his mount up a rise and stopped to close his eyes a moment, sending his thoughts out to Lunyrr.

Images flashed into his mind and he smiled. The Duldarians had a little run in already with one of the mountain clans, and most entertaining of all was the River Drake that had harrowed them. Now, the pair of city dwellers found refuge in a small cave, beleaguered by their experience. Redeyes grunted once more, more out of amusement.

Opening his eyes, blinking, and casting his gaze to reacclimate himself, Thwark led his pack deeper into the midst of the Spines of Zhul'Tarrgan. After an hour, dark clouds blew in from the east, the air became colder and with it came the rain. A storm had blown in, and by the scent it carried, it was going to be a big one.

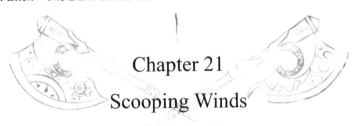

Chapter 21
Scooping Winds

Flinn woke to a rough shake, opening his eyes to see Joden already walking back towards the cave entrance. The sound of steady rainfall could be heard beyond and occasional flashes of lighting. There blew in a brisk chill to welcome the Druid's son as he sat up, stifling a yawn. He groaned, never recalling such a time his body felt so overworked and uncomfortable.

Another sound of discomfort escaped Flinn, using the rough cavern wall to help pick himself up and guide him over to stand beside Joden. The seven-foot-tall Duldarian stood with hands to his hips, a lifted chin down which eyes gazed down the slope of a broad nose.

The moon was full, then again it was always full. Every night, one after the other, said to be the watchful eye of Wulndar himself. Said to be privy of the dark happenings of the nights, during times where unspeakable things occurred.

"The rain will mask our scents, if by a little," Joden confirmed without looking to the young man.

The Warlord kept his eyes to the mountains across from the cave, scanning over the crags while drinking in the vibrancy of Zhul'Tarrgan's kingdom. Everything seemed to be infused with newfound life, heightened by the early evening shower. But the unnaturally cold air dampened the joy derived from such a sight. For beyond those serrated peaks the river would once again be sighted, and all they had to do was get around the lengthy pass. They would follow it eastward, until they reached a bridge that would take them to the western side before reaching the ruins of Duldar's Keep.

"Ye fought well earlier, lad," Joden nodded and stepped out from the cavemouth.

The Druid's son stepped up beside him. "It wasn't me," Flinn admitted, though loathe was he to do so. He knew he had no fighting spirit in him and no proper training. If it were not for the Twins, Flinn would never have had survived that skirmish with the Ghar'tul, or anything else leading up to that.

Joden decided it was time to go. Using the night as cover, sticking to its shadows, keeping from walking openly beneath the full moon's light. He led a cutting a swath between the dark crags as thunder rolled and lightning flashed. But that was when the wind howled most, haunting the hollows amid the rocks, echoing woefully their sorrowful sound. Flinn's eyes darted warily about, reminded of the Banshee and half expecting the Abominable to come crashing towards them.

A long time had passed with nothing other than the storm to hunt them. Weaving their way through the winding mountain pass as the rain fell harder. Drumming from the heavens beat the canvas above, reverberating to roll over the peaks of the Spines of Zhul'Tarrgan. Flinn heaved a sigh through his nostrils, his jaw tightening with a fate-accepting frown. Joden glanced back at him once, making sure that he was close.

On through the storm they traipsed. Soaked, tired, and hurt. The rain stung at their face, like needles while the wind yammered offensively. Unpredictable lightning flashes lit up the bloating black clouds, sometimes screeching and screaming with imperial maliciousness. Flinn happened to glance into the mountains at such chance, catching a streaking glimpse of such spearing power.

With those flashes of light, however, also came the silhouette of a familiar image watching up on high rocks above them. Perched high in silence. As always, the shadow-wolf cast its amber eyes over Flinn. They almost appeared to have a glow of their own, so piercing was its gaze. Within the small number of blinks during the flash of light, the shadow-wolf had vanished.

For a moment, the young man stood there in the storm, eyes to where he had seen the shadow-wolf, but Joden's booming voice called for his apt attention. He stood several strides away, waving the Druid's son to follow him, and shouting something about standing in the open. Flinn could not make him out through the storm. He cast one last look to where he the shadow-wolf had been, then pressed on.

Up ahead it appeared that the pass sloped down into a canyon, but it could not be seen for sure. At least, not from where Flinn was. Joden kept leading them forward and the ground noticeably changed. Rock walls leaped up flanking the Duldarians, as though about to pass through a great gate into the unknown.

And that was when it happened. A flash of light erupted, sending a bolt straight into the right side of the cleft, and with it came a rumbling tremor as portions of living stone broke free. Joden and Flinn bolted to run back up the slope, while tumbling rock echoed aggressively behind them. Had they been any closer both men would have been buried and ground to a pulp.

When at last the tumult from the blast subsided, leaving only the thundering of the storm, the Duldarians looked back down to see the path partially blocked. Most of the mountain had slid down the slope. They both stood still for several moments, trying to hear above the storm for any warning signs of further collapse.

Nothing was apparent. And the Warlord led the Druid's son down the slope once more, only this time picking and climbing over the rubble. In some places, the debris made for an easier descent into the canyon, while others required a moment of forethought.

Not a word was shared between them as the canyon swallowed them up and trudged on. The heavy rain filled in some places along the path, creating deep puddles, as the sound of riverbed stones crunched beneath their boots. It was apparent that the tributary they walked was unused to frequent running water, but not unfamiliar.

The canyon continued, stretching endlessly while it turned here and bent there. Joden appeared as though he was looking for something in the canyon walls, judging by how close he walked along them, trailing the rock with his fingertips. Flinn watched him, a quizzical expression knitting his eyebrows together. They leaped up, suddenly, and the young man stopped mid-step at the sight of Joden walking into the canyon wall itself!

The Druid son's eyes were playing tricks on him again. They had to be. He wiped the rainwater from his face, then looked at the canyon wall more intensely. Until Joden poked out from the wall once more and waved the young man over.

A sizable crack in the rock wall provided some shelter against the storm, deep enough to house the Duldarians, but too small to move about freely. Joden explained that they needed to wait the storm out, and Flinn accepted that. He was only glad for the respite. He moved as far back as he was able, the rain now just sprinkling him, and slid down the concave wall. He rested his head back against the cold stone, grateful for the rest.

Chapter 22

The Pack Fears Naught

Much ground had been covered. The rain continued. Harsh and unmerciful to match the viciousness of the storm, but The Pack kept their pace. Normally, they would have stopped for shelter and wait for the rain to pass but Thwark Redeyes did not allow it. Where scent was hampered, the Pack Master's black beauty made up for in sight. Lunyrr kept the trail, following along with the pair of Duldarian city dwellers.

Their paths would soon cross, and once the Duldarians came out from the unused tributary, they would have to trek downriver to get to the Northern Crook Bridge. It would be long before they reached it, however, for their road would soon collide with the Wolf-kin. Thwark looked forward to that crossing, more so to cross weapons with the legendary Joden Bear-Blade. Thwark had been young during that time, back when the pack was under the leadership of his father.

Yet, there was something else Lunyrr kept watch over, something unnatural and ancient. He could feel her angst, her sense of caution and desperation to avoid crossing paths with whatever it was that made her feel such unease. But from those emotions alone, Thwark understood that there was something else on the Duldarian's trail. Something of Desdemona's own perverted making.

Redeyes kept on and as they ventured to cut the Duldarian's off, there came the most horrifying wailing howl far in the distance. Thwark brought his pack to a halt, stopping as one while their ears, eyes, and noses reached out around them. Their mounts lowered their noses to the ground, flattening their ears against their heads, and issuing froth disapproving growls.

"The Abominable," one of Thwarks' captain's gasped.

Without warning, Thwark unsheathed a dirk at his hip, and in one swift movement thrust the blade through his captain's throat. He then leaned in, reaching to grip him by the jowls, pulling him in close so their noses touched. Redeyes growled, "Wolf-kin fear nothing, The Pack *fears nothing*."

He guided his sputtering, gurgling commander to slide from his mount, and wrenching free his dirk at the same time. Thwark turned to the others, casting his eyes to meet any who dared meet his gaze. But there were none who made the mistake of doing so.

"There is no room for fear," Thwark told them, "fear causes cowardice, cowardice causes panic and panic delivers death. We are not prey. We are *predators*."

Redeyes allowed a moment for his words to sink in. His pack watching him, their amber eyes catching the light of the moon, reflecting her glory back at him. In that moment, another nightmarish roar echoed through the Spines, and Thwark marched determinedly in its direction.

Flinn had fallen into half sleep, standing wedged into the concavity of the mountain wall, all while Joden stood resolutely vigilant, until a terrible roar woke him fully. Joden had stiffened at the sound of it, throwing an arm across Flinn and giving him a shake. They had to be quiet. The sound had come too close, assuring that whatever made the sound was coming this way.

"It's the Abominable..." Flinn breathed, fear gripping him.

"Those that die to yet live wish to embrace that which they lost—even if it means their final end," Joden's recited lowly, causing Flinn to glance at the Warlord in a new light. He was quoting something, something familiar, but from where he could not recall.

"Chin up, eyes open, boy-o," Joden whispered, "the rain will mask our sound and scent, so long as the thing stays far enough away."

If that were true, Flinn thought, then why was the beast here in the first place?

As if on cue, there came heavy footfalls, as the Abominable came into view near where the Duldarian's hid. They shallowed their breathing, keeping eyes locked on the gargantuan antlered beast.

For a blink, Flinn thought they had been seen when the twin pair of glowing blue eyes turned in their direction. For what felt like long moments, the Abominable stared, leaving Flinn certain they had been spotted. Joden gripped his arm, giving it a reassuring squeeze.

The Druid's son closed his eyes, trembling from the fear that had taken hold of him, until he placed his hands over the heads of his axes. Reinforced confidence and calm settled over his heart, giving him courage with a renewed perspective. He watched now as the beast went about its way, following down the tributary, its nose to the stones trying to pick up a scent before letting loose a skin crawling wail.

It nearly seemed that the beast would move past them, until it stopped mid-step, backed up and sniffed erratically in a small area which led its nose further away and back towards the canyon wall. A low grunt escaped after lifting its head, eyes transfixed in the general direction where the Duldarians remained hidden.

Joden tensed, his feet already shifting to compliment his adjusting stance. Slowly, his hand reached for his claymore, while Flinn's axes slipped slowly from their holsters. The familiar sensation of excitement overcame him, the Twins pumping adrenaline into his veins. It was no longer clear if it was him or the axes anymore that made him feel this way. But any excuse to wield the weapons now was sought after.

The Abominable sniffed the ground again, never taking

its glowing eyes away from the rock wall and lifted its head only to lower it again to search for the smell that would lead it to the Duldarians. That was a fact that neither of them could deny. It was only a matter of time now.

As the Abominable followed its nose, migrating ever nearer to where Flinn and Joden hid, the Druid's son envisioned himself running out to meet the creature head one and if not for Joden being in the way he would have certainly done so. Yet, he dared not make a move as the grotesque antlered reared up after a deep discovering inhale. Its eyes were fully locked on them now.

This was it. This could possibly be the height of Flinn's challenges, if he could best this monster and live to tell the tale, his name would be chanted from the roof tops. Joden alongside him be damned, Flinn wanted the glory for himself! Maybe it was the Twins thinking on his behalf, but what did that matter now? Live or die, this was the moment he read about in so many stories.

Just as the muscles in his body tenses, readying to send him forward, there came a howl—a familiar howl—splitting through the rain and the winds as keen as any blade through flesh. It was echoed by several others. And if the gods cursed him for it, so be it, but Flinn found himself affected by those sounds. It was not fear, although he knew the dangers that followed those calls, but something else inside of him triggered a sense of relief.

Suddenly, the idea of locking himself into a fierce battle with Wolf-kin and the Abominable excited him. Flinn licked his lips, then tightened his jaw as his breathing became excitable. It had to be the influence of the Twins, because never in all his years had Flinn felt such a thing.

He glanced over to Joden, finding that he already locked eyes on him, something in his stare assured the Druid's son that he was not the only one who shared in the feeling. He was a Warlord after all, the title spoke for itself.

"Tonight, we may dine in the halls of Wulndar, Flinn Druid's Son," Joden's voice was low, foretelling of a sealed fate. Before Flinn could even muster a response to that, Joden rushed out with a roar that rivaled the Abominable's own.

The unholy creature came back down to all fours, waving its antlers in answer to the challenge before pushing from the ground to rear back up again. Its roar filled tributary, bouncing from between the rock walls, and echoing down in both directions.

Joden came in hard, drawing the beast's attention to him at the same moment werewolves rushed through the thick curtain of rain. Flinn had no idea where they had come from, the storm too thick to see any great distance, no matter the direction. But he saw their hulking dark shapes lumbering their mass towards them Joden and the Abominable.

Between the charging Duldarian and the werewolves, the antlered monster chose the closest of foes. Flinn screamed, so hard that his throat nearly split as he ran in with the Twins held out to either side. A werewolf's snarl caught his attention to his left, he stopped, pivoted, and gave himself fully over to the handling of the axes.

"Delthos seeks us!" Flinn shouted, giving praise to one of the Fateful Saints known between here and Es'lyhn. Truly, it was the only thing that came to his mind while his heart knocked against his chest, and his stomach tied itself in knots while the Twins guided his attacks.

They pulled him away from mortally wounding claw swipes, yanked him off to one side and drew up into his chest to push him further backward, enough to evade the swing of a clobbering arm.

He ducked another overhanded swipe, came up swift with Ursarctos, biting its edge deep into the mosnter's ribs with a powerful swing. The werewolf yelped, cringed, and threw itself away with a snapping of teeth. The beast came back in, claws reaching, but Flinn closed the gap, shouldering between the monster's claws and lowered himself just enough to throw his shoulder into the monster's mid-section.

Joden danced about the Abominable nearby, delivering great swings of his claymore and scoring deadly strikes that would have felled any living creature.

A grunting snarl escaped the werewolf, bringing Flinn's attentions back to it fully, in time to follow the guidance of the Twins already leading him away from the beast's reaching claws. The axes then directed him off to the monster's left, using the change in its stance to guide him around its blind-side. Wulfaxe swung up on an upward-cutting angle, Ursarctos mirroring the movement but slightly more elevated. Both weapons bit deeply, causing the monster's flesh to sizzle which suddenly caused the runes to emit a black light.

The bone handles had warmed with each stroke that followed as Flinn kept moving in a circular motion around the werewolf. Moving just as the Twins wanted him to, positioning himself precisely in the way they visualized. The monster had entered a blind rage, both from the frustration of not landing a single strike and from the irritation Flinn had caused by not remaining still.

A glance had shown Joden disengaging from the Abominable, darting to intercept werewolves on their way for Flinn. The Warlord beheaded one, the Abominable giving chase from behind, and skewering another of the Wolf-kin. The Warlord wung his blade around to clip another werewolf just beneath the jaw. That only bought him enough time to draw the attention of the Wolf-kin further, leading the Abominable in after him, and once again thinking to use the beast unerringly against the new threat.

But as it were, the Wolf-kin had the numbers, and the Abominable was a tireless thing. How long could the Duldarian's last in the tributary? Flinn's mind had been reeling, too caught up in the exhilaration of the skirmish he found himself engaged with.

He took a slashing claw-swipe across his chest, of which could have been much worse had the axes not pulled him back by the arms. He staggered slightly as he glanced down at the wounds across his chest, becoming dreadfully sickened by his own blood spilling forth. The werewolf leapt from left to right tauntingly, slavering at the maw before three others of its pack joined the fun.

More of the Wolf-kin appeared, both in their lesser and hybrid forms, leading with weapons and claws alike as they split themselves into two groups. One harassing the Abominable while the other engaged with Joden and his powerfully wild swinging claymore. The abominable took two or three Wolf-kin down at a time, but their numbers proved greater as they synchronized their attacks. Rotating offensively. Three would lash out, scoring hits, directing the Abominable's attention onto them, as three others attacked from another angle.

Thus, was their tactic, round, and round, but with no true pattern the creature could cipher. And through it all watched Thwark Redeyes. Staying off at the edge of the exchange, flanked by a handful of his most trusted captains. He observed Flinn specifically, making note of the twin axes that guided his death strokes. He had heard tales of those axes, wielded by the hands of one like the youth who swung them about now.

An agonized supernatural scream resounded, bringing the hairs on all, especially Flinn's, to stand on end. The sound was followed by a howl and the ring of steel. The battle with the Abominable was far from being over, and the Druid's son wondered how Joden faired. But he dared not take his sights from the trio of werewolves circling him. With the Abominable pre-occupied with the assailing Wolf-kin and the Warlord, there were no interruptions here between these four.

Flinn suddenly lunged, Wulfaxe faking a thrust and causing the werewolf to bring up a forearm to shield itself, but Flinn was yanked and forced to leap to the left, swinging up and around with Ursarctos to score a slashing blow to the monster's elbow. A chunk of its flesh along with some of the bone flung away cleanly.

Having enough of the game of tag, the three other werewolves roared before rushing in, but Flinn back pedaled of his own accord with no urging from the Twins. There was a sliver of doubt that squirmed its way into his heart, unsure that even the axes would be able to take on three werewolves at a time. And as if to defy that doubt, the Twins yanked his arms forward, pulling him towards the beasts as though to prove him wrong.

Flinn fought to relinquish his grip from the weapons, but found his hands firmly held in place. Panic overtook him as he dug his heels into the river-stones, fighting against the power of the Twins as they reached out for their foes.

In that same moment, the Abominable was now focused more on the werewolves than it was on the singular warrior who always seemed to dance out of reach. The beasts clambered over it, clawing, and biting and tearing away chunks of rotted flesh, snapping at exposed bones. The monstrosity struggled against them, battering them away, grabbing at some and tossing into the rock walls like sacks of wheat, but there were always more to take their packmate's place.

Joden danced outside of the melee, clipping, or swinging at any who came too near and worked his way to aide Flinn. He was left awestruck, however, to see the Druid's son utilize the twin axes firsthand was... something else entirely.

Flinn continued to fight against the pull of the Twins, hungry as they were for the confrontation. The werewolves, even with their injured kin, rushed forward. One leapt high, covering the gap and landing just a hair too late. Flinn was thrown in a none-too-graceful evasive maneuver, evading being pounced upon entirely by the beast. It turned, answering with swiping claws, but were just out of reach as the Twins pulled him Flinn out of harm's way.

Spinning violently in a cyclone-like manner, the Druid's son managed another daring feat of evasion as another rushed him with a series of reckless claw attacks. Maybe due to his defiance against the Twins and the vying of control over his arms, he was too slow to dance out of reach of the last few attacks. The beast managed to clip Flinn at the shoulder and again as he spun with the blow, receiving another before spinning to the ground of the tributary, crashing into the stones, and sliding a few steps away.

Lightning flashed at the same moment, as if the gods themselves were aghast. The rain fell harder, the thunder drummed loudly overhead, adding further to the morose atmosphere that would be Flinn's dismal end. Here, as seemed proper, was a sacrifice to Zhul'Tarrgan himself. Another flash of lightning lit up the tributary, outshining the moon above, and with it came the silhouette of the shadow-wolf looking down from the escarpment from up high. Perhaps it had come to watch the last moments of Flinn's existence expire.

The quartet of werewolves closed in around him, forcing the Druid's son to get to his feet quickly and turn in place, trying to keep them all within sight at once. He found that the Wolf-kin were far different than the Ghar'tul. They were more calculative and not as reckless as the goat-folk.

Flinn screamed his own agony as Ursarctos stubbornly rose defensively, bringing Flinn's wounds to mind now that some of his adrenaline had subsided. He bled freely, furrows left behind across his flesh, leaking his life's essence. They were deep, for sure, but somehow Flinn still stood strong enough on his own two feet.

Uncertainty clouded the Druid's son's mind, unsure how much longer he could last. Especially now that the Twins proved to have a total disregard of his own hurts, fearing that they would use him up entirely until they could no longer.

Then, a great defiant roar shook the canyon with rumbling force as Joden Bear-Blade shouldered in from behind one of the werewolves circling around Flinn. He swung his sword down over another and severed its head clean completely, then pivoting after a single step forward as he brought his claymore around from a backhanded swing. The Blade cleaved another one of the beasts through the mid-section until the last two broke away from circling the smaller Duldarian. Joden coming to stand between the Druid's son and their foes once again.

A sharp whistle pierced the night, recalling the two werewolves from the Duldarians, but not without snapping their jaws angrily towards Joden. A roar disrupted their focus, pulling their attention towards the Abominable and the relentless Wolf-kin. Fighting to pull werewolves off itself, killing some, wounding others enough to ward them away, but ultimately the Wolf-kin were too many for it to handle.

Joden pulled at Flinn, leading him wide around the tumult, placing the Abominable and the Wolf-kin between they and their Pack Master. He recognized Thwark indefinitely, perhaps not knowing of him specifically, but he remembered the one who sired him. The likeness to his father was undeniable, and the same exudence of superiority radiated from his son as it had from him back in years past.

The antlered monster finally lost footing, slipping on loose stones and forced to its hindquarters. It shuddered beneath the conjoined efforts of the werewolves as they tore into it with gnashing teeth, and slashing claws. Their Pack Master watched with his captains, but his eyes were not for the Abominable; his eyes were for Joden Bear-Blade and the scrawny lad in his company.

He let them run with no worry of the Duldarians gaining significant ground. He did find satisfaction, however, in how Joden recognized his presence. Yes, he derived much pleasure from such a reaction.

Desdemona's abomination was nothing more now than scattered debris before the Wolf-kin had finished their work. Leaving it in pieces like discarded refuse, further testament that the pack's numbers proved the stronger. It only bolstered Thwark's confidence that they would have no issues overpowering Desdemona herself when the time came. He called out long and loud, sending his howl into the night sky. Lunyrr appeared moments later, and Thwark climbed atop her barebacked.

He led his packmates onward, spitting at Abominable's corpse as he urged Lunyrr forward, and started to the path after the Duldarians. They would not have gotten far on foot, and nowhere fast enough to outrun the Wolf-kin on such a straight run. There would be no other place to hide here on out, for soon they would be left with little choice but to face The Pack.

And to make things more interesting, the Pack Master sent a handful of his fastest runners ahead, trusting in their own fear of him not to lose their self-control. Of course, he was unable to hide his smile at the thought that they may happen to kill Joden on reaching them.

It would be the longest night of Flinn's life, as he and Joden ran down the tributary as it wound northward and then gradually curving west. Canyon walls ran by them, Joden's pumping powerful legs through the constant rain. Flinn fought to keep pace with him, but his shorter strides, though quick of foot, were able remain just behind him. The storm, meanwhile, had not relented and the cold came with a numbing bite now. The longest, dreariest night of Flinn's life.

Out of habit, the Druid's son cast a look over his shoulder, seeing no sign of the pursuit. Not to say that it was not underway. He had no idea how long the Abominable kept the Wolf-kin occupied, unsure if they had brought the thing down under their numerous might. Or if by any luck, both had wiped each other out. Wishful thinking, Flinn realized. Focusing again ahead of him, with Joden gaining a bit more ground, the Druid's son picked up his pace.

Howls broke through the storm behind them. It was just a matter of time before they came upon the Duldarians. "They're coming!" Flinn shouted as a loud crack of thunder muted him at the same moment.

The wind shifted along with the rain, bringing a colder air along with it. Flinn glanced back once more, revealing a small group of werewolves in a flash of lightning, trailing behind them and closing fast.

"Joden!" Flinn called in warning nervously. He did not dare reached for Twins again to sooth his angst, at least not yet, not while they were trying to make an escape. The moment he had regained control of them he slipped them back into their belt loops. The feeling not being in control of himself disturbed him, and the axes certainly stripped that ability away from him earlier.

Joden grumbled something, acknowledgement maybe. It was hard to tell through the storm.

As they gained more ground, now with the Wolf-kin not far behind, the canyon suddenly came to a halt, having eroded to fall away into a deep channel below, running south as the river could be seen rushing below cliff fall. To their right, southward, was enough room to travel along the escarpment, a ledge wide enough if they kept their backs to the rock wall. Flinn was unsure which idea he liked more, staying to face down the werewolves, take another risky plunge into the river below, or walk the precarious ledge with no promise that it would take them anywhere.

Joden slowed before reaching the cliff's edge, turning back whence they came, and hefted his claymore into a two-handed grip, wringing tightly its hilt. He met Flinn's eyes, only grunting and gesturing with his bearded chin towards the narrow ledge that wrapped around the mountain face.

Flinn screwed up his face with incredulity, "Ye can't mean to stay here and fight them!?"

The howls grew closer, more sounding further in the distance, as the troupe sent ahead of the pack would soon be upon them. "Go, lad," Joden reversed his hold on the blade, thrusting it down into bare rock. The act ignited the black-light runes as its steel caused sparks to fly as the metal drove into the stone floor.

"I can't just leave ye here!" Flinn protested, but his

eyes went sharply to where the Wolf-kin's howls issued form the tributary, just making out their forms through the rain. His hands lurked near the Twins, ready to slip them free with a thought. They wanted him to, he could feel their energy itching at his fingertips so nigh.

Then Joden did a strange thing, unfastening his wide leather studded girdle to toss it off to the side. He went about removing his great kilt from around his shoulder and let the thick garment drop around his feet. He stood naked there before Flinn, leaving the Druid's son with a confused expression over his face. "Go," Joden waved Flinn away, "go now, lad."

The Wolf-kin emerged fully into view, howling, and snapping their teeth excitedly as they spread from one another to surround the trapped Duldarians. Before Flinn could protest any further, Joden suddenly shouted out in agony, arching his back, and throwing his eyes to the full moon. His joints popped out irregularly as muscles swelled and contracted beneath his flesh. Fingernails became thick claws shredding through fingertips, and toes, as he reached and clawed towards the night sky.

"Go!" he roared, taking a lumbering step forwards while his physical form continued to take on a new and hulking shape.

Flinn, startled by what he saw, shuffled back, unsure how to register what was happening to the Warlord. He was no druid, last he checked, believing that only they possessed the ability to change. But what if Joden was not merely a warrior?

The next words that issued forth from Joden were not words at all, instead a froth-spitting roar towards the werewolves that shook the mountains. Flinn gazed on the werebear in awe, hardly believing it. As the werewolves scurried back a bit, hesitant to engage but eager at the same time, Joden Bear-Blade turned his large head onto Flinn, with piercing wild eyes of burnt umber and released another frightening roar.

Flinn took to the pass, taking the hint, and made it to

the narrow ledge. He hugged closely to the mountain wall, hoping to the gods that the storm's wind did not blow him over. Joden's roar shook the mountain again, answered by the gleeful sadistic howls of Wolf-kin.

Thwark reached his runners not soon after they had caught up to the Duldarians, calling them off at the sight of the werebear. He barked a command for three of his warriors to go after the youth, and as they bound forward with Joden moving to intercept them, Redeyes rushed out to cut him off. Joden kept on, however, regardless of the wicked bearded ax pointed at him.

"Bear witness the fall of Joden Bear-Blade!" Thwark proclaimed, twirling his weapon, before moving in to do battle.

Joden fought to get past but realized there would be no way around his foe other than to clash with Thwark and be done with it. He could only hope that Flinn would make it to the bridge, buying him the time he needed. Yet with those three Wolf-kin after him, the chances were slim, and that is even if he does not risk falling first.

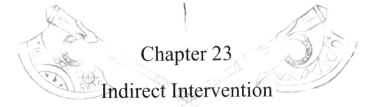

Chapter 23
Indirect Intervention

Joden took a leaping step, coming down with a powerful clawing swipe. Thwark dipped and rolled beneath it, unafraid of the gargantuan beast's size or strength. He kept close, forcing Joden to turn and keep the Pack Master in front of him. He stepped in behind the swing of his ax with the focus of felling a strong oak.

Joden bound outside the reach of the vicious weapon he lashed out and clip the haft of the ax, sending Thwark stumbling forward and turning from the force of the blow. Staggering away a few steps, the Pack Master balanced himself, planting his feet firmly into the stone and pushed off his lead foot and launched himself at Joden in a rush of advancing steps.

Thwark Redeyes feinted high with a thrust of his weapon at Joden's wide face, ducking right beneath two swiping claw attacks that would have felled someone slower. The Pack Master was quick, however, of both wit and in reflex. He continued forward to roll under the attacks, popping up behind the werebear and swinging a hamstringing blow that brought the beast to its knee.

His sanguine eyes flashed through the hard storm and beamed with victorious strike, bringing memories back of the olden days, where the clans fought against one another. A reason to fight, to kill, a reason to conquer.

And then the rain stopped. The dark clouds no longer alight with bright flashes. The thunder rolling away distantly, no more than a giant's whisper. The chill air remained, heightened more so since the rain, making a forlorn battlefield of the escarpment, ripe with woe and festering with encroaching death.

Thwark had not removed his eyes from Joden, nor had he in turn. His wound bled freely, having severed the tendon gruesomely. It would heal, but not fast enough to end this fight. He watched as Thwark made casual steps towards him, keeping just out of reach even should Joden decide to lunge for him. Any attempts to pick himself up resulted in losing beneath the brunt of his weight, his leg could not support him.

"Why won't ye join me, Bear-Blade?" Thwark asked over the space between them. "I know ye feel it, the shift, there's naught ye can do now. Another age is upon us…"

Joden snorted through his nostrils, shaking his head defiantly and releasing a roar equally refuting.

"Suite ye self," Thwark snarled before speeding forward to finish his downed foe.

The Wolf-kin watched anxiously, too enraptured by the sight. There was no avoiding this confrontation, bound as it was by the Fates. And just as Thwark came close enough to swing his ax for the execution, a violent a tremor shook the mountain that threw all present off their feet. Thwark scrambled to regain his footing, while Joden took the opportunity to pulling himself rapidly towards the Pack Master.

There came a break in the precipitous pass hugging and jutting around the mountain side. A gap lay before Flinn, the path having given out after an explosive lightning strike. He nearly lost his balance, if not for bracing against the rock wall. When everything settled, and the last few bits of loose rocks tumbled past, Flinn measured the stretch of the gap. He did not think he would make it, even if he tried.

Was this the end of the road then, Flinn asked of himself, at the same time contemplating how best he should approach this unforeseen obstacle. There was much more of the path to take ahead, beyond the gap, which made it that much more difficult to accept that this was the end. Flinn thought back on the Warlord, wondering how he fared against the Wolf-kin. Hoping that the werebear he had become was enough to fight against them.

The young man felt confident in Joden's abilities, certain that the werebear would surprise him somewhere down the road, catching up to him eventually. Back to the dilemma at hand, Flinn brought his attentions to pass. Just looking at it made his breathing erratic. Knowing also that the hazardous repercussions from making the risky leap could be dire.

But what courage the Druid's son lacked, or what boldness was absent, could easily be found in the Twins. Flinn's hands brushed over them lightly, too nervous to rest them completely over their cool heads. Even by that slight touch, their ravenous appetites nearly overwhelmed him. He pressed himself against the mountainside, bracing himself against their overpowering influence. When Flinn felt secure enough, he let his hands fall over the Twins and pressed his palms into their silver surface.

He received the courage he sought and more. Thinking himself the fool to even doubt his abilities in jumping over the small expanse. Any runt could do it, which meant he was being a child in his over-analyzing. But why go back at all, when Flinn could join Joden in battle, and let the Twins slake their thirst in blood, swept in the beautiful dance of battle?

The same uncontrollable feeling swelled up from his hands to travel up the lengths of his arms, a feeling that frightened Flinn. His fear overruled the Twin's pressuring. And just as with the first time, he did not like it now. Realizing too, he did not have their qualities, needing them to continue.

Mentally, Flinn forces the axes to understand his need to get across, that there were more battles yet ahead. They relinquished their rising hold over him lightly, allowing the Druid's son to channel their strengths for what he needed to leap across.

Haunting winds howled, blowing frigid air into his face, and making cold his bald pate. He ignored those ghostly supernatural sounds, positioning himself a bit closer to the gap's edge. And just as Flinn's muscles summoned the confidence to leap the space between, a most stomach sinking sound caught his ear and forced him to look nervously back the way he had come.

There, now far behind, were Wolf-kin who inched their way nervously for him. When seeing him, one of the warriors clacked his teeth together tauntingly. "Here I come, city dweller, nowhere t'go now."

Flinn could see in his eyes that the Wolf-kin believed he was done for. There was nowhere for him to go other than over the gap. The Druid's son watched helplessly as they inched their way closer with every shuffling step. It was now or never.

"Come now, laddie, with me or over th'edge…"

"If the Gods are listening, help me!" Flinn turned from the Wolf-kin, leapt over the gap, and landed on the other side with a bewildered expression left on his pursuers faces, including his own. He glanced back again, feeling foolish for having thought it had been impossible to fathom, and quickly reminded that the axes were the ones who made it possible.

But that was not all. A low rumbling could be felt, a tremor from the mountain itself. Flinn pressed himself against the rock wall, glancing up to watch for any falling debris and to the Wolf-kin who clutched the rocks, fighting to keep from falling over. Then, like lightning, a screech split the air but there was no flash. Instead, a descending streaking fissure shot down the mountain wall, stopping halfway up above the gap in the pass.

Tumbling stones came down, like boulders heaved by giants, crashing along the mountain wall during their descent, ricocheting outward as well as collapsing parts of the pass from where Flinn had just leapt. Larges stones fell over the Wolf-kin, toppling them and sending them down below screaming their ill luck.

After several long moments, the tremors ceased. Loose bits of smaller stones tumbled here and there was replaced a stillness along the path. Now, with no way feasible way to get back to Joden, the only way for Flinn to go was forward.

Thwark stood over Joden's motionless form, riddled with the marks of his packmates, both from steel and claw. A bloodied unconscious mass of hulking strength reduced to nothing beneath the might of the pack. He did not play by the normal standards as they had in olden times. The Wolf-kin surrounded the werebear, sniffing his body, and one inspecting the warrior's runic claymore until Thwark called for it. He settled the blade beside the warrior, giving orders not to disturb his body further.

Then moved to where he had seen the Druid's son last. The narrow pass had gone, apparently having collapsed during the sudden tremor. Turning back towards the war-party, Thwark issued another order, back tracking to take a different pass. Thwark nearly laughed aloud, reflecting on Joden's foolishness for leading the lad to the cliff and to his own end. Redeyes was no native to the Spines, but he knew the mountains well enough.

Leading his pack away from the dead-end escarpment, Thwark only hoped that Zhul'Tarrgan found Joden Bear-Blade a worthy sacrifice, and took his time returning to North Crook Bridge. The boy had only one route from that narrow ledge and that led him straight to the other half of his pack. That is, of course, if the lad had not fallen to his death already.

Meanwhile, the moon gazed down on Joden's body, showering its grace and power over his imposing form as he lay there alone and bloodied.

Chapter 24
Fatigued

Flinn's steps carried him quickly around the mountain's bend, which soon led him to less treacherous ground. The narrow path offered points from which to descend a bit lower, bringing Flinn gradually level with the rushing river and soon followed along its length. All he knew was he had to get to some bridge if he remembered Joden's words correctly. The fatigue that seared Flinn's every aching step slowed him, and with that came his anxiety. Constant glances over his shoulder proved tiresome as well, to a point where he had no care if the Wolf-kin descended upon him.

He reminded himself of Joden and the sacrifice he made. That alone kept him going. Flinn could not give up just yet, not while he felt that he was that much closer to his goal. He had to quicken his step, however, apply some measure of urgency in his travels. He focused on getting to the bridge, imagining it without ever seeing what it looks like. Any bridge would do, really, and so he kept an eye out for anything even remotely close to it.

A bend in the river rounded the mountains this side of the river, disappearing into the crags, traveling by light of the full moon but still having to be mindful of his footing. Flinn tried to pick himself up into a light run whenever the terrain allowed, then having to slow his progress again when it changed.

Flinn was unsure if he heard correctly, thinking perhaps that the sounds of heavy breathing were his own. After a look behind him, his stomach like a lead weight. A lumbering shape clambered over the rocks after him and having a struggling time of it. One of the Wolf-kin must have survived the fall from the collapse, for there were no signs of the other two.

Groaning at having to deal with the Wolf-kin, Flinn's hands went reluctantly to his axes, removing them from their holsters and kept on toward the bend. He wanted to at least make it around before having to engage his pursuer, the relentless bastard that he was. And naturally, the Twins wanted him to stop and face the brute, but Flinn resisted their desires.

With the river to his left, the Spines of Zhul'Tarrgan to his right, Flinn was caught between elements of water and earth with only one road open to him. He could continue to run until his legs gave out, or he could give into the nagging of the Twins and simply face down the Wolf-kin.

Flinn was too tired, his legs wobbled beneath him, and he could barely keep himself upright the further he went. But he held firm his axes, confident that he would make it around and still have enough energy left to stave off the one who hunted him. A glance showed that the warrior was gaining on him.

He rounded the bend just-so, feeling his legs grow heavier and heavier with every footfall. Flinn could feel his locomotion slowing, the fatigue of the worst night of his life finally bringing him down, but he had to keep running. He picked up his pace, forcibly now, taking large awkward steps while threatening to collapse. The Twins would be of no use, all they did was instill in him quality characteristics he did not have in himself, flailing his arms about during battle like some puppet on the strings.

Clearing the bend at last, the bridge came within sight. The sudden bubble of elation Flinn felt seeing the bridge in the distance had just as quickly popped. Wolf-kin guarded the bridge, too many to count in the night, but their dark shapes could not be mistaken. The moon's light shown them clearly enough, and the sight of them crushed the Druid's son utterly. He fell to his knees in defeat, exasperated, and with nothing left.

Behind him he heard his pursuer, breathing just as raggedly as Flinn. "Ye're. Quick. I'll give ye that…"

Not the firs time Flinn had heard someone tell him that, and right now he did not care. He slumped his shoulders, resting the Twins over his lap, and listening to the crunch of approaching steps from behind. If this was his end, then Flinn would have to make sure it was worthy of story. And as the Wolf-kin approached, close enough to feel the warmth of his presence standing over him, Wulfax shuddered in his grasp, bringing him up to one knee in a single backhanded swing that buried deep into the Wolf-kin's sternum.

Ursarctos brought Flinn up further, swinging in suit and bringing the Druid's son to his feet, sinking deeply all the way to the butt. The warrior sputtered out blood, disbelief in his amber eyes before sinking to his knees. Flinn let the axes remain, keeping just enough strength in his legs to hold him aloft, and finally being the one to tower over those always taller than he.

A dark shape caught his eye askance. Approaching from the same direction the Wolf-kin had come. There was no doubt what it was, and Flinn watched as the shadow-wolf slowed her approach as she neared.

She never stopped after the young man, as the brash and crude Thwark had bade her do and continued to shadow Flinn even after separating from Joden. Finally catching up to him just as he downed Thwark's packmate.

There was no more fight left in him, plainly, going down with the toppling warrior he had just slain. The bits of his axes lodged deeply, pulling free from the young man's grasp, as he collapsed to lay on his side, eyes aflutter only to close. He would dream now, Lunyrr knew, and no longer would they need to chase after him. Thwark was right in knowing that the lad would come straight to them. He just needed a little urging is all.

It was a shame, however, that Joden had fallen. Yet, Lunyrr had known the Duldarian to be strong in times past and knew further that his strength had not diminished. He was just dealt a bad hand, as many sometimes were.

The black wolf yowled high to the moon, calling for the nearby Wolf-kin by the bridge yonder. Before long two warriors along with a werewolf arrived, answering the summons. Lunyrr lowered her head with warning growl, standing over Flinn's unconscious form, which caused the werewolf to slow his approach. Until given the signal to scoop the young man up in its powerful arms, and for the axes to be collected carefully, they all made the short trek back to North Crook Bridge, where they would wait for Thwark and the hunting party to arrive.

Chapter 25
The Face in The Dark

Even if there was no sound, sequestered entirely amid total and utter silence, there would be heard the rushing blood in one's ears. Or perhaps it was the sound of silence itself? But that low, continuous whirring of whispered warmth brought the Druid's son back to consciousness. He was unsure when he had lost it, and the only thing he recollected was seeing the black wolf before collapsing into complete darkness. And how his body *screamed*.

He sat himself up from the cold cell floor as damp straw clung to him, exuding a strong smell of ammonia, but there was something else that threatened to empty Flinn's gut.

By the soft glow of torch light creeping through the cast iron bars, and by following the stench of decay, there was found a partially illuminated dark shape slumped and leaning in one of the far corners. The half rotting corpse, bloated and staring blankly with clouded eyes bulging from their sockets, was a macabre mockery of the life it had once known. A panoply of festering horror that instilled in Flinn despair. But the more he looked on the poor bastard the more the Druid's son realized it was not Joden, and a wave of relief washed over him.

He whispered a short prayer for the fool who had gotten himself stuck in a cell, and then brought himself up to his feet, brushing piss-ridden straw bits from his person and moving towards the bars, distancing himself as much as possible from the rotting corpse.

Shadows danced in tune with the silent song of the orchestrating torchlight, illumining a narrow hall beyond the dark iron bars that kept Flinn from leaving. His weapons were gone, that much was obvious, along with his silver-plated girdle. Even his mother's dagger he had tucked in his boot, unless he had lost it long before now and never realizing it. In any case, Flinn was amazed they left him in his kilts.

"How like you your lodgings, Wulndarian?" a sly voice from across his cell slithered questioningly.

Flinn glanced through his bars trying to peer and make out a face across the narrow hall. The shadows played too heavily across the way, however. But there did appear a pair of pale ashen hands that gripped at the bars, but only a pair of cold sapphire rings floated in the darkness back at him.

The Druid's son had seen that haunting glowing color once before, the eyes in the alley, but these were not the same eyes. The warning registered, however, not to get too friendly with whoever it was across the hall. The pale ashen hands receded into the nothingness, replaced by an amused giggle, disturbingly lilting and candid.

"You're new here," the darkness peeled away to reveal a face that continued to press uncomfortably into the bars of his or her cell. It was difficult to differentiate such fine features, such as this person possessed. For they were strangely sharp, and angular, vibrant with an alien youthfulness, and emanating a deranged gauntness. Black tresses of raven hair fell over the bruised orbits of almond shaped eyes, entirely black save for the blue glowing irises.

could not truly tell if this were a man or woman, boy or girl, for so fair were the features. Almond shaped eyes turned in towards a slender-bridged nose, but the orbits looked hollow as if they were simply holing into some fathomless abyss. Flinn had to believe otherwise, for how could that even be?

"Have a name?" his voice was an elevated whisper, his eyes darting to Flinn's left, straining to look down the hall.

Flinn was silent, not feeling at all comfortable consorting with the stranger, and still at a loss for what the hell he was. He had never seen anyone like him before in Wulndar.

"I am Razjil Sha'et Moonglade," the strange fellow introduced after settling his eyes over Flinn once more. He pressed his faced further against the bars, poking his delicately pointed nose through with eyes flashing with a sinister hunger. "You must be of great import for them to throw you in *that* cell—"

Razjil sniffed intrusively in the young man's direction, appearing taken by a perverted ecstasy. "So sweet you smell," his words were whispers now, "I can hear your blood flow."

Flinn stepped back instinctually, causing Razjil to smile, revealing plaque-ridden teeth. But the elongated canines are what alarmed him most. Razjil shushed him softly, pulling away from the bars to let the darkness of his cell swallow him whole.

No sooner had a heavy creaking moan of hinges echo down the corridor to Flinn's left, bolstered by heavy plodding bare steps. Thwark Redeye slid into Flinn's view, causing him to step back with wide eyes. Thwark chuckled, watching as Flinn tried to save face and straighten himself fearlessly.

But Redeyes could smell that fear clearly, an intoxicating scent he had known in the old ages of Wulndar when the cycle shifted favor as it did now. He glanced over his shoulder and then slowly back to Flinn, stating, "Careful, lad, ol' Razjil's been here a *long* time—even before *my* time." He smirked, tilting his head judgingly with scrutinous eyes.

Flinn met that red-eyed stare head on. He would not allow this beast-man to see he was frightened. Defiance would be a shield, but by the gods, he fought from pissing himself.

"Ye failed, boy-o. Yer bloodline held no potency to aid ye, and yer Warlord's left sprawled over the Spines." Thwark said the last words were said with a curl of the lip, recalling the sweet taste of victory. "Soon Desdemona's army will march over Duldar's Port, and ye'll be here when it happens."

It took all Flinn's mettle not to show that he was disturbed by what the Pack Master said to him. Especially at mention of Joden. The news came with a great sorrow and a gut punching feeling of loss. Flinn recalled how he felt when he held the Twins in his hands, trying to recreate that feeling to keep him steadfast. But for all of him, he could not.

Flinn stepped forward, coming right up to the bars, unafraid that Redeyes could reach through at any moment and take him by the throat. He narrowed his visage, glaring up from beneath his brow and whether it was that look alone, or maybe it was something in the Druid's son's eyes, he could see that Thwark was confused—no—surprised by his action.

"Before my time is done, I'll see ye dead for what ye've done."

Thwark lifted his chin, looking down nose as the shadows played against his dark skin. He smiled, four sets of canines bright enough to be seen before releasing a bellowing laugh. Just as unexpectedly, he reached through the bars of Flinn's cell, yanking him face first into the cold iron. Bright lights flashed over his vision, his head thrumming as if he had taken a solid punch. In fact, he would have much prefered that instead.

"Make sure ye don't disappoint me, then, laddie," Redeyes' wolfish grin never left him, shoving Flinn back and stumbling. The Pack Master stepped back slowly, sizing the Druid's son up before he turned and disappeared back down the corridor, bare feet sending echoing slaps that grew distant until the door opened and shut.

Flinn groaned quietly, rubbing his face and the bridge of his nose. Lucky that he had not made a bloody mess of it, with so narrowly missing a break. Leaning back into the wall, the bars of his cell at his left, he rested his head back and wondered how he was going to get out of this one.

A clucking tongue brought Flinn's attentions back to the cell across from him. Scowling at the hushed sounds of disproval. "You have powerful enemies, young man," Razjil observed.

"Enough from ye, I don't need yer yammering madness," Flinn waved the prisoner away and turned from the bars of his cell. He had nearly forgotten about his rotting company, then thought better to go any further.

"Mad? No, no, no, no, no. Not *mad*," Razjil protested frantically. Then became silent before adding, "… maybe a little—but, no more than Desdemona or any others who fall sway to the dark ways, then again, *my* people have a certain... susceptibility to the Arka'nym."

Flinn scoffed Razjil away with another wave of his hand, having no idea what he just referenced. Setting his back to the bars, trying to blow the scent of piss and death from his nostrils, Flinn could feel the dampness squish beneath his boots and turned his nose up towards the ceiling with an exasperated exhale. Just how the Hells was he going to get out of this, he thought again? He was stuck, worst yet, that Razjil across the hall was batshit crazy.

Long hours passed, with Razjil still going on and on about how he had come to Wulndar from across the Blood Sea centuries ago. A laughable claim, to live for centuries. Then again, Flinn thought back to Joden, having to be at least over a century old himself. The thought was baffling. Flinn only half listened now, catching something about a hidden forest on Es'lyhnn, a place none knew of and shrouded in a magical haze.

"Will ye *shut up*!?" Flinn spun about, gripping the bars of his cell, and allowing his impatience to take precedence.

Razjil went silent, perhaps thinking Flinn had something worth-while to say. When nothing of interest was forthcoming, he resumed talking.

"I—I can see things, you know?" Razjil said feverishly, wringing the bars tightly so that his flesh rubbed against the iron loudly. "That's why she keeps me here. I am the first she'd ever seen… and the last she'll ever know. And at one time, after turning me, I was her most prized advisor." Razjil's words trailed off sadly, his blue irises shifting to the floor of the corridor, staring blankly as he recalled older times.

Flinn squeezed his eyes shut, shook his head, and sighed. This was torture. In fact, he would much rather *any*thing else aside from what he was enduring at this very moment to occur. Maybe that was the cause of death for his cellmate? He hoped not.

Then those blue rings flickered back to Flinn, and Razjil went on, "But I can't see *you*—that's why you bother, you see, along with other reasons. After she found you, she came to me, asking what I could see. And when I could not see, she threw me down here."

Now this did interest Flinn, clearly showing it by his sudden change in posture, but his eyes held reserved pessimism.

Razjil managed a weak smile. It faded immediately after Flinn brought his eyes to leery slits. "What I mean is, I can see the outcome of one's greatest triumphs, or greatest failures—I cannot see these things with you. Yet, you radiate something, something that not even you have yet discovered," Razjil nearly giggled with excitement.

"Did she make ye this way? Crazy? Or maybe that's the true reason why ye're down here?" Flinn asked, pushing away from the bars again. Clearly, Razjil had been locked up for far too long.

Whether Razjil did not hear his words or chose to ignore them, Flinn could not tell, because the crazed man just kept yammering on. "Don't you see?" he tittered, "you are special without knowing it but now *she* knows it and has no idea what to do with you! Could he be friend or foe, an advantage to her cause or the end of it!?" he laughed now, full heartedly.

"Then why does she keep ye alive done here, then?"

Razjil tilted his head hard to the side, looking back at Flinn sideways, wearing a thoughtful smile. Turning his head again proper, the strange man answered, "She means to starve me here. Until I am but a dried husk, mindless and ravenous."

"Starve ye to death?" Flinn raised his eyebrows at that.

"Not to *death*, you innocently ignorant young man," Razjil shook his head, still smiling, "she means to starve me so that I am lost to myself."

"Ye make as much sense as a rock singing a diddy," Flinn let out a restless sigh, both tired and too afraid to sleep.

If Razjil was right about the Pale Lady not knowing what to do with him, then what was Flinn to do with this information? And if he knew such things, then maybe he could help him in other ways. Flinn, after all he had to find a way into the ruins of Duldar's Keep and retrieve the Dark Tome, right? And it could not get any clearer that he was had arrived, of course maybe not precisely where he wanted to be at present, but he made it in one way or the other.

Razjil opened his mouth to say more, but went suddenly quiet, and swiftly receded into the swallowing darkness of his cell once more.

The distant, yet familiar, heavy creaking of an opening door echoed down the corridor with a resounding shutting weight that followed. Even before the quiet could settle, there came the whispering approach of several feet.

Chapter 26
Regrettable Decisions

It was hard to believe that a woman could look both erotic and dangerous at the same time. Both beautiful and ugly. Her very posture portrayed a wicked intent, using the allure to bind and snare any man's attention. This woman, whose dark hair fell over her slender shoulders to frame her soft deathly pale face, reminded Flinn of a dark spider found in the darkest of cellars. Her eyes permeated with a cold glare, reaching out to grasp at men's hearts in a frozen fist.

Flinn had to step away from the bars, getting just out of reach from the clawing frigidity that seemed to radiate from her, and nearly pressed into the back of his cell. Two guards, or maybe priests by the look of their garb, stood flanking her a step behind. Their pointed hoods dipped forward as they kept eyes to the bottoms of their robes, their feet hidden beneath the heavy folds as the stood towering like flanking spires to either side of her.

"Do you know of me, Duldarian?" the woman, so diminutive even when compared to Flinn, spoke in a piously commanding tone betraying her size. But her accent was off, not sounding from the land.

She tilted her head to the right, turning her chin up to the left just-so, the makings of what could be a smile pulled at the corner of her tantalizing lips. While her glacial eyes flashed brighter, they only complimented an almost withholding expression of amusement.

"You *do* know who I am," Desdemona allowed her smile to take full flight, "then you know also I am aware you are here to take the Dark Tome from me, perhaps use it for yourself or against me or whatever other plans you may have?" She righted her head and narrowed her gaze, the smile on her face had gone and was smeared with a disproving frown. "I don't like it when others try stop me from doing what I enjoy."

Flinn found her glowing eyes half-lidded as Desdemona stared at him with all sense of amusement drained away. Was she going to cast a spell on him, some dark magic from the book? Or would she send in her towering guards to drag him out and beat him into a bloody pulped slab of tenderized flesh? Whatever her intent and no matter how fearful he felt, the Druid's son swallowed hard and stood a little straighter. He would have to treat this woman as he had expressed defiance against Thwark.

Perhaps perceiving such inward struggles within him, Flinn watched the smile on Desdemona's face reappear along with an entire change in demeanor, presenting herself a bit more warmly after smoothing out the black dress she wore. Her actions drew his eyes to how well the dress complimented her figure. A large V cut in the front provided ample vision of her full breasts, coming down to meet at just below her navel. Her hips were aesthetically wide, but that only made the Druid's son wonder about her backside. He blinked away his sudden lustful thoughts, chalking it up to whatever dark charms Desdemona had already spun around him.

Her girlish giggle brought Flinn's wandering eyes back to meet her own and instantly regretted it. He found her artic orbs held him in place, sending her mind probing his own, feeling her hands that rested clasped just below her chest, cascading down the length of his body down through his toes. How she did such a thing frightened him, but with her echoing words without ever moving her lips, she soothed him. Relaxing him utterly.

He panicked, fighting to gain control of his body while his mind pieced itself back together slowly, and with every renewed piece, the urgency to reclaim himself screamed louder. Flinn struggled once he felt he could focus on turning his head away from her. He could *feel* the command being sent, but it was as though his face had been caught in a cold death-grip, preventing him from the act. Not even his facial expressions betrayed his angst. He had been completely paralyzed.

He fought and fought and fought. Every now and then Flinn could feel crinkles generate from a slowly knitting brow. Felt the wrinkling of his nose as his lips peeled back and felt a low growl reverberate up from his chest, at last to bar his grinding teeth.

The Druid's son felt a sudden surge of energy overwhelm him, warming his face and aiding his mental strength. If he could not turn his head, or move his extremities to break the hold, then he would focus on something a bit less physically demanding. With the resurgence of power gained with sheer will alone, Flinn began working his eyes until they slowly disengaged Desdemona's incredulous glare. That was all he needed, just to look away from her, to break the chain of sight between them.

But it was that act that released him fully from the witch's ocular trap. It did not happen all at once, but regaining control over himself bodily happened faster than he had expected once he severed the sight. Once feeling tingled back into his spine, arms, and legs, Flinn nearly stumbled forward into collapse, but he managed to summon the strength needed to keep from falling to his knees. Something inside of him raged against the mere image of prostrating himself in any way before Desdemona, and he held onto to it indomitably.

"Impressive," Desdemona remarked, accentuating her words with the delicate arch of a single eyebrow, "perhaps I was wrong to judge your insignificance…" a momentary pause lapsed between them before Desdemona turned away with a flippant hand-gesture to her acolytes, "Show our guest the meaning of subservience to his Queen," her voice echoed behind her as her priests parted from her path and retained a deep bow until she had left.

Only then did one of them remove a single key from

his sleeve, while the other removed twin daggers from his own.

"It'll be quick and to th'point," the priest said, his voice held a disturbing amount of excitement. When he stepped into the torch light, his smile could clearly be seen from beneath the black hood hanging down past his nose.

Flinn watched him fiddle with the lock, his cohort behind him rubbing the blades of his daggers together, one over of top the other in menacingly soft circular motions. The Druid's son's attention went back to the acolyte busying with unlocking the cell door, taking notice of the symbol stitched just above the cuff of the robe's sleeve. That of a grotesque demoniac undead hand, as two fanged icicles dripped from a severed wrist, with a third like a frozen tear—or drop of blood—falling further between them.

The tumblers clicked, but it was not the offered welcome of release that that sound offered. Flinn's heart raced, quickening with the screeching squeal of rusty iron hinges. Perspiring beads ran down from his brow, streaking down his filth ridden face. The acolyte pushed the door inward slowly, purposely, while his companion snickered behind him.

Flinn knew he was in a heap of trouble now, with bad going to worse in seconds. He had to escape, but it would not be an easy task. If only Flinn had the Twins with him, those hungry and feral axes, to use their influence—Hells, even better, if Joden was here—but he had only himself and the time that worked against him.

By this time, the door to the cell was wide open, torchlight backlighting the pair of looming shapes crowding before the open portal, making of them nightmarish shadows. "Worry no', lad, if ye fight us or no' makes no difference to us—it's fun either way," said the dagger wielding acolyte.

Flinn's mind worked frantically now as the acolytes shuffled into the small cell, trying to calculate how he would use this opportunity. Should he act now, risk a tussle with these larger hooded men, or should he wait a moment longer and bide his time? He had to think quickly and decide on the spot. He felt like a rat staring into the excited dilated eyes of a cat.

A warmth grew out from the center of his gut, and the closer he came to impending harm the faster that warmth boiled inside of him, jetting up into a roiling storm of swirling flames. Something inside of Flinn splintered from himself, into something else.

Flinn pushed from the wall, tucked himself tight and led with his dominant shoulder, slamming hard into the nearest of the occultists. He pumped his legs, driving the acolyte back into his armed fellow, but never ceasing the driving momentum of his pumping legs until he pinned one acolyte between the other against the bars of Razjil's cell door.

His pale, clawed hands lurched out from the darkness, taking the knife wield by the arms to begin pulling them achingly through the bars. The acolyte lost the hold of his daggers, clattering noisily and echoing against the stone floor, adding to the disturbance with the snap of bones and tearing of wet flesh. He screamed, blood splattering over Flinn's face, and too focused to notice.

Flinn gave the occultist in front of him a hard right-hand, followed by a heavy left hook, causing the acolyte's head to snap one way and then the other before being shoved to the cold stone. He lay there unconscious while Flinn quickly collected the daggers from the man screaming agony.

The first that came to Flinn's mind was to silence the occultist and did so without thought to thrusting one of the daggers through the man's throat. His screams ended with an abrupt gurgling.

Razjil's face appeared, inhaling deeply. His eyes flashed and rolled up into his head out of some euphoric perversion before pulling back on the occultist's arms to tear them free sickeningly. Blood splattered the floor into great pools, as the armless priest e slid down the bars lifelessly.

Flinn, daggers gripped tight in his hands, his mouth agape at what he had done and at what atrocities Razjil committed. He stood shaking in the hall, the adrenaline ebbing from his body and leaving him to question who he was. But this was not the time to think, for there was still much more for him to act on. A glance behind him showed him the long torch-lit corridor lined at either side with steel barred doors. At the end of that dank and moist hall, the stonework slick and glistening, was the way that would lead beyond the large door at the end.

"Free me," Razjil's voice startled Flinn, glancing back to the prisoner's bloodied face staring at him from behind his cage. "I can help navigate through this place; I can show you the way out!"

Flinn stared long and hard on Razjil, deliberating what he should do. Letting the strange individual out could go either way, but then again, Razjil had been here for an exceptionally long time and would be his best bet for getting out of here.

"Release me!" Razjil begged, "I swear I will not betray you, see, I helped you!" he gestured to the corpse sitting against the bars with a glance.

"Aye…" Flinn was skeptic.

"You'll never make it out of here on chance alone, Wulndarian," Razjil warned and his eyes flickered only once at the key that still remained in the keyhole of Flinn's cell door, "But you must kill *him*…" and then his eyes went to the priest moaning with a slow hand to his head.

The Druid's son glanced between the key and the priest, to the door down the hall, surprisingly not having swung open yet. He rushed for the key first, pocketing it before he came to stand over the priest, holding tight to the twin daggers he held. A battle of objective consciousness warring clearly within his eyes. Instead, he tucked one of the daggers away and reached for the key he had stored and held it up for Razjil to see and then made it disappear into a strong strained fist.

"I will do no such thing, and neither will ye, is that understood?" Flinn said as he stepped over the occultist and gave him another hard right that put him down again. "Promise and I'll set ye free."

"Fine, fine!" Razjil said with no small amount of irritation, "but I will do what I must to ensure our escape—is *that* agreeable?"

"There's one last part of the bargain, Razjil," Flinn eyed the stranger for a hard moment, keeping that icy-ringed gaze of his, "Tell me where I can find the Dark Tome."

Razjil appeared hesitant before answering. But before the moment grew too long, he acquiesced to the demand. "Agreed."

With a heavy sigh, and a scrutinizing stare, Flinn moved warily to unlock the cell door, but before he turned it all the way he captured Razjil's eyes with all attempts to ignore his bloody face. "In exchange for yer help," Flinn felt the need to reiterate their bargain before turning the key.

Razjil nodded before stepping back from the cell door, watching Flinn finish the last turn with an audible tumbling click. The Druid's son pocketed the key once again, preferring he be the one to secure it, and stepped away from the iron barred door.

The odd little man pulled on the bars, opening the door inward, before stepping out. He stood much shorter than Flinn, extremely so. But his short stature did nothing to soften the hideous smile wrapped around his face, showing off his elongated canines. His movements were akin to shadows seeping from within themselves, sinister, yet graceful. Clad was he in dark and tattered garments, hemmed with silver stitching crafted by a fine hand, while grey and white patterns swirling a quarter way up the sleeves of his time eaten robes. The images reminded Flinn of blowing wind through wisps of cloud, but the grey gave up a stormy air about it or most akin to a heavy fog.

His frame was both frail and lithe. He could not have been any taller than five feet. His raven colored hair spilled down his head and past his shoulders in knots and tangles. While long-pointed ears sliced through them, sweeping back gently with a slight rotational flare. Flinn had never seen anyone like him before and could not help but stare back into the dark orbits of Razjil's eyes that made it nearly seem as though he only had empty sockets.

Just when it did not seem possible, Razjil's smile grew wider and appeared to strain his facial features beyond reason. The sight of it, along with a sudden flourishing bow, caused Flinn to step back into a guarded stance, bringing the daggers up with uncertainty. Time was being wasted, and the Druid's son would hate to get into a mix up with this one. He looked dangerously unpredictable and proved as much already.

"Razjil Sha'et Moonglade at your service, once again." He straightened, taking a moment to relish Flinn's apprehensive manner. "We must get to a particular chamber so that I can collect my instruments and you your belongings—I know just where they keep them!" he whispered the last part as if sharing a secret.

"We made a bargain, Razjil," Flinn reminded, "do not make me regret having done so." The conclusiveness of his words was like the glinting edge of the daggers he held, dangerous and radiating ill intents.

"No, no," Razjil put up a protesting hand, assuaging the young man's trepidation by patting the air, "once I make a bargain, *barbarian*, I maintain the accord unless breached by the other—you kept your end, and I shall keep mine." He winked before casting a longing glance down at the unconscious occultist. It looked as though he was battling some inner struggle before wrenching away with a disappointed hum and turned to skitter down the hallway. "Follow me, Wulndarian."

Flinn shook his head, already cursing himself for a fool. He followed the madman down the torch-lit and shadowed corridor. What had been done to that acolyte was unnatural, but a lot of what was happening lately dealt with that overall theme, so it came with little surprise. As far as Razjil was concerned, he had been locked away for a reason. And Flinn knew that later, after all was done, there was an extreme possibility he may have to pay for that later.

Chapter 27

A Hopeful Outcome

It was no wonder anyone had not been alerted to the raucous back in the dungeons, for there were a series of winding stairs leading up from the depths into various chambers, into more corridors, ending with more halls both small and great. Most surprising of all, there no guards anywhere so far along the ascent. And it was an achingly long climb, Flinn feared that his legs would be no good to him once they reached the top of the next stairwell. And happening often, Razjil kept disappearing into the shadowy spaces between the blue torchlight. Setting that oddity aside, the last thing Flinn wanted was to lose sight of the diminutive lunatic and did his best to keep up.

There was a draft along the stairs, like a cool whisper from behind, tickling the length of the spine up until it caused the hackles on the back of the neck to rise. Every once and again, Razjil's face would appear from the shadowed areas between the light, a peeking measure to make sure Flinn was not far behind. So far, the Duldarian managed to maintain the pace set by pointy-eared man's gait, skittish and excitable as it was.

Flinn stepped as quietly as he could while watching him, it almost felt like he was simply floating three steps at a time. It was a taxing endeavor that seemed to stretch on endlessly. Just how far down had Flinn been kept and did the ruins go even deeper than the dungeons, he wondered?

Razjil slowed their pace, casting a glance back to Flinn from the cloak of shadows enshrouding him. "A bit more to go yet, and I'm afraid we'll need tread more carefully now."

Before going any further, the pale ashen-skinned prisoner placed a boney finger to his blood-stained lips, and then turned back into the darkness to appear in the next glow of torch light up ahead.

Letting go a distressful sigh, the Druid's son followed, thinking on the Priest they had left behind and wondering if he had regained conscious by now. Perhaps even already underway to catch them or raise the alarm. Such thoughts caused Flinn to constantly look over his shoulder, but he found looking behind down those steps was more frightening. It reminded him of when his father used to send him down to retrieve something from the cellar back when he and his brother were young.

The memory of Nelvedias caused Flinn to smile, nearly having forgotten about him during all the chaos. Wondering where he was now, or even what he was doing this very moment. Was it just as harrowing as what Flinn experienced, maybe worse?

He followed for a while longer before rounding the next bend in the cold winding stairwell, stopping only because Razjil placed an alarming hand to the Druid's son's chest. His touch was deathly cold, which made Flinn suck air through his teeth and step away.

Razjil only smiled, offering a shrug but immediately tapped his ear and cocked his head to listen. Flinn strained to see if he heard anything himself, but for the life of him there was nothing to indicate imminent danger. No descending footfalls, no bantering, nothing. Only the silence and the faintest draft that haunted the spiraling stairwell.

After several more blinks of passing, Razjil finally gave a satisfying nod to himself before continuing up. Before long, the stairwell coming to an end, the pair of escapees greeted by a large, iron banded wooden door. It stood barring any further progress, heavy and appeared ungiving.

"There are things in this keep that should not be, Wulndarian," Razjil turned before trying the door, his visage became a mask of solemnity, eyes boring into Flinn's own.

"Be on your guard, Warrior."

Flinn was about to say he was not anything of the sword, but he recalled those he had felled with the Twins. And having had to put one of the priests out of his misery after the cruel way he had been torn apart. He flinched from the memory of it. During, Razjil started opening the door, expecting it to creak and moan as the other had deeper within the dungeons. Thankfully, it did not, opening quietly and without resistance.

Peeking through the small space Razjil created, he looked back to Flinn with a crazed smile and a crooking finger to follow. The way he did so was more than off putting, making Razjil even more devious and harder to trust. The Druid's son had to open the door wider still, for the space Razjil made was only wide enough for himself to pass through.

Cursing under his breath, muttering about following child-sized folk, Flinn widened the door and pass on through into a vast pillared hall of shadow, scarcely illuminated by braziers giving off eerie blue light. This hall was by far the largest he had yet seen. The braziers were placed between every third pillar, allowing for vast pockets of darkness to consume much of the magnificent yawning expanse. The pillars themselves were thick and bulbous, ugly in design, with swollen upward spiraling stonework reaching up into a nonexistent ceiling. If there was, it could neither be seen nor fathomed how far up it went. As though the darkness above was more than what it was, it made Flinn feel he was being watched from what hid in the suspended void.

Razjil moved to the right, his stride swift and covering distance efficiently. He moved with a nimbleness Flinn had never witnessed, not even from the most graceful of beasts. Trying to keep up with him, Flinn fell behind him between the wall and the pillared hall at either side to rush up and press against the nearest of spiraling columns

"Are ye sure it's nearby?" Flinn had to ask.

The lunatic pressed a thin finger to his lips, eyes wide

and reprimanding. Razjil gestured to follow, with his dark robes fluttering hauntingly silent behind him. He glided across the dark marbled floor, traveling the twenty or more so strides it took him to move from one pillar to the next. The pointy-eared man's movements were so rat-like and quick. Each time they arrived behind a column, Razjil would cock his ear as if listening for something until he took off again and creep to the next.

He stayed clear from the flames within the braziers, however, Flinn made note of that again, having witnessed do the same with the torches in the stairwells. At last Razjil led Flinn to a great black wall of solid obsidian stretching left to right. Further to the left, a few strides away, a black door could be seen, cast in a cool light from flanking braziers. It looked so plain and oddly placed, and there was nothing about it that made Flinn want to investigate it.

Razjil turned slightly, whispering back to the Druid's son through the darkness, "Through that door they keep all assortment of things, it's there we'll find what you seek."

Flinn noticed Razjil's hesitancy. Something unnerved the little man, looking feverishly about across the open space that spanned between the columns and the door yonder. What was it they were waiting for? Flinn was seconds from asking.

"Stay close," Razjil whispered with one last look about, and then skittered across the hall to the door. The Druid's son rushed behind him and felt immediately vulnerable. Maybe that was what the strange man was feeling. It was a further distance than Flinn anticipated, while instilling a dire need to reach the door to whatever was on the other side of it.

They stopped just before the radius of the brazier's light, staring at the black door I front of them. Flinn constantly looked over his shoulder, feeling watchful eyes bore into his back. He saw nothing looming from the shadows, however. He could very well blame his mind for playing tricks on him, but after all that Flinn had seen, he was not taking any more chances.

"Well, what is it?" Flinn pressed, he was getting anxious and his tone came off a little irritated.

The long-eared man paid it no mind and simply pointed to the door, "You must go, I cannot get too close to their warmth. But you can go, I will alert you of any danger."

"What, why me? I don't know what's in there!" Flinn snapped.

Razjil only smiled and brought his hands together with a bow of his head. He was about to speak when there came a heavy, slithering noise from their right, followed by a hollowed exhaling rasp. Flinn heard it too and twisted around to see what it was that made such a sound. His hands reached instinctually for the Twins, reminded immediately of their absence. All the reason to open that door and get inside.

Along with the dry sound scraping paper, and hollow rasping, a twin pair of glowing blue orbs rose high in the darkness. Razjil moved himself to stand beside Flinn, who had turned fully to face the noise as both looked on in suspense. From the shadows of the pillars, a large swaying shape eventually slithered into the blue light's radius.

Flinn's eyes widened, once more left baffled by the existence of yet another unseen creature. He could feel his entire body tighten, the hairs on his flesh standing on end and an overwhelming need to relieve himself overcame him. He had never seen anything like it before.

"Now would be a good time, Wulndarian." Razjil hissed harshly and shoved Flinn behind him towards the black door, "what you seek is within that room! Look for a green strung bow, a quiver of the same color! Bring those to me after you find your own!" Razjil turned to face the towering, half-man half-serpent undead creature as it continued to slither hypnotically towards them, releasing a drawled hiss.

The Druid's son staggered back a few steps, unable to take his eyes from the entrancing sway and the gleaming blue eyes of the scaled abomination. He had no idea that Feral Folk took such shapes, but this thing was something else entirely different altogether. It came nearer and nearer with no rush at all. There was no sense of urgency in its gait, unbothered with the time it would take for it to reach them, but there was certainly plenty of intent that came with it once it did.

"Don't look at it, just go!" Razjil rasped aloud, the loudest Flinn had yet to hear him, and caused for him to shake himself from the hypnotic trance.

Forcing fear down deep for later day, Flinn made for the black door at an awkward run. A loud hissing filled the immediate area, glancing to see Razjil strafe out of reach of a swiping clawed hand. It nearly appeared that the pointy-eared man became shadow itself. Flinn had no idea if what his eyes witnessed were true or not, but he knew the predicament he found himself in was real enough.

There was little time to slow his momentum fully, as he crashed into the thick door shoulder-first. The jolt of the impact rang through Flinn's body with but cursory recognition, the adrenal-dump that coursed through his veins staunched any pain or injury ordinarily felt. Immediately, not wasting even a blink of time, Flinn fiddled with the iron ring that was the handle—when the door did not budge one way, he instead pushed—and rushed into the next room without any care for danger in wait. He closed the door behind him in that same moment, just in time to capture most of Razjil's hideous laughter before it became muffled.

With his back pressed to the door, Flinn's eyes immediately searched the room. It was large, dimly lit with an eerie cool glow coming from crystals fixed in each corner. The small chamber was reminiscent of a small shop found on the docks of Duldar's Port, a small business dealing in strange things found and traded by seafaring merchants. The walls were lined with shelves and housed all sorts of different weapons, armors, and tools in no order or placement.

But there were cloths neatly folded on tables, or roughly thrown into discarded piles along with shoes and other vestments. Flinn swallowed even when he saw children's toys, add to the twisted perverted shrine of the lost and found. Stories of missing children came to mind, yet another reason now none in Duldar's Port were permitted beyond its walls. But these things all looked old, worn by time, dust ridden, and forgotten.

There were several chests differing in size spread throughout the chamber as well, each one closed with no visible locking mechanism. The chances of his weapons being in one of them was possible, and it made sense to check them first. With one last wary glance about, ensuring nothing lurked in the shadows, Flinn hurriedly pushed from the door, leaving the muffled sounds of combat behind to begin his search. A green bow, arrows of the same color, the Twins, his girdle. That was all he needed, but as he flung open chests, swinging their lids back hard on their creaking hinges, the more he felt he would not find them fast enough. So far, each chest revealed anything *but* what he was looking for.

He rushed over to one of the nearest tables, upon which an array of items was found. His eyes scanned them from top to bottom and left to right, as he ran down the length of the table itself. Still, He did not find what he was looking for. He combed the chamber, moved towards the left-most wall and checking everything in between from the front to the back of the room. He scanned the walls nearest him, still with no luck of finding what he sought.

Hope was draining. What if Desdemona had his weapons kept someplace else in the Keep? The thought made Flinn uneasy, but maybe he could at least find Razjil's bow and quiver.

A vicious exchange drew the Druid's son's attentions back to the black door, hearing the battle rage beyond. How the long-eared man faired would be anyone's guess. Flinn just hoped he did not wind up getting himself killed before leading him to the Dark Tome.

Flinn continued looking, intent on finding the axes as well as the bow. He searched as quickly as he could, sweeping back the way he came, offering another onceover while gradually making his way to the other side of the room. Flinn prayed to Wulndar, Augustinah, seeking their guidance—

Hells, he even prayed to Zhul'Tarrgan—but what he asked from any of them was to help speed his search.

The chamber suddenly crashed open, only to slam shut. Flinn, fear stabbing needles into his back, spun around at the clamor and froze in place. He relaxed slightly at the sight of Razjil, who fit a plank across the door to bar it shut, then spun himself around against it heavily. The portal itself shuddered violently, with the undead serpent-creature obviously trying to get in from the other side. The door looked as though it would hold, but as to how long...

"Nothing?" Razjil spoke, removing himself from the door to help in the search. Not so much as sweat beading from his brow. His robes however appeared to be smoking, and where his pale ashen skin was exposed, he sported small blisters.

"Nothing yet, I still haven't looked in the far corner," Figuring Razjil's wounds a resulting combination from battling with the serpent and perhaps the heat from the braziers, Flinn pointed askance while continuing his search of the place, making his way there himself.

In that corner, however, there was a divider of what may have been cherrywood, and as to what it hid behind it was yet to be discovered. Flinn had paid it little mind, placing most of his focus with what was immediately clear around him. Yet, Razjil moved to it the moment Flinn pointed it out. Traveling through shadow itself, the strange man became a wisp of the trailing stuff that moved faster than the eye could blink. Yet, it was not just all shadow, it was mixed with a fog-like substance similar to that found blanketing over the Moors outside Duldar's Port.

"Here!" he announced excitedly, stepping from around the divider with his bow and quiver in hands. His mood had shifted entirely with the finding of the bow, for it was itself a prize to be had with ends capped in blackened tin, fitted with small emeralds and a green sheen over the polished wood when the light hit it particularly well.

"The axes, my belt?!" Flinn's queries were nigh

hysterical.

Razjil shrugged, shaking his head but looked no more concerned about it now that he had his own belongings back in hand.

Flinn could hardly contain his anger at that and had half the mind to rush the little man and punch him square in the jaw. But before he could take that initial step forward, he noticed the tall closet not far from where Razjil stood. "Check in there!"

Giving into a slight bow, with a stupid grin fixed to his lips, the ash-skinned man did as was bade of him and opened the closet. At first, Flinn's stomach lurched hopelessly when he saw the dusty and moth ridden clothes inside, some stained with old blood. Yet, the longer the Druid's son watched Razjil search the confines of the stand-alone closet, the more doubt of discovery settled.

"Ah, perhaps these?" Flinn's eyes lit up, as Razjil rifled some more through the closet, pulling forth a silver-plated girdle housing two axes. He dropped them with a sharp intake of breath when the silver touched his bare flesh, his eyes flaring angrily. "You keep dangerous tools, Wulndarian!"

Flinn quick-handedly retrieved his belongings, buckling the girdle about his waist securely. A smile started tugging at his lips, the first bit of good luck he got since coming to this damnable place but cleared just as quickly at the loud crash at the door. Worry marred his visage on seeing the plank set across the portal bounce and shudder in its iron hooks. Another crash shook the door, rattling its hinges, the blackened wood finally splintering and threatening to break completely soon enough.

"Stay behind me, friend," Razjil said cheerily.

Flinn needed no other urging.

Stringing his bow with one skilled fluid motion, Razjil plucked the string as a musician would his instrument. He cocked his ear to its thrumming note, a look of euphoria washing over his features before reaching for a slender arrow with green and black-striped fletching. The wood of the arrow had the same green gloss over the shaft as the bow, ending in a serrated-edged arrowhead curling like barbed fishhooks at corners from the tip. And though the arrowhead itself was blackened, there glistened a filmy putrid green coating its surface. He knocked it, caressing the green fletching betwixt middle and forefinger until they settled on the bowstring itself.

A scaly rotted fist punched through the splintered door, coming back out and reaching back through with both hands, tearing the hole bigger, frantically working at stripping the portal down. When the hole looked seemingly large enough, the serpent made several mindless attempts to fit through it but proved too broad of shoulder and bulky of rotted torso to gain direct passage. It thrashed violently until freeing itself to slither away from the door, preparing to charge through the mangled barrier.

Razjil hummed a strange tune as he pulled back on his bow, drawing it until his two first knuckles brushed past his delicate ear. The reversed hold on which he pulled back the bowstring was strange to Flinn, but it looked as though he gained more efficiency from doing so.

A sharp whistling from the arrow split the air as it sped straight and true. It passed through the torn door, just as the sound of the slithering monster's charge initiated. Razjil's arrow remarkably landed between the monster's eyes, shooting through it and into the hall beyond. The half-man half-snake abomination was left unphased, continuing its purposeful advance and forcing itself through the smaller portal.

Razhil's incredulity came in the form of a muttered curse and was all the signal Flinn needed to bring his twin axes to bear. He let out a breath, steadying into calm and allowing the instilling abilities of the Twins to flood through him. Closing his eyes, imagining both Wulfaxe and Ursarctos each ran from Flinn's rock-like fists, climbing the lengthy mountain passes of his arms, to stand up on high upon the peaks of his shoulders.

Flinn opened his eyes in time to watch the long-eared

man draw another arrow with blinding speed. He let it fly, striking true and this time not going all the way through the beast's head. From the arrow, however, there came a toxic glow that dripped from the embedded head of the missile, sizzling, and burning the undead flesh of the snake-man, eating away at its anthropomorphic serpentine face.

Razjil let loose several other arrows, all resulting in the same way. Whatever magical enchantments either the bow or arrows had, they worked. But its momentum took it through the door, crashing with a spray of splinters and bolts and iron bands. The acidity of the enchantments ate away the monstrosity, slowing it down as it lost pieces of itself while deteriorating. Half its face was nearly gone as pushed itself through into the chamber. Its momentum had slowed considerably, but the abruptness of the halting progress made the abomination teeter and sway idiotically.

After a few blinks, the undead creature managed to get to the center of the room, crashing into whatever got in its way before dropping to the floor.

The raven-haired little man stepped around the husk, staying clear of the acidic splashes on the stone floor.

"Mind your footing," he warned.

"We need to move, there could be more," Flinn said in a hurry and moved to the door Razjil currently was peering through. An arrow had already been knocked into his bow.

"We find the door leading up from this place, yes, and then get you out of here," Razjil answered as he stepped lightly over the shattered remains of the door. His steps reminding Flinn of an alley-cat picking its way around refuse. He led them back into the darkened hall and zipped past as fast as he could between the braziers in a cloud of shadows and mist.

Flinn remained vigilant against his situational companion. Just because they worked together now did not mean anything was guaranteed for later. For all he knew, Razjil could very well turn on him at any given instant. The fact that he had not already was surprising to Flinn, but most likely because the pale ashen man was accumulating enough trust to use against him in the end. Fire may well be a valuable ally in that instance.

"How far?" the Druid's son asked, following along the obsidian wall behind Razjil. They kept the pillars to their left.

"If we do not run into trouble, not *too* long," Razjil crept along the path, keeping the bowstring semi-taut and ready as his eyes scanned ahead, sweeping from left to right and back again.

For a time Flinn followed in silence, but something was unnerving him about his escort. He had no idea who he was, what he was or where he was from. Certainly, he was no native to Wulndar, for he lacked both size, physique, and features of such a strongly built people. No, Razjil came from somewhere else, somewhere far and having no business in these lands. Flinn tried to remember what he had been saying about a magical forest someplace secreted away on Es'lyhnn.

They kept going, moving wide of similar doors along the wall. There were no guards about, of which Flinn found strange. Yet, Razjil made them stop and duck behind the shadow of a pillar across from the wall. That same dry sound could be heard whispering in the darkness, slithering across the floor.

"What else is done here?" Flinn asked aghast, unable to see anything but hearing plenty of it.

"Where I come from, there small lizards who skim the waters of our ponds," Razjil whispered only after the slithering had passed. He turned his glowing eyes to Flinn then, twisting his neck impossibly to look over his shoulder much like an owl. "Perhaps once a distant relative?"

Razhil shrugged, righted himself and pressed, taking point once more. Flinn found out more about him in that instant than during the entire course of their time together.

Flinn shook his head, his thoughts were confusing enough already, he did not have the luxury of being distracted by them now. He had to get the tome, escape the Keep and make it back to Duldar's Port before it was besieged. And right now, the only hope of doing so was with this strange little man with a toxically enchanted bow and a hankering for blood.

As the pair used shadow and darkness to cover their path, Flinn's mind wandered once more not long after refocusing. He wished Joden was here with him and wondered what fate he had met at the hands of Thwark and his Wolf-kin. Did he kill many of them before he himself fell to their fangs and claws, or did they dishonor him by their overwhelming numbers, flooding him relentlessly and tossed him over the mountain's edge down into the rushing river below? Flinn's throat tightened, saddened by the Warlord's absence, and in never knowing how he had ended.

With a resigning sigh, the Druid's son focused on following Razjil, all while allowing the swell of anger and retribution flow from his axes and meld with his being. Flinn vowed to avenge Joden Bear-Blade, and to ensure that his memory lived eternally.

Chapter 28
A Bit Further

The image reflecting at Desdemona, looking into the wall of high polished obsidian, revealed Baar'Dahl standing in his hunched way. The Ghar'tul War-Chief wore his more monstrous hybrid form, as others of his clan milled about behind him against the backdrop of dark forest. A bright full moon hung in a black night sky, an eager waiting eye.

"Are you in position, Dark-Brow?" Desdemona referred to him by his clan name, for her to address him otherwise was beneath her. *He* served *her,* not the other way around.

Baar'Dahl dipped his great horned head, smeared across the brow with dark warpaint, as like the rest of his clansmen. "We oversee last minute preparations, but we are in position, Dreaded One," he bleated, beating a strong fist against his bulging chest as emphasis.

Desdemona glared with sharp eyes and nodded approval. She then started pacing within the limited view of the mirror, a delicate hand framing her chin thoughtfully.

A large firepit roiled behind her, silhouetting her frame against the blue light, and setting her apart from the overall shadowy hall of her throne room. Straight columns stood erect around the large rectangular parameter, holding up the second floor. Beneath the colonnade was only darkness, but the scarce light that was able to reach it revealed a writhing consistency.

She turned once more, still thoughtful, as she walked from beneath the colonnade and into the center of the Hall towards the dais upon which her waited. The mirrored wall detached itself with the chipping of stone, following behind her as if Baar'Dahl was there to move it. After situating herself on the plush cushioned seat, Desdemona chose that moment to break from her contemplation.

"You will wait until Redeyes and his pack arrive, whether he gets there tonight, or tomorrow or even the next day—"

"My Lady, you *promised*!" Baar'Dahl interrupted her, and his long floppy goat ears drooped soon after he blurted the words. His eyes lowered, cursing himself for a fool.

Desdemona offered the faintest murmur of a smile, much like a wolf who watches the unwary doe from the shadowy brush.

"So, I did," she said more to herself than to her general. "Fine. Launch your attack. But I will require a harassing approach. Sporadic and periodic attacks only, keep them on their toes until the bulk of my forces gather for the final assault," Desdemona paused a moment before adding, "should you see mobilize and strengthen, break them and disengage. I want their spirits shattered at the folly of their resistance."

Baar'Dahl bowed his head, accepting the order without protest. He would have preferred to take Duldar's Port before the next sunrise, but there were only three different clans who had agreed to unify beneath Desdemona's banner, and none of the Mountain Clans were among them. Maybe there were not so foolish to bend their knee for a second time before the Pale Lady, and each encounter with her left Baar'Dahl strengthened that sentiment.

Then again, Desdemona hardly needed them at all, not with the undead forces that beckoned her call, despite their small but nightmarish numbers, the Dark Tome empowered the Pale Lady's abilities. Baar'Dahl shivered at the thought of those abominations flooding the city streets, not fully trusting Desdemona's control over them. He gathered enough of his courage, and dared to ask, "Will that be all, my Queen?"

Her eyebrow arched, along with the faintest of smiles. She was amused by the Ghar'tul's discomfort and relished in his anxiety to rid of their exchange. "For now."

He gave into a low bow and then made to turn from her but stopped when Desdemona called out to him.

"Oh, Baar'Dahl…" her smile returning fully with a gentle tilt of her head, "Redeyes will be the one to kill High Lord Ranarek."

Baar'Dahl visibly bristled, infuriated by her decree, and looked as if he was going to protest. Before he could, Desdemona dispelled the communication mirror. It broke inward to crumble and shatter.

She laughed. Delighting at her enabling, enjoying her instigating, swimming in the pool of her chaotic influence over the simple-mindedness of the Feral Folk and taking pleasure in the smaller reprimands she handed out.

During her time since her reawakening, Desdemona's power had grown daily. It took time to regain its full height, which is why she had to act fast in taking Duldar's Port, the Wulndarian youth and that city posed her greatest opposition from Wulndar's total domination. As for the Feral Folk Clans of the wilds, they could be handled easily enough. She would off one last chance for them to follow her, should they refuse for a second time… then, so be it.

She could rest assured now that she had young Duldarian captive, who would have otherwise been a problem in her schemes. But, with him in her possession, Desdemona was free to continue with her plans without worry. Razjil's inability to foresee his part in all of this had ruffled her considerably, which left little room for chance. Perhaps she would keep the Duldarian youth as a plaything, that is if her priests had not beaten too harshly.

Whatever they were, the things kept crawling and clambering over one another trying to get to Flinn and Razjil in a hurry. Before reaching the other side of the vast pillared hall, their presence had been discovered by emancipated and raggedly clad hairless creatures slavering at the jaws. They were of all sizes, of both Feral-Folk and Duldarian, but they all shared the same pale flesh that pulled taut across their bones and with the same burning frigid hunger in their eyes. The snake folk had been but a taste of the horrors that roamed the massive hall, and now were privy to the presence of life wandering its pillared expanse. They came from their shadows in hot pursuit of Flinn's warm flesh and blood all of the sudden, surprising even Razjil.

Flinn followed the pointy-eared man at a hard sprint, following the wall west until a pair of standing braziers revealed a shadowy portal with steps leading up. Both made for it, this time Razjil was heedless of the burning he felt from the proximity of the brazier's light and the Druid's son was not far behind him as his companion physically started smoking after passing between them.

The clacking of anticipatory jaws echoed up behind them as the pair ascended yet again another winding stairwell. Flinn wondered if that was all this keep was made up of, vast halls and spiraling steps. It was enough to make him sick and eager to leave the place. But he had to retrieve the Dark Tome. That was his whole reason for being here, even though he had no intention in arriving in the way that he had.

Claws scrabbling in the darkness sent shivers up Flinn's spine, he could feel that the scurrying undead fiends were close. He dared a glance, saw one of the pale things round the bend of the stairwell wall, and the sight of it was something a child would have nightmares about. Hells, *he* himself will have nightmares. More of them pushed and shoved, climbing, and clambering over one another in a frenzy, snapping at each other as they went, having no qualms in expressing violence against their own.

Higher and higher up the stairwell Flinn and Razjil raced, the ghouls getting closer, until Flinn felt his ankle pulled back and out from under him. He pitched forward, hitting hard his knee into the next ascending step, and stumbled down hard to the stone. He half turned, already knowing what had hold of him, and chopped into the ghoul's outstretched arm. Hacked and slashed, furiously now that the ghoul took hold with both clawed hands. Its long fingers curling around the toe and heel of Flinn's boot, pulling him back as the rest of its horrific ilk closed in from behind it.

Rotted, chipped, and serrated teeth bit down over his boot while cold eyes burning with a ravishing hunger for flesh.

The sharp whistle of Razji's arrow streaked a mere inch from the Druid's son's head, lodging right into the ghoul's brow, snapping its head back and sending it to crumple into its filthy kin. That gave Fliin just enough time to get to his feet, scrambling up the stairs. Razjil let loose two more arrows in quick succession of one another, each finding a mark and all of them deteriorating their targets.

"Best not to fiddle with these ones, Wulndarian, their bite is worse should they find your flesh and you'll not like what changes come thereafter," Razjil let go two more arrows before he spun on his heel and took off up the steps, slowing the undead creatures only briefly, jamming them up while fighting over the slain, and long enough for Flinn to generate distance as he continued on.

There was no time for thanks, Flinn quickly reminded himself what could happen should the undead dig their hooks in the living and he had no wish to experience *that* again. The ghouls continued to swarm up the steps after them, taking up the chase anew, but it would not take long for them to reach the escaping duo.

Before long, the top of the stairs came to view, leveling out into a small landing where a door awaited them. Razjil made for the door quickly and gave it a push. It opened easily, revealing dim illumination and a sudden gust of cool air beyond. Flinn pushed from behind, both slipping into the next chamber, and slamming the door shut behind them. Razjil bade Flinn to maintain pressure, fighting to do so the moment the crazed little man removed himself to lift a bar latch and drop it into place across the door. He gave a nod, signaling it would hold for the time being.

Scrabbling and pounding sounded on the other side as Flinn pushed away from it, but he was not shaken by fear, not while gripping tight the bone handles of the Twins. He was ready should they break through, wielding the axes and satisfying their lust for battle. But he was surprised they had not tried and convince Flinn of fighting along the stairwell. Perhaps they felt his overwhelming desire not to engage the undead creatures.

Turning his gaze to Razjil, hardly breathing or not at all it seemed, he impatiently gestured for the Druid's son to follow him. The room was some sort of ritual chamber. A colossal bronzed basin sat at the centermost area of the large room, resplendent with a high dome-tiled ceiling above and painted masterfully in a mosaic image of a woman with widespread arms, gowned in cool colored robes of blues and greys.

Her face could not be seen, hidden behind a great horned mask. Flinn swallowed hard, looking away from the ceiling to the lines of pews set to face a large podium elevated atop hewn obsidian overlooking the chamber itself. A single steepled archway led into darkness behind it and to either side an ascending flow of steps leading up from the apparent congregational area.

Yet, it was the banner hanging from the precipice. Black as the night, with the same symbol Flinn had noticed on the priest's sleeve back in the dungeons. He wondered about that same man now, curious whether he caught up to the undead mob assailing the door presently or had been torn apart by them along his way. Glancing back to the portal, watching for a moment as it rattled against the latch-bar, Flinn hoped it would hold, not wanting to share in the same possible fate as the priest.

"They'll not get through, or at least not yet—this way, Wulndairan," Razjil's assuring tones brought Flinn back from his dead stare.

The pointy-eared man walked down the center isle

towards the precipice, bow at the ready as he stalked towards the left-most stairs. Wary of their sudden luck at relieving themselves of the ghoulish menace, Flinn followed with keen eyes and an ear for the slightest sounds, though he was sure that Razjil would hear anything long before him with those long, pointed ears of his.

Up the short narrowing flight of stairs and to the steepled opening behind the podium, Razjil led Flinn further along a straight hall leading away from the chamber. "We're getting closer," he said without a backward glance.

Following in silence, Flinn's thoughts kept him from a response. Having gone this far along his journey, and with what Razjil informed, he was ready for anything at this point. If they were closer to his goal, then they were that much closer to being away from this forsaken place. Yet, something settled uneasily in his gut.

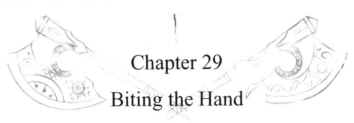

Chapter 29
Biting the Hand

Thwark Redeyes stood staring into the fireplace of blue flames, casting its light into lounge on the main floor of the Keep. Paintings hung from all four walls of maddening motifs, nightmarish images of abominable creatures, and a large painting of Desdemona that hung just above the fireplace. The main portal divided from the outer hall by silken curtains of sanguine, pulled back and kept in place with silver braided cords looped over small hooks in the likeness of skeletal hands. The room felt alive with writhing shadows, keeping Thwark and two of his captains' company.

Redeyes trusted Desdemona as much as he would trust a goblin, and that was not at all. His captains fidgeted, openly uncomfortable waiting in this ghastly room. Thwark thought he would have been ordered out of the Keep and sent towards the city by this time, but Desdemona wanted a word with him.

Speaking of the whore herself, Redeyes spotted her at the doorway after a casual glance, momentarily caught unaware of her presence. A supercilious smile creased her lips while her eyes took in the trio before her. Thwark stared, waiting for her to speak, or say *something*, but she appeared content to make them uncomfortable.

"You will lead the main assault when the time comes, leave Baar'Dahl and the rest of the Ghar'tul to harass the city until I give the word," Desdemona dipped her chin down softly, glaring intensely, "is that clear, Redeyes?"

The Pack Master lifted his chin, curling his upper lip slightly. "And the High Lord?"

Desdemona rolled her eyes and shook her head with a

dismissive hand, "Yes, yes, yours to do with what you will. Now will you do as I ask, or shall I inform Baar'Dahl to reap that glory as well?"

Thwark grunted acquiescence, irritated that he had waited so long for so few words.

"You can be quite the insufferable, flea ridden beast," Desdemona commented aloud, not bothering to mask her disgust and turned away back into the main hall to leave the Wolf-kin alone.

Redeyes stared after her listlessly, find that hate was too soft a word to describe what he felt for her. If he had half the right of mind to tear her apart, he would have done it just then. He signaled to one of his subordinates, who moved quickly to the portal and peek beyond, after a brief observant moment, he glanced back with an affirming nod.

Thwark nodded and led his captains out into the ruined long hall. Not many guards were posted, perhaps fewer than two hands on the main floor. The second floor would have to be found out later, but there was one place Redeyes knew a good majority of Desdemona's followers would be found. It was well into the night, and many would find rest in these wee hours.

While most of Desdemona's deadlier forces were underway to lend aid to the Ghar'tul, it was a prime time to take advantage of a rare opportunity. Thwark gestured for one of his captains to make for the main doors, the guards watching him curiously as they allowed him to slip past.

Redeyes's Pack were just outside, gathered in a massive courtyard and playing as though they were preparing for the trek to Duldar's Port. But they would not reach the city this night, waiting instead for the Pack Master's word.

Redeyes knew that once he had that black book in his possession, Zhul'Tarrgan would find him worthy again to receive more blessings of power. To rule all Wulndar as it was meant to be. He had no care for Duldar now, that would come later. With the power of the Dark Tome, the strength of The Pack and the grace of the full moon, Zhul'Tarrgan would shower Thwark in with his boons boundlessly. There would be naught to stop him after that.

Thwark and his remaining captain crossed the expanse of the Great Hall to a great wooden door on the other side just beneath the colonnade supporting the second floor. Redeyes opened it, stepping inside to a large dimly lit. Rows of beds lined to the left, right, and back walls. Most of occultists were sound asleep, while others looked up from borrowing their noses in old books or from reciting dark prayers.

"Seek ye a bed, Wolf-kin?" an acolyte asked. He made no effort to hide the insincerity from his voice.

Redeyes looked back to his captain, stepping in from behind and shutting the door. Without notice, he locked the latch in place, giving it single tug to ensure that it was secure. There were no guards in this room, a pity for these poor fools who sought rest during such tumultuous times. Redeyes, while holding confused stares, took two powerful steps forward, eying the occultists who now felt something was off with the Pack Master's demeanor.

The scrape of steel against leather sounded as Thwark's captain unsheathed an identical pair of board swords form his hips. Seeing this, one of the priests nearest Thwark half stood, worry on his face. "What's happened, have the Duldarians marched on us?"

Redeyes looked to his left, eying and smiling at the priest as those others who were awake waited for an answer. Thwark's only response was a quick single-handed upward swing of his weapon to the nearest to the priest. The bit lobbing off half of his head away from chin to crown, and it was all the signal needed to commence the slaughter.

From behind the closed door, back in the long hall, howls sounded as the sounds of battle ensued. All while Thwark and the captain went about the massacre of the priests and acolytes, cutting down those who stood to oppose them easily, and with far more ease as they executed those too slow in waking. What better time than now when such betrayal was least expected?

The guards had little time to organize as the decrepit hall suddenly became flooded with Wolf-kin, their shapeshifted packmates making quick work of Desdemona's followers, then bounding to climb their way up to the second floor. Desdemona came rushing out from her private chambers, the railing stopping her from going over completely and looked down over the chaos. Her enraged gaze swept left to right, with a face contorting to compliment the burning cold of her eyes.

"Foul dogs!" she screeched, raising her left hand as a swirl of frost gathered within clutching fingers, "you're all filth!" Desdemona's arm swung down, tossing the gathering sphere of cold and setting it loose down into the Wolf-kin mob, heedless whether her own followers were caught in the blast.

The swirling mass only grew as it flung over the Wolf-kin and her guards, consuming them in a storm of snow and ice. Some slipped on moss-colored stones, losing their footing, and making an easy catch for the mini snowstorm that crackled over them, encasing them in a tomb of ice.

"Ungrateful mongrels!" Desdemona levitated up and over the railing, drift down from the second floor like an apparition, shooting conjured spikes of ice aimlessly without a care who they speared.

Those Wolf-kin who fell before her had risen from their deaths with but a graceful sweeping of Desdemona's hand. She had only look upon their corpses and willed the breath of life to reanimate their husks, illuminating their eyes with the same frigidity filling the hall. But they were mere fodder to be flung against the surging Wolf-kin still pouring through the ruined Keep's doors.

"I'll put you *all* down like strays!"

Desdemona moved through the tumult, searching

furiously for the only one responsible for this betrayal, and knew further this to be a battle now for supremacy. She cursed herself for the fool, knowing she should have laid the filthy Pack Master low, should have forced the Wolf-kin to her heel with more force!

Anger only heightened her rage as she searched for Thwark, but he was yet to be found. Until realization dawned. Redeyes meant to take the Dark Tome! Desdemona threw out a repulsive power of cold, sending Wolf-kin and undead alike outwards in a ten-foot radius. Leaving in its wake horrific ice sculptures lost to time.

Making for the door set behind her throne, Desdemona shot upward and flew down the long hall over the battle. More of the filthy beasts came in from the outside, making it apparent that there was hardly any opposition stopping them from coming in. Once again, she cursed herself for being so lax. This would not have happened had she taken the proper precautions, especially when dealing with Redeyes and his father's pack those many years ago. She realized Thwark did not share his father's loyalties, again she cursed herself for a fool!

Once behind her throne, she immediately saw that the door had been forced inward, with two of the guards she had left there torn apart. Their blood smeared the floors and walls, leaving their bodies mutilated from brutal deaths. Desdemona wasted no more time, shooting through the open portal into a small round chamber where a columned wall of stone greeted her at the center, from which a flight of spiraled stairs both led up and down. She glided up the winding stairwell, intent on getting to Thwark before he laid his filthy hands on the book.

If Flinn never climbed another stairwell again, he would be happier for it. They had been climbing for longer than Flinn cared for. Until Razjil held up a hand, slowing their pace. The Druid's son fidgeted with the Twins. His heart beating hard and quick, listening to catch sounds of battle echoing down to them, as well as with the all-too-familiar howling from the Wolf-kin.

There were no torches here along the stairs, only the light that poured in a few steps ahead of them, but that did nothing to ease Flinn from the ghastly image Razjil painted as the ash-skinned man looked back at him. Those glacial eyes sparkled in the darkness, floating rings within the shadows as though there was no face there at all.

"Continue up these stairs, they will lead you to where the book is kept, but from here we part ways. But I do thank you for your aid." Razjil said.

Flinn opened his mouth in protest, made to take a step closer as if he were to rush the strange man, but those twin glacial eyes suddenly winked out of sight, stopping him cold. That was it then. Flinn was on his own here on out. He moved cautiously up the stairs after a collecting moment, amazed how swiftly Razjil had vanished and how quick he was to leave Flinn's side. He supposed it was better than having the strange man turn on him completely, and technically speaking, he *did* uphold his end of the bargain after all.

He heard a trailing whisper further up the stairs, "Fates favor you, Wulndarian..." Then nothing but the song of death, rage, and iron.

Flinn blew out a breath of irritation, "Shit."

His eyes followed the steps to where the blue light could be seen, where he was sure Razjil had gone and no doubt without notice. It must be nice to have supernatural abilities such as those he possessed, but if it was at the same cost Flinn had witness of the pointy-eared individual, then it was probably best he did not have any. An archway came into view ahead, and from beyond it the sounds of battle came clearer. Pressing himself against the inside wall of the stairwell, Flinn would have to be quick in passing, fearing he may be noticed going up the stairs if not careful enough.

"Damn everything," Flinn cursed under his breath.

But he had a duty to his father, he had a duty to Duldar's Port and the hundreds of people who depended on him. Even if he felt out of place in the city, he still had a love for it. Even the thought of the Dock Master's sons being harmed by the hands of Desdemona's abominations, or the fangs of the Wolf-kin unsettled him. It was time for Flinn to see this to the end, for if he did not, the fate of Wulndar hung by a taught thread ready to be cut.

The battle sounded relatively far enough away, but that did not mean it could not spill out to him at any given moment. Swallowing down his nervousness, taking heart that the Twins were in his possession, Flinn made the decisive decision to rush past the archway and continue up the winding stairs. Behind him he could hear a struggle beyond the chamber leading out to the main hall, heard too a door crash open followed several battle cries, and those of the dying as well. Flinn pumped his legs hard, taking two, sometimes three steps at a time, moving as fast as he could with hopes that his passing had gone unnoticed. There was no telling what waited at the top of these stairs, and there was certainly no excitement in finding out.

Up, up, up he went, until he climbed high where the only light came from the moon outside, filtering in through arrow loops to Flinn's left. His legs started burning, still unused to so much physical duress. He had never run so much in his life, had never been chased in fear of being killed before and had never exerted so much energy in just trying to stay alive! The stairs went higher and higher, round and round until they could take Flinn no further.

Another door at the top of the stairs, thick of wood and banded with black iron and hinges, yet they were rusted and worn. Moss grew from the stone walls, slick and slimy, glistening should the outside light hit it. Flinn swallowed, approaching the last the door where on the other side the Dark Tome waited.

Commotion echoed back up to him from further down the stairwell, forcing Flinn to make the final decision and reached for the rusted latch, lifted, and pushed the door open with a disruptive groan. A short flight of stairs yawned open before him, leading up from the floor to a large circular room filled with black light, and a large conical roof above. To the right there was a large winching mechanism fashioned into the stone wall, and a series of large gears and chains that ran up to a similar mechanism to disappear into the shadows of the rafters. At the center, levitating inches above a busted lectern, was the Dark Tome.

Flinn closed the door quickly behind him, already feeling the pressure from the immense power radiating from the book. The sound of rushing feet echoed from beyond the door, forcing Flinn to find a hiding place. Moving quickly, ducking behind the winching system, he crouched low behind the large rusted gears. Just as he situated himself, the door burst open and a pair of red eyes came up the small flight of steps.

Flinn would never forget the face that condemned Joden to death, and so was again the same face of Thwark Redeyes who climbed the last step straight for the Dark Tome. A small handful of Wolf-kin clambered up, spreading out but kept clear from the permeating power of the black book. It probably would not take long before they noticed Flinn, but he made no sound whatsoever, fighting the urge to leap out and cleave the Twins into Redeyes' skull. He gave their handles a reassuring squeeze, asking for a bit more time.

The Wolf-kin moved further into the tower spire, casting their eyes about, but never directly over Flinn's. Two of the warriors stood to either side of the steps leading back out of the room, two others stood a few steps behind Thwark, keeping a reasonable distance from the Dark Tome and the corrupting power it permeated.

As Flinn let the building courage and battle lust rise within him, a hideous screech shook the tower. Dust shifted down from the rafters, rattling lightly the chains above, just as Desdemona floated up the steps between the two left to guard the door.

"I'll dry your hides in the sun after peeling it from your bones, you treacherous dogs!" Her hands shot out to either sides, expelling jets of ice into the guards. They backpedaled, throwing up their arms to shield themselves, but they were left frozen. "Did you believe to best me, Redeyes, you and your pathetic uprising will be crushed beneath my heel!"

This was an unexpected circumstance not yielding to a favorable outcome, Flinn clearly made that summation. While in his mind he rambled over several different scenarios, none of which seemed to end well. His concentration was broken under the weight of her diabolically laughter, leaving Flinn baffled that such a tiny woman could sound so cruel.

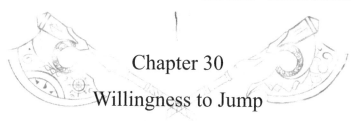

Chapter 30
Willingness to Jump

Livid certainly was not enough to describe the twisted features contorting Desdemona's face, her burning eyes were all for Thwark the moment the ugly bastard came into her view. The last remaining dogs accompanying him waited for his command to be set loose. She wanted him to give the word, so that she could dismember them in a wash of blood and wet flesh. And afterward, Desdemona would see that Thwark Redeyes did not even have a chance to gurgle his agony.

"Traitorous wretch," she spat the words venomously, each emphasizing her hatred, "you and *all* your ilk will pay dearly for this." She laughed and Thwark's signaling grunt sent his remaining escorts upon her.

Flinn watched as she snatched one of his warriors up without touching him, and with but a discarding wave of her clutching hand, the Wolf-kin was flung up and through the wooden planks of the roof, with naught but splintered debris and dust trailing beneath the monster. Its snarling sounds, yips and yowls grew more distant by the second until nothing.

The second came upon her, rushing forward, but stopped dead in his tracks within her stare; one Flinn had suffered once before himself. Her eyes burned brighter as she held the Wolf-kin's gaze in her own. He reversed the hold on the blade of his broadsword, placing the tip into his belly meticulously before shoving it through himself. Blood spilled from his mouth, flowing over his thick wiry beard before falling to his knees and topple over.

Thwark looked on. If he was afraid the Pack Master

did not show it as he stood facing down the Pale Lady as he moved around so that the Dark Tome was between them. Desdemona stalked towards them. Her every step graceful and purposely set, moving via Thwark, with neither of them wise to Flinn's presence, praying to that it remained to be a while longer.

"What wasn't enough for you, Redeyes?" Desdemona asked, now pacing, "did you not have a big enough part, or were you so hungry for power you would do anything, even if it meant the slaughter of your entire pack?"

Thwark stood strongly defiant, his posture proud and reminiscent of Joden. There was something about Thwark that set him apart from his kin, though, and maybe it *was* that defiant glare he sent back to the Pale Lady.

The Twins were getting restless, that much could be felt. But Flinn kept reminding them just a little while longer before they could feed and get their fill. It was understood now that they truly were sentient, in a manner of speaking, and like the great beasts they were so too did they require sustenance to stay strong. What that meant for later days, however, Flinn was unsure. He just wanted to wait a bit more, see how this exchange played out and taking advantage of the time it took before being noticed by either Desdemona or Thwark.

The small statured woman threw one insult after another towards Redeyes, hoping his own anger would blind him into acting impetuously. Flinn had to admit he was impressed at the Wolf-kin's resolve, for neither did he make for the tome or move to attack.

"Your filthy paws aren't worthy to possess such power!" Desdemona snarled with a curling upper lip, "do you truly think that the blessings given to your father were passed down to you? The gods do not work as mortals do; they bestow their boons on those worthy enough to receive them. And certainly not to those who slay their kin to possess their power for themselves."

Thwark sucked at one of his upper canines, wiped at

his mouth with one hand casually and then spat at the floor to his right. Desdemona's words seemed to have little affect over the Pack Master. But not once did he remove his eyes from her.

Thwark's right hand tightened around the long haft of his bearded ax, the head of which resting on the floor. Flinn held no doubts that the Pack Master could heft that weapon up within a blink, as well as with minimum effort.

"Tell ye what, lass," Redeyes's voice rumbled out, "Ye turn around, go back down to the cellar and get back in ye're casket—and then maybe, if ye play real nice, I'll let ye up every once in a while for supper."

Desdemona lifted her chin at that, lifting a single eyebrow. "Oh, such words are like a blade thrust into my already decayed heart." She laughed, a cackling unlike anything Flinn had heard before, turning his blood to ice. After her merriment subsided, Desdemona cocked her head to the side looking Thwark over before her eyes flared and flew across the space between them, knocking over the lectern to send the tome floating off to the side.

"I'll just rip and tear you apart for fun," she reached out with clawed fingers and a demented smile marring her pretty face.

Flinn felt sick simply looking on her now, but he could not tear his eyes away, he could not waste a moment should the opportunity present itself and it surely would be soon. He could feel it in his gut and with the tome no longer between them, the Druid's son may have a chance to make a grab for it.

But suddenly, a few strides away from Desdemona's reaching hands, Thwark smiled. "Don't worry, I'll make sure ye get a big enough piece," and just as he finished his words Redeyes strafed to his right, grasping the long handle of his ax in two hands and stabilized his footing for a huge up-and-over downward chop as Desdemona's reaching fingers came nigh for his throat.

The blade severed her at the forearms, the limbs plopping to the floor. She screeched, but not from pain, for her agitation was too clear to see. And before Redeyes could wind up and finish the job, Desdemona's form became vaporous and rose as if lifted by fire's heat. Flinn followed the vaporous cloud, only able to make out the glowing pair of glacial eyes as the transformed woman shifted like a cloud by strong winds.

"Face me, Witch!" Thwark boomed and then made to seem as though he was going for the tome.

The vaporous cloud let loose a shriek and dropped from the height of the ceiling, going for the baited trick Flinn Thwark's movement to be, intent on swallowing both Redeyes and the tome. Instead, Flinn watched as Thwark spun and brought his ax about, only to cut through her vaporous form harmlessly. An echoing laugh followed at the attempt.

"Fool!" she rasped before rushing away from Thwark towards the tome, solidifying along with both of her arms grown as though they had never left her. She looked desperate and that desperation made her seem less powerful in Flinn's eyes. The simple way that she looked reminded him of a child realizing her toy was about to be in the hands of another. Was Desdemona so dependent on the black book that she threw away all caution to the wind?

Thwark must have thought so too, for he had rushed her in an instance, preventing her for reaching for the Dark Tome, deceiving her with a thrust to push her back, only to come back down with a hacking chop that drove her to the floor. The bit of the weapon had been driven deeply into her shoulder, the force of which driving her to her knees. Thwark wrenched the ax free unkindly, before he could swing down a second time. Desdemona's form vaporized once more and dispersed like a stream of pipe smoke blown into solid stone.

Once more, Desdemona's vaporous form shifted and drifted frantically from side to side, up and down until she solidified a few strides away from the cranking mechanism with her back to Flinn. He immediately swallowed, for she was far too close for his liking and she kept gliding backwards until all she had to do was turn around and reach for the handle of the crank. Without looking, she did just that, and began to turn the mechanism that initiated the clanking of gears as heavy chains rattled. Flinn held his breath, fearful that his exhale would tickle her flesh as a fly tickles the strands of a spider's web.

A wooden wall lower, opening outwards from the tower. As it opened further and further, the light of the full moon poured its light into the spire, revealing beyond the canopies of Howler's Wood.

The Dark Tome drifted towards, as if by some lunar magnetism. But somehow Flinn knew it was not simply just the moon that empowered it, for the tome itself held power all its own. Perhaps even a mind expressive of its own will.

"No!" Thwark started after it but stopped when the book suddenly moved out quickly in response, almost appearing to enjoy the chase, if that could be possible.

Until Flinn realized it was the book that moved on its own, nor the moon that pulled it, but Desdemona's outstretched hand using whatever malign, unseen powers to push the tome out of Thwark's reach. Her glittering eyes shifted onto Thwark, her smile daring him to pursue the book further.

"I can simply float down and get it, but you—" Desdemona smiled, "such a fall would leave you broken and mending for days—I doubt the son of a murdered champion could survive even that—but, I'll prolong your miserable existence longer after that, Thwark Redeyes I've had plans for you for some time yet."

If Flinn could afford to curse, he would, but he feared drawing attention to himself. But this suddenly became a far more precarious situation. Unless he acted right this moment. Even so, what in the Hells did he expect to accomplish. There was no way he would be able to fight both the Pack Mastr and the Pale Lady.

The book was too far, Redeyes and Desdemona both were in the way, and yet Flinn still held the element of surprise. For once, he was thankful for his shorter stature and smaller frame. There would be no way for an average Wuldnarian to hide where he currently hid.

He heard Wulfaxe's distant howls, commencing the thrill of the hunt, he heard the echoes of Ursarctos' mountain trembling roars, trumpeting empowerment. They called from within, causing the ax handles to vibrate and create an almost numbing sensation in Flinn's hands. He felt it in his arms, jolting his shoulders and reverberating his eyes. Everything appeared clearer with heightened definition, his nose was sharper and was able to smell the covering perfume that tried to hide the stench of decay from Desdemona. His heart beat faster, causing a deep drumming of war that rushed his blood into his ears, allowing him to pinpoint every utterance of sound with profound accuracy.

The time for waiting had ended and it was time now to change the course of Wulndar.

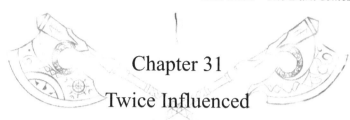

Chapter 31
Twice Influenced

Desdemona pushed the book a little further out, maintaining her smile over Thwark. Nearing the edge of the overhanging platform, the Dark Tome threatened to go completely over. The Pale Lady could see Redeye's hesitancy now, torn between what he wanted to do and what might happen should he risk doing it. Reminding her much as a dog would, wanting the bone at the same time its master tells it to heel. Oh, how she enjoyed watching the squirming wave of emotions crease his brow.

"What*ever* will you do?" she cooed, bringing her freehand to her breast in mock fear.

Redeyes bit his inner cheek, clearly fighting indecision. Then, as if he had to even think about it, Thwark rushed towards Desdemona with his wicked ax trailing behind him.

The Pale Lady's eyes widened for just a moment, slightly surprised by the Pack Master's decision but no less prepared. Letting loose a maddening laughter, she spun away like a dancer and just in time to evade the Pack Master's attack. The bit of the weapon clanged into the gears, bouncing off from them and sent sparks flying. Flinn jolted, his axes crossing to form a defensive **X** in front of him. He only hoped that his own actions had not been noticed.

But Redeyes went with the momentum of his attack, swept up in the moment of it, taken by the powerful force of his swing and followed the ax's trajectory into the stone floor. The shock of the impact hurt his hands, sending pain halfway up forearms. But then, the hackles on the back of his neck rose and causing his muscular back to tense. He turned slightly, enough to lay eyes on the Druid's son.

The young lad held frozen for just a moment, until Thwark mouthed the words "help me" before spinning off and launching himself into a charge towards Desdemona. Yet, as Flinn watched the Pack Master at work, with his seemingly reckless swings and misses, in how the Pale Lady edged closer and closer with every dodge and evasive maneuver. Until Flinn realized that Redeyes was herding her towards him.

Shit. Flinn cursed. It was bad enough that Thwark knew he was there, but if Desdemona became aware of his presence then things would get a little hairy.

Flinn waited until she was drifted closer to him, amazed at her ability to deftly retaliate or counter any of Thwark's attacks. She continued to wear that horrid smile over her tantalizing lips, taking humor in how pathetic the Pack Master's efforts were. She was toying with him, Flinn could see that plainly, and where Thwark once had the upper hand it was the Pale Lady who was now unrelenting. She slowed her pace now, watching as she relished Redeye's growing fatigue. Delightfully turning aside one lazily lobbed strike after another.

She clapped her hands together gleefully, turning them to interlock her fingers and pointed them directly towards Thwark. From their tips a small sphere of cold manifested and shot forth an arrow's width beam of frost.

Redeyes took the beam directly to the groin, causing him to grunt painfully and double him over. Desdemona laughed pleasingly, the frost spreading through his hips, down his legs and up his torso. Each step he took to get closer to the witch was harder than the last, until Thwark was eventually left frozen in mid chop right before he reached her. The ice stopped just below his bone-pierced earlobes, leaving his nostrils clear.

Flinn knew that Redeyes was now at the mercy of the Pale Lady, but he was one less problem to worry about, for Desdemona was clearly more of a dangerous threat. The Druid's son bided his time, he had one chance to deliver a significant blow, and if he botched the only opportunity he had, then all Wulndar would suffer for it. It was not until that moment he realized much hung on the balance, solely based on what Flinn decided to do next.

"So close," Desdemona made a pouting face and lifted a hand to trace her finger over Redeyes' brow. She smiled, giggled a little. "You see—"

Desdemona's eyes bulged with confusion, slender shoulders leaping up to her ears, while small body went stiff. The Pack Master stared wide-eyed, not quite sure what had happened himself, until Flinn wrenched free the Twins from either side of Desdemona's neck. He brought them down again, wasted no time in felling the small woman. The Twins had full control of his arms now, unrelenting in their hacking, splattering the Pale Lady's dark oily life force over his face. Flinn found himself lost in the killing, as Desdemona shrieked beneath the silver biting of Wulfax and Ursarctos.

She was unable to turn and twist to see her assailant, but the wild attacks denied her. All she could experience was a bombarding savagery, one that had finally blossom, and was empowered by a relentless fury. Every time one of his axes came up to take a breath before plunging into undead flesh, Flinn thought of when he last saw his father. Another hack brought the great Warlord Joden Bear-Blade vividly to mind, recalling the powerful werebear he had him become. He recalled his brother, unsure if he would ever see him again. And it angered him.

So much that tears began to swell in his eyes. Not to be mistaken with sorrow, for this was no time for weakness, but of a raw, primal hate for the creature who sought to take it all away from him. *Had* taken some of it already.

Desdemona lay face down in a pool of her own blood as a barely recognizable minced mess. She attempted once at an incorporeal form. Whatever supernatural magics were at her disposal were thwarted by the silver blades of the Twins, however. Their runes aglow with the same burning black light as the Dark Tome.

The muscles in his forearms bulged, a vein in his forehead popping out like a great **Y** as he found himself towering over The Pale Lady, heaving heavily from the exertion of her butchering. Flinn had lost himself. His eyes now stared maddeningly down at the mutilated woman and swung down into the back of her already battered skull for good measure. An act, Flinn might add, of his own volition.

Before long, Flinn stood amidst bit of flesh, splintered bone, gore, and brain matter. His muscles burned, his eyes rolled wildly and distant, shinning like a beast in the shadows reflecting light.

And then it was gone. As quick as that, the feeling left him, whatever it had been. Flinn blinked himself back to the present, looking around him confusingly and then glanced down at the bloody, fleshy mess at his boots. He nearly wretched, almost emptying his stomach, heaving as he staggered back into the winching system and almost slipping on the mess in the process. Then suddenly remembered about Thwark Redeyes, the Dark Tome, and the Wolf-kin below.

Thwark's mouth was covered with ice, preventing him from speaking, but his strained muffled sounds were frantic. Flinn instead moved to the stairs and cocked an ear, listening. The sounds of battle were still carried up from the first floor, distant as they were but leaving the Druid's son satisfied tha he had enough time yet while the battle raged. Flinn bolted and hurried past Thwark who was trying to get the lad's attention but Flinn stopped short of the overhanging platform where the Dark Tome remained floating just near the edge.

Panicked noises drew Flinn's eyes to the Pack Master, glaring at him from his frozen encasement. There was no time to waste on him right now, returning attentions back to the tome and inched his way out on the rickety platform. The closer he got to the book, Flinn realized, the more it sounded as though whispers escaped it, but he could not even begin to fathom what they said.

Before he knew, the Dark Tome was but a reach away, but he could not part his sights from it or make any other movement as the tome rose eye level with the Druid's son.

Flinn had slipped the Twins back into their belt loops, nestled safely and fully sated. He reached out his hands mesmerizingly, feeling a pulling force emanating from the tome and sending tremors through his outstretched fingers.

The book floated towards him, its light just barely touching his hands before they suddenly clamped around the tome within a blink. Drawn to him as though two pieces finally finding their fit.

An unspeakable force vibrated through his body, thrumming with an indescribable feeling. Images flashed through his mind's eye, of heroes both wretched and righteous, stretching wilderness and high mountains. Images of robed and hooded individuals give the book praises, above them Augustinah and Zhul'Tarrgan both. But they were larger, colossal even, with the blackness of the void as their all-encompassing cloaks, the Dark Tome lay within their reach, but neither moving to take it.

Then, time wound backwards, a colossus with a great midnight beard stood amid the open sea, arms outstretched and up to the sky. He released a sonorous bellow as light shot from his eyes, nose, and mouth. The light exploded blindingly after it had increased in volume, and then there was nothing.

Darkness encompassed everything save a blood moon, offering a soft sanguine luminance while bathing Zhul'Tarrgan and Augustinah in its glow. When they spoke, they spoke as one. "Rare is our unity, but greater when our wills combine," their voices sounded feminine and bestial all at once, making it impossible to distinguish which voice belonged to whom.

They then pointed directly to Flinn, "You shall be our preserver, making it so that civilization does not ruin the natural order. You, and you alone, must unify Wulndar to live cohesively—should you fail in this, then all Wulndar will die and his sacrifice will be for nothing!"

"Whose sacrifice?!" Flinn shouted back in desperation.

With that they both pulled back into the void, leaving Flinn alone in the moon's light. Until it flared so bright that it could have blinded him. As hot as the moon burned, there was only a showering warmth that enveloped the Druid's son. He felt stronger, larger than what his size betrayed and now he knew that he had been chosen. Not by one, but by *two*!

But when they left, there could be felt another presence. An uncomfortable sensation that made Flinn's skin crawl. The Dark Tome called to him, offering power, riches, and abilities that defied reason, but with it came the knowledge of the Void, an understanding of magical energies suffused in all things. And though it did not clarify, Flinn knew it all came with a price. This book was not of the gods, it was something that surpassed even their vast knowledge.

Then it all stopped, that last thought throwing him out of whatever reverie he had fell into and left Flinn momentarily dazed. It was not until after that he realized he teetered dangerously at the edge of the platform. He stepped away quickly, The Dark Tome thrumming in his hands. Despite the inherent darkness felt in the relic, Flinn had to admit that he felt incredibly powerful while holding it. With this book he could do *anything* he wished.

No! Flinn could tell that it was the book making feel that way, not unlike the axes and there was a reason why the Druidic Circle wanted to lock it away. Only they would be able to contain and safeguard it from others. Flinn had to get the Dark Tome back to his father, and fast.

Perhaps this was why Flinn had been tasked in retrieving it, due to his ability to analyze and be objective. Yet there was no telling what could happen so long as the book was within his possession. More reason to rid himself of it as quickly as he could. Flinn tucked the book under his arm, feeling its thrumming power against his body, fight against its enticing whispers. He made it back into the tower chamber, Redeyes making another attempt to break loose, only resulting in a laughable failing effort.

The Pack Master brought his eyes to slits when Flinn moved passed him, noticing at the last second that the Dark Tome was in his possession. A sudden burst of energy overcame the Pack Master, as he fought against his frozen encasement, muffling what Flinn assumed were displeasing protests.

Kill him. Avenge Joden. He deserves death! This time the whispers, harsh voices of many, were as profound as an approaching storm.

They forced Flinn to stop mid-step, turning on his heel to face Thwark as one of his hands absently rested atop one of the Twins, and stepped back around confidently looking up to Thwark's hulking form.

"I should kill ye," Flinn said evenly, "settle the score once and for all."

A short-muffled response came almost as a growl but in that instance Thwark had gone abruptly silent with widening eyes. He noticed a reddish-green glow reminiscent in the lad's eyes, leaving the Pack Master to wonder if it was perhaps the book that made them so? Also, the scent of the Duldarian had strengthened, overbearingly and could not be mistaken.

Flinn stepped back, glancing to the minced form that once was Desdemona before returning his eyes back to Thwark. He was the reason why there had been so much death, seeing the witch's work done in her name, but only to betray her in the end. There was no room for those who would bite a helping hand, regardless to how it went lent.

"If this is the way of it, then ye're what's wrong with Wulndar also," Flinn's voice was flat, matter of fact and remorseful as he slipped Wulfaxe free from its resting place.

The Pack Master screamed behind his frozen prison, making violent efforts to break himself free. Flinn twirled his ax, never removing his eyes from Thwark, remembering the sacrifice Joden had made for him. All as the Dark Tome thrummed joyously beneath his arm.

Chapter 32

Preserving the Land

If there were any more of cultists, or undead soldiers guarding the ruined Keep, then there was no sign of them. Either having receded back down below, or ran off into the surrounding wilderness, but there was no one else to be found. Both first and second floors had been secured by the Wolf-kin, along with the outer bailey and the immediate surrounding land just outside the crenellations. The tower was assumed to have been taken over by now, Desdemona slain by the hands of Thwark Redeyes and the Dark Tome now in his possession.

All they had to do now was wait for their Pack Master's return. And wait they did as they posted in the long hall, sifting through the dead and those who had died again. Taking their slain to line them up just outside the Keep's doors. Guards posted to watch the stairs leading deeper into the ruined keep, for sounds haunting, eerie sounds rose from its depths.

It had been a long nigh already, and The Pack had yet to march on Duldar's Port. Before that could happen, the Pack Master would have to first return, and after a while of Thwark's absence, the commanding officers left behind became troubled. Desdemona was, after all, a powerful witch, and so a small detachment was led by one of the higher-ranking warriors. They made their way for the tower stairwell, nearly rushing halfway up the steps, some on all fours, but stopped less than half-way up, taken unawares.

A black-lit glow preceded the man coming down one step at a time, haggard, restless, and drained of all expression. The Dark Tome floating behind and a little above his head, crowning him in an eldritch halo. In one hand, gripping up thick mohawk-dreads of hair, swung Thwark Redeyes' head, his lifeless eyes wide in disbelief of the fate he suffered. As Flinn descended each step he seemed to emanate an unseen, but very much felt force radiating a pure aura of ferocity.

The Wolf-kin separated, pressing themselves to either side of the stairwell as this youthful Wulndarian approached warily, he deliberately took his time moving between them, half expecting to be attacked and look every bit the ready for it. He held tightly to Wulfax, preferring its quick speed over Ursarctos' power. And though the Wolf'kin outnumbered Flinn considerably, they could do nothing other than look on him with incredulity. Flinn glared at them and wherever the torch light hit, the strange reflection of his feral eyes flashed hungrily. The Wolf-kin closed in behind him, following in his wake, making the Druid's son peer warily both from behind and in front of him.

Reaching near the bottom of the steps to the first landing, Flinn found his path blocked by the largest of them. There was a reason behind why these Feral Folk had not yet torn him apart. It came as a feeling, at first, only to be reinforced with revelation.

The commander never removed his eyes from Flinn, but neither did he move from out of his way. If he were to stop the young Wulndarian, now would be the time to do so and yet he appeared to teeter between how he was to act. It was in the eyes, however, something that foretold of deeper reasonings. The Druid's son could hear the Wolf-kin's breathing, all of them, never two were the same of rhythm. He could smell the scent of their anxiety, were they contemplating overwhelming him and take the book for their won, and once accomplished would they fight one another ownership?

The large warrior offered a nod and stepped aside, surprising Flinn further.

As far as the Wolf-kin were concerned, Flinn Druid's Son had bested their Pack Master and claimed the Dark Tome for his own. Presuming that he had slain Desdemona, for she was nowhere to be seen. Taking to the main floor, Wolf-kin trailed behind him at a respectable distance, as Flinn walked on through to the long hall and into a slaughterhouse. He walked up and over the dais to the front of the throne, taking the steps down. He slipped his ax into its holster and walked out of the ruined Keep, using Thwark Redeye's head to split the Wolf-kin like a parting river as they stared in disbelief.

With the Dark Tome nearby like a witch's familiar, Flinn headed south towards Howler's Wood. He had to stop the Ghar'tul from slaughtering innocent people, and he doubted very much they would be selective about it. Maybe, with the book in his possession, he could turn the tide and right a grievous wrong before it occurred. The question was, would these Wolf-kin take up arms and pursue him once their disbelief left them, and aid in the destruction of Duldar's Port, or would they feel broken and scattered without direction?

The gates leading from the outer wall were blocked, however, by a dire black wolf. She stood strong and noble, amber eyes keen on the head held in Flinn's hand. He stopped, remembering the wolf, had seen it time and time again sporadically, nearly throughout his entire trek through the Feral Lands.

Flinn could feel the Wolf-kin huddling behind him, keeping their distance with anxious movements between them. Several other dire wolves positioned themselves adjacent the night-colored beast. Supported further by four of some of the largest and fiercest looking Wolf-kin he had ever seen. This was his final test, Flinn thought, he would have to fight his way through.

Before he considered launching the offensive, Flinn instead tossed Thwark's head to land sickeningly and tumble across the ground until it stopped rolling just short of the black wolf's paws. She padded forward few short steps, lowering her head to sniff at the head of her former rider and then rose to glare across at Flinn.

His hands hovered by the Twins, ready to slip them out and allow them power to guide his strokes. But she only slowly approached, lowering her head with ears flat and turning her muzzle just-so to bare her fanged teeth. Flinn slipped the Twins free, shuffling back into a stance which gave the dire wolf pause and causing the Wolf-kin surrounding them to ripple as they shuffled back themselves.

"No," came a voice from behind him, forcing Flinn to glance at the warrior who spoke, "she answers to ye now, lad," and with a spread of his hands he added, "as do we all..."

Flinn's eyebrows met, his eyes squinted confusingly with a disbelieving frown on his face. He looked back to the dire wolf, who had somehow wound up right in front of him without notice. He stiffened, remaining still while his heart quickened as she leaned and sniffed at him. The beast towered over Flinn, already being of short stature as it was, but did not feel that she meant him harm.

I am Lunyrr, a soft and dominant feminine voice echoed into Flinn's mind, *I welcome you, Pack Master.*

Is this really happening? Flinn thought.

Yes.

And to punctuate that point, Lunyrr threw back her head to send a long, harmonic howl to the full moon, echoed by the rest of The Pack.

Come, Champion, if we go now, we may be able to reach the city before too many are lost to the Ghar'tul and the undead abominations.

Lunyrr nipped at Flinn, pushed up against him and turned to lower herself. He glanced around him, around what had been the enemy for days, pursuing him, killers, and murderers all. Just what in the Hells was happening to his life?

Lunyrr eyes held Flinn's, as if entranced by an unknown power. *We must hurry, Druid's Son.*

Heaving a sigh, and honestly seeing no other faster way to get through Howler's Wood, he clambered awkwardly up into the dire wolf's saddle.

Hang on. Lunyrr was off in an instant before Flinn was able to secure his grasp over the pommel of the saddle. She sped from the fortress, darting through the chill night air, and into Howler's Wood. Flinn closed his eyes, allowing himself to enjoy a once in a lifetime experience, something he had only dreamed of doing. Pacing sounds opened his eyes as he glanced all around him to find dark shadows spread to either side of him and deeper into the forest. Behind him he saw more, and it was a magnificent sight.

Lunyrr made sure that she kept Flinn at the head of the Pack, leading them towards Duldar's Port. He wondered, though, as their sleek forms sprinted through the dead of night, rushing past trees, bushes, would they be too late, or maybe this was all a ruse

No, Lunyrr answered his thoughts, the ways of Wolf-kin are both simple and with depth—you slew Thwark and therefore ended his leadership. The Pack respects and follows those who are strong.

She dashed between trees, leapt from small elevations, and ran up ravines, Flinn happened to glance up into the trees, watching hulking shapes fling themselves from one to the other, their amber eyes aglow. Werewolves scaled the trees from above with surprising stealth, appeared to run alongside him before veering off. It was almost as if they wanted to get a good look at the Druid's son for themselves.

Flinn gripped tighter to the pommel of the saddle, lowering his body to press it closer to Lunyrr. Everything was happening to him so fast, within a few short days his entire life had made one drastic change after another. Just wait till his father heard about it all.

We are your family now. Lunyrr's voice was a gentle wind and but there was something behind her tone that worried Flinn, something he could not place. And as he had felt with Razjil, so too did he feel with this sudden turn in events. As he was taken south to Duldar's Port, a host of Wolf-kin and werewolves in his shadow, the Dark Tome remained close with unrelenting whispers.

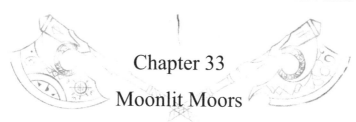

Chapter 33
Moonlit Moors

The fog-covered moors stretched out from Duldar's Port's high crenelated walls. Looking outwards to the wilderness beyond, an expanse that roved into the Highlands further north and into the darkness of Howler's Wood northeast of the city. wrapping around to the west of the city walls. Scouts reported seeing activity near the forest's edge, coming back in bravely from being out in the Moors. High Lord Ranarek made sure ships were ready to evacuate the city should there be need to do so, for an attack was imminent.

It was a cold night, much colder with the blowing pale wind. Duldarian guards, heavily armored in spiked plates held by thick leather harnesses, naked all else above the waist other than their kilts. Around which some huddled around the brazier fires, large stone bowls meant to keep the walls illuminated.

One such guard, accompanied by two others, kept a fur hood up around his head, peered away from the flames in the brazier, casting his eyes out into the darkness. There was a lot of talk of something dark on its way. The guards had been tripled on the walls because of it, the streets heavy with patrols, and alarm posts had been placed all throughout the city.

The Druidic Circle had forewarned High Lord Ranarek of dark portents to come, and something about tonight felt especially off. The High Lord had conferred with his advisors, Hrothnir chief among them, and only affirmed their Lord's concerns that this may be the night city was tested.

A single guard strutted up to the small group who

sought the fire's warmth, armed with a large iron maul whose head resembled a bear's. "Make ye rounds," he said, dismissing those around the braziers. They reluctantly peeled away from the warmth of the fire but ultimately dispersed, leaving the newly arrived guard by himself.

His vision was not so good these days, not to say he could not see but being of an age that most Wulndarian warriors considered veteran, the guard had certainly suffered his fair share of wounds from past battles. But his vision did not go so far anymore, and because of that, he did not notice the shadowy figures slink out beneath the full moon's light from Howler's Wood and into the fog over the Moors.

The guard's eyes went back to the flames of the brazier, studying the fire with outstretched hands, and hoping that the night proved uneventful...

The Ghar'tul horde drove their forces into the fog. Their focus on the towering walls of Duldar's Port, eager to raze the city. It had been an eyesore for the Feral Lands far too long, and at last it would fall.

Their hooves beat into the soft earth, hardly making a sound and kept low as they rushed through the cloaking fog. They angled their approach towards the doubled-door gates. Ghar'tul suicide-archers and shield-bearers kept pace with ramming teams. Their supernatural strength made it easy for them to carry the large constructs, fitted with iron ram heads at one end and a counterweight on the other.

Brute squads, armed with heavy concaved round shields, flanged maces in their hands and wearing heavy leather studded shoulders and harnesses over their great kilts, formed the next line. But with each squad there were a handful of lightly armored Ghar'tul, smaller in their frames and armed with short sword and daggers. As they approached the outer walls, these small groups sped forward ahead of both the brute squads and ramming teams.

In their hands they swung small circles with their grappling hooks and the moment they were close enough to the walls, the spinning circles grew larger and let go to sail up and over the walls to find purchase and quickly yanked back to find purchase.

But the main force of the Ghar'tul would only just arrive as the walls were cleared by their kin who scaled the sheer face of the walls. This would be the first of many smaller assaults, just as the Pale Lady had ordered. They would attack, kill, retreat at the signal. It had all been discuss, laid out carefully for all to understand. If there were those too stubborn to follow the order, then they would be left behind to their fate.

But there was another force that they had sent long before their grapplers took to Duldar's Port's walls, and even now scaled the walls without the need for grappling hooks. Ghouls. Some had been Wulndarian once, while others were more like animal carcasses that had been altered defilingly.

They made no sound as they reached over the edge of the wall, staying clear of the braziers. Their blue eyes were as twin flames swimming in pooling voids, penetrating the night unblinkingly.

Hunched, emancipated and hairless creatures scurried in either direction. They moved like rats and swarmed the guards without a sound, for some could not make noises at all without their throats. Some fed on the warm flesh, savoring its delectable warmth and chew. But the undead creatures did not dally long, for their hunger for fresh kills overcame them and off they went in search of more prey.

Before long, their presence was made known but most of the guards who came to answer the alarms and shouts and clang of battle, were soon fiercely engaged with the ghouls and Ghar'tul who now clambered over the walls themselves. The Northern Gates were suddenly assailed not long after, as alarms now rang all throughout the city. High Lord Ranarek had made a decree long ago for all able-bodied men of age to undergo routine drilling, in preparation for inevitable assault. Guard, noble and citizen alike. And since the Druid's son had left, they only tripled their efforts. Duldar's Port was ready to defend the city to the last. The militia was quick to act, having practiced the motions without fail, and soon joined up with rushing guards who led them to the outer streets.

Guards fought fiercely atop the battlements, organizing into tighter groups until those with shields took to the front and spearman kept close behind. Any of those who were not likewise armed kept to the rear, both moving forwards and backwards. These Duldarians began pushing into the invaders; either spearing, bashing, lifting to throw them over the walls, or hacking them into pieces, the abominations were swept from the crenellations and ran down with disciplined ferocity. It was not long before the rest of Duldar's Port organized, and those in the streets who had been battle-ready formed up with others and pressed to engage the ghouls that now began penetrating deeper into their city.

High Lord Ranarek had ran from his keep with due haste, armored and prepared for war, flanked by an elite guard clanking in heavy plate and chain mail. The moonlight reflected off his iron breastplate, embellished with a powerful rearing bear overlooking the Spines of Zhul'Tarrgan and trimmed in gold with a consistent flow of etched knotted design.

Wishing Joden was with him, he was glad that Hrothnir ran alongside him. They three, once had been four, held a history to the erection of this city, and it was they alone who had been able to establish civilization long ago. To live in harmony and without fear of being preyed upon blindingly. Now, here they were again, just the two of them.

But there was doubt in the High Lord's heart, as he stole a glance to his comrade, his friend rushing beside him to take their place at the northeast gate. He could see the worry in Hrothnir's eyes, the look of earnest as if time were running out. He hoped Joden was still alive, along with his friend's boy, for it would be they to save this city from complete obliteration.

They ran through the city, their pace quickening when there came a resounding and explosive thunder-smack that echoed back to them. While ghouls and Ghar'tul terrorized the outer streets, one of the city's gates were under siege! Another thunderous explosion, and another after another, each holding their own note seemingly.

"If they get into the city, we're doomed!" Hrothnir reached into his satchel as they sprinted, pumping his legs amid tangling robes and threw up a handful of small black feathers.

High Lord Ranarek and Hrothnir both, along with their armored entourage, became much faster and seemed nearly to fly through the streets on unseen wings. Those who witnessed their passing roared, emboldened by the sight and took off to follow.

"The Druidic Circle convenes even now, preparing," Hrothnir shouted, a step ahead of the High Lord.

Ranarek only grunted, too focused on trying to keep his breath. He was not as young as he once was and nearly three times larger. Living a civilized life had fattened him up a bit, and if he and his two comrades survived this nightmare, he would not hear the end of it. He was still strong and able, though, that much was clear, using that same strength to push on.

"Yer age is showing!" Ranarek shouted over his shoulder, gaining more ground, and soon enough was leading the entire contingent. Most of the forces were keeping to the outer streets, pushing into place mobile barricades fashioned out of supports and fitted with round shields. And fought back the ghouls from getting any further into the city.

If Flinn did not return before the coming of the Red Moon, Hrothnir was unsure as to what would happen next. But it *would* happen, that was for certain, not only due to Flinn's dreams but a myriad of other portents that only Druidic eyes could see.

Chapter 34
Bear's Might

Lunyrr sped through Howler's Wood, carrying Flinn astride her back while trying to keep from falling from the saddle. She leapt over and glided under downed tree, made sharp last second pivotal turns, every time nearly flinging the Druid's son from her back. But his grip was sure enough and the fear of falling did not pervade him, in fact, it was thrilling. The high moon was bright and beautiful, and the Dark Tome all the while never left the Druid's son's side, somehow maintaining its proximity of orbital magnetism. Its dark glow was the beacon to which The Pack followed, enveloping their Pack Master in its aberrant light, and bouncing off the black coat of the dire wolf he rode.

The song of night heralded their coming, who at last matched Lunyrr's pace, spreading to either side like a cavalry hunting for a fox. Their eyes caught reflected the moon, twinkling ominously in the dark, as the Wolf-kin were carried on deft paws. The edge of the forest was coming into view, they could all see it. Their hearts beat faster, their minds linked with their mounts were abuzz with anticipatory excitement. The time was near for battle, it did not matter to them the goal, so long as it bolstered their strength by doing so.

Fires could be seen distant as they came to Duldar's Port in flames, drowned in battle's song. "We're too late," Flinn nearly dropped from the saddle.

Not yet. Lunyrr's thoughts promised.

She rushed out into the Moors at a hard sprint, with Flinn hugging tight to the saddle and conforming to her shape as much as possible. The Pack were close behind, bounding hard for the city with equal urgency, mounted or running as half beasts in werewolf form.

The fight pushed further into the streets, the ghouls driving back the defensive lines as the Duldarians fought with just as much savagery. All the while, the Ghar'tul were given time enough to splinter the large double doors of the northeast gate. Taking any more punishment from the alternating rams would result in a breach, and once they were through, they would splash into Duldar like swamp water.

But Hrothnir, swinging a two-handed flail in his hands, directed the mighty runic weapon in wide arcs and circles. Any time the heavy flanged head hit one of the undead creatures, they shattered into fragmented pieces of petrified stone. The runes on the head of the weapon flared bright with black light, sending showering sparks as from a smithy's hammer over hot iron. But for every ghoul, every Ghar'tul too slow to evade the powerful swings he delivered, there were more to contend with.

High Lord Ranarek, along with his elite guard, continued to lead his contingent towards the gates, while waving a great sword about with heavy swings. He lobbed the heads off from Ghar'tul, split in twain the torsos of undead fiends, and cut in half any of the two fool enough to get in his way. His weapon bore no runes, a simple blade of tempered silver, but did just as well had it been enchanted. In truth, the undead melted before its biting silver edges easily.

"They keep coming over the walls, and the gate's just about to give!" Ranarek shouted above the din of battle, "we'll not be able to hold them off much longer!" he brought down his mighty blade, hewing a Ghar-tul warrior in its hybrid form, "Hrothnir, ye need to do something, lad!"

"The Druids are doing just that!" He shouted back, clobbering a ghoul to the street. He stepped forward, twirling the flail around him, and taking another undead abomination after bashing half of its skull.

One of Ranarek's guards moved to intercept an incoming ghoul on route, but before he could take another step, there were others who swarmed in from alleys surrounding the troupe. The guards chopped with their swords frantically. Others were taken down similarly, ravaged as if by a pack of rabid dogs. The ghouls tore into any exposed flesh they could get to, arms, legs, thrusting their clawed hands and spear through soft bellies, pulling out bloody wet innards. The poor warriors who fell beneath the ravaging undead screamed the terror of such agonies

High Lord Ranarek and Hrothnir stepped in behind several others, sweeping their weapons like farmers tending fields. Cleaving and bludgeoning the ghouls aside with powerful strokes. It was too late for some of the men, their flesh had been gnawed away, deep furrowing claw marks rending their flesh, their bowels strewn about like macabre streamers.

On reaching the gates, the scene was no different than what they had left behind. The only difference was the Ghar'tul presence. They bleated and cursed as they fought, noticeably keeping distance from the ghouls who fought with them. But above it all came the successive pounding of the rams outside the gates. There was a big enough space now to see the Ghar'tul at work, their archers peeked through to let loose their arrows when they saw an opportune moment. For High Lord Ranarek, he knew the odds were against them, not looking the least bit hopeful that the city would last the night.

There was one element missing from all of this, however, a detail that both Hrothnir and the High Lord noticed. The Wolf-kin were not present during the attack. Not even a single dire wolf could be found among the Ghar'tul and undead assault.

"Let's reinforced that gate, lads!" Ranarek shouted the order.

Ranarek held up his sword, shouting for his warriors to

rally to him, and formed a wedge to fight their way closer to the gate were a huge chunk of the battle was fought. The Duldarians formed shield walls stretching left to right, crossbowmen positioned behind them to let loose thrumming twangs and sending bolts into the invaders, and duel-wielding warriors hacking and slashing with both sword and ax.

But it was not just here the fight took place, in either direction, further down the outlying streets, the battle continued and to Ranarek each would pose their own problems, their own challenges. He hoped his warriors were stout enough to hold the enemy from getting further into the city. There were women and children to protect, those too weak to fend for themselves.

"It is as it was at Duldar's Keep," Hrothnir fell into step alongside Ranarek, sweeping his great war-flail to plummet from right to left as it pummeled and smashed anything that did not call Duldar's Port.

"Gods, I hope not. If so, then we'll end it just the same," the High Lord swallowed hard after that, letting loose a reinforcing war cry before bulling forward into a sprint, those who followed shouted in response, emboldened as they likewise mobilized.

Ranarek, Hrothnir and their force of elite warriors, along with the militia, joined their brothers-at-arms by the gates and fought for their very lives. The gates exploded open then, dashing hopes of reinforcing it, the battering teams following through into the city, leading with the siege weapons, and barreling warriors over, friend and foe alike. When their momentum had ended, the Ghar'tul pressed into the melee.

"Hold them, lads!" came a shout up and down the defending line, "Gates, to the gates!"

But that was the least of their worries, for from outside, slinking through the battered gates, came the slithering half-man half-serpent folk known as the Shess'H'ssh. They were what remained after the Pale Lady's deceptive rule more than a century ago.

Hrothnir's beating heart felt as though it had been constricted within a cold grasp at the sight of them, their large slithering forms breaking through and widening the breach of the gates, allowing more of Desdemona's forces to seep inward. He watched as the abominations swept aside the defenders as easily as a child knocking over the pieces of a chess board. Their horror-stricken expressions reflected Ranarek's.

Feeling Hrothnir's eyes on him, he glanced his way and gave unspoken command. A plea for action. The Druid nodded, knowing that the Druidic Circle needed more time, and stepped back behind the holding lines of Duldarians. He let go his flail, falling heavily to the street. His eyes kept on the tumult. The leather studded armor he had been wearing over his chest had simple fastenings, making it easy to shed away. And he walked into the fray as he discarded his kilt-like robes.

With a glance to the moon, Hrothnir called upon her power, tapping into the spirit realm where Zhul'Tarrgan answered the call and offered himself willingly to accept his gift. The Druids of Duldar's Port were not entirely without the feral savagery of the wilderness, but low were they to call upon that influence, for it did demand a heavy toll be paid.

The moon's power showered over Hrothnir's naked form, altering his body to take shape and gain strength beyond that of any Wulndarian. As the large old man sauntered deeper into the melee, he moved and twisted his body just enough to evade incoming attacks from the enemy. One such Ghar'tul, in his lesser form, rushed for the old man, its armed lifted and ready to deliver a bludgeoning blow with its war-club.

Hrothnir caught the goat-man by the wrist, pulling him along and flinging him out over the battle as thought weighing no more than a child. The Ghar'tul's surprised bleating trailed after it, crashing in the distance. Hrothnir's flesh tore free like ripping paper until the werebear ran rampant in all its raging savagery.

The hunched-back monster swung left and right with

grate wide clawed hands, toppling three and sometimes four of the invaders at a time, delivering one mauling attack after another tirelessly. He charged into tight groups with wide open arms, pulling them into his deadly embrace, crushing them as their bones broke. His great gaping maw opened wide, clamping over heads to crush skulls as easily as a melon, emitting resounding dense pops.

Hrothnir, old in his years, eldest of the champions who founded this city in their comrade's name, showed none of his age while in his hybrid form. And where there was fur, there could be seen streaks of silver that glinted in the moons pale glow, serving further as a banner for the defenders.

The werebear moved through the enemy as through a rushing river, an uncontrollable storm amid the chaos of battle. As the moon bounced from his tawny hide, a shimmer of hope swept over the Duldarians whenever they caught glimpse of his passing. High Lord Ranarek held up his sword once more, calling for his warriors to press the offensive. Their war cries paled against the werebear's own, as Hrothnir flexed and roared to the moon with a collecting of piling bodies, forming a halo of death around him.

Lunyrr ran towards straggling groups of Ghar'tul, still filtering in through the ruined gates of Duldar's Port. Flinn kept a firm hold on the bridle, Ursarctos slipping it into his right hand and clipped a passing Ghar'tul at the back of his head. The warrior pitched forward, face down and motionless as Lunyrr left him behind dead in the Moor. The first of many, Flinn knew, using the power swings of the axe to deliver monstrous blows until he was carried on through the gates.

Wolf-kin swarmed the rest from behind, flooding through the gates and now pressing the Ghar'tul and their undead allies from two sides. And while the the cataclysmic war raged between monsters and men, Flinn held his place astride Lunyrr, lending both ax and fang to the defense of Duldar's Port

Then suddenly, he realized that the Duldarians were attacking the Wolf-kin as well. Killing the aide that had come to bolster their chances of survival. In this part of the city, it was naught but pandemonium and Flinn knew he had to be the one to make the Duldarian's see.

"We have to find my father!" Flinn shouted down into Lunyrr's ear, "they don't realize ye're here to help!"

I will run up and down the length of the fight, but the rest is up to you, her voice came in the form of an irritated snarl. When no argument issued from the Druid's son, the dire wolf turned about and charged through the masses. Never staying in one place long to be overwhelmed, picking through the battle

As she sped through the battle, Flinn occasionally chopping down with his ax if the enemy came too near, he shouted for the Duldarians. "The Wolf-kin have come to help! The Druid's Son returns! We have it! We have it!" As if the Dark Tome hovering about his head was not sign enough.

It took several more announcements and passes to garner enough attention to get the message across. The Dark Tome not only caught the awestruck Duldarians but also those of the Ghar'tul along with their undead allies

By the Moon! Look! Lunyrr's exclamation brought Flinn's eyes to the werebear and at first thinking it was Joden! But the more he examined the beast, he noticed the discoloration of its hide. No, it was not the Warlord, but no less of a hulking beast. After a strenuous struggle between one of the familiar Snake-folk, it was at last brought down ferociously. The beast turned in place, swatting at ghouls and Ghar'tul alike, until its eyes locked onto Flinn.

Lunyrr veered away towards the outskirts of the battle, resuming in making sure that the Duldarians did not attack their unlikely allies. Until they were suddenly speared from the side, sending both mount and rider to topple over one another several times. Lunyrr scrambled to all fours, lowering her center mass with raising hackles. She positioned herself over Flinn's sprawled form, groaning from the impact and rolling over in a daze with a hand groping the street for Ursarctos.

Rising above them was serpentine abomination responsible for the blindsided attack. The Shess'H'ssh slithered towards them casually, swaying like a hypnotic horror. It pulled the length of its body across the stone, arms hanging loosely at its sides and its tongue flickering. Lunyrr stood defiantly, a warning growl escaping her.

Feeling her new rider starting to collect himself, she stepped forward slightly to give him room enough to get up. Flinn got to his feet, both axes in his hands, and at last aligned himself enough to focus on the behemoth before them.

Flank it and divide its attention! Lunyrr already bolted into action before Flinn could even comprehend what she had just relayed. But his latent locomotion was no more than a blink in time before he rushed opposite her. The Shess'H'ssh swayed towards Flinn, finding him the smaller target and seemingly the easiest

Faster than Flinn anticipated, the Shess'H'ssh was on him in an instant. Darting to one side, forcing Flinn in the opposite direction and then sending the rest of its length like a whip. Flinn dashed back the way he had come, but the serpentine monster was already rearing above him, diving back down with fangs leading.

Lunyrr appeared in a single upward leap, her jaws open and clamping down over the Shess'H'ssh's thick neck. Consequently, the impact drove the abomination off course from Flinn, giving him the time need to move. While the undead monster fought to tear the dire wolf free, rushed in toward the horror. His axes guided his hands, biting into the decayed flesh, tearing into the scaly hide as a hot blade burning through leather.

Bombarded by two different assailants, the Shess'H'ssh flailed about aimlessly. Allowing time and time again for Lunyrr to simply disengage before being caught, then rushing in and finding a new area to tear into. Flinn had to back away several times, else risk being caught himself by the monster's powerful thrashing. But the Twins were fanatic in their desires to hack this abomination into pieces.

The axes pulled Flinn forward, rushing him in towards the monster, heedless of its forward spiraling tail lashing for him. It snapped out violently, colliding into Flinn's advance, but instead a sudden flare from the Dark Tome created a translucent shield of dark light, absorbing the impact. What could have been a crushing blow only succeeded spinning Flinn away harmlessly away.

He thought he was in the clear when another one of the undead serpent-folk came in fast with a strong backhanded swing. Flinn was sent sailing through the air, his body feeling the full brunt of that attack, and more. He crashed into the wall and plummeting down to the street, the Dark Tome with a sudden snap of tethering energy, and winked out completely upon impact, tumbling away beyond reach.

The Twins had been lost also, thrown from Flinn's hands upon impact. He tried picking himself up but was quickly denied any control of his body. Severe pain could be felt all along his spine, accompanied with a swift realization that in some places he felt completely numb, his neck being chief among them. He could not even move his head. Suffice it to say, all he was able to do was lay ironically facing the battle.

I've failed, he thought, *I've failed ye, father!* A depressive guilt pressed down on him as he looked to finally see that the Wolf-kin and Duldarians fight alongside one another, putting down the undead scourge along with the Ghar'tul menace. But the battle was far from over. Flinn's eyes blurred with tears, blinking them away.

Dark Tome suddenly levitated from its back, tilting until it was upright as thought looking straight at Flinn. That was when the night fell beneath a drape of sanguine light, replacing the pale glow with one of blood. The Dark Tome, though, remained untouched by the new light, its own aura unwavering and strong. Slowly, Dark Tome floated towards Flinn. As all around him every swing of a sword, every biting fang or sweeping claw moved at a snail's pace. Seemingly by the book's will alone, or was it in conjunction with sanguine light?

Stopping before him, positioning higher until Flinn could no longer see it, something else had occurred. Zhul'Tarrgan moved through the battle as it caught in a slowed time warp, sometimes tilting back to move past the downward chop of an ax, or casually duck beneath the pole of a spear, until soon the Lord of Beasts stood not six paces from the Druid's son. Perhaps this was what death is, Flinn thought, perhaps Zhul'Tarrgan had come to take him away.

The Lord of Beasts wore a battle raiment of thick leather armor, with an ornate circlet crowning his horned head, while carrying over one shoulder a strong oaken branch riddled with strange inscriptions, each symbol wriggling with black. At the thicker end, fastened by a bolted cap of bronze plating, there dangled a seven-linked chain with an egg-shaped weight of spiked iron. It swung side to side like a clock piece, as if ticking down Flinn's last moments here on this plane of existence.

"Will ye preserve my Feral Lands, Flinn Druid's Son?" His voice echoed, trembling the streets, shaking the foundations of the long houses, sending tremors through the slow movements of the warriors who inched nearer in delivering their death blows.

As he lay there, unable to move even if he so desired, threatening to black out from the pain, Flinn growled acquiescence and somehow knew that Zhul'Tarrgan understood.

Augustinah appeared clad in a cuirass of shimmering gold fit over loose earth-toned robes. She kneeled beside Flinn, the tips of her fingers caressing his brow to follow the line of his face. She was crowned with a myriad of flora. But it was her long fiery locks of red hair that stood out most.

"Promise to maintain natural order."

Flinn managed to grunt another affirming response, bearing the pain of his broken body as waves of agony came to him in waves, threatening to send him into darkness.

Zhul'Tarrgan gesture Augustinah to step aside and said, "Rise then, Champion." he swung his great flail up and over to send it over Flinn's broken back.

A flash of searing pain racked his body, but soon became a smoothing and revitalized warmth in the blink of an eye. A sudden brilliance of dark light, no doubt the Dark Tome in response to whatever power bestowed, illuminated to lay a dark glow over Flinn's form. The Gods had vanished, the battle continued as if it had never been slowed, but the sanguine glow remained. Confusingly, all feeling came back to Flinn, in fact, he felt stronger than ever before. He picked himself back up unsteadily at first, swooning for a moment from a rush of light-headedness.

His eyes went searching for the Twins, locating, and gathering them up quickly before stalked off, hoping to find his father, or even High Lord Ranarek. The Dark Tome hovered nearby, orbiting the Druid's son protectively.

The battle for Duldar's Port continued, and before Flinn could even take two steps to lend to the city's defense, and excruciating cramp squeezed his gut. He dropped to his knee, the Twins clattering to the stone as he wrapped his arms around his midsection. And as the Dark Tome oddly pulsed along with the pain felt, Flinn could feel his temperature rise from within him.

Seeking an easy kill, Ghar'tul split off to put the lad down, and take the book for themselves. Any who came within teen feet of the Druid's son, however, meaning to do him harm were struck by a bolt of black light that vaporized them instantaneously. The Dark Tome pulsing brightly with every bolt it sent.

Meanwhile, the sanguine moon angrily down at Flinn. His situation only worsened as time progressed, making seconds feel like hours of torment. Flinn felt his flesh burn like parchment held by flame, felt his muscles slide around with a mind of their own, stretching themselves beyond their limits, or bunching up elsewhere, shifting and spasming. But all of that was nothing when compared to sudden snapping and popping bones, breaking down his skeletal structure while his entire anatomy reshaped itself.

Before too long, the werebadger pulled itself up beneath the blood moon. The last known descendent of the Te'lidae Clan thought to have ended with Duldar's death.

Blessed be. Lunyrr had watched the transformation from afar, was under way to aid him until she saw there was no need. Her echoing words entered the beast's mind, causing the feral creature to snap its gaze to her. The Dark Tome infused his hybrid form, making his eyes glow like twin black flames and limned his frame in a black light as a second skin. Smaller than a werewolf, as tall as the tallest Wulndarian, the werebadger released a bestial roar, surging with the power of the Dark Tome. Like flames, that black light of power ignited around his clawed hands to travel away up to his shoulders.

What once had been Flinn now charged Lunyrr in a blinde rage. She was not fool enough to stand against that monster, there were few who could against their unbridled aggression. She turned and broke into a sprint. She had been in worse situations, but with Flinn being a descendent of the Te'lidae Clan *and* in possession of the Dark Tome; well, that made things *slightly* more complicated.

Chapter 35
Unhinged

Strength, power, and a rage beyond comprehension assailed Flinn, empowered tenfold by the Dark Tome. His massive arms, gnarled by pounds of thick muscle, enveloped in flames of black light while the rest of his body was outlined in the eldritch glow as the Dark Tome maintained proximity of its possessor. Whispered words wriggled into his mind, like too many poking fingers hooking and jabbing and burrowing into his brain. *Kill all*, they said, *avenge, eradicate*, they commanded.

You must fight now, Preserver! Fight now alongside me! Lunyrr's words were but a trailing echo in the vast corridors of Flinn's mind as she turned and took off. She sensed the hunger in Flinn, the burning rage that would not be able to be tamed. There was only a berserk chaos that swam in the werebadger's eyes as it gave chase.

Lunyrr would not be able to face Flinn while empowered by the Dark Tome, she knew that as well as any. That was not to say that he could not be beaten, but that would require a combined effort. Neither were the case now, and the best that the black wolf could was to lead Flinn on a wild chase, maybe try leading him into the fray. She knew by doing so would cost the lives of many warriors on all sides, but she saw no other option than facing the werebadger down herself.

Flinn's rushing movements from behind twitched Lunyrr's ears that way, though she dared not look behind her in fear of slowing her momentum. Leading the werebadger away from the battle, she circled out wide until circling back around the way she had come. And left surprised at how well

Flinn shifted his trajectory, pivoting instinctively to rush her from an intercepting angle.

Pumping her legs harder, forcing herself to run faster before being speared by the beast, just barely missed being swiped by his long knife-like claws. The last thing she wanted was to be wrapped up in a tackling embrace at the mercy of a frenzied first-time shifter. The dire wolf remembered well how savagely the Te'lidae Clan fought and protected their territories. Their berserkers were unrivaled in combat, the most ferocious and unyielding in all Wulndar.

Gaining some headway, and only by so much, the pair finally caught up with the current battle, dashing between friend and foe alike. Close enough now to send mental warnings to The Pack. They had to steer clear of the werebadger, some incredulous thoughts rebounded back to her, but Lunyyr's frantic messages convinced them the truth of it. Cutting tightly among a skirmishing group of Ghar'tul, the black wolf purposely ran between the lot of them as they swung at her in surprise, even made to chase after her, until one of them bleated out a warning too late received.

Rushing forward on all fours, springing up and crashing down, the werebadger slammed into them. The flames on Flinn's arms flared, as he toppled over one of the goat warriors, slashing its face to bits. He reached out to another, swiping out his throat. But from that flaring glare, flame-like tendrils had simultaneously flickered outwards to simply touch those Ghar'tul too slow in moving. And they were immediately vaporized in an explosive dust, leaving residual stains where they once stood.

Flinn turned, all snarls and growls, as feral eyes searched for prey. He launched forward, claws reaching, and sliced through into the back of an unsuspecting Wolf-kin warrior. He tried to turn free, but suddenly went completely stiff after making the mistake of peering into the werebadger's gleaming eyes, filling the warrior's own with the black light. Flinn tilted his head, opened wide his jaws, and clamped down over the Wolf-kin's face, crushing his skull in a single bite.

The Druid's son turned in place, letting the corpse fall at his feet, as the battle around him widened into an avoiding messy circle.

Dark energy crackled and snapped from around Flinn's outlined body, his arms burning continually but otherwise left him unharmed. The tether from the Dark Tome blinked every so often, as if wanting all to know that its power was in use. Flinn roared before charging back into the chaos.

Those aware enough to keep out of reach, either turned and fled or attempted to throw the nearest enemy in the monster's path. There were still some undead that aided their Ghar'tul allies, but those that moved to meet the werebadger were swiftly taken down by a single bolt of dark flame that shot from the book itself. And long were they disposed of before they even made it within reach of Flinn.

Flinn was lost in his own rage, gone with the lust for blood and battle, and driven further by the dark whispers of the black book. The Druid's son roved the battlefield like a hound from the fiery depths, in search for his next victim.

Ghar'tul, Wolf-kin, undead abomination, or Duldarian, it did not matter to the werebadger. They all suffered the creature's rampage. Any time an attempt was made by either the Ghar'tul or the Undead to overwhelm Flinn, the Dark Tome saw to evening the odds. Some were reduced to clouds of dust, while others ran aimlessly screaming aflame. One Duldarian defender had the misfortune of watching his flesh slough from his bones, the moment one of the tendrils of dark flame reached out to touch him. This new arrival turned the tide, for all parties involved. Flinn was out of control.

Light from the Dark Tome shone as a black-lit stain amid the sanguine glow of the night, an ugly splotch emanating a wilder force of power that knew no bounds. Beneath it, tethered to it, the Druid's son in all his monstrous glory. Even if by some fat chance the three armies joined, they would still lack the strength to sever the link between Flinn and the Dark Tome.

Lunyrr half-expected this to happen and was left

admittedly aghast by the werebadger's empowered assault. He had to be stopped, however, the tether between he and the Dark Tome had to be severed somehow.

While the battle raged, so too did Flinn. To him all were prey, the whispers told him so, the Dark Tome *convinced* him of it. The Druid's son directed his ire onto any who crossed his path, closing the gap in a few short loping bounds to tear their limbs free in arcs of spilling blood, pulling heads from shoulders, disemboweling to throw their insides to the city streets.

Attackers and defenders alike combusted instantaneously if too near the black flames that arched from the book., leaving haunting cries of despair echoing on the night's wind. For a moment, unless it was an illusionary effect from the sanguine glow, Zhul'Tarrgan could be spotted among the fierce battle, drawing the werebadger's dark-lit eyes to him. That one he knew, for there came a great sensation of reverence towards that great Lord of Beasts. He stood there in his battle raiment, eyes glowing brightly, with a satisfied grin beneath a narrowed horned brow. His eyes were only for Flinn as he watched the magnificent creature, then offering an approving nod. Then just like that, he was lost amid the flow of battle.

Massive chest heaving with great hyperventilating breaths—all while the beast turned slowly—Flinn sniffed up at the air, inhaling deeply of blood, sweat, and fear. Snarling and licking at its bloodied maw at the Ghar'tul and Undead that lay strewn about; mangled, mauled and torn, the beast-man regarded the wide circle now surrounding him. The combatants doing their best to keep clear of the monster while dealing with one another. Flinn bound forward, choosing any direction, and leapt into the fray. Some tried to fight back, pathetically, and were quelled by the circulating streams of dark flames and berserk nature of the Druid's son.

Those misfortunates not obliterated by the streams of flames, were now close enough for Flinn to tear apart. Their efforts were of no avail when pitted against the sheer ferocity of the Te'lidae berserker and were soon naught but discarded refuse beneath his clawed feet.

War drums, beating resonantly somewhere in the distance, caused the werebadger to cock his ear up and turn an arrow-shaped head to their sound. Excitement rose from the monster's depths as the sanguine glow reflected from his silvery back, bouncing off from the white and black striped patterns on his face and shinning off from his brownish underside. It was a wild emotion that overcame him, burning bright from Flinn's center which sent him deeper into his frenzied state. He leapt from one group to the other, forcing himself into tight ranks and sent them screaming as he felled them.

A sense of urgency, of warning, caused Flinn to whip himself around in time to spot a large group of werewolves headed his way. They wedged themselves through the throng of warriors, forcing a path and dispatching any who got in their way with extreme intolerance.

Their scent was too strong to ignore, bringing the werebadger's nose sniffing their direction. A low growl rumbled from Flinn's depths, his lips peeled back against bloodstained fangs, as he squared himself and bolted forward to meet the charge but stumbled as a bright flash of light exploded above the battle. Flinn brought his arms over shield himself from the sudden burst.

The flare blinded everyone, even the undead abominations, but for them stagger soon afterwards, some crumbling into dust, others so disoriented that the defenders quickly made short work of them. Great drums of thunder and screeching lightning preceded a heavy rain, bringing with it earthy, refreshing aromas. Aside all this, it was the severing Flinn felt the moment the rain touched him. It was as if something had been taken from him, like a mother's babe from her bosom, wrenched violently free to leave behind the emptiness of the void. The disconnection was tangibly noticeable.

The flare of light had dissipated, leaving behind the

soothing glow of the sanguine moon and the continuous tranquility of the rain. But there was also left behind a momentary lull in the battle as warriors on all sides reoriented themselves confusedly.

The werebadger did not feel as infuriated, some of the rage having left him it. And the black flames that had encompassed his arms and limned his body had gone also. The Dark Tome lay on the street, and though it rained, not a drop fell onto the book itself. But there it lay, spine up and cover splayed open as it lay face down. It now appeared like any other book found on a shelf, save for its blacker than pitch nocturnal binding. The dark-lit aura that usually emanated brightly from it had dulled considerably; its radiating power now dormant.

Flinn paid this no mind, but he turned sanguine glowing eyes onto those getting their bearings and felt his muscles tense as he prepared to launch himself into an attack. That was until there barreled through a behemoth of a monster that stopped the werebadger short of his intended prey. It towered twice that of any werewolf. A great mountain of hulking muscle that let loose a thunderous, deafening roar of challenge.

If the werebadger was expected to balk beneath such power, the attempt failed utterly. Flinn rushed the werebear, launching up high and come down with large raking claws across the tough hide of the larger beast, leaving deep furrows of pink and red flesh across the werebear's chest and midsection. Digging those claws into flesh as if scaling a mountain, Flinn clambered up and around to the werebear's back, evading his foe's frantic reaches, and sunk his fangs into a shoulder thick with knotted muscle.

Large clawed hands finally found hold of Flinn, ripping him free to leave behind grievous wounds. In a rush of air, the Druid's son was thrown to the pavestones and pinned beneath the strength and weight of the hulking monstrosity atop him. Fight as he may, Flinn did not have the strength to free himself. The werebear roared again, victory at hand.

The battle for the Ghar'tul had pivoted horribly in their disfavor, and the one who led the united lowland clans watched in defeat while his forces retreated. Baar'Dahl, with his most trusted captains, watched safely out of range of the fighting, in a ransacked building. The family who had called it home died with children in their arms. Baar'Dahl made sure the wee ones died quickly but had left the parents for last. He had taken a personal liking in the agony they felt witnessing their children's murders. Especially when he realized that the battle was not going as planned.

"What now?" one of his captains asked but was soon clobbered over the skull with a morning star, splattering brain matter and bone fragments in a spray of gore. Baar'Dahl sniffed, returning his gaze back over the battle.

"We go," he answered. What had supposed to be a hit and run skirmish to harass the Duldarians launched into a full-scale attack. The undead minions were all but slain, the Wolf-kin had switched their allegiances, and the young Duldarian managed to get the Dark Tome. Once again, Desdemona failed in delivering on her promise. This battle was lost.

The werebadger thrashed wildly, much as a child throwing a tantrum, with claws and fangs swiping and snapping at the parent. It took little effort on the werebear's part, but the monster must have known there would be no use stilling the uncontrollable behavior of Flinn. And so, with a meaty, club-like fist, Flinn was knocked unconscious from a heavy blow to the head.

All Flinn knew then was the darkness and a woman's soft echoing whisper. *Do not become blinded by tainted power…*

Birdsong and windblown leaves caused for Flinn to blink awake. Shafts of sunlight filtered in through a window on the other side of a small moderately furnished bedroom. The cool breeze occasionally blew the white satin curtains into a billowing dance of welcome, or like the ghostly remnants of spirits. Flinn blinked his eyes from them, something about the curtains reminding him of something, but he could not recall. His mind felt blank, his body felt unbearably sore and achy, and his head suffered a splitting headache.

By the bedside, set atop a small set of drawers, were a matching pewter bowl and decanter. White strips of fresh linen cloths had been stacked and folded beside them. But his attentions were draw to the door that opened with a light creak. A nursemaid entered before his father stepped in after her. He wore thick earthy toned robes that hid his frame, but he walked stiffly and if he moved too quickly, a whisper of a wince marred his features.

"Ye're awake, boy-o, that's good," Hrothnir smiled, dragging a small chair along with him from by the door. The nursemaid had walked over and went about fussing over Flinn's head. She handled him none too gently.

"Quit yer fussin', ye'll only make it harder." she scolded while she worked.

After the nursemaid had finished changing his bandages, Flinn looked to the bowl she picked up to see it slosh thick with bloody cloths wavering about in darkened water. His eyes went wide and flickered to his father worryingly. Hrothnir patted his son's leg, a warm smile dressed in his thick greying beard.

"Ye'll be fine, boy-o, no need to worry," the Druid's smile kept strong before asked, "tell me, can ye remember anything?"

Flinn opened his mouth to answer but confusion shadowed him when he tried to recall anything at all. His memory was as foggy as the Moors beyond Duldar's walls. "I-I don't know, Da," Flinn finally said, his brow furrowing hard to recall his memories. Yet, any images in his head that did flash by were but mere blinks, never tangible enough to focus on.

"That's alright," Hrothnir soothed his gently, "ye've had quite an experience, Hells, we all have."

There was one thing that did come to Flinn's thoughts, and those were concerning the whereabouts of the Dark Tome.

"The Druids have it secured away, laddie, don't ye worry," Hrothnir informed and then asked, "do ye not remember what happened to ye?"

Flinn slowly shook his head, unsure as to what his father referred. He had a feeling that it was anything but good.

After listening to his father's retelling of events, up until his arrival with the Wolf-kin, the blood moon, his son's consequential change, and how the battle had turned in the city's favor because of his deeds. But when he described Flinn's uncontrolled bestial animosity, and the many warriors who had been killed unwittingly by his hands, he regrettably explained what needed to happen next. It all left Flinn feeling appalled and disheartened at once. At least, he tried to make himself feel better about it, Desdemona's possible returning rule had been dashed to the dirt.

"And now there's the matter of what to do from here," Hrothnir leaned back in his chair, exasperated, bringing his arms up and interlocking his fingers behind his head. "Don't worry, we've got time." The Druid reached forward and patted his son's leg before standing up from his chair.

Flinn watched him head for the door, opening it and just before leaving said a few last words, "I'm proud of ye, son, as proud as any da can be." The Druid stepped out after that and closed the door behind him, leaving his son to ponder and rest.

Night was fast approaching, Flinn noticed the subtle shift of the faintest of shadows. The Nurse Maid had stoked the fire burning low in the hearth. Brought him a book to occupy his mind, telling him it was one that her father used to read to her. She had even gathered fresh candles and set them by his bedside. His eyes went back to the story, a telling of the adventures of two fantastical characters. One being a Firbolg and another a warrior, who both scoured the Feral Lands fighting Drakes and serpent-folk and other such nightmarish things. But they were not merely fairy tales to Flinn, not anymore, and though his memory was still coming back to him in waves, each one affirmed that revelation.

Flinn had set that book down after five pages. He had no desire to read of things he now knew were out there. He relived the horrors he had experienced and those of which his father said he had committed and having no memory of the latter.

Turning in his bed, his body extremely sore, Flinn wiped at his brow, feeling the slightest tickle of perspiration running down the side of his head. Perhaps maybe the fire in the hearth was giving off too much heat, but the flames burned reasonably low, and surely the candleflames alone could not be a possibility.

The day waned, falling to dusk, and then into the night basking in the sanguine glow of the moon filtering in through the bedroom window. Flinn's his eyes widened with self-induced terror. His heart suddenly started pounding, raising his blood pressure considerably. He leapt from the bed, his aching body not deterring him in the least when he pulled back the covers and fell in a heap right there at the center of the floor. Familiar cramps gripped his gut, the heat rising painfully, causing him to snarl against the pain.

Flinn pulled at his face while his brain felt as if it were

boiling inside of his skull, becoming nothing more than hot goop. He tried getting to all fours, nearly managing it, but toppled to his side. Reaching out for anything with no luck for purchase. A wave of unbearable pain racked him, resulting in a blood curdling scream that escaped him.

The Door burst open, swinging violently into the room. Hrothnir ordered the two guards accompanying him to hold Flinn down, while all three of them rushed towards his son. The Druid held a length of sparkling chain in one hand that sent wisps of smoke slithering from between clenched fingers, his fist trembling with the efforts of holding it aloft.

Kneeling beside Flinn, as he was being held securely beneath strong hands as his body threatened the bounds of flesh, the Druid threw the silver chain over his son's head and held the large pendant against his bare chest. Pressing it down as the smell of burning flesh came first, followed by long agonizing moments that reversed the shifting. Whatever crazed spell he had fallen under was knocked clean from his body, leaving Flinn catching his breath in the blood moon's light.

The Druid looked up to a third guard near the door, wearing plainly all the fear he tried to keep deep inside on his face. "Tell High Lord Ranarek that we cannot wait another night."

With a swift salute the guard was more than happy to be away from the room.

"Oh, boy-o, I wish there were another way," Hrothnir said softly under his breath, placing a loving hand to the side of Flinn's flushed face. And no matter how much the pendent burned into the palm of his own hand, the Druid kept it between him and his son, sharing in pain until Ranarek arrived.

Chapter 36
Raising the Horn

Wind chimes played, bringing a renewing feel with the chilled wind playing through their brass lengths. There were several hanging between the pillars outside on a colonnaded porch. The sun was bright that early morning, but the city of Duldar's Port was eerily quiet. The air was still chilly, but the grey skies seemed to have been lessening by the day. Only bird song could be heard echoing through the streets and not a soul to be seen daring the cobblestone ways. Flinn, with Hrothnir to his right and another robed and hooded Druid to his left, stood before the great obsidian doors to the Hall of Lords.

It was set apart from the Keep and sunken into the earth purposely. It was said it had been here before the city was been built, and one of the reasons why it had been built around it to begin with. There was something otherworldly about it. Only the High Lord and the Druidic Circle were permitted to walk freely of its massive hall. Said to be built with hewn stone blocks, placed by strength that no man should be able to possess. Flinn had never seen the inside of it, not once.

As far as last night, Flinn was unable to forget the painful transformation that was referred to as Shifting. Nor did he soon forget the pain delivered to him that balanced back the scales between man and beast. The pendent had been removed from him immediately when the blood moon was no more, replaced by the new morning sun. He kept it safeguarded in a small leather pouch, tucked into his silver plated and studded girdle, while the Twins rested unbothered in their belt loops.

Absently, Flinn rested his hands over their heads, dissipating the butterflies that fluttered in his gut, but he sucked through his teeth at the burning sensation they gave him, forcing Flinn to remove his hands from the axe heads. That was something new entirely, and he had a feeling he knew why.

Hrothnir placed a comforting hand to his son's shoulder, giving it a reassuring squeeze. The secondary druidic brother cleared his throat abruptly, prompting for Hrothnir to remember what this was all about. Patting Flinn's shoulder he said, "Time to enter, lad."

Two teams of two guards stood at either side of the large ornate doors, embossed with gold against blackened iron. As the trio approached the last few strides, each of the guards took hold of two sets of chains and turned to pull on them. Even with two seasoned and strongly built Wulndarians, the amount of strength shown pulling the great doors was made clear with the strain of their efforts. The doors groaned on giant hinges, wide and beckoning with a great inhale to venture into the fire-lit hall.

Flinn glanced up, towards a large domed roof of stone, coming to a small tapered point. The three entered through the yawning doors, already being pushed closed behind them. The hall was dark and sparingly lit, shafts of light beamed down in no pattern through almond shaped apertures. Making the smooth black slated floor seem awake with endless watching eyes.

Pillars circled around a cairn and at the center there was a dais where High Lord Ranarek and the rest of the Druids stood, forming a ring around a large obelisk of dark amethyst. Giving off a light of its own, the narrow gem stood taller than a Wulndarian, jutting up on an easterly forty-five-degree slant ending in a geometric point.

Flinn approached slowly, not knowing exactly the formal rituals required in a situation like this. His father had told him just to be himself. Let them see him as the Flinn they all know, and nothing more than that. But the knowledge of what he had done, both good and ill, continued to grate on the

Flinn's mind. Was he hero or a berserker whose rage knew no bounds, and was he any different than the Ghar'tul or the Wolf-kin?

The Dark Tome had been collected, however, but there were no thanks from the Druids. The only praises he received were from his father, and those words always had a twinge of sadness behind them; so, it was hard for Flinn to take comfort in just that. Something was amiss, Flinn could feel it, the city felt different for him now. Unwelcoming, maybe?

There was a heavy incense in the air, spicy on the nostrils and causing a slight burning of the eyes. Even the air felt oppressive to him, yet he realized that none of the others around the obelisk appeared bothered by this. His father and the Druid escort made the same squinting eyes and covered their noses and mouth with their sleeves as they continued towards the dais, both urging Flinn along hurriedly.

When the trio stepped up onto the platform, the discomforts from the hall vanished. The spiciness and burning sensations had completely gone, as well as with the lightening of the atmosphere. Adjusting himself, Flinn soon realized that all eyes fell to him. Eyes Laden with intensity by those who hid beneath the overhang of their hoods, while High Lord Ranarek gazed beneath a thick studded leather headband crowning his head.

A terrible, nerve racking silence stretched among them, and so uncomfortable that Flinn found his hands over the Twins once more, pulling them away after another itching burn

"Druid's Son," Flinn's eyes snapped to High Lord Ranarek, "much has happened when ye left the city, and yer da has filled me in on the lot of it." His eyes leveled on the young man, much as a father would before admonishing his child, "but you saved this city, as much as it would feel otherwise to you, and made yer da and me both proud. That warrants acknowledgement and praise."

Along with the High Lord, Hrothnir and the Druids, a thunderous call went up to fill the hall with their booming voice, "Hail, Flinn Druid's Son, Preserver! Hail!"

Flinn's heart rattled against the inside of his chest, like a caged beast demanding release. This felt good to him, more so than he had originally thought. Perhaps this meeting was not so bad after all. And he even dared a creeping smile, creasing his face as sign that it would only deepen with age. They repeated the praise twice more before they quieted.

"And praise be to Joden, who fell for this cause, may Wulndar hold him high as we burn a reaching pyre in his honor tonight," the High Lord bowed his head, along with the hooded figures surrounding the obelisk.

"Now, there is a matter to be resolved," High Lord Ranarek's baritone voice jolted the Druid's son from his thoughts, looking up to meet the leveled gaze of the larger man. "The Dark Tome will be kept here, within this chamber. Heavily guarded and never to be used by anyone, myself included. None will be permitted within these halls, not unless it is in the direst of circumstances—under penalty of death."

Flinn was relieved by this decree, but shocked also by the merciless consequence. Maybe that was for the best, then that way no Duldarian would dare be tempted to take whatever power that book held. He certainly did not want to find out on his own, for what the book showed him was enough to make any Wulndarian mad for power. That damned book caused too much suffering already, and because of it Joden and others had lost their lives because of it.

"We are grateful for your sacrifice, Flinn Druid's Son, do not ever mistake that for anything else," the High Lord's eyes softened, almost pitying, "but ye're Feral Folk, worse yet, a Berseker. We lack the knowledge to teach ye such things and for ye, there are none left who remember how…" High Lord Ranarek's eyes flickered briefly over Hrothnir after that, both sharing a momentary sadness.

The Druid's son's face grew long. He knew what was going to happen, he felt it the moment he walked into this hall and felt their eyes on him. His father had mentioned it just the other night, but it did not seem to Flinn as if it were a possibility.

"Yer place is to protect this city from without, to keep order yonder wilderness," Ranarek lifted his chin, honoring Flinn's fate with emphasis on pride, "Ye're the Preserver, boy-o, and as such, these stones walls are no place for ye to grow into what ye're destined to become."

Flinn bore witness to his entire world shatter into a million different pieces, blown by the winds and scattered across the Blood Sea. His throat tightened and could feel the welling of tears gather on the lower lids of his eyes, and no amount of influence from the Twins could sweep his heartache aside. He fought them back by not blinking, fought hard not to let a single tear stream down his face. He would not show weakness; he would not be pathetic as to whimper like some kitchen girl, scolded for not hanging a pot correctly. No. Flinn would remain stolid and accepting of his Lord's ruling.

"Have ye anything to say to that, lad?" Ranarek asked, surprised by the amount of discipline, and control the young man demonstrated.

"What of the Wolf-kin?" Flinn asked, not surprising Ranarek with the inquiry.

"They claim ye to be their Pack Masker, I'm told," which brought the High Lord to his next topic, "I can't have ye stay for the night, boy-o, it would be too dangerous and if things slipped out of order…" he shook his head as if seeing some unseen horror, "I canno' have that on my conscious, lad."

It was understandable. Given the circumstances, Flinn would not bother to argue over the decision. He was a liability, any coming of age man would see the logic of that. At least, any honorable and sensible thinking man. But Flinn was no mere man, was he? He was Feral Folk. A Wulndarian truly connected with the Wilderness, blessed by the moon and harmonious with the spirits of the beasts. But were they even safe from him?

"We will honor you here in Duldar's Port, boy-o, a statue made in ye're honor, a memorial and reminder that there is one Duldarian who braces the Feral Lands and protects our city," Ranarek smiled, sticking his thumbs into his studded leather girdle. "This will always be ye're home, lad, and though we canno' have ye here with us, doesn't mean we won't be able to call ye're name from the walls in praise—the rest of this month will be known as a month of festival—all for ye and into the next to span the length of such."

Flinn realized his shoulders had been sagging and pulled them back to straighten his posture. He did not want to seem depressed by any of this, and though he was truly hurt—truly and indescribably hurt—he had a duty to his father, his brother, to this city, and to Joden.

"I will keep the city safe from without, High Lord," Flinn said, "just be sure your archers don't stick me full of arrows, should one night I happen to pass through the Moors."

This brought laughter from Ranarek, even a few chuckles from the Druids that lifted the burdened atmosphere. "Aye, I'll be sure to let all in Duldar know of that decree, as well!" The momentary relief dissipated, replaced once more by a dour air. "Now, we'll leave ye here with yer da; for there is more to be said that only a father and son must share."

Ranarek bowed deeply towards Flinn. The High Lord barely bowed his head lower than his shoulder, but to flourish so before the Druid's son was a true honor. The Druids mimicked their Lord before he gestured for them to take their leave until only Flinn and Hrothnir remained. Before he slipped from the hall, the High Lord glanced once over his shoulder for but a moment.

He knew Flinn was destined to be great, but he feared that the Feral Lands would fully take him; doing away with all his civilized knowledge. Then again, he knew that he had descended from a strong warrior. A reassuring smile appeared on the High Lord's face, knowing he had no need to worry. *A strong warrior, indeed.*

Once they were alone, Flinn spoke before his father had a chance to, "He's right, da, I'm too dangerous here in the city. There's no other way around it, I mean, he could have caged me up or something but…" even the Druid's son seemed confused the more he thought on it. The deeper he analyzed; the more layers of perspective surfaced.

Hrothnir simply looked on his son with the same smile Flinn had grown accustomed to seeing. It all still felt like a dream. There were moments where he would think back, to the time spent with the Firbolgs, the encounter with the Banshee and her Dead Sinners, the River Drake, and as much as he would like to forget, the Abominable. All feeling like a vividly lucid dream. Gods! He was living his own Fairy Tale!

Flinn felt a sudden overwhelming sadness when he looked on his father's face. He knew how this could go, the eventuality of their contact with one another would inevitably grow smaller and smaller as years passed. Unless Flinn was able to gain control of the beast within him, maybe become something like Hrothnir!

"Don't worry, boy-o, we'll be seein' one another," said his father as though reading his thoughts, "we'll set up weekly visits and help ye control yer feral side—there are those still out there who know the ways, I'm sure of it. And I'll be the one to help ye find them."

Flinn's eye brightened with a returning smile and spoke excitedly, "So, you *can* teach me!? We can tell High Lord Ranarek, and maybe before nightfall ye can have me go out into the Feral Lands and—" but his smile slowly faded the moment he noticed that his father did not share his mirth.

"No, lad." the old Druid's voice held the same weight of sadness pulling at his heart, "ye don't understand, lad, ye're ancestors are no more, as far as we can tell, for there have been no sightings of the Te'lidae to show ye their ways. Ye and I are not of the same blood…"

Flinn swallowed, stricken dead cold by what Hrothnir omitted. "Then...?"

Hrothnir's features tangled themselves up angrily, "But, make no mistake, just because we're not of blood does not mean we're not kin!" he gripped Flinn by the shoulders then, holding him tightly as he looked down on him. "Look at ye! The last known descendent of Duldar, the blood of a champion coursing through yer veins!"

So many more questions began to formulate for Flinn. Who his true parents were, how did he happen upon Duldar's Port, and why was it that Hrothnir raised him under the watchful eyes of High Lord Ranarek and Warlord Joden? Nothing made sense to him and he felt like he did not even know who he was. His smile dripped away, speechless and staring hard into Hrothnir. Several times he opened his mouth to speak but just when it seemed he collected himself and his thoughts, he clamped it shut, unable to process anything further.

The Druid watched him carefully, witnessing the myriad of different emotions playing over Flinn's face. His heart went out to him, as nonchalantly as he was able to break this news to the young man, he whom Hrothnir raised as his own son in honor of a lost friend. To witness the changes from boy to man and help shape Flinn into the very Wulndarian who stood before him now. Hrothnir knew Flinn had countless questions, and he may well have most of the answers, but it was not now, not here. For it was not for Hrothnir to explain and felt he would only confuse the lad further.

"I love ye, boy-o. Don't ever forget that," Hrothnir pulled Flinn into his hard hug, keeping him him close.

Tears streamed down Flinn's cheeks, but he did not cry aloud or whimper. He set his jaw, furrowed his brow, and roused an inner bestial rage to do away with the weak emotion. Dragging it down, mauling it until it was no more, as he held his father tightly, not wanting to let him go.

"What were their names?" Flinn's voice was low to

mask any quaking in his words as he pushed away enough to ask.

The Druid lifted his chin, sad to answer, "I cannot answer that for ye, lad."

"How did ye know what and who I was?" Questions just started spilling out from Flinn, but he had to know something, anything.

"Oh, boy-o, I knew the moment I smelled ye scent, and when ye had yer first tantrum—only a Te'lidae can throw a fit to rival that of a bear's," Hrothnir smiled.

They both shared a much-needed laugh and embraced each other a bit tighter before letting go to stand at arm's length from one another.

That was it then. There was no knowledge of his parents, only that he was left outside the city gates, and there was no knowledge if the Te'lidae even existed anymore by how they were referenced and Flinn was to live outside Duldar's Port. With Wolf-kin of all creatures.

"There *might* be someone who may be able to shed light on yer lineage," Hrothnir explained, not wanting any more of the sadness to weigh down on his son's shoulders, "some call her the greatest Druid among Druids, others say she is a witch with no care for those other than herself. I do not know much of her other than she can be found living a solitary life, far to the south between Wulndar's Feet."

Flinn somberly listened. Inside of him, however, emotions waged war on his mind and heart.

"Seek the Firbolg's, lad, they will teach ye the ways of balance, while ye wolf-kin show ye the rest—but, be warned of them, they are wild beast-men and take joy in the thrill of the hunt. Do not allow one side of ye to weigh heavier than the other, for to do so would see one half forgotten," Hrothnir's worry was clearly heard and Flinn knew better than to ignore such a warning.

"Ye'll stay before the red moon rises," the Druid revealed, "plenty of time to pack what ye need. Now, stand ye tall, Champion—pouting's for wee kits."

Flinn stood straight, pulled his shoulders back and stuck out his chest out. He held his father's eyes, accepting every word bestowed on him. But knowing that he would never see the inside of the city again, no longer hear the echoes of his boots. Never again to step foot on the cobblestones and pavestones to wander its magnificence. He would never see the many new and strange peoples who came and went from the wharves and walk its length of small coastal shops abundant in all its trade, nor marvel at the lavish interior of the long houses.

"Shall we enjoy the rest of the day together?" Hrothnir waved a hand towards their only exit.

Flinn smiled, but before acquiescing, he had to ask, "Why has all of this been kept from me, and why for so long, da? Why did it all have to happen this way?"

The Druid nodded solemnly, only further validating Flinn's justifiable inquiries and instead pointed to Flinn's feet. Not just *at* them, but to the polished stone beneath. Encircling the obelisk were obsidian slates, all cut in a trapezoid fashion. Each slate, however, had been worked into with runes. Their grooves filled in with pure gold.

"These tell the story, but they are not for me to read out—only the Preserver can read them and only to himself," Hrothnir explained, watching his son's head shake confusedly. "When ye touched the Dark Tome, lad, when your head was filled up with but a taste of its power, did ye not think it would not leave its mark on ye?"

The runes shimmered in the pulsating glow of the obelisk, casting its nightshade light all around and throwing shadows up against the cairns. At first, they appeared indecipherable, but after a few blinks of adjustment, Flinn could read them.

"Start there, lad," Hrothnir pointed to a slate tile to his left, more at the other side of the obsidian circle.

Taking a hip-width stance, the slate tile between his boots, Flinn looked down on the sparkling runes beneath him. The way they were cut into the stone was precise, using thin lines that read right to left. The first few lines explained the conflict of balance, between chaos and order. Always being one to champion the other, but whichever is more strongly influenced will be victorious.

Flinn looked up to his father, who only pointed at the next tile counterclockwise. That one describing the ways since the making of Wulndar, a powerful Greater God sacrificing himself to be that which fathered all life on the island. Flinn remembered the tales, of how Wulndar came down from Beyond, kneeling in the Sea to thrust his own sword into himself. When he laid semi-fetal, his blood pouring into what now was the Blood Sea, his body becoming rock and earth.

And each tile spun a tail along a timeline, every hundred forty-three years there came a shift in balance. The telling of how the Desdemona came to power, how Duldar stood against her, until it had been razed during her rule, the telling of how the Te'lidae had been all but wipe from existence. Up until recent events.

Then, a prophetic figure was mentioned. A descendant of Duldar to be bestowed upon the city, and he alone would champion the new age to ensure its preservation but it was not for good or for ill that he would do this—simply to preserve the natural balance. It was Flinn the runes were describing, up until the moment he succeeded in gaining a foothold amid the chaotic shifting of the balance. But that was it, only the coming was foretold and the hope of rectification. After the fifth tile, twelve in all, they continued only to be blank. Flinn knew then that was why he had not noticed the runes, for only half the circle was written.

"Why're those empty, da?" Flinn looked up to his observing father.

"Because the new Eld is not yet foreseen and so cannot yet be written." Hrothnir smiled with his words, the sparkle of optimism in his eyes. "Come on, boy-o, lets enjoy the day with one another and among those who love ye."

Together, they both stepped out from the cairn stones, away from the obelisk and into the discomforts of the watching hall. The doors opened, moaning expectantly as if sensing their approach and allowed for the day's light to shine through. From the colonnaded balcony onto a stretching causeway that led out and then up, Flinn followed his father up a steep climbing flight of stairs that took them to a large door at the rear of the High Lord's Keep.

There, they were greeted by Ranarek himself with several heavily armored Honor Guards. The Druids stood outside around the perimeter of the small chamber, which acted as a small private room. Large shields and weapons, flanking long black and gold bordered banners, hung from the walls. Torches, standing on tall stems, were set in the four corners of the room where a large centered fire roiled.

The door behind them thundered shut heavily on its hinges, nearly causing Flinn to flinch. But he remembered all that had happened and all that had yet to be. There was no room for fear now, and there was still the fresh anger over Joden's death that continually peeked through his emotional curtain.

"Walk with me, Druid's Son," Ranarek stepped aside, sweeping his arm back behind him to the portal that led into a short hall and then into the Long Hall of the Keep.

Flinn gave his father a glance, who in turn offered him a reassuring nod, before he moved to stand beside the High Lord. Ranarek draped a heavy arm over Flinn's shoulders, keeping him close and leading him out. Everyone else followed them but kept a few strides back.

"I'm going to show ye something that is going to make all of this worth it, lad," Ranarek whispered to Flinn, "and knowing yer skepticism, I hope that this reaffirms yer purpose and belief in ye self."

As they walked the Long Hall, guards posted at every support thudded a saluting fist into their breastplates as the pair passed them. And each guard they passed shouted, "Hail, Flinn Druid's Son. Hail!"

When at last Ranarek and Flinn came to the large doubled doors that led out from the Long House, the guards quickly reached for the thick iron ring-handles and pulled them open with minimal effort. When the doors had opened wide enough and the light of morning illuminated the city beyond, Flinn could not believe his eyes.

The streets were filled with Duldarians, all looking up excitedly or turning eagerly to see who was coming out. When they saw Flinn beneath the High Lord's arm, their cheers were a deafening storm!

"Hail! Flinn Druid's Son! Hail!"

"Hail! Preserver! Hail!"

Ranarek pulled Flinn close, leaning to say loud in his ear, "Ye see, lad! Ye're a hero!"

Even the howls of the Wolf-kin could be heard from the northern walls on the other side of the city, heightening the overwhelming feeling Flinn felt in his chest. What a sight! There, right at the front of the gathering, Ortheim and Horthgir with their father Jordt! Even they shook their fists, holding them high as they cheered and honored Flinn's name.

High Lord Ranarek guided Flinn to the top of the large stairs, using it as a platform from which to speak. He held up a strong hand, culling the uproarious crowd. When all was silent, not even the noisome barking of dogs, did the High Lord speak.

"Let this day, forever more, be known as a holiday!" he shouted jovially.

The crowd was hysteric with cheers.

Quieting them once more, Ranarek went on, "This day hence until equating a full month, shall be known as the Druid's Son's Festival!"

This time, the High Lord did not bother to calm the crowd down now as they cheered, shouted, and sang their praises. Playing music and spreading out to make room for dancing. Tables had already been set among the streets, filled with trays of food, kegs of mead and games for the children. Ribbons fluttered, banners waved, and flower petals fell from the high windows by buxom maidens calling for Flinn's attention.

Ranarek descended the stairs, looking back to Flinn with a great smile and waved him along before skipping his large girth the rest of the way, eager to join in the festivities. But he stopped mid-way when everyone quieted as they noticed Flinn raise his hands and shouted above the din of gay pageantry.

"Hear me!" Flinn shouted, "Hear me now, please, all of ye!" The crowd shushed and attentive. Flinn suddenly felt meek and abashed.

He felt a touch at his back, turning to see Hrothnir standing not far behind him. The old bear smiled, nodding for his son to go on now that he had everyone's attention. Turning back to the giant gathering, Flinn scanned through to see not a one of the Wolf-kin among them.

"Before nightfall, I must leave," Flinn's voice did not mask his sorrow, "but before I leave, I want this moment, if it is indeed to be a day remembered, shared by all." He then looked directly to the High Lord with an unspoken request.

Ranarek eyed the young man for a hard moment, looking as if to protest, for he knew damn well what it was Flinn was asking. His smile spread open his thick mustache and then turned quickly to address the crowd, "Call the Wolf-kin! All shall share this day!"

At first, the crowd looked shocked, a dread silence hanging over them. But from somewhere in the crowd a voice shouted, "For the Preserver!" and then the raucous began anew!

Ranarek dispatched a small escort to fetch the Wolf-kin before joining the rest of his people. Flinn stood where he was, unsure of going down and mingling with anyone. What if there were other emotions or things he could not control and feared the possibilities. His fears melted away at the hand that laid gently atop his shoulder, turning to see Hrothnir's thick whiskered mustache spread wide with that familiar smile and with eyes beaming with pride. He gave his son's fiery goatee a playful tug.

The two of them descended the steps together and once

among the rest of the citizens of Duldar's Port, long drinking horns were thrust into their hands. Every single person had one, raising them high around the pair.

"Hail! Flinn Druid's Son! Hail!" and every one of those gathered that morning drank until the kegs ran dry.

Flinn brought his horn to his lips, halting as a soft feminine voice entered his mind.

Blessed be the Preserver. Lunyrr's praises entered the emotional halls of his mind, sounding close but nowhere to be seen in the crowd, but her words left behind them a reverberation of unease and wariness. There was lot of work ahead of Flinn concerning the Wolf-kin. Showing them a different way of thinking, a way taught to him by his father. A Druid's way.

But now, such matters deserved little thought, and Flinn threw his head back and downed the contents of his horn. For those select few who knew the Druid's son well, knew too his love for mead.

The revelry did not cease as the day waned, the streets filled with dancing and carts with all manner of stuffs from food, drink, and random things enticing any who happened by them. Children rushed by, trailing black and gold ribbons behind them and many tried to stay as near to Flinn as they could. Asking him all manner of questions, challenging to display his strengths and some even pretending to be a beast-man themselves before taking off chasing down one another. Their parents kept them in range of sight, however, especially when around the Druid's son.

It pained him to see the uncertainty in some of their faces, while others wore their fear plainly. But they always gave him a nod when they had chance to meet his reddish-green eyes, that seemed to glow even in the light of day. Or perhaps reflecting its glare. None could tell for sure.

Wolf-kin stood in groups to themselves, very few mingling overly with the Duldarians but there were interactions to be seen in small amounts throughout the city streets. The Dire Wolves had left outside from the walls, led on by Lunyrr after kindly declining to remain in the city. She was an impassive shadow as she lounged outside the gates.

Several of the Wolf-kin gathered near enough to Flinn amid the revelry, found themselves swept up by the dancing. A circle had formed as a pair of the beast-men fell into a ritualistic war dance made more intense as one of their own began beating drums. The minstrel was more than giving when passing the instrument to the warrior, and though he fought behind a forced smile, it was plain to see that he was very intimidated by the request to use it. The people began clapping, stomping their feet, and more of the surrounding Wolf-kin fell into the circle right into the next step of the dance.

Flinn watched in awe. Finding the war dance stunningly powerful, exuding strength of sure foot, nimble turns, and pivots, sweeping arms and sharp tearing motions with occasional chest beating. The crowd loved it as they cheered them on.

The mead flowed, the food had no end and soon all the Wolf-kin found themselves caught in boisterous laughter shared between they and the Duldarians. On one street there was a wrestling contest, on one corner a drinking game. Across the street a dagger throwing lane had been set. It seemed that the festival carried on in every direction, two streets over or three. But the day did wane. Midmorning stepped down to kneel at noon and would eventually recline into the early evening.

The festival kept on, however, as throughout that entire day groups of men had been dispatched by High Lord Ranarek, preparing the three honorary pyres to burn soon when night fell. To honor those who had fallen during the battle, including the Wolf-kin respectfully, and one built specifically for Joden. Flinn knew that he and the Wolf-kin would not be present to witness such an honor. Instead, they would watch from outside Duldar's Port's walls.

The Druid's son detached himself from the festive gathering, seeking solace at the city square where the three pyres were being erected. The square was large enough to accommodate fifty pyres if they so wished. There were too many bodies and burning three pyres was just as well symbolically. Flinn tucked himself away, leaning against the corner of an alley, and watched the Duldarians at work.

But the day did wane.

And it was not long before Flinn was found and approached by one of High Lord Ranarek's personal guard, asked to follow him to the Northeastern Gate where the High Lord, his father, and a large contingent of Duldarian warriors waited ceremoniously. And no matter what fancies they found themselves caught in, the Wolf-kin dropped everything at Flinn's approach, and some even released echoing howls at his passing. Alerting others not near enough to see and soon all within the city had come answering.

Armored warriors formed flanking columns of three lines at either side of the gates, creating a path to the colossal doors. A team of six men looked down from the ramparts, each with a series of cranks connected through thick chains. Ranarek and Hrothnir, with the Druidic Circle bunched to either side of them, waited as Flinn walked that path while the Wolf-kin kept a respectful distance behind. Among the Wolf-kin stood a banner bearer, holding up nothing than a dark tattered hide that sometimes caught the cold wind. On the banner, when chance met for it to be glimpsed, a blood red symbol.

Flinn glanced back, never noticing the flag before now. It looked relatively new, and likely done during their remaining days here in the city. Yet, it was the symbol that truly piqued his interest. A blood moon over two crossed axes.

"Flinn Druid's Son," High Lord Ranarek's voice brought Flinn back around, realizing he would have run right into the large man. "The time's come for ye to take yer place and see to yer duties beyond this city. Are ye ready and willing to accept that which the Gods themselves have charged ye?"

"Aye," Flinn gave a curt nod, forcing himself not to glance to his father until the time was right. He could feel Hrothnir's eyes on him, though, and that of every Wulndarian gathered.

"We would give ye a horse, but the animals are skittish in the presence of wolves," Ranarek smiled with a wink, accompanied by the warm chuckles from the onlookers, even from those of the Wolf-kin. "However, we offer ye this as a parting gift and token of ye status as well as a reminder that Duldar's Port will always be yer home," the High Lord beckoned with a hand for one of the Druids.

The hooded man stepped forward, a slenderly long ornate box of polished birch. Inlaid with gold corners with engravings of the wilderness carved into the wood itself by an artisan's hand. Opening the box, the Druid holding it revealed a short bow of beautifully carved willow wood. A remarkable tool and strongly built with great care as to the bow's intent. It was held out for the young man to take, as the Druid bowed his hooded head.

Another stepped from behind the High Lord, bearing a sealed quiver no less decorative than the bow case, hinting at the quality of the arrows therein. With great thanks, Flinn took up the bow and its matching quiver, graciously.

"May these serve ye in times of need," Ranarek declared.

Hrothnir stepped forward then, placing a passing hand to the High Lord's shoulders and came to stand over Flinn and gestured with a glance to the small pouch containing the pendent. "Mind its use, lad, for whenever ye wear it to suppress ye're wilder ways, it will lose its influence that much more". Then, with heavy hands over his son's shoulders, Hrothnir pulled the young man into a bearhug. The After releasing him, the Druid looked Flinn over proudly for a moment, then proceeded to spin him around to all those gathered behind him.

The entire city now had come to the Northeastern Gates. All of them quiet, looking from the edges of the outer city into the vast open spaces, some hanging out of windows from overlooking houses, and children along with their parents climbing lantern posts to get a better view. Flinn was shocked he had not noticed their approach, perhaps too caught up in the ceremony or perhaps not allowing himself to be openly keen of his surroundings, but they were here to see him off. He had half expected to be hunted and cast out like a leper, but there was a heavy air of awe permeating from the crowd as they looked on.

"Hail! Flinn Druid's Son! Preserver of the Wilds!" Hrothnir shouted loud behind his son, thrusting a strong fist to the sky.

"Hail, Flinn Druid's Son. Hail!" the combination of the unified sound of the Duldarian's echoing praise, the Wolf-kin's howling and the banging of sword on shield filled Flinn's chest with a burning warmth that nearly took his breath away. That paled under the clanking and cranking of gears and rattling of chains issuing from the opening of the gates.

As they creaked and moaned on heavy hinges, Flinn's memory fell back to one night. A night long ago in his earlier years when the young men came of age to share mead with the veterans of the city, gathered at the local pub and listen to the eldest of them tell fantastical stories. Watching those great gates open, Flinn recalled one such beguiling adventure of a prophesized warrior. But it was the closing poetic chant that always stayed with him and became more prevalent while watching those gates open.

And Lo He stood before those Gates,
With chin held high,
Never frail,
In knowing beyond them He must go.
To follow wild and twisting trails,
Where foul beasts freely roam.
Out where howls echo late,

Where shadows shamble Undead Sinner's gait.
But beneath the Moon's baleful gaze,
Only strongest wills resist such seething hate.
Beware the Feral Lands, all ye who know this tale,
Or succumb to the Feral Craze
That turn teeth to fangs and claws to nails.

Epilogue

Licking flames reached well over the walls of Duldar's Port, flickering high like stretching, grasping hands towards the sanguine moon in perverted praise. Dark was the sky, not a cloud to be seen and if by chance one happened to pass, it skittered quickly across the glaring blaze of that bloody eye. Amid the mist blanketed moors, Flinn watched as the pyres burned in the distance in what once had been his home—but never again would he walk its city streets. Never again would he gaze out into the Blood Sea from the wharf, nor help his father in his study, pouring over old tomes on herbal mixtures and learning of olden days before there was ever a thing as a city.

Flinn continued to observe in silence, his face giving off the faintest expressions of discomfort at the silver pendent that itched and burned against his bare chest beneath his shirt. No doubt it would leave a searing imprint on his flesh, but the Druid's son would not dare remove it. Yet, he kept close to mind what Hrothnir had warned of the constant use of the magical trinket. There was no desire, however, to turn into the monster Flinn had become only nights past. He could feel it, though, clawing and scrabbling up the walls of whatever pit was containing the beast.

For now, Flinn forced that fear away with the aid from the Twins with but a touch, now seeing how long he could keep his hands over them before the burning became too much. He watched on alongside Lunyrr, contrary to his wishes, while the rest of the Wolf-kin returned to Howler's Wood and there would they remain until his approach. But she was able to sense the young man's acceptance of his new position. Dealing with his own incredulity of it and of the power given over The Pack was still prevalent, despite the many times she assured him that he had nothing to fear so long as she was by his side. It was all she could do while the Druid's son watched with sadness in his eyes, yet it was a mixture of anger as well.

The black dire wolf sat quietly beside the Preserver, both watching the city as plumes of smoke rose and the aroma wafted back to them. All those of Wulndar and those who sailed the Blood Sea were sure to see that beacon of flame, and purposely so. For this nigh marked the beginning of a new age for Wulndar, but that did not mean that all would be as one hoped. These were still dark times. An entire age of darkness was to be had.

The coming of the Sanguine Moon foretold such. And how the Preserver would grow into himself was still to be determined, for not *all* Preservers were known to be alike. Flinn could still be shaped, he could still be molded to fit the ways of the Wilds. Duldar's Port still stood as an oppressive reminder of what could eventually happen all throughout Wulndar. And that thought alone did not settle well with *any* of the Feral Folk. Not even the Firbolgs, with all their mysticism and beliefs in balance, dared not upset the Feral Lands with stone walls and industry.

Lunyrr would have to be subtle with Flinn. Pushing him too far to one side could risk much, but not pushing him far enough would garner too little. She watched him, knowing that he paid her no mind, and knew in time that he would learn to trust her, and with that trust Lunyrr would be able to lead the Preserver on a path most beneficial for The Pack.

The Druid's son glanced over to her, meeting her intense gaze, making it seem he had heard her own contemplations. But that was ridiculous, for he was hardly a novice with the link between them. Besides, it was *she* who established it. Just as she had done with Thwark before his thirst to rule everything his red eyes laid upon.

A long silence stretched between them, neither seemingly wanting to be the one to disturb the quiet. Flinn looked as if he wanted to say something yet lacked either the confidence to speak or did not have his thoughts entirely together.

Looking away and back towards the city, Flinn asked, "What now?"

Lunyrr cocked her head to one side, surprised he asked for her direction—she had not expected it to be so quickly sought.

It is what you will, Preserver. So long as you maintain the natural balance here and protect the Feral Lands, whatever decision you decide will be met with obedience from The Pack. What does your heart tell you, what words are carried to your ears by the chilling winds? How does the earth reverberate within your spirit?

"I don't know what any of that means, or what it's supposed to mean," Flinn shook his head, letting go a deep sigh.

The dire wolf shifted her weight, repositioning herself more comfortably before her response echoed through Flinn's mind. Sometimes the paths we take are like many branches of a tree, each leading straight on until they split and veer into different directions. Revelations often come at junctions, or until we are faced with the decision as to which splitting branch we should take at the divide. You will know when the time comes...

Looking down between his boots, Flinn took in another deeper breath before letting it out with an accepting nod. He then asked, "Then first, we will build a totem to honor Joden where all can see, here in the Moors. So large it will tower over the mist."

The dire wolf dipped her head, acquiescing.

"But it will be built at the hands of the Dishonored," Flinn added, labeling those who had been responsible for the Warlord's death and laid an unblinking stare over Lunyrr. "Gather them for me."

As you wish, Pack Master. she dipped her head once more and kept his stare a few moments longer before being released from Flinn's gaze.

Flinn, looking back on Duldar's Port, imagined building the largest and most extravagant totem ever seen. Those constructing it would sweat and bleed until it was finished, and when it finally was complete those who built it would be responsible to watch over it. Isolated from their kin, never to be part of The Pack again. And should they refuse the Druid's son's commands, he would kill them outright but that would be a decision they would make for themselves.

The rest of that night was spent in silence, with Flinn's memories cataloguing all that he had yet experienced. While lost in his own contemplations, Lunyrr watched him for a bit longer before laying down.

That next morning, having spent the night on a constant vigil, Flinn and the dire wolf made their way through the misty moors back north towards Howler's Wood where the Wolf-kin waited. A new chapter in the Druid's son's life had begun and it as time now to think on his plans, of what he wanted to do next after the order to build the totem was given. Afterward, he would set a course to locate the Firbolgs and see if they knew anything of an old crone to the south. After that, who knows. Perhaps rebuild Duldar's Keep, cleanse it of any lingering undead abominations, use it as both shelter and as an anchor to retain whatever semblance of civilized lifestyle he risked losing in the wilds.

But as for what the future held, or what was truly required of him, only time would reveal. For no one's path was ever clear to them and Flinn only hoped that as the days passed, he did not become lost to the Shift. That exact thinking struck fear into the Druid's son's heart. For down amid the depths of his being, he could feel the hunger of that monstrous beast as it continued to claw up. It wanted to be free, to run wildly beneath a blood moon.

I bring you the Dishonored, *Pack Master*. The black beauty's voice heralded Lunyyr's approach with twelve warriors trailing after her. They seemed nervous but tried to mask it with their strong physical presence.

For long moments, Flinn quietly studied them each in turn, as they stood gathered around him in the dense forest. The Druid's son fingered the pendent he still yet wore, biting his lip against the searing pain pressing into his chest. Shifting shade drew Flinn's attentions upward, finding that the sun's light filtered down through the trees to dapple Howler's Wood with shadows. But so too did a shadow lay over Flinn's visage when he reapplied his eyes to the twelve before him.

He took one long inhale, taking in their smell. And mingled in their scent, although faintly, Flinn could make out Joden's own. Jaw tensing, teeth grinding, and red-green flames flickering in his angry glare, Flinn soon found himself delighting in the scent of the Wolf-kin's fear.

End

Acknowledgements

I would like to acknowledge Shalina Hubbs, who expressed her belief in my abilities and helped support my dream. Not to mention, giving me that little kick in the ass I needed to get moving!

Also, I want to acknowledge Wes Hancock, my illustrator, and all his hours of hard work trying to capture my creative vision. You have done phenomenal work. You're the man, bro'!

I would like to acknowledge Mirav Tarkka, my publisher and who has been a profound help along my journey. I am looking forward with continuing our exchanges and our corresponding business together. You have been an extreme inspiration and a huge help in getting my stories out there! Toda!

Lastly, I want to extend a big thanks to all my supporters who have been waiting to read my work and get lost in the labyrinths of my mind. Fret not, this is but the first of many, for there are other tales to be told!

Made in the USA
Middletown, DE
15 October 2023

40870352R00195